Balancing Act

A Lake in the Clouds Novel

EMILY MARCH

FOREVER

New York Boston

Copyright © 2023 by Geralyn Dawson Williams
Reading group guide copyright © 2023 by Geralyn Dawson Williams and Hachette Book Group, Inc.

Cover art and design by Nicole Lecht. Cover images © Getty Images; Shutterstock. Cover copyright © 2024 by Hachette Book Group, Inc.

Forever
Hachette Book Group
1290 Avenue of the Americas, New York, NY 10104
read-forever.com
@readforeverpub

Originally published in trade paperback and ebook by Forever in November 2023

First Mass Market Edition: July 2024

Forever is an imprint of Grand Central Publishing. The Forever name and logo are registered trademarks of Hachette Book Group, Inc.

The publisher is not responsible for websites (or their content) that are not owned by the publisher.

The Hachette Speakers Bureau provides a wide range of authors for speaking events. To find out more, go to hachettespeakersbureau.com or email HachetteSpeakers@hbgusa.com.

Forever books may be purchased in bulk for business, educational, or promotional use. For information, please contact your local bookseller or the Hachette Book Group Special Markets Department at special.markets@hbgusa.com.

ISBNs: 9781538707418 (mass market), 9781538707425 (ebook)

Printed in the United States of America

BVGM

10 9 8 7 6 5 4 3 2 1

Praise for Emily March

"Feel-good fiction at its finest."
—Susan Wiggs, *New York Times* bestselling author

"A brilliant writer you'll love."
—Susan Mallery, *New York Times* bestselling author

"Emily March's stories are heart-wrenching and soul-satisfying."
—Lisa Kleypas, *New York Times* bestselling author

THE GETAWAY

"Readers looking for feel-good fiction about a big, loving family will enjoy this...March creates believable characters, and the Prentice family is an easy one to spend time with."
—*Booklist*

"An intellectually engaging and psychologically probing novel about a family returning from a dark place to a better one."
—*New York Journal of Books*

Balancing Act

Also by Emily March

The Getaway

For Emmie
You're the sunshine in my sky.

Balancing Act

Prologue

August
Eternity Springs, Colorado

WILLOW ELDRIDGE STOOD IN the dining hall of the Rocking L Ranch. She told herself that she absolutely, positively couldn't cry. She had to show courage and project confidence. She had to paste on a smile and be happy!

Heaven help her.

This was so hard. Willow didn't know if she could do it. The what-ifs swirled through her head like scraps of paper in a funnel cloud. Today, she was dropping her son, Drew, off for a week at summer camp. This would be the first time they'd spent a night apart since his father died over a year and a half ago.

"Mom, how far away is Nana's house again?" Drew asked.

"Lake in the Clouds is less than one hundred miles from here." Barely. Ninety-eight point six, to be exact. With much of it over winding mountain roads. "I can be here in no time at all if you really need me. But you're not going to need me. You're going to be too busy having tons of fun."

He sighed. "I guess. I'm a little scared."

Me, too. "That's normal, buddy, but you'll be fine. You're just about the bravest boy I know."

"You don't know any other boys."

"That is not true. What about Jackson and Aiden and Ethan?"

At this mention of three of his friends, he shrugged. "They're all braver than me. I'm a wussy."

"Andrew John Eldridge! You are not a wussy."

"Nathan Campbell says I am."

"Nathan Campbell is a bully, and you do not need to listen to anything he says."

"He's my friend."

"Well, he's not a very good friend," Willow retorted. The child was a mean little tyrant, and Willow wanted her son out of that boy's orbit. She had her fingers and toes crossed that Drew and Nathan ended up in different classes this year. That might not solve the problem, but it certainly should help.

A teenager approached wearing khaki shorts and a green T-shirt sporting the Rocking L Ranch logo. They'd met Sean Rafferty upon their arrival ten minutes ago, and he was to be one of Drew's cabin counselors. "All right, Drew. I have you all checked in. You're going to be in Black Bear Cabin. If you come with me, I'll show you where to stow your gear and introduce you to your cabinmates."

Willow swallowed hard and willed away the tears that threatened. Then, leaning down, she gave Drew one more hug and said, "I'll see you in a week, Drew. Have a fabulous time. I love you."

She waited, hoping for an *I love you, too*, but Drew *was* an eight-year-old boy. He wouldn't get mushy in front of his counselor. So instead, he gave her a wave and a shaky smile and said, "Bye, Mom."

She allowed her eyes to water only after he had walked out the door. She turned around to head toward her car and discovered the camp director watching her, his dark eyes warm with understanding, his smile sympathetic. She'd liked Chase Timberlake when she'd spoken to him on the phone earlier this week. Meeting him today reinforced that positive impression. He struck her as capable and caring. Drew would be in good hands.

Approaching Chase, Willow said, "Thank you again for making room for him."

He gave her an easy smile. "I'm thrilled we had a bunk for Drew. We rarely have a last-minute cancellation, so I think this was meant to be. He'll have a great week and come home with tales of grand adventure. So don't worry about him. We'll take good care of him."

"I know you will. Everyone I've spoken with raves about what a special place the Rocking L Ranch is and how much good you've done for troubled children in the years you've been in operation."

"Camp is a labor of love for many of us in Eternity Springs," Chase replied.

The camp had been founded by local philanthropists with the vision of serving children who had suffered a significant loss. Two weeks ago, a friend of Willow's aunt had suggested that Drew apply for a place in the camp's final summer session. The phone call from Chase with news of the opening had come earlier this week. Life had been a mad rush of camp prep ever since.

Someone called Chase's name, and he excused himself. "We'll see you next Saturday, Willow. Don't worry about him. Drew is going to have the time of his life."

"I know he will—if he manages to not hurt himself. Word of warning, Chase. The child is accident-prone."

"Noted. We'll keep an extra-close eye on him. You have my word."

Willow believed him. The Rocking L Ranch had an excellent safety rating.

She returned to her car with her tears mostly vanquished and looking forward to her afternoon. Willow and Emma, her four-year-old daughter, would be joining Willow's mother and aunt for High Tea at the upscale resort where they'd booked rooms for a girls' weekend in this picturesque little mountain town. Emma had picked out the cutest little hat to wear, and she was very excited. It promised to be a nice family getaway. Willow regretted that her sister Brooke wasn't able to join them.

They'd be staying at Angel's Rest Healing Center and Spa—she loved the sound of that. Who knows? Maybe after a healing soak in the hot springs she'd finally find her courage and tell her mother about life in Nashville and the circumstances surrounding her husband's death. Willow knew she couldn't make things right with her mother until she did that.

She also knew she couldn't turn back the clock. She wished she hadn't been so blind, so trusting. If only she'd used her brain instead of following her heart.

This stupid heart of hers. Seriously, it wasn't to be trusted.

And yet she wouldn't trade Drew and Emma for anything.

Willow gazed out at the towering mountain peaks surrounding her and her lips twisted in a wry smile. She definitely had the proverbial hill to climb. She had a lot to make up for where her mom was concerned.

Genevieve Prentice was a good mom. An excellent mom. Willow had not been a good daughter. Not for the past ten years, anyway. She wanted to fix that.

Willow wanted to fix herself.

The most difficult step would be to come clean, to explain why she'd erected this wall between herself and her mom for the past decade. She needed to be honest with her mom about why she didn't move home to be closer to her family after Andy died.

Maybe I'll do it this weekend.

Yeah, right. And maybe little piggies would fly, and Drew would never have another cut, scrape, or broken bone, and Emma would suddenly decide she likes green vegetables after all.

"Baby steps, Willow Eldridge," she murmured. Baby steps were progress. She and her children were here in Colorado. Hopefully, upon their return to Nashville in two weeks, they will have made significant steps forward in repairing relationships and healing broken hearts.

By the end of their spa weekend, Willow was optimistic. She'd definitely made progress. She couldn't remember having laughed so much with her mom in years. Monday evening, as she watched her mother cuddle and love on Emma as she read the four-year-old a bedtime story, Willow's heart overflowed with love.

Genevieve Prentice rocked being a grandmother. She

adored Drew and Emma. She was patient, caring, and kind—always willing to listen when one of the kids wanted to talk. She never gave the appearance of favoring one grandchild over the other. She played pirates with Drew— his latest obsession—and stacked blocks with Emma. This afternoon, Genevieve had glowed with happiness when she allowed Emma to play in the best toy box in all the world: Nana's jewelry box.

On Wednesday afternoon, Willow received an e-mail from Drew. Short and filled with misspellings, it nevertheless reassured her that he was indeed having the time of his life.

"You miss him terribly, don't you?" Genevieve observed when Willow read it to her. She stood at her kitchen sink, adding water to a pitcher filled with hummingbird food concentrate.

"Like my right arm." Willow gave a little laugh, lifting her gaze from her phone. "I'm torn. On the one hand, I'm thrilled for him to be having such a wonderful time, but on the other hand, it makes me sad that I'm not there to share it with him. It's different from sending him off to school. I know what his day is like at school. But this week, I'm clueless. There's a big event in his life that I know nothing about."

Her mother's smile turned bittersweet as she stirred the bright red sugar water with a spoon. "Oh, that emotion I understand all too well."

At that moment, Willow felt an urge to explain herself. Maybe, just maybe, she had the gumption to do this.

She cleared her throat. "Mom, there's something I need to say to you."

The light in Genevieve's green eyes turned wary.

"Something's wrong?"

"No," Willow assured her, though, in all honesty, that wasn't the truth. Something *was* wrong. It had been wrong for years. The time had come to make it right.

How to start? *You were right, and I was wrong, and I'm sorry? I've been a horrible daughter. Please forgive me?* Or maybe, *Guess what, Mom. Turns out I was married to Mr. Wrong.*

Before she could decide which tack to take, her phone rang. Glancing down at the screen, she spied a name that struck fear in her heart. Rocking L Ranch.

Willow's gaze flew up to meet her mother's. "It's the camp. Why are they calling me?"

Her heart in her throat, she thumbed the green button. "Hello?"

"Mrs. Eldridge? Your son is okay. However, I'm afraid there's been an incident."

Chapter One

New Year's Eve
Lake in the Clouds, Colorado

SEATED ON A SOFA with her feet propped up on an ottoman in front of a crackling fire, Genevieve Prentice wiggled her toes. The jingle bells on the tips of her woolen WORLD'S BEST NANA slipper socks jangled.

Her sister, Helen McDaniel, was sitting beside her and jangled her own slipper bells in response. Her socks read AUNTIE! LIKE MOM, ONLY COOLER. Both women wore pajamas as they sipped their nightcaps and watched the clock tick toward midnight.

"So, admit it," Helen said. "You're glad I dragged you kicking and screaming to the party, aren't you?"

"I wasn't kicking and screaming."

"Sure you were. You've never liked New Year's Eve parties, but you enjoyed yourself at this one. Admit it."

"I enjoyed myself," she deadpanned.

"Oh, quit being such a scrooge."

"You're a whole holiday behind, Helen. New Year's Eve is a fat little cherub in a sash."

"Well, you don't have chubby thighs, and no one has ever accused you of being an angel."

Genevieve snickered and sipped her cognac. "You're right. I did enjoy myself. The party was fun. Your neighbors at Mountain Vista Retirement Community are interesting people. Of course, the whole celebrating by London time was different, but it makes sense for partygoers who need to be in bed by seven o'clock."

"Now, that's mean. The party didn't end until ten."

"I was speaking about myself."

Helen leaned away from Genevieve and gave her a considering look. "Hello. Light bulb moment. You have a big birthday coming up this year, don't you? You're bothered by it."

"No, I'm not," she lied.

"Balderdash."

"Now, there's a word right out of the old folks' lexicon," Genevieve grumbled.

"Oh, stop it. Sixty is the new forty. It's middle age today."

"There's some new math. Imagine how loudly my knees will creak if I live to be one hundred and twenty!"

Helen tapped her lips with her index finger. "We should do something special for your birthday. Throw a big party."

"I do *not* want a party. Of any size."

"Spoilsport. Something else, then, to mark the occasion. Maybe finally take a hot-air balloon ride with me? You'll love it as much as I do, Genevieve. I promise."

Genevieve snorted. "It'll be a cold day in Austin in August when I go up in one of those death traps."

Footsteps descending the staircase provided a

welcome distraction, and Genevieve smiled up at her daughter, Willow. "Everything okay with the children?"

"Emma is fine. Sound asleep. Sledding with her uncle Lucas today wore her out."

When Willow didn't immediately follow up with a mention of her son, Genevieve's stomach sank. Poor little Drew had been having a time of it since summer camp. "And Drew?"

Willow sighed. "He's awake. He says he had a nightmare about the accident."

"Which one?" Helen asked.

"It was a combo nightmare about his dad and camp. And just when I'd begun to relax, too."

A burning log split and fell in the grate with a *thunk*. Flames flared, and sparks rose up the chimney. Genevieve lifted her gaze toward the second-floor bedroom occupied by her grandchildren during this holiday visit. They'd all worried that a return to Colorado might trigger another panic attack for Drew, a malady he'd suffered numerous times since that unfortunate business at camp this past summer.

Drew had been sitting at the poolside when another boy thought it would be funny to pretend to drown. Frightened children screamed as the lifeguard dove into the water. The child standing behind Drew was jostled by the crowd and spilled a cherry snow cone all over Drew.

That had triggered a flashback to the car accident that had injured Drew and killed his dad. Reliving his terrors, Genevieve's grandson had lost his cool.

"That poor child," she said now. "He's had too much trauma to bear for someone his age. My heart aches for him."

As Helen nodded her agreement, Willow said, "When we get home, I'm going to see if I can't find a new counselor for him. Dr. Harris is nice, but I don't think she's helping."

"He has seemed a bit withdrawn during this visit," Genevieve observed.

"Withdrawn?" Helen repeated with a scoff. "Are we talking about the same boy I watched ride a snowboard yesterday? He attacked the bunny slope. Defeated it, too."

"Colorado has been good for him. He loves it here," Willow said. "But Mom is right. At home, he's been acting clingy and timid like he did in the months right after his father died. He keeps his feelings bottled up inside."

"I honestly didn't see that from him this trip." Helen swirled the cognac in her snifter. "Not like I did during our visit to Nashville in October. In fact, yesterday on the slopes, Drew reminded me a lot of his father."

Genevieve nodded in agreement. "Yesterday, Drew did seem to act more like his old self, and yes, he did remind me of Andy. That man lived life big."

"Drew will rise above these challenges, Willow," Helen said. "I'm sure he'll follow in his father's footsteps."

Willow turned toward the fire. Genevieve thought her daughter sounded a touch forlorn as she said, "We will see. In the meantime, I'm hoping tonight's bad dream is just a blip and that Drew continues to build upon the progress he's made while we've been here."

"Well, listen to your instincts, Willow," Genevieve suggested. "They're good ones."

"I don't know about that. However, I am going

to listen to them. My deaf ear is flipped to the on position."

"Good girl." Helen patted the seat beside her. "Now, grab a glass and come sit with us. Let's cheer in the New Year together."

Genevieve added, "I suggest you give yourself a generous pour. Helen convinced me to allow her to set up all of the gifts she gave the family this Christmas to ring in the New Year. They're in the dining room."

On her way to her mother's liquor cabinet, Willow froze. She glanced at her mom with eyes rounded slightly in alarm. "The cuckoo clocks? All eight of them?"

"Yes, all eight of them."

"Won't it be glorious?" Helen beamed. "Forget 'Auld Lang Syne.' I can't think of a more appropriate way to put a period on this year and say hello to the next, can you?"

Willow met her mother's gaze, and the two women exchanged silent identical looks—semi-amused horror. Then, Willow's expression relaxed, and she turned to Helen and smiled. "No, Auntie, I can't think of anything more appropriate."

Genevieve silently toasted her daughter. Then, taking a sip of the cognac, she savored the French liquor. She'd brought out the good stuff for tonight. Why not? Why save anything at this point in her life?

Ticktock to Helen and all her clocks.

Ticktock to my big six-zero.

Ticktock to being six feet under.

Genevieve tossed back the remainder of her drink, then rose to get a refill. "Less than ten minutes to go now. Anyone want to commit to a New Year's resolution?"

"Not in this life or the next," Helen shot back. "I gave up New Year's resolutions at the turn of the century."

"The turn of the century," Genevieve repeated glumly. "That makes us sound so old."

"Not old. Vintage? Or MCM, remember?"

Midcentury modern. Genevieve snorted and kissed her daughter on the cheek as they passed, going to and from the liquor cabinet. Then, carrying a glass of scotch neat, Willow took a seat beside her aunt and said, "I have a New Year's resolution."

"Oh?" Helen asked. "Do share."

"I alluded to it a moment ago. I'm going to start listening. To my instincts. To my mother."

Following a moment of shock, Genevieve and Helen both burst into laughter. Genevieve filled her snifter. Willow wrinkled her nose at her mother and aunt. "All right. Maybe I deserve that."

Helen clapped a hand to her breast. "Maybe? You think? Willow, my love, you have been butting heads with your mother for a decade. She says black. You say white. She says night. You say day."

"Well, things are changing. I'm changing. My guiding word for the year is *listen*."

"A guiding word, hmm?" Helen considered the idea a moment, then nodded. "I like that. Having a guiding word for the year makes more sense than making a resolution you never keep."

"I keep my resolutions," Genevieve protested.

"That's because you only resolve easy things. So what *is* your New Year's resolution this year, Gen?"

"To exercise every day."

Helen met Willow's gaze. "She proves my point."

"Exercising every day isn't easy."

"But you already do it daily. Ergo, it's an easy resolution."

Genevieve made an exaggerated roll of her eyes and addressed her daughter. "Have you ever met another person who actually uses the word *ergo*?"

"One of my professors in college used it." Willow toasted her aunt. "Here's to the vocabulary queen. You've always inspired me."

"Thank you." Helen added an aristocratic nod to her acknowledgment of the compliment. "Maybe I'll make *ergo* my word of the year. I'll use it once a day."

"I think *argue* is more appropriate," Genevieve observed.

"I won't argue that," Willow quipped.

"Traitor." Helen exaggerated a scowl toward her niece.

"Not because you're argumentative, Auntie—"

"Which she is," Genevieve teased.

"—but because guiding words work better if you can act on them. Ergo"—Willow shot her aunt a grin—"choose a verb."

"I concede the point." Helen tapped her index finger against her lips. "Hmm. All right. I think I'll go with *climb*."

Genevieve and Willow both took a moment to consider it. "Interesting choice," Genevieve said.

"It suits. It's uplifting. A friend of mine likes to say that we all can use a little more skyward in our lives. I think she's right. So this year, I'm going to concentrate on climbing to put a little more sky in my life."

"And you said you won't make resolutions."

Helen gave a nonchalant shrug. "Your turn, Genevieve. Share with the class."

Genevieve sipped her drink and considered. "I don't know. I'll have to think about it. Is there a rule that your guiding word must be chosen by New Year's?"

Willow shrugged. "There are no guiding-word police."

"I volunteer for that job," Helen said, raising her hand. "My first policing act is to declare that yes, you must choose before the little birds coo."

Genevieve glanced at the clock and winced. She should run upstairs in the next three minutes and grab her earplugs from her nightstand drawer.

"Ticktock, sister."

"Oh, give me a minute." Ticktock. That should be Genevieve's guiding word. However, she knew if she proposed that, Helen would give her grief. She'd already picked up on Genevieve's birthday bum-out.

"You have two minutes. It's almost midnight."

"Okay...okay. My word is..." *Old. Decrepit. Over-the-hill*. Not verbs. *Fade. Shrivel*. No, Helen would slap her upside the head if she rolled that out.

Genevieve would have to pick something halfway positive, or her sister and daughter would bug her the entire year.

"Ticktock, ticktock, ticktock."

Genevieve shot her sister a look. "*Murder*."

"Har har."

"Okay." Genevieve went with the next verb that popped into her head. "*Breathe*."

"*Breathe*?" Helen pursed her lips and considered it, then nodded. "That's acceptable. A bit zen-ish for you. More like something I'd choose."

"I'm so glad you approve," Genevieve deadpanned as the minute hand reached its zenith.

The cuckoo clocks began to chime. One after the other, not in rhythm. Not in unison. Eight of them. An entire flock of cuckoo clocks ushering in the New Year.

"Happy New Year!" Helen crowed.

Genevieve covered her ears with her hands. "I'm changing my guide word."

"Too late," Helen declared.

"No, it's not too late. The birds are still screeching."

Willow laughed. "She has a point, Auntie. What's your word, Mom?"

Genevieve needed peace and quiet. She needed her aching, aging joints to stop screaming at her. She needed the freight train speeding toward her that was her upcoming birthday to stop blowing its whistle so loud!

She wanted the damned birds marking the time to shut the hell up.

"*Muffle*!" she exclaimed. "My guiding word for the next year is *muffle*!"

Into the silence that marked the New Year, her sister said, "Seriously, Genevieve? And here we've all believed that I was the one who's gone cuckoo."

Willow awoke on New Year's Day to the sound of Drew picking on his sister. *Oh, joy.*

No surprise, really. He'd be grumpy in the aftermath of the nightmare. The best thing Willow could do for everyone was to find a distraction fast.

Quickly and quietly so as to avoid waking her mother and aunt, Willow bundled the children up and headed out. Their destination was Raindrop Lodge and Cabins

Resort, the lakeside property purchased and renovated by her mother and aunt over the past year. Since Genevieve's three-bedroom home couldn't comfortably sleep everyone, Raindrop had served as overflow lodging space for Willow's siblings during their holiday visit. Maybe one of them would be up early, too, and provide Drew with a distraction from his mood. If not, well, she and the kids could take a hike through the woods until the family began to gather. Today, the Prentices planned to assemble at Raindrop for a traditional New Year's Day dinner and a football-watching party. Everyone would go their separate ways tomorrow.

Willow had mixed feelings about the ending of the holidays. She'd survived Christmas again, not an easy feat considering all the bad-marriage baggage the season ushered in with its red-and-green cheer. But once she'd soldiered through December 25, and excepting Drew's nightmare last night, she and the kids had a fabulous time.

Honestly, Willow dreaded going home. She was happy here. The kids were happy here. On Christmas morning, Drew had said Nana's house was the best place on earth, and he wanted to stay forever. Emma had enthusiastically agreed.

"So why are we leaving?" Willow wondered aloud as they arrived at the Raindrop property. Maybe the time had come to put Nashville in their rearview mirror.

She turned her rental car off the main road leading to the lodge and headed for the dozen or so small log cabins snuggled in the woods where her sibs were staying. Neither Jake's nor Lucas's place showed signs of life, but a golden glow in the window of Cabin 8 suggested that her sister was awake. Upon noting the footsteps in the fresh snow, Willow concluded that Brooke had gone on her customary morning run.

After making the loop past the cabins, Willow continued on to the lodge and pulled to a stop in the parking lot beside it. The kids bailed out and ran over to a snowdrift, where they began making ammunition for the snowball fight their uncles had promised. It was a beautiful morning, cold but clear and almost windless, with only a handful of puffy white clouds floating against a bright blue sky. Willow watched her children with joy in her heart and, for the first time, seriously considered the idea of relocating her family to Lake in the Clouds.

It was time to make a move. She was ready. The kids were ready. But where should they settle? What would be best for the children? Heading home to Texas was an option. It would do Drew and Emma good to be around their aunt and uncles. Also, their father's parents lived in Texas. Willow had a decent enough relationship with Maggie and Tom Eldridge, though it had been difficult since Andy's death, given they'd never revealed knowledge of their son's sins, and Willow had no intention of cluing them in. Honestly, she liked having a few state borders between her and her children's paternal grandparents.

Willow was distracted from her musings by the arrival of her siblings and her brother Jake's fiancée, Tess, and the snowball fight that ensued. It wasn't until midafternoon with the family congregated in the lodge's second-floor media room to watch the grudge-match game between Texas A&M and the University of Texas that she had another moment to herself to think.

Halfway through the first quarter, Drew looked at

his mother with puppy-dog eyes. "Will you make the cheese dip now, Mom? I'm hungry."

"Already? We just had lunch."

"It's never too soon for cheese dip," Lucas observed.

"He's right," Jake agreed. "Besides, it's not a Prentice-family football-watching party without cheese dip."

"Please, Mom?" Emma added.

Willow surrendered and headed downstairs to the kitchen. She had just removed a glass bowl filled with melted Velveeta from the microwave when a cheer erupted upstairs. She picked out her son's gleeful voice and rolled her eyes. The little traitor was rooting for the Aggies over Willow's beloved Longhorns today.

As she opened a can of Rotel tomatoes, she got a little teary-eyed. She did dearly love her family. Being around them soothed a wounded spot in her soul. She wished she'd listened to her mother and moved the kids home to Texas after Andy died and before Genevieve up and moved to Colorado. They'd needed the family that Willow had pushed away. In her defense, she'd been such an emotional wreck at the time. Making any decision, much less one as big as moving, had been a hill too high to climb.

She'd been grieving. She'd been angry and afraid and ashamed. The anger and fear were bad enough, but the shame had debilitated her. She'd worn it like a pair of concrete sneakers—big sneakers, like size eleven. She'd found it nearly impossible to do more than shuffle around Nashville, much less move home to Texas. Home to her mother.

Who had been right about Andy Eldridge all along.

Willow dumped the tomatoes into the melted Velveeta, picked up a wooden spoon to stir the gooey combo, and sighed. She had yet to have that talk she needed to have with her mother. Drew's panic attack at camp had ended any attempt last summer, and in the months since, she never found a good opportunity for it. Didn't help anything that she dreaded the conversation like the bathroom scale following a chocolate binge.

"Well, it's New Year's Day," she murmured. "A new year. A new beginning."

She'd talk to her mother and talk to the kids. It was time to bust up those concrete sneakers and move forward with her life.

Another roar exploded from upstairs. Sounded like she was missing a good game. Willow gave the cheese dip one final stir and set down the spoon. With the bowl in one hand and a bag of chips in the other, she headed back upstairs.

In the media room, her brothers reclined in the armchairs in front of the big screen. Her sister, who liked her team to win in a blowout, nervously paced the back of the room. Tess sat between her mom and Aunt Helen, but instead of watching the big screen, the women huddled over Tess's phone. Looking at something wedding related, Willow surmised. The big day was only three months away now.

"There you are," Jake said, rising from his seat. "We've been wondering what was keeping you."

Brooke delightedly eyed the bowl that Willow set on the snack table. "I'm going to make a pig of myself. I figure calories today are free due to all the skiing I've done since Christmas."

"I agree," Tess said. "Today we splurge because tomorrow we all start our wedding diets."

The bridegroom paused while reaching for a paper

plate. With alarm in his voice, he asked, "What wedding diet?"

"I'm going to lose eight pounds before your wedding," Aunt Helen announced. "I have three months. I can do it."

"I don't want to hear about a wedding diet," Jake insisted.

Not taking his gaze off the game, Lucas smirked. "You have packed on a few pounds over the holidays, bro."

Shielding the action from Emma and Drew, the groom flipped his best man the bird.

"Consider it a wedding health plan, honey," Tess said, giving Jake an encouraging smile. "You and I have been working way too hard."

"Hey, don't blame me. You're the one who brought three new projects into the firm in December."

"I know. But between work and the wedding prep, for the next few months our stress levels will be through the roof. That's why I think a diet-and-exercise plan focused on health is a good idea for us."

Jake scowled and returned his attention to filling his plate with chips and slathering them with dip. Aunt Helen asked, "Aren't y'all using a wedding planner? How much prep do you have left? I'll be glad to pitch in to help. I wouldn't mind making a trip or two to Austin, and I know Genevieve would be happy to step up what she's doing on your behalf, too."

"Thank you," Tess said. "I may take you up on the offer."

Watching the game, Drew shouted, "Fumble!"

"Who's got it?" Jake asked.

Every Prentice in the room shouted, "Nebraska!"

Tess looked at them like they were crazy. "Nebraska?"

Grinning, Genevieve explained. "It's an old family joke that no one recalls exactly how it started. I'm afraid it's the first of many you'll encounter."

"Mom's right." Willow snagged a pretzel from the snack table and added, "Welcome to the family, Tess."

At that point, everyone's attention returned to the game, and bickering over football resumed. One set of downs later, Tess's cell phone rang. She checked the number and frowned. "Speak of the devil. Why is my wedding coordinator calling me on New Year's Day?"

Lucas suggested, "Let it go to voice mail."

All the women in the room exclaimed in protest. Tess walked toward the door as she answered the call, saying, "Happy New Year, Megan. What's up?"

The Aggies were driving downfield when Tess returned less than five minutes later, her expression strained, her eyes wide and shining with tears. Seeing her, Jake momentarily froze before shoving to his feet, grabbing the remote, and switching off the game. Lucas protested, "Hey—"

"Sprite?" Jake asked, moving toward Tess. "What's happened?"

Lucas's complaint died on his lips when he, too, caught sight of his sister-in-law-to-be. He asked, "How can we help?"

"It's okay." Two fat tears overflowed Tess's eyes to roll down her face as Jake reached her and pulled her into his arms. She spoke against his chest. "I'm okay. No one is hurt. I didn't mean to scare you. I'm sorry. This isn't the end of the world. Nothing insurmountable. I'm being silly. Emotional and silly."

"About what?" Genevieve asked, voicing the same question flashing through Willow's mind.

"Talk to me, sweetheart," Jake urged Tess.

"It's our wedding." Tess swiped the tears away from her eyes. "Our venue. Last night after a New Year's Eve party, it burned to the ground. Megan has been on the phone trying to find a place for us that's not already booked, but this late, she hasn't had any luck."

"Oh no!" exclaimed Genevieve.

"That's terrible," Brooke agreed.

Aunt Helen clicked her tongue. "You poor dear."

Jake, ever the manager, summed up the problem. "So we don't have a place to get married in Austin on our date."

"Not a place that we'd want," Tess said. "We'll have to push back the date."

Jake frowned. "I don't want to push back our date."

"Me, either. But I don't know what else we can do."

"How about we change the venue?" he suggested.

"We *have* to change the venue!" Tess exclaimed. "That's the problem."

"No, I mean completely change it. We considered having a destination wedding early on in this process. I know it wasn't our first choice, but..."

"Maybe it's our only choice." Tess closed her eyes and massaged her temples. "If it's even a choice. The destinations we considered will also be booked this late in the game."

Willow asked, "Were you thinking beach resorts?"

"Not necessarily. Mainly, we wanted something affordable for our guests. That's the problem I have with destination weddings. Too often, they're prohibitively expensive to attend."

"How do you feel about an outdoor wedding, Tess?" Aunt Helen asked.

"Depends on whether or not an alternative sheltered spot is available in case of rain."

Willow saw her mother and aunt exchange a look. A message passed between them. Willow wasn't the least bit surprised when her mother smiled at Tess and suggested, "Why don't you have the wedding here in Lake in the Clouds?"

Helen jumped in. "The end of March isn't a busy time for Raindrop Lodge. The innkeeper we hired has today off, but I know how to access the reservation system. So, say the word, and I'll check our occupancy around your date. Between the lodge rooms and the cabins and rentals that friends own, I'll bet we can offer complimentary lodging to almost all of your guests in order to lessen travel expenses."

"Helen is right," Genevieve continued. "If a lakeside ceremony doesn't suit you, you have multiple choices for a spot with a breathtaking vista as a backdrop. I'm sure Gage would open the Triple T Ranch for us."

"Inspiration Point," Tess said to Jake, exchanging an intimate smile with him.

Some history between them there, Willow thought.

"You get a lot of rain here in spring," Jake observed. "What about indoor places?"

"You could hold the ceremony at St. Vincent's, where we went to church on Christmas," Helen said. "I doubt they have a wedding already scheduled since the church mainly serves locals. I don't know of any local weddings scheduled for the last weekend in March, do you, Genevieve?"

"I don't," Genevieve confirmed.

Tess's eyes lit up. "Oh, that's a lovely old church."

"The parish hall is too small for a reception, but

we always have the lodge to offer. If you'd prefer a reception venue less rustic than our lodge—"

"Yes," Brooke interjected. "Something without cuckoo clocks."

"It's possible we could hold the reception at The Emily if we can get our contractor to speed up our renovations."

Willow's mother had partnered with rancher Gage Throckmorton to renovate an old movie theater in Lake in the Clouds. They'd renamed it The Emily after Gage's late wife. Willow nodded her agreement to the idea. "The Emily would be a beautiful indoor reception venue."

"The stage would make a great dance floor," Helen added.

Genevieve nodded. "All the theater seating will be out for refinishing in March. We could bring in tables and chairs."

"Isn't the floor sloped?" Brooke asked.

"I'm sure we could overcome that issue with some temporary flooring. In fact, that might be something Gage and I should discuss. It would certainly make the facility more versatile. There might be other appropriate places available, too, if you think Lake in the Clouds is an option."

"Maybe. Although, Raindrop Lodge is special to us. I don't have a problem with rustic." Tess considered a moment, then groaned. "I don't know. I'm over-whelmed. I don't see how Jake and I can pull this off with our workload. Megan is an excellent wedding planner, but asking her to start over with our event and do it long-distance? I doubt she'd have the time or the desire to work for us."

Willow looked at her son and then toward her daughter. An idea began to form in her mind. Then, speaking to Tess, she asked, "Details like that aside, would you want to get married in Lake in the Clouds?"

Tess and Jake exchanged a look, then Tess nodded. "We fell in love here. I think it would be very nice to get married here, too."

Willow nodded. "Then let me be your wedding planner."

"Great idea!" Brooke exclaimed. "Willow is a fabulous event planner. She's won all sorts of awards and recognition."

Tess folded her hands prayerfully. "You would do that for us? Seriously? Oh, Willow. That would be fabulous."

"Sure you want to do that, sis?" Jake asked. "Might be challenging to do from Nashville."

"It probably would, yes." Willow couldn't have received a clearer sign for the answer to the question that had plagued her today. *It'll be Christmas morning déjà vu for the kids.* She drew in a deep breath, then planted her flag. "That's why I'll do it from here. Mom? Auntie? Could the children and I stay here at Raindrop Lodge? Do you have a cabin available for a long-term rental?"

"Absolutely!" Helen exclaimed.

"We'll need it for the spring semester. Beyond that, well, we'll see how it goes."

"But what about your work?" Brooke asked.

"I haven't booked many events this winter." Between the proceeds from Andy's life insurance and the inheritance she'd received from her grandfather, Willow didn't need to worry about finances. She worked because she enjoyed it and because she needed some adult interaction in her life. She kept her schedule light because she wanted to be available to meet her children's needs. "I can take care of the commitments I do have from here."

"Hold on. Wait a minute." Drew scrambled around in his chair and sat on his knees, his eyes wide with hope as he met his mother's gaze. "We're gonna move here? To Lake in the Clouds? Will I go to school? Where?"

"Yes," Willow responded. "I don't know where yet. I'll want to look into the public and private elementary schools, see what's available, and determine which would be a good fit for you."

Genevieve spoke softly. "I can't believe you want to move here."

Willow froze. Was that dismay she heard in her mother's voice? Surely not. Genevieve had always bemoaned that she lived so far away from her only grandchildren.

Of course, that was before her big getaway last year when she'd totally upended her life, sold her house and most of her belongings, and run away from her family.

Willow bit her bottom lip as doubt assailed her. *Dang it, dang it, dang it.* Maybe this was a bad idea. She shouldn't have acted so impulsively. She should have spoken to her mother before jumping in feetfirst. Visiting was one thing. Genevieve might not want Willow and the kids to follow her to Colorado to live.

Except…her mother might have changed, but she hadn't altered her DNA. Genevieve Prentice would love to have her grandchildren living close. Willow was sure of it.

Mostly sure.

Well, Mom's a big girl. If she doesn't want us here, she can just tell us.

Willow met her mother's gaze, took a deep breath, and leaped. "Drew and Emma should see you more than they do now. Is this plan okay with you?"

"Oh, Willow!" Genevieve clapped her hands and beamed. "This is the best idea ever."

Okay. Good. *Whew.* "So we can rent a cabin?"

Aunt Helen didn't hesitate. "Of course. I think the new one, don't you, Genevieve? Cabin 17? Zach finished it right before Christmas. It's a three-two. We haven't begun renting it yet, so we won't need to move any guests around. I think you'll enjoy having the extra bath. It's too bad Cabin 18 is still a work in progress. The kids would love the loft."

"Seventeen is perfect for them," Genevieve agreed. Glancing toward Willow, she added, "Unless you'd want..."

When she hesitated, Willow thought she knew what words her mother had been about to say. *Unless you'd want to move in with me.*

Genevieve Prentice, before her getaway, would have asked. However, Genevieve Prentice of Lake in the Clouds, Colorado, valued her independence. Willow was okay with that. She felt the same way.

"...the cabin you stayed in last summer because it's closer to the main road," Genevieve continued. "Seventeen is at the edge of our property. The other cabin would be five to ten minutes quicker getting Drew to school."

Willow considered the question. "Five to ten minutes can make a big difference in the morning, but I think the extra bathroom will be handier in the long run. We'd love to stay in Cabin 17."

"So it's settled?" Helen asked.

Willow nodded. "It's settled."

"Hurray!" Drew shouted.

"Hurray!" Emma repeated. "We're moving to Lake in the Clouds!"

"Fabulous," Lucas piped up. "Now, can we please turn the ball game back on?"

Chapter Two

NOAH TANNEHILL DIED IN his dreams again last night. Third time this week. Waking in the morning should have brought relief. Instead, he met the day with regret.

He should be dead.

His crewman was dead. His brother was dead.

Some days, Noah still wished that he were dead.

This cold, gray February morning was one of those days.

It took serious effort for Noah to drag himself out of bed, pull on clothes and outerwear, grab his hiking sticks, and head out into the intermittent snowfall. He took his usual route through the forest, which right now was a four-mile circuit with plenty of hills. He added a little distance each week. The plan was to start jogging in spring and running in the summer. So far, he was a little ahead of schedule in his rehab.

Back at his cabin, he finished off at the woodpile.

That, too, was part of his recovery effort. Swinging an axe damned near did him in, but over the past month, he'd built a decent little woodpile. By the time he headed into the house, he was exhausted—and still cranky. Ordinarily, strenuous exercise and frigid air helped him beat back the blackest of his moods. Today, even after the walk and a session with the axe, he still felt mean as a bear with a broken toe.

Give him shattered bones over nightmares any day.

Noah reconsidered making the run into town that he'd planned for this morning. Better he eat beans for dinner than bite someone's head off because he had his grizzly on. However, he'd already put off the chore twice, and he could delay a visit to the post office no longer.

He'd found the stack of journals in a trunk in the attic last week. That had been a summer activity for the two brothers one year. Having them around exacerbated his nightmares. He wanted to read them. However, reading them would kill him because doing so would resurrect memories of that summer and his brother, and Noah couldn't deal with that.

Besides, Daniel's journals needed to go to his widow. She would be thrilled to receive them.

He exhaled a heavy sigh and hit the shower. Half an hour later, he pulled his truck into the post office parking lot and grabbed the box from the passenger seat. After eyeing his cane distastefully, he elected to leave it behind. Unfortunately, that turned out to be a poor decision. He'd hit rush hour at the post office, and he had to stand in line behind three other people.

Three chatty other people. Doing business with a chatty postal worker. Chatty chat, chat.

Noah wanted to snarl.

Instead, he kept his expression impassive and stared out the window toward the Lake in the Clouds town square. The snow had stopped, and the sky cleared to a brilliant azure blue. With the improvement in the weather, people had started emerging from their homes like ants after a rain.

Great. Just his luck. The grocery store would be swarmed. Probably with chatty people. Lots of chatty folks in Lake in the Clouds.

Noah shifted his weight from one leg to the other. Stepped wrong and set his teeth against the stab of pain. Maybe he'd skip the groceries. Beans for supper didn't sound that bad, did it?

No, it didn't. However, beans for supper, breakfast, lunch, and supper again tomorrow didn't sound all that great. Better he suck it up and soldier on. He would ratchet up his don't-mess-with-me attitude, brave the crowds, and stock his larder to overflowing. With any luck, he wouldn't need to speak to a stranger again for weeks.

Ten interminable minutes later, Noah approached the post office window with his package. The postal worker, whose name he recalled was Liz, beamed at him and spoke in a chirpy tone. "Hello, Mr. Tannehill. It's so lovely to see you again. It's been quite a while since you stopped by to send off your boxes to fire departments. Becky and I have worried that perhaps you've been having trouble with your poor hands."

Noah very deliberately did not look down at his burn-scarred hands. He did not bother to mention that he now scheduled pickups from a private shipper when he had a load of inventory ready. Instead, he ignored her question and stated, "I need to send this package overnight."

"Overnight? Good thing it's so small compared to what you ordinarily send. It'd cost you an arm and a leg to express ship your usual boxes."

Liz waited expectantly, but he didn't respond.

Finally, she picked up her tape and measured his package, her lips pursed as if she were sucking a particularly sour lemon. She informed him of the mailing cost before asking begrudgingly if he needed stamps. Noah nodded and requested one roll. Rather than the flag stamps he'd expected, she handed over yellow roses. He counted bills from his money clip and slid them across the counter.

Noah hesitated. Perhaps because the rose stamps reminded him of his mother, and he knew what she would have said about his behavior, which he acknowledged was rude. It wasn't the clerk's fault that he felt like a grizzly.

"Keep the change." Noah turned to leave.

"What? No! Mr. Tannehill, stop! It's against our rules! And...you have more than twenty dollars coming back."

"Order a pizza for the office for lunch." He stepped outside the post office and filled his lungs with icy winter air. His shrink had given him a series of deep-breathing exercises when he needed to chill. He'd run through them in his truck before braving the grocery store.

It didn't help. Noah lost his zen before he'd made it through the produce department and cut his shopping trip short. By the time he wheeled his purchases out the front door, he was back in bear mode. A traffic jam caused by a fender bender near the entrance to Raindrop Lodge didn't improve his mood. They seriously needed a stop sign at that intersection.

When he returned to the cabin, he would call Dr. Hardesty's office and schedule a tele-doc appointment. As much as he hated the idea, if he talked about the nightmares during the daytime, perhaps he could avoid revisiting them in his sleep.

Finally, he made it home. He hauled his meager purchases inside and put everything away. Then he grabbed his phone and headed out to the back porch to sit in the sunshine and soak up some vitamin D while he made his phone call. He'd no sooner taken a seat in his favorite porch rocker when movement in the window of his workshop caught his eye.

An animal?

Then, a flicker. A flame. A frickin' flame!

His heart pounding, Noah shoved immediately to his feet. Within seconds, with his firearm on his hip, his cane in one hand, and his phone in the other, he descended the back steps and headed for his workshop. The structure had been the original barn on the property, which his father had expanded into a large storage facility, apartment, and garage. It stood some fifty yards or so away from the new place. Noah planned to assess the situation and call for help if necessary.

Urgency pulsed in his blood as he covered the distance as quickly as he and his cane could manage safely. The last thing he needed was to slip and break his leg again.

Once more, he spied the flutter of a flame. Small. Not spreading. He smelled no smoke in the air. Good.

Mentally, Noah envisioned the fire extinguishers he kept in the shop. One on the wall beside the door. One on the wall near the power tools. He would go inside, grab an extinguisher, and put the fire out.

He would.

I will! I won't freeze and fail to move. I can do this! I will do this!

Then, a shadow moved across the window. A small shadow. Small could be good—or not. Had Noah left the doors unsecured the last time he exited the shop? He didn't think so. He was conscientious about such things. It was still early in the season for a bear to be about, but a small black bear could do plenty of damage. Hell, raccoons could do a ton of damage.

But they didn't start fires.

Odds were his intruder walked on two feet rather than four.

Noah had to be smart so this situation didn't flare out of control.

The recent snowfall served Noah well in that it muffled his footsteps. He approached the building at an angle that he knew made him difficult to spot by anyone—or anything—inside. Drawing close, he stopped and listened. *Click. Click. Click. Squeak. Swish. Squeak. Swish.*

In an instant, Noah recognized the sounds. The click was a lighter. The squeak and swish were the opening and closing of a door on one of his dollhouses. What the hell? The structures were created to be set ablaze but at a fire station, not in Noah's workshop.

Angry more than afraid at this point, Noah strode toward the barn's front door and shoved it open. What he found inside stopped him in his tracks.

A kid. A little boy. Seven or eight years old, he'd guess, wearing outdoor gear. Blond hair peeked out from beneath a red stocking cap. Carrying a BIC lighter in his hand, he stood looking at the shelves lining the wall where half a dozen dollhouses in various stages of construction sat. Finally, the kid jerked his head around to stare at Noah, wonder and excitement glowing in his big blue eyes.

Noah growled. "Who the hell are you?"

The boy's expression quickly transformed from wonder to accusation, and he declared, "You're not Santa Claus!"

Genevieve crossed the fingers of her right hand behind her back as she observed Gage Throckmorton flip through the stack of French movie posters that she'd stacked on her dining table. She'd asked the Colorado rancher to drop by her house this morning on his way to his standing weekly appointment at the barbershop. Gage wore his poker face, so she couldn't judge his reaction to her purchase based on his expression.

She'd spent a pretty penny on the posters, an unexpected find during the sisters' trip she and Helen had taken to Germany to visit the Christmas markets in December. After discovering a pair of vintage posters at a booth in Bonn, she'd learned that the vendor had an entire collection of French posters of classic American film noir movies. Knowing they'd be perfect to grace the walls of The Emily, she had met the vendor at his shop and agonized over which posters to choose. Finally, an impatient Helen convinced her to buy them all. Genevieve had shipped them home and waited on tenterhooks for the box to arrive in Lake in the Clouds.

Like almost everything she and Helen had bought

on their Christmas market extravaganza, the shipment home had been slow to arrive. She hadn't told Gage about her purchase, and she was worried he wouldn't love them as much as she did. The man had been surprisingly opinionated about interior decorating choices for the theater. After butting heads with him repeatedly, Genevieve challenged him about it. He'd explained that he was making selections he believed his Emily would have made.

Genevieve quit arguing with him after that. But oh, she wanted him to like these posters.

However, he'd worked his way halfway through the stack and had yet to speak a word. Genevieve's nerves were stretched tight.

If he hates them, I'll resell them on eBay. It'll be no big deal.

No, I won't resell them. The Emily is my project, too. So I get to have some say-so.

Compromise. We will simply have to find a way to compromise.

She crossed her left-hand fingers, too.

Finally, having studied all twelve posters, Gage let out a low, slow whistle. "Genevieve. I am in awe."

Her tension eased. "You like them?"

"Like them! *Le Faucon Maltais. Le Grand Sommeil. Les Enchaînés.* Bogart. Alan Ladd. Orson Welles. Bacall. Ingrid Bergman. Veronica Lake! It's a treasure trove!"

Whew. "We talked about tracking down vintage posters for musicals, but we never discussed detective movies or film noir. I didn't know how you felt about it."

"Love it. I don't think you can beat Bogart and Bacall. This was a great find, Genevieve."

Genevieve beamed from the praise. "They've given me all sorts of ideas about programs for the theater. Depends on which direction we want to go with it."

He looked up from the movie posters and pinned her with his crystalline blue-eyed gaze. "What do you mean?"

Goodness, the man is fine to look at. Genevieve forced her attention back to the matter at hand. "This theater project began on a lark."

He shot her a grin that made Genevieve's toes tingle. "Actually, it was more of a lie at the time."

"That's harsh, Gage." What happened was that Genevieve had conceived of the idea on the spur of the moment to ward off gossip about Gage's presence at her home very early one morning. It had been an innocent visit. Gage had been widowed less than a year and was still deeply grieving his wife. But small-town tongues like to wag, so Genevieve gave them something positive to wag about with her theater-redevelopment partnership plan. "I like to think the idea was inspired."

"Okay, yeah. I'll give you that. So, tell me what's on your mind about our direction with The Emily."

"I think we have some mission drift, and it's my fault."

Gage removed the reading glasses he'd donned to study the posters and slipped them into his shirt pocket. "Mission drift?"

"Yes. If the weather doesn't cooperate for an outdoor event at Raindrop Lodge, our first event in The Emily will not be a salute to classical movies but a wedding reception. That leads to this question. Is The Emily going to be a theater or an event center?"

"Can't it be both?"

Genevieve nodded. "Yes, but is that what we want?

We never sat down and discussed it. You agreed to allow Jake and Tess to use it for their wedding reception. Since then, the focus has been on flooring and flowers instead of playbills and popcorn."

"I'm not focused on flowers," he replied, flashing a grin. "That would be you. It's completely understandable since you're the mother of the groom and the wedding planner's contact person."

Not to mention being her nanny.

Something in her expression must have telegraphed her displeasure, because Gage arched his brows and asked, "Do you regret offering the theater to Jake and Tess?"

"No, not at all," Genevieve truthfully responded. "It's a perfect solution, and chances are we won't need to use it. I just didn't think..."

"You didn't think what?"

She'd be so happy? So resentful? So fulfilled? So uncertain? So torn? No way was Genevieve going to express the thoughts tumbling around inside her. They didn't make sense to her. Everything was at odds. She *was* thrilled to have Willow and the children living here in town. That was a truth. She loved her grandmother role. However, she'd also grown to love the new version of herself that she'd been creating here in Lake in the Clouds. Honestly, right now, Genevieve didn't know *who* she was. Or, more precisely, who she wanted to be.

She couldn't admit that to the confident man standing in front of her. Instead, she deflected. "I guess I'm simply the type of person who needs a little more organization with my projects. I think we need a mission statement. We need policies and procedures. Otherwise, I'm afraid we will look up one day, and we won't have time on The Emily's calendar for a film noir festival because we're booked to the rafters with weddings."

"I'm a rancher, Genevieve," Gage said. "I don't write policy and procedure manuals."

"I know that. That's not what I'm asking. I want a meeting. A brainstorming session, if you will, where we discuss our vision for The Emily going forward. We did that last year when we first began the project, but a lot has happened since then."

"I don't have a problem with that. Let's get it on the calendar. Who do you want to attend? Willow might be good. She's an organizational whiz, from what I hear around town."

"No," Genevieve responded, more sharply than she liked. "This is our project, yours and mine. I think we should get a good grasp on what we want before we offer the rest of the world an opportunity to tell us what we want."

Gage eyed her speculatively. "Something has put a bee in your bonnet. Want to share with the class?"

Genevieve sighed, closed her eyes, and shook her head. "I'm sorry. You're right. I'm in a mood, but it has nothing to do with The Emily or you. I'm feeling a bit overwhelmed at the moment. Lots going on."

"Understandable. The wedding is, what, a month away?"

"Six weeks." And in all honesty, she wasn't very involved in the wedding planning. Which was fine by her. Truly.

"Well, I'm happy to sit down with you and talk about The Emily." He reached into his pocket, pulled out his phone, and scrolled to his calendar app. "So, sometime in April, then? After the wedding?"

"Do you have any time this week?"

Gage glanced at her in mild surprise, then returned his attention to his phone. "How about this afternoon?"

"I can't," Genevieve responded with genuine regret. "I'm watching Drew and Emma this afternoon. Willow has vendor appointments."

"Lucky you. I don't get to see my grandson again for almost a month. Looks like tomorrow afternoon and Friday morning are best for me."

Genevieve had promised to drive over to Eternity Springs with her sister on Friday for a day of shopping and to have lunch with their friend, Celeste Blessing, and Genevieve couldn't cancel. They'd already rescheduled the trip once because the ballet class Emma attended scheduled a mini-recital for grandparents that Genevieve had wanted to attend. "Tomorrow afternoon works for me."

"This sunshine we have now is supposed to hold through the end of the week. Want to come up to the Triple T? I'll introduce you to Jarvis."

"Jarvis?"

"My blue-ribbon bull. He's a special one. Blue ribbons everywhere we showed him."

Genevieve laughed. "Well, I can't pass up that opportunity."

"Come for lunch. Around twelve thirty or so?"

"Sounds great. Thanks, Gage."

"Now, I'll drive by the theater when I leave here. Want me to drop these posters off there? Or would you rather keep them here?"

"I'll keep them, thanks. Helen is stopping by later to take another look at them. We've both been frustrated that our purchases have been dribbling in since January.

But one good thing about it is we can revisit our sisters' trip when each box arrives. We enjoy that."

"Do you have another vacation lined up?"

"No. We're talking about it, though."

"Where do you want to go next time?"

Genevieve smirked and said, "My sister hasn't convinced me yet. We're discussing the South Pacific."

Gage said his good-byes, and Genevieve shut the door behind him. She liked Gage Throckmorton. He'd become a true friend the past year, and she enjoyed working on the theater project with him. He was good company. And then there was the whole Kevin Costner doppelgänger thing he had going on, which set the hormones Genevieve still had left aflutter. Of course, it didn't hurt that a time or two, she'd caught masculine appreciation in his gaze as he gave her a surreptitious once-over.

Not that he ever came close to doing or saying anything flirtatious. Genevieve was good with that. At this point in her life, she needed friends more than she needed a lover.

At least, that's what she told herself.

She returned to the dining table, where the posters lay neatly stacked. She began to flip through them again, her mind racing with ideas for a film noir festival at The Emily. Then Genevieve heard a car door slam in her driveway, and she assumed that Helen had arrived. As she turned toward the door, intending to greet her sister, Genevieve's cell phone rang.

Willow. Genevieve glanced at the clock on her wall. She still had forty-five minutes before she needed to leave to babysit the grands.

Her daughter probably wanted to ask Genevieve to

arrive early. *Well, dear, you're out of luck.* Helen had dibs on Genevieve's time for the next little while. She was not bailing on her sister or rushing her along to play the grandmother. She'd done it twice last week. Although Helen refrained from saying anything, Genevieve had picked up on her sister's disappointment.

Genevieve had sworn to be more aware going forward. However, the transition to local nana from long-distance one had presented some unexpected speed bumps. Learning to balance Genevieve the sister, Genevieve the grandmother, and Genevieve the woman was challenging.

"Hello, Willow."

"Mom, where are you?"

Genevieve straightened in alarm at the tight, anxious tone in her daughter's voice.

"Are you at the lodge?" Willow asked. "Is Drew with you?"

"No. I'm still at home. Why are you asking about Drew?"

Willow exhaled a troubled sigh. "That boy. He asked to walk up to the lodge to buy a candy bar in the gift shop with his allowance money. He should have been home half an hour ago, so I called the shop. He never came in."

"Oh no!"

"I'm not frantic about this," Willow continued. "He's probably sitting somewhere playing his Switch and lost track of time. I need to go look for him, but Emma's asleep. She felt a little warm when she went down for her nap. I think she's having a hard time shaking this ear infection, but I can't be one hundred percent positive about that. I'd planned to check her temp at the top of the hour and cancel with you and the vendors if she's febrile. I don't want anyone to catch something from us. But now, oh, Mom, you understand how it is. Could you come over early so I can look for him? Or, if you don't want to get near Emma, could you go look for him for me?"

"Of course." Genevieve walked toward her kitchen and gathered her purse and keys as her sister swept into the house. Helen's wide smile died a bit as she spied Genevieve lifting her keys from the key rack. To Willow, Genevieve said, "I'm not worried about being around Emma if she's feverish. I'll be there as fast as I can."

When she ended the call, Helen asked, "Now what?"

"It's Drew." Genevieve quickly summarized the situation. "I'm sorry, Helen. There's probably nothing wrong beyond a boy lost in his video game, but I can't tell Willow no."

"I know that."

"Would you come with me? We need to catch up. We haven't talked all week."

"And whose fault is that?"

"Mine. I know. I know. Come with me, Helen? Please?"

Helen hesitated. "I'll join the hunt for Drew. I don't want to babysit."

"I'm not asking you to babysit. I can multitask, you know. But I'd like some sister time."

"I'll take my own car," Helen said, pivoting to leave. "This is Drew, after all. It might be handy to have an extra car in addition to extra hands if a rush trip to the doctor for stitches or a cast is on the docket."

Genevieve grabbed her purse and followed her sister outside. "I'm hoping he's outgrown that."

Helen paused as she opened her car door. "I like your positive thinking, Genevieve. However, I wouldn't count on that. You know that bad things always come in threes."

"Threes!" Genevieve's purse slipped to the ground. "He hasn't had a single accident since they moved to Colorado!"

"Well, in order to get to three, there must be a one and a two." Helen slid into the driver's seat.

"Aren't you just Miss Merry Sunshine?" Genevieve grumbled as she bent and scooped up her bag.

"No, I'm Betsy Boy Scout. I believe in always being prepared." Helen started her car. "Face it. Drew has a history of being snakebit."

"He's never been bitten by a snake!"

"You know what I mean, sister, and if you're gonna be Nana-on-Call, you'd better be ready to earn your badges." With that, Helen finger-waved good-bye, pulled the driver's door shut, then drove away.

"Nana-on-Call," Genevieve muttered as she climbed into her own car and started the engine. At times like these, that's exactly who she wanted to be, and she was grateful for the opportunity. Truly. Never mind how many ones, twos, and threes.

Bad things always come in threes.

"Please, God," she prayed aloud as she backed out of her driveway. "Keep our precious little guy safe."

Always.

Chapter Three

AFTER SPEAKING WITH HER mother, Willow set down her telephone with a sigh. Single parenting was not for the faint of heart.

She told herself not to worry about Drew. Hadn't she spent the past six weeks shooing him outdoors to play? Wasn't she determined not to be a helicopter parent or a snowplow parent or whatever was the label du jour of the overprotective progenitor? Yes and yes. It was a challenge in today's dangerous world. Not for the first time since moving into the Raindrop Lodge cabin, Willow wished she'd rented a place in the middle of town.

She'd wanted to nurture a sense of independence in Drew, to encourage him to get off his Switch, get outside, and explore. She'd believed that to be easier—and safer—to do on property owned by her family than in a neighborhood where she didn't know another soul.

Willow was so worried about Drew. But landing the

helicopter-mom chopper was easier said than done for a mother who carried around the baggage that she did.

Willow's teeth tugged at her bottom lip as she checked the clock, glanced at the window, and looked back toward her daughter's bedroom. Then, switching her worry from her elder child to her younger, Willow decided to sneak into Emma's room and take her temperature.

This risked waking her. Emma was a light sleeper. If she wasn't ill and Willow woke her prematurely, the child would be grumpy and clingy for the rest of the day.

But Willow didn't want the responsibility of getting her mother sick. She had enough guilt where her mother was concerned. She didn't need more. If Emma was ill, Genevieve could choose whether or not to stay with her.

Willow sent up a quick prayer that her daughter wasn't ill.

She followed that with a prayer that Drew was all right.

She added a third prayer that she wouldn't backslide into the kind of behavior that was destructive for her children and herself. Once the praying was done, she made a mental note to call her counselor's office and make a virtual appointment.

Drew wasn't the only family member who'd suffered from PTSD after the auto accident that killed his father and left Drew bleeding and traumatized. No one in the Prentice family knew that a bomb had gone off in Willow's world a week before the wreck when she'd learned that Andrew Eldridge was a cheat and a thief. During the weeks and months after the collision, she'd been dealing not only with Andy's betrayal and death and Drew's injuries but also with her own self-doubt. How could she have been so wrong?

Her instinctual response was to gather her babies and hold them close. Instead, she all but squeezed the life out of them.

Willow had tended to hover over her kiddos even before the crash happened. Afterward, she'd been afraid to let her children out of sight.

In the months following his father's death, Drew's behavior swung from clingy and fearful to willful reck-lessness. Trips to the doctor for stitches and sprains became commonplace. Willow held her baby tighter.

It hadn't helped the situation that he'd been upset by a fake-drowning prank the first time she let go and sent her baby off to camp.

It took the clarity of hindsight, history, and a new psychologist in Nashville to identify that Willow's hov-ering only worsened matters for her traumatized young son. Drew responded to her cues. He clung because she clung. Drew had come to associate a physical injury with the sense of safety of being in his mother's arms. They'd both be healthier, mentally, living with an in-dependent mindset.

She was trying. Though days like today made the task easier said than done.

Still, sending up the bat signal for Nana's help was being a responsible parent, not an overprotective one. At least, that's what Willow told herself as she removed the thermometer from the bathroom medicine cabinet.

Everything she'd done since August was aimed toward walking that tightrope between smother and support. She'd enrolled both children in activities that encouraged independence and self-reliance. Swimming, T-ball, karate—hadn't Emma looked too cute in a gi? But organized activities needed to be balanced with free play and exploration. Lake in the Clouds offered that opportunity.

She hoped exploration hadn't taken Drew somewhere he shouldn't be playing.

Stepping cautiously, Willow entered her daughter's room and approached the bed. She carefully placed the thermometer close enough to Emma's forehead to get a reading. Normal. Thank heavens. Her poor ear had been giving Emma fits with a series of infections. On this last visit, the pediatrician warned Willow that tubes were likely in her daughter's future.

Well, that's a worry for another day, Willow told herself as she successfully exited Emma's room without waking the girl. Now she could focus all her fretting on her son.

More than likely, Drew's adventure today was simply that—an adventure. Willow needed to celebrate it, not rush to secure his safety.

Something else that was easier said than done, especially for Andy Eldridge's widow. The echo of her husband's voice floated through her head. *Life isn't safe! It isn't meant to be safe. It's meant to be lived.*

The man had undoubtedly done more than his fair share of "living." Right up until the moment he crashed his car and died.

And almost took their son to the grave with him.

Her phone rang again, the generic ringtone rather than one she'd assigned to a contact. Hoping for news about Drew rather than wedding-related business, Willow rushed to pick it up. An unfamiliar number showed on the screen. Ordinarily, she would ignore the call. Today, she answered it immediately. "Hello?"

"Willow Eldridge?"

"Yes."

"I have your son. He's lucky to be alive. You need to come get him."

Willow's grip crushed her cell phone, and she closed her eyes, catapulted into the past and another call. The words hadn't been quite the same, but close enough. Close enough.

That's all it took. In her mind's eye, Willow saw red-and-blue flashing lights. She heard sirens. She rushed through automatic doors and into a crowded room where she knocked over a Christmas tree when she turned toward a reception desk.

In her ear now, a stern voice said, "I'm sending you an address pin. Here, talk to him."

"Mommy?"

Sweet Jesus, thank you. The panic flooding through Willow eased at the sound of her son's voice. To some extent, anyway. "Drew Bear, where are you? Are you hurt?"

"I'm not hurt. I don't know where I am. The sign said 'Santa's Workshop,' but that was a big fat lie. Mom, you have to come and get me. He won't let me leave."

"What? Who is he?" *Please, God. Keep my baby safe.*

"He's not Santa Claus."

"Give me the phone, kid." The deep voice sounded hard and harsh. "Your kid trespassed on my property. You need to come get him. I won't let him go back the way he came because I don't want to be responsible if he falls through the ice."

"Ice? What ice?" Willow's voice rose an octave.

"Come now. I'll send you the address."

"Is he okay?" Willow demanded. "Is my son all right? Who are you?"

The stranger disconnected the call without further response.

Even as she stared in shock down at her device, Willow received a text from the stranger's number showing an address. Her hand shook so badly she could hardly read the screen. *This is what I get for letting go and encouraging independence. This is what I get for landing the damned helicopter.*

Her brow furrowed as she tried to make sense of what she saw. The pinned location was nowhere near Raindrop Lodge.

"Oh, wait." She zoomed out. Okay. This wasn't far from the lodge, after all. If you went over a mountain and walked on a frozen waterway. "Andrew John Eldridge, I'm going to skin your hide."

Willow took just a moment to consider her next move. Genevieve was probably still ten minutes away. But as much as she hated waking Emma from her nap, Willow dared not wait until her mom arrived to go for Drew.

Or could she wait a few minutes? Drew hadn't sounded scared on the phone. He sounded annoyed. Petulant, almost. Was it reasonable for Willow to conclude that the stranger had no intention of hurting her son? After all, the bad-tempered stranger had called for her to come get Drew.

And yet...stranger danger. Should she call the police?

Calling the police on a Good Samaritan neighbor wouldn't be nice. Distant neighbor. Who was this man?

Willow decided she would steal a minute for a quick

call to someone who was as good as a cop in this town. She scrolled through her contact list and phoned Zach Throckmorton, the contractor her mom and Aunt Helen had hired to oversee the renovations at Raindrop Lodge. Gage Throckmorton's son, Zach, had been born and raised in Lake in the Clouds. He knew everyone.

A deep, masculine voice said, "Hello?"

"Hi, Zach. Willow Eldridge here. I have a quick question. Do you know who owns the property at 4743 Running Elk Road?"

"Running Elk Road is the boundary line between Triple T property and some acreage owned by a guy out of Denver. He has a vacation home on it that's been in the family for a while. Place is called the Hideaway. It's the only property on that road that doesn't belong to our ranch."

"Do you know his name? The guy from Denver?"

Zach thought a moment, then said, "David, maybe? Something biblical, I think. Jeremiah? No, it's Noah. Noah Tannehill."

Noah Tannehill from Denver. "What do you know about him?"

"Not much. Why do you ask?"

Willow explained about the phone call and her dilemma. Zach said, "Too bad I'm not at Raindrop today, or I'd come down and stay with Emma. I don't really know him. Guy keeps to himself."

A recluse. Willow decided to wake her daughter up and head for Running Elk Road immediately.

Zach continued, "He's a second-generation owner. Maybe third. I know that Dad has offered to buy that piece of land in the past, but the family refused a strong offer."

Walking toward Emma's bedroom, Willow asked, "Any reason to suspect that he kept the property because he needs a place to hide the bodies?"

Zach laughed. "Nah. In fact, it sticks in my mind that there's something about him that's positive. Makes him a good guy."

Okay. Well, that's encouraging. "Does he live there alone?"

"Don't know for sure, but the few times I've seen him in town, he's always been by himself. But I wouldn't worry too much, Willow. I honestly believe Tannehill is a good neighbor."

"He didn't sound very neighborly when he called."

"Could be he was afraid for Drew."

Willow's spine stiffened. "Why do you say that?"

"To get from your place to his place on Running Elk Road on foot, Drew must have followed Silver Creek. Being February, it's frozen over, so he may well have walked on it. However, there are a couple places along that stretch where pools are deep, and hot springs keep the ice slushy. So it's not safe for him to have made that hike by himself."

Willow closed her eyes. She'd brought this on herself. She'd sent him off to explore, and explore he did. If he'd fallen through the ice and drowned or frozen to death, it would have been her fault!

No, it would not have been her fault. The only exploring Drew had permission to do this afternoon was along the path from their cabin up to the lodge gift shop. He'd had permission to spend his allowance on a candy bar, not wander off to another mountain entirely across a frozen mountain stream.

Reaching Emma's room, Willow saw that her

daughter had awakened from her nap. Good. "Thanks for the intel, Zach. Just one more thing. Is Noah Tannehill an older man?"

"No. He's around my age. Maybe a couple years older."

Well, hmm. So age didn't explain the Santa comment. But some men did go prematurely gray. And if Noah Tannehill was a recluse, he could definitely have a beard.

Willow ended the call with Zach and smiled at her daughter. "You had a good nap. How are you feeling?"

"I'm okay. Can I get up now? Can I have a snack?"

"Yes and yes. Let's get your shoes on, and I'll grab the snack bag on the way out the door. We're going for a little drive."

Willow sent her mother a quick text explaining the new development, grabbed the snack bag, and ushered Emma to the car. As she buckled her daughter into her car seat, Willow's thoughts returned to Noah Tannehill's phone call. Drew must have had some reason to bring up Santa Claus. Wonder what it was?

"What happened to your hands?"

Noah ignored the question and turned a scowl toward the boy seated at the small table in the kitchen section of his workshop. "Do you want warm milk or hot apple cider?"

"Can I have hot chocolate?"

"No." Noah didn't have any hot chocolate. "Milk or cider. Those are your choices."

"Milk, I guess. I'd rather have hot chocolate."

"Beggars can't be choosers."

"What does that mean?"

"That a boy who needs something warm to drink should be satisfied with what he gets even if it's not exactly what he wants."

"I like milk, too." The kid—Drew—rifled through a container filled with screws that Noah had sitting on the table. "I just like chocolate milk better."

Noah filled a brown earthenware mug with milk and set it in the microwave. While the oven did its thing, he folded his arms and studied the boy. Noah's temper had risen from simmer to stew when he learned that the boy had come from the lodge by Mirror Lake instead of wandering off the Triple T Ranch. While the chance of falling through the ice in one of the few deeper sections was minimal, Drew could have easily gotten wet up to his waist.

Hypothermia could have killed the kid. Noah did not need another senseless death anywhere close to his world. "What made you think it was a good idea to go off in the woods alone? Not to mention walking on the ice."

"I dunno." Drew shrugged his shoulders. "I just needed to be by myself for a little while. My mom worries about me a bunch, and sometimes that makes me want to be away from everything."

That took some of the heat out of Noah's irritation. *Been there, done that.* He'd never forget the look on his mom's face that one Easter dinner when he, Daniel, and Dad had all been called into a four-alarm downtown. The weight of a mother's concern could be a heavy burden. "Why does your mom worry about you?"

Again, that little shrug. "It's complicated."

Okay, this kid was too young to say something like that.

Ding. Noah turned back toward the microwave, removed the mug of milk, and placed it on the table in front of the boy.

"Thank you." Drew tugged off his hat and gloves and stuck them into his coat pocket.

"You're welcome. So why aren't you in school?"

"We're already done for the day," the boy replied. He lifted the mug and took a sip. "I'm homeschooled. When we moved here in January, I was going to go to St. Luke's School, but they didn't have room for me. I didn't want to go to public school because I was bullied at my school in Nashville and the third-grade teacher in Lake in the Clouds scared me, so my mom said she'd teach me. She's really good at it, but she says I try her patience. If we're still here next fall, I'll go to St. Luke's because I'm smart and exhausting and need kids to play with. How come the sign outside says 'Santa's Workshop'?"

It took Noah a moment to catch up with the whiplash-speed change of subject. Drew divulged a lot of information that piqued Noah's curiosity. Thinking of the one-by-two-foot sign hanging on the cabin's front porch that he'd carved in middle school woodshop and given to his parents for Christmas, he corrected, "It says 'The Hideaway.'"

"No, it doesn't," the boy insisted. "It says 'Santa's Workshop.' It's kinda hard to read because the *k* has a big splat of bird poop on it and there's a big crack in it, but that's what it says."

The bird-poop comment triggered Noah's memory of the contents of his scrap lumber pile stacked out of sight against the far wall of his workshop. "Oh. We're talking about different signs. My dad made the old 'Santa's Workshop' sign."

"Does your dad live here?"

"No, he's gone."

"He's dead? My dad is dead, too. How did your dad die? Mine had a car wreck, and I was in the car with him, but I didn't get hurt too bad and everyone said it was a miracle because I wasn't buckled in. I need more miracles 'cause I break things all the time."

"What sort of things?"

"Bones. I broke my right arm twice and I thought I broke my ankle, too, but it was only a sprain. I broke a tooth, too. Are you going to answer any of my questions?"

"No. I can't get a word in edgewise."

Drew didn't pause. Instead he asked, "What happened to your dad?"

"He died from lung cancer."

"Did he get it because he smoked? Cigarettes are bad for you."

Noah shook his head. "No, my dad didn't smoke. He was a firefighter, and they have a higher risk of dying from cancer than the average person."

"A firefighter!" Drew's eyes rounded. "Oh, wow. So he was a hero?"

"Yeah, he was a hero. Now shut up and drink your milk, kid."

His mouth in the mug, Drew muttered, "It's not nice to say shut up."

"I'm not a nice man." Noah checked his watch. How much longer until the boy's mom got here? He wasn't accustomed to this nonstop chatter.

Noah strode to the thermostat on the wall and punched the heater up a couple of degrees. Ordinarily, he kept a fire burning in the woodstove while he worked, ensuring the shop stayed warm. His trip into town this morning meant that the place was chillier than usual. Noah didn't mind, but the kid needed to warm up.

At the table, Drew Eldridge slurped a long drink of milk. Then the chatterbox started up again. "How come your dad made a 'Santa's Workshop' sign?"

"It was part of our holiday lawn decorations."

"You had lawn decorations this far from town?"

"In Denver. That's where I grew up. You sure are a nosy kid, you know that?"

"I'm a little nervous. I always talk a lot when I'm nervous."

Noah was taken aback. After those first few minutes, Drew hadn't seemed to be frightened. Noah hadn't intended to scare the kid. Maybe he was just out of practice being around people. "Am I making you nervous?"

"Nah. Well, maybe a little bit. I'm mostly worried about what my mom is going to do. She's going to be mad because I didn't go where I said I was going, and she'll probably punish me."

"Does she ground you?" Noah asked.

"No. She'll take away my Switch. It's her new favorite thing to do. She used to not do it because I played *Animal Crossing* with my grandmother when we lived in Nashville. Nana really loved doing that, and Mom said she couldn't punish her when I was the person in trouble. But now that we live in the same town, we hardly ever play. I see her almost every day. She babysits a lot."

"Your grandmother plays video games?" Noah folded his arms and leaned against the counter. "That's cool."

"Yeah. She's cool, I guess." The boy took another long drink of milk, then set down his cup with a bit of a bang. "Oops. Sorry. It slipped. Don't worry. I didn't break it."

"Good. It's my favorite mug."

"Whoa, you're lucky. I probably could have broken it without meaning to do it." The boy wiped his mouth with his coat sleeve and added, "My mom sometimes calls me Andrew-the-Accident-Waiting-to-Happen. She'd never give me her favorite anything to use."

He paused and giggled softly. "She *did* let me help hang the cuckoo clock Auntie Helen gave us for Christmas, and I get to wind it every week."

Noah put two and two together. Stifling a grin, he clarified. "Your mom wants you to break the cuckoo clock?"

"Maybe. She doesn't like it very much. But I'm really careful. My sister and I both love Cocoa. That's what we named our cuckoo bird." Then, in an abrupt change of subject, he added, "I'm not cold anymore. Will you show me how the dollhouses work now?"

Noah released a long sigh. When the kid first showed up and quizzed him about the contents of Noah's shelves, he'd begged to see a dollhouse in action. Noah had put him off, saying truthfully that Drew needed to stay inside and warm up first.

Noah had an old house he wouldn't mind sacrificing for the effort. Besides, lighting a fire might be the only way to put a lid on the motormouth's questions.

"Okay. Let's do it."

"Hurray!" Drew scrambled out of his chair. "I love playing with fire!"

Noah turned his most ferocious gaze upon the boy and stepped right up to him. Looming above the boy, hands braced on his hips, he put a stern note of threat into his voice as he said, "Stop. Right. There. We already talked about the lighter you used earlier. Fire is not a toy. Never under any circumstances is fire something to play with."

Drew's eyes went round. "I know. I didn't mean we're actually going to play with fire. That's just an expression."

"Don't care," Noah snapped. He wanted to put the fear of God into the boy where this subject was concerned. He'd lost track of the times he'd seen when mixing children and fire led to heartache. "Don't even say such a thing is fun, you got it?"

Drew nodded and said, "Yessir."

Noah held the boy's gaze for a long moment, then nodded and took a step back. "All right. Put your hat and mittens back on, and you can hold the door while I get the dollhouse outside."

"They're not mittens. They're gloves," Drew corrected as he tugged his outdoor gear from his pocket. He studied the shelving. "Can I pick which one we burn?"

"No." Noah intended to use one of his early, basic structures, which he mainly kept for scraps, not the more elaborate designs he built today and gifted to fire stations around the state for training purposes.

"Okay." The boy pulled on his hat and gloves. Excitement glimmered in the gaze he turned toward Noah.

To his shock and surprise, Noah was tempted to smile as he donned his coat. He liked that the kid had accepted the no rather than whine. Made him think he probably heard the word quite often.

Noah absently rubbed his aching thigh as he walked to the shelves at the back of the workshop where he stored the completed houses ready for shipping. Then, like an excited puppy, Drew scampered around Noah. He asked, "Which one is it? Is it heavy? I can help you carry it. I'm pretty strong for a kid my age."

"I can tell. You've got some guns for a, what, ten-year-old kid?"

"I'm only eight."

"Ah, well. You look older than eight." Seeing the proud lift to Drew's shoulders and the self-satisfied smirk form on his lips, Noah couldn't help but smile. Probably the first one he'd cracked in weeks. Maybe months. Hell, had he smiled even once since his personal Armageddon?

That thought wiped the smile right off his face. Gruffly, he spoke to Drew. "It's this one here. It's not terribly heavy, just bulky. And I'm not going to carry it. I'm going to wheel it out in this."

Noah gestured toward the four-wheeled collapsible wagon he used to tote items around his property. He couldn't carry very much when he needed a cane to walk.

The boy eyed the dollhouse critically. "That's not very fancy."

"It doesn't need to be fancy. It's supposed to be functional. Here, you get the top right corner." With Drew's help, Noah lifted the dollhouse off the shelf and set it into the wagon. "Go get the door, son."

Outside, Noah set the dollhouse atop the old iron barrel. It was a two-story structure made of plywood with a pitched roof. The interior contained four separate rooms and an attic space with sliding panel doors to access each. This particular dollhouse stood forty-two inches tall and thirty-six inches wide, which made the structure slightly smaller than a Barbie Dreamhouse. "You gather some fuel while I get my torch."

"What sort of fuel?"

"Anything that will burn. Forage around below the woodpile. Pine cones are great for this purpose." Noah slid open the door on the bottom right. "Put them in here. This is our burn room."

"Okay!" Drew scampered off.

Noah went inside to get his blowtorch, a spray bottle of water, and a fire extinguisher. When he returned, the boy had a nice pile of tinder in the dollhouse. Noah pointed toward a log a safe distance away. "You go sit over there. Watch and listen."

"Can't I—"

"No." The boy did as he was told, and Noah nodded at him. He realized he kinda liked this kid. Go figure. He didn't like anybody anymore.

He began his lecture. "Like I told you earlier, my dollhouses are training tools for firefighters. The better a firefighter understands what the fire will do next, the better he can fight it. Using this house, we can demonstrate fire flow path."

"What's that?"

"Behavior. I'm going to show you fire behavior."

"I know how fire behaves. It makes smoke, and you can die from smoke. You don't have to be on fire and burn up to die."

"That's true," Noah agreed. "But did you know that opening the wrong window in a burning house can speed the fire's growth? Or that opening the right window can make the fire go where you want it to go?"

"Why would I want to make a fire go anywhere but out?"

"Well, because first, you must rescue the people inside."

Concern glimmered in the boy's eyes. "And the pets," he insisted. "You can't let their dogs die."

"People and pets are first priority," Noah assured. "You buy yourself time by controlling the flow of oxygen to the fire and, thus, controlling the fire."

Drew frowned as he studied the dollhouse. "What if you keep all the windows shut?"

"Well, why don't we see?"

Noah lit his propane torch and set the tinder in the burn room afire. For the next ten minutes, he showed his young trespasser how fire moved from room to room, how introducing oxygen gave it fuel, and how removing it killed the flames. While he hadn't given a demonstration like this in forever, it came back to him easily. He talked about the science of fire behavior, smoke patterns, smoke colors, and air patterns.

The boy was captivated. And smart. He asked the right questions, but Noah realized he was missing an opportunity. He'd satisfied the boy's interest in the dollhouses, but Drew Eldridge didn't need to know about firefighting science. He needed safety knowledge. "Do you know how you would get out of your home in case of a fire, Drew?"

"We don't really have a home right now," the boy responded with a shrug. "We're living in one of Nana's cabins at the lodge until we decide where we want to live forever. We might go to Texas to be near my uncles and Aunt Brooke if we decide not to stay in Colorado."

"Okay, then, do you know how you'd get out of your cabin?"

"From my bedroom?"

"From every room," Noah said. "You need to know two ways out of every room in your house. Actually, every building you enter. You should make it a habit to take notice of exits every time you go somewhere new."

"Like my nana's house. I sleep over with her a lot."

"You should definitely have an escape plan for everywhere you sleep."

"We had one at our old house." Excitement and pride gleamed in Drew's eyes. "It was two stories, so we had ladders to hang from our windows. Mom even had us do fire drills like we did at school."

"That's good. Do it for your new place, too." Noah closed the sliding doors on the dollhouse, leaving only the burn room window cracked. He nodded toward the boy. "Come here, Drew."

He sprang from his seat on the log.

"Now, do what I do." Noah placed his fingertips against the left top slide. Drew repeated the motion. One by one, they tested the slides. Noah lifted Drew to reach the attic and roof vents. He saved the burn room for last.

Drew touched it, then quickly yanked his hand away and backed up, putting distance between himself and the dollhouse. "It's hot!"

"The fire behind it is actively burning. The lesson here is that if you're ever in a burning building, before you open a closed door, touch it. If it's hot, don't open the door. Find another exit. Because remember—what happens if you open that door?" Judging the boy to be far enough away for safety's sake, Noah slid the burn room door open.

"Kaboom!" Drew exclaimed when the flames flared.

"In a manner of speaking, yeah." Noah opened all the dollhouse door slides. Soon, the house was ablaze.

"Wow. That's really so cool. Thank you for showing me, Mr. Tannehill."

"You're welcome. So, tell me what you've learned."

"Stay low to stay out of the smoke. Touch doors to see if they're hot before you open them. Then, get out, stay out, meet up where planned."

"That's all good, but you left something out."

"I did?"

"You did."

Drew furrowed his brow. "I don't— Oh! Two ways out! Always know two ways out!"

"There you go." Noah picked up his fire extinguisher and asked Drew, "Have you ever used one of these?"

"Nope."

"Okay, then." He walked over to the boy and handed the extinguisher to him saying, "Lesson number two. With a fire extinguisher, you want to remember P.A.S.S."

Drew studied the piece of equipment with wide eyes. "Like a football?"

"If that'll help you remember, then sure. Pull, aim, squeeze, and sweep. Back up some more. You need to stand eight to ten feet away."

"Okay."

Drew moved back fifteen feet. Noah took him by the shoulders and guided him to where he needed to be. "Now, don't do anything until I tell you. I'm going to describe what I want you to do first. Okay?" He waited for the boy's nod, then continued. "First is P. You're going to pull the pin on the fire extinguisher. You know what the pin is?"

"This thing?" Drew gripped the end of the pin between his thumb and forefinger.

"Yes, that's it. When I tell you to do it, you're going to pull that pin. For A, you want to aim the nozzle low toward the base of the fire. S, you're going to squeeze the lever to discharge— No! Not yet. What did I tell you?"

Drew grinned sheepishly. "Sorry. I'm supposed to wait."

"Then do it." Noah took a breath to collect his thoughts before he continued. "Okay, once the foam begins to flow, you're going to sweep—the second S. Sweep the nozzle from side to side until the flames are extinguished. Got it?"

"I think so."

"Then practice. We're going to go through it once pretending."

"But the house is about to burn up!" Drew exclaimed. "Shouldn't I hurry and put the fire out?"

"I think you should do what I say. Practice. What are you going to do first?"

"I'm going to pull this." Drew pretended to pull the pin with a flourish. "And then I'm going to aim this hose, and then I'm going to squeeze this trigger, and then I'm going to spray from side to side like this. Can I do it for real now?"

Noah figured he had a fifty-fifty chance of getting hit in the face with foam. "Go for it."

Drew couldn't get the pin out. Noah put his fingers over the boy's and helped. "Aim the nozzle."

The lever proved to be too stiff for the boy, too, so Noah helped him squeeze. "Woo-hoo!" Drew called as the white foam arced toward the fire.

"Keep it low at the base of the fire, remember? And don't forget the second S," Noah cautioned.

"Sweep!" The boy gleefully extinguished the fire, continuing to spray until the canister had emptied.

"Good job, Drew."

"Thanks, Mr. Tannehill. That was fun. How do you know all this stuff? Are you a firefighter?"

Noah went still. Now, there was a kick in the balls disguised as an innocent question.

His mood returning to black, Noah snapped out, "No."

Then he walked over to the tree stump where he'd left his cane, picked it up, and added, "Wait here. Your mother should be arriving any minute. Don't touch anything."

"Where are you going?"

Noah didn't respond as he started toward the house, then stopped and reconsidered. He returned to the burn site, bent, and scooped up his blowtorch. Sound floated toward him in the brittle winter air. An automobile headed in his direction.

"Mr. Tannehill? Mr. Tannehill, wait!"

He didn't wait. He picked up his pace. He didn't want to look at Drew's bright, curious eyes or see his wonder and ready smile. He didn't want to hear any more about his having lost his father or answer any more of the kid's incessant questions. He damned sure didn't want to speak to the mother. He wanted to shut himself in his cabin, alone.

Alone. That's what he needed.

What he deserved.

Less than a minute after he entered the house, he heard a knock at his front door. "Mr. Tannehill, can I come in? I need to use the bathroom. I gotta go really bad. Number two. And you're out of toilet paper in the bathroom in your workshop."

Noah thumped his head on the nearest doorjamb, then headed for his back door.

Chapter Four

"IN A QUARTER MILE, turn right onto Running Elk Road. Your destination is on the left."

Willow let out a relieved sigh. What should have been a thirty-five-minute trip had taken almost an hour due to an accident on the road near Raindrop Lodge and a stubborn herd of mountain goats who created another roadblock a mile back.

Seated beside Willow in the front passenger seat, Aunt Helen observed, "Something I've wondered about—is there a way to make your GPS speak in a masculine voice instead of a feminine one?"

From the backseat, where she sat next to Emma, Genevieve replied, "Surely there is."

"Remind me to google that later," Aunt Helen said, glancing down at her phone. "I don't have any bars here."

They were out in the middle of nowhere, Willow thought. Her grip tightened around the steering wheel.

How could she have brought her children to a place where cell phone service didn't exist? What kind of mother was she?

Not as good a mother as her own—that's for sure. Willow could always count on Genevieve Prentice. She always did what was best for her children. Even when she'd had her own little personal crisis, flipped out, and moved to Colorado, that had been the best thing for the family because it led to the truce in World War Prentice.

No matter how hard she tried, Willow would never be as good a mom as Genevieve.

She didn't have her mother's strength.

Genevieve hadn't retreated from the world when her husband died leaving her with not two, but four— FOUR—children to raise. Nope, she squared her shoulders, lifted her chin, and charged ahead. Fearlessly. Unlike Willow, who was afraid. All. The. Damned. Time.

Willow had been so relieved and grateful when her mother had arrived at the Raindrop Lodge cabin with Aunt Helen just as Willow started her car to retrieve Drew from the address on Running Elk Road. Genevieve had a knack of being there when Willow needed her. At least, she was there when Willow wasn't pushing her away.

While Emma played with Willow's tablet—screen rules be damned under these circumstances—her mother and Aunt Helen chatted almost nonstop. The conversation centered on the women's ongoing feud with the county employee in charge of permitting and provided Willow a welcome distraction. Despite the primarily positive intel from Zach about Noah Tannehill and the fact that Drew had sounded just fine when she spoke to him, Willow's worry and concern ratcheted up with every minute that passed. By the time she reached the entrance gate at 4743 Running Elk Road where a sign read THE HIDEAWAY, she was strung tight as a guitar string.

Her son had been alone with a stranger for more than an hour. What if...

Stop it.

She followed tire tracks through the snow toward a large, attractive log mountain home. A second building on the property appeared to be what was popularly called a barndominium these days. Her gaze darted between the two structures. She was desperate to see her son.

Willow recognized that her anxiety level was overblown. Her mouth shouldn't be this dry. Her heart shouldn't pound this way. However, this is what she'd been dealing with for the past few years. *Mrs. Eldridge, there's been an accident. Mrs. Eldridge, I'm so sorry to have to tell you this. He wasn't buckled into the car seat, Mrs. Eldridge. Your son is lucky to be alive.*

"There he is," Genevieve said from the passenger seat. "Near the barn. What is that thing he's holding?"

Willow heard the click of a seatbelt release, then Aunt Helen scooted the center of the backseat and leaned forward. "It looks like a fire extinguisher to me."

A fire extinguisher! "What is he doing with a fire extinguisher?"

"Better than a fire starter, I'd imagine," her aunt observed.

The tire tracks continued toward the house, but Willow veered off in the direction of the second building.

She was thankful she drove an SUV equipped with snow tires, especially when she stomped on the brakes and the tires slid a bit before the vehicle came to a complete stop.

She cut the engine and bailed out of the SUV. "Drew, baby. Are you okay?"

"Don't call me a baby, Mom," he protested as she threw her arms around him and clutched him tight. "I'm fine."

Thank you, God. Relief made her knees weak, but rather than collapse like she wanted to do, she rode the motherhood roller coaster and did her job. "Actually, you're not fine. Andrew John Eldridge, you are in so much trouble! You had permission to walk up to the gift shop. What made you think it was all right to take off into the wilderness all by yourself?"

"I didn't mean to go into the wilderness, Mom. I thought I was taking a shortcut, but I got lost. I didn't know which way to go. Then I found the creek, and I thought it would lead me to Mirror Lake, only instead, I saw this house. I was going to knock on the door and ask for help, but I got distracted by the North Pole."

Santa Claus. The North Pole. "What are you talking about, Drew?"

"Look! I'll show you!" He dropped the fire extinguisher and dashed around the corner of the building. Willow trailed after him, a follow-up question about the fire extinguisher on the tip of her tongue.

"See?" Drew pointed toward a wooden sign that read SANTA'S WORKSHOP. "I knew it wasn't real, but I couldn't help myself, Mom. I went inside."

"Oh, Drew."

"I know it was wrong to snoop, and I'm very sorry. I

apologized really good to Mr. Tannehill." Drew paused a moment before adding, "He doesn't like Christmas at all. He's like the Grinch when it comes to Santa Claus."

Willow sighed. She could relate. Though she pasted on a happy face each year for the children's sake, Willow would be content to skip the Christmas season entirely. The worst time of her life was tied to the holidays. She'd discovered her husband's affair during a Christmas party. She'd made her decision to leave him while watching Drew's rehearsal for the Christmas pageant at church. Andy had wrecked his car with their son aboard and died on December 14.

Distracted by thoughts of grinchery, Willow was slow to pick up on the tale her son had begun to relay about setting a dollhouse on fire.

"What? Wait!" Willow held up her hand, palm out. "Wait a minute. You set a toy on fire?"

"Not me. Mr. Tannehill. And it wasn't a toy or an accident. He did it on purpose. And guess what, Mom? He let me put it out!"

So, the Grinch of Lake in the Clouds played with fire? And he'd encouraged her son to join him?

Anger flashed through her and, on its heels, concern. What sort of man set toys on fire to entertain a child?

Serial killers set fires. They tortured animals.

Drew continued in an excited rush. "He taught me how air is fuel for a fire and P.A.S.S to put it out. And if you're ever in a burning building, touch the door to see if it's hot before you open it!"

Willow walked up to Drew and took him by the shoulders. "Stop. Drew, hush. I need some context here. I want you to start at the beginning and tell me what happened. Slowly."

He did his best. When he was finished, all Willow knew for sure was that her son had trespassed because a sign had been too tempting for an eight-year-old Santa believer to resist. Why he and his host had spent the better part of the hour occupied with fire, she still didn't understand.

She knew she didn't like it. Drew got into enough trouble on his own without encouragement from an adult. So why in the world would Noah Tannehill play with fire with Drew? Her gaze shifted from the workshop to the house and then back to her son. "Where is Mr. Tannehill now?"

"He's in his house. Guess what? He has a cuckoo clock! I saw it when I went inside to take a poop. It was almost three o'clock, and I wanted to stay and watch it and see if it sounded like any of Auntie's clocks do, but he told me I had to wait for you outside because he could hear your car, and you were almost here."

"I see. Okay, then." Willow made a scooting motion with her hand. "Go get in the car with Nana and Auntie and your sister, Drew. I need to thank Mr. Tannehill for helping you."

And maybe give him a piece of her mind about mingling children and fire.

Not that she had much of a mind left to be doling out pieces of it.

As her son scampered away toward the SUV, Willow turned to the house. She was facing the back of it and could easily follow the footsteps through the snow to the back porch steps, but this didn't feel like a back-door sort of call. She decided to walk around to the front.

The house was dark. She heard no music nor the sound of a television drifting from indoors. Certainly didn't hear the barking of a dog or the mewl of a cat. She'd have believed the house to be empty had Drew not insisted that the man was inside.

Willow climbed the front porch steps, and when she didn't spy a doorbell, she rapped three times on the door.

Nobody responded.

She knocked again, harder this time. *Rap. Rap. Rap.*

Silence.

Well, what now?

Good manners demanded she not leave without thanking him, but honestly, that was just an excuse. She wanted to meet this man in person. She wanted to look into Noah Tannehill's eyes and take the measure of the man.

As best she could, anyway. She hadn't always been the best judge of character, had she? *Hello, Andy Eldridge's ghost. I'm talking about you.*

Willow remained haunted by the mistakes she'd made where her husband was concerned.

Stop. Don't go there right now. This isn't about what happened in your marriage in Nashville. It's about today in Lake in the Clouds, where it's time to play Mama Bear and make sure everything is on the up and up here on Running Elk Road.

She wanted to assess this stranger whose space her son had invaded. She needed to reassure herself that he'd had reasons for playing firebug with her son that went beyond psychopathic tendencies.

Knock. Knock. Knock.

Nothing.

"Okay, then," she murmured. She'd approach this from another angle.

Willow pulled out her phone and scrolled to Recents. Finding Noah Tannehill's number, she typed out a text. This is Drew's mom. I'm standing on your front porch and want to speak with you.

At least half a minute ticked by before her phone pinged with a response. Why?

I want to thank you. Among other things.

No need.

Well, yes, there is, too, a need. I can't leave without speaking to you.

I'm busy.

Busy doing what? Torturing an animal? Setting another fire? Please. It'll only take a minute of your time.

Another half a minute passed before he texted back. Did your kid get his stubbornness from you?

I'm afraid so.

Willow stared down at her screen, holding her breath. Finally, she heard footsteps approaching. She pasted on a smile as the door swung open. Her smile abruptly faded.

A fallen angel stood glaring down at her.

It was a fanciful notion. Ridiculous, really. Likely it popped into Willow's head as a result of that paranormal romance she'd read last week. He did look a lot like how the main male character was described.

Noah Tannehill was absurdly handsome. His thick mahogany hair brushed the collar of a gray flannel shirt. His eyes were mesmerizing, a glowing cat's eyes amber, though that didn't come close to describing them. Willow figured she would need at least a dozen more adjectives to adequately do that job. He had strong, sharp bones and a complexion that appeared tan even in the middle of winter. His mouth was...well,

Willow couldn't tell how it was shaped because, at the moment, it stretched in a grim line to match his furrowed brow.

She was tall, but he towered above her—six foot three or four, Willow guessed. As he folded his arms across a broad chest, his shoulders appeared to be as wide as the front range of the Rockies.

Even with all that angry on, he was a beautiful man.

Okay, maybe he was a Ted Bundy type, after all.

"Well?" he asked.

Off-balance, Willow stuttered out the first thing that popped into her mind. "I'm a grinch, too. In fact, my sister calls me Grinchette upon occasion."

"Excuse me?"

"Drew said you're a bah-humbug type when it comes to Christmas, and so am I, so we have that in common."

He folded his arms. "This is why you badgered me to answer the door?"

"I didn't badger," Willow defended. "I texted."

"Multiple times," he shot back. "That's harassment. All because I played Good Samaritan to your kid."

"I know. I'm a pest. It's part of the job description when you're a mother in today's world." Since she'd already dipped her toe in that particular pool, she might as well jump all the way in. "May I use your bathroom, please?"

Noah's mouth gaped. "What *is* it with you people?"

"I have my grandmother's small bladder. It's a trial."

He hesitated for a long moment, and Willow wondered if he'd deny her request. *What are you hiding, Mr. Tall, Dark, and Cranky?*

Finally, he exhaled a little sigh, stepped back, and opened the door wider. "Fine. Be my guest."

Willow darted indoors before he could change his mind. The inside of the house was neat and clean but sparsely decorated. It reminded Willow of how her brother Lucas decorated his home. Everything was functional, with leather and earth-tone fabrics. He kept no pillows on the sofa or throws draped artfully over the back of a chair. She noted the paperback book lying facedown and open on a table beside a chair and came to a complete stop. It was the same paranormal romance she'd read last week, the new release in a popular series.

Noah Tannehill reads romance novels?

Maybe he had a wife, after all. Or at least a girlfriend. *He surely has a girlfriend. All Roman gods do.*

Ted Bundy had girlfriends.

"The bathroom is the first door on the left," he said, gesturing toward a hallway.

Willow offered up a smile and made her way to the indicated door. The bathroom reflected more of what she'd seen—practical and plain. Feeling a tad bit guilty despite her Mama Bear intentions, she snooped in the cabinet. Basic cleaning supplies and toilet paper. No tampons or makeup. No bloody knives or whips or chains.

She stared at her reflection in the bathroom mirror. Her eyes did look a little wild, her mouth pinched. *Willow Eldridge, get a grip.*

She exited the bathroom to find Noah Tannehill with one hip propped on a bar stool, drumming his fingers against the granite countertop. His expression, already dark, had turned thunderous. "Just what is it you suspect me of doing to your kid, lady?"

Willow opened her mouth to automatically deny the accusation but then hesitated. Had she been that obvious, or did he have a guilty conscience? Psychopaths didn't have a conscience.

But she'd probably been pretty obvious, too.

She decided to play it down the middle. "Willow. My name is Willow Eldridge, and I sincerely want to thank you for calling to tell me where my son was. I also wanted to meet you in person. Drew wandering off the way he did this afternoon scared me to death, and when I'm scared, my mind can go to some very dark places. He's only eight and—"

"I didn't touch your kid," he snapped.

"Oh, no no no. Not that sort of dark. I never went there." Although come to think of it, she probably should have gone there instead of where she went. "But when Drew told me you'd been setting toys on fire, my brain went to torturing animals and Ted Bundy."

He gaped at her. "You decided I'm a serial killer?"

She shrugged. "You are terribly handsome. Is your name Theodore, by chance?"

"Noah." He chuffed a laugh. "You're crazy."

"I'm a mother." Willow gave a dismissive wave. "Crazy comes with the territory."

"And I wasn't setting a toy on fire, either." Now his voice held a note of defensiveness. "I demonstrated a firefighting training tool!"

"He said it was a dollhouse."

"That's what they're called."

"Why?"

"Because they look like a dollhouse. I make them in my workshop."

"I meant why did you do the demonstration?"

"I had to do something to keep him occupied until you got here. The kid is curious."

"So you thought it would be a good idea for him to play with fire?"

"I *found* him playing with fire."

"What!"

He explained about Drew and the lighter and how his shop was filled with wood, sawdust, and other flammable materials. Again, Willow's knees went weak. She stumbled toward his sofa, asking, "Mind if I sit down?"

"Could I stop you?" he grumbled.

"If your shop is such a flammable place, why do you leave lighters lying around?"

"I don't. My torches and tools were properly stored in my shop. Your kid snooped. Like mother like son, it appears."

Willow buried her face in her hands. "Is it Friday? I really wish it were Friday."

"It's Wednesday."

"I was afraid of that."

"Why do you want it to be Friday?"

"Martini Friday. It's so much better than Taco Tuesday. I limit myself to one martini on Friday evenings, but I could really use a drink today. That boy is going to be the death of me."

"So this isn't the first time he's wandered off?"

"Actually, it is. And honestly, it's a victory of sorts for both of us. Drew has been a clingy child."

The look Noah gave said he didn't believe her.

"It's true. I'm sure it was my fault. He was involved in a serious automobile accident a couple of years ago, and afterward, I hovered. I'm trying to reverse that habit. Just like I'm trying to encourage the curiosity he's currently exhibiting. But I'm learning that a curious child is a parenting challenge. I've traded one problem for another."

And she didn't know why she was babbling on about this. And yet she couldn't seem to stop. "It's hard being a parent in today's world. Danger comes at your children in every direction. A mother hen gets whiplash trying to watch out for her chicks, and she ends up with scrambled eggs for a brain."

"So that's your defense for snooping in my bathroom cabinets?"

"How did you...never mind. I'm trying not to be an overprotective helicopter mom. No snowplowing the road ahead of my children. It's one of the reasons we've come here to Lake in the Clouds. I want Drew to learn independence and self-reliance, and I thought it was safer to do that in the mountains than on city streets. But then I give him permission to walk by himself to buy a candy bar at the lodge, and he ends up treading thin ice. It's disheartening."

"I imagine so." He hesitated a moment before adding, "Nothing wrong with watching out for your kid, Willow. Stranger danger and all of that."

Willow shrugged. "But how do I raise children who aren't fearful? I want my children to be safe, but I also want them to be strong and bold and brave. I want my kids to be brave. I want to be brave. If I'm always harping about safety, how will they have the courage to take a risk? How do I balance the message? My great-grandmother was only sixteen when she immigrated to America all by herself. What courage that took! And my grandmother used to send her children outside to play in the morning, and she'd tell them not to come home before dark. Such independence that fostered.

Maybe my mother is so strong because she wandered the neighborhoods when she was young. That's what I want for my children, but it'd be irresponsible to do that in Nashville. Maybe it's irresponsible here, too."

"If that's what you want, then walk the walk."

"What do you mean?"

"They'll learn more from what they see you doing than from what you tell them to do. You want 'em to be brave, then show them how brave you are."

"That's just it," Willow said with a hint of a wail in her voice. "I'm not brave."

"Sure you are. You just talked your way into a serial killer's home to check for tortured cats."

Her smile was slow in coming, but it dawned bright. "That's the nicest thing anyone's said to me in a long time. However, I didn't say anything about cats. Though I guess I should make an excuse to check out your basement."

"Be my guest." He made a flourishing gesture toward a staircase. "I have a nice-sized attic, too. Been a while since anyone's been either up or down, though. I live alone. Blessedly alone. Might want to take a broom with you to knock down the spiderwebs. Maybe some bug spray, too. Critter spray, just to be safe."

She gave him a long look. "Are you looking for a cleaning lady, Mr. Tannehill?"

Maybe...just maybe...she saw the flicker of a genuine smile on his lips before he shrugged and said, "If the dust rag fits."

He wasn't a serial killer. He probably didn't even have cobwebs in his attic. But after the past hour, Willow felt like she had bats in her belfry.

Finally confident her knees would once again support

her, Willow rose from her seat on his sofa. "Another time, perhaps. I have a couple of appointments I'm late for already. Also, my mother and her sister are in the car with the children, and they'll wonder what's keeping me."

"Brought along reinforcements, hmm?" he observed.

"I might be crazy, but I'm not stupid."

"Won't they be worried that you've been inside Jeffrey Dahmer's lair for so long? Will they knock down my door and come after me with baseball bats?"

Willow smirked. "Have you met my aunt Helen? It's not beyond the realm of possibility."

"In that case, allow me to usher you quickly toward the door."

She laughed. "Here's your hat. What's your hurry?"

"I'm not stupid, either. Your car is out back. Go this way and save some steps." He escorted Willow through the kitchen toward his back door.

Before he opened it and allowed winter inside, she extended her hand. "It's been a pleasure to meet you, Noah Tannehill. Thank you for your kindness to my son and for being a good neighbor and Good Samaritan. Please let me know if there is anything I can do for you. I owe you."

He hesitated a moment before extending his own hand. Only then did Willow notice the burn scars. *Oh great. How appropriate that I'd end this encounter with a faux pas.*

Because it wasn't in her to ignore another's pain, she asked, "Does it hurt?"

"Not anymore." He clasped her hand and shook it. "Good-bye, Willow."

"Good-bye, Noah. I'll let you return to whatever you

were doing before we invaded your world. But before I go, may I ask…do you make the other kind of dollhouse? My little girl turns five soon. I think a dollhouse would be a perfect gift for her. She's just the right age."

"Sorry, I don't," Noah said with a note of finality.

Willow shrugged. "Hey, never hurts to ask. Thanks again, Noah. Maybe we'll see you around town sometime."

"Don't count on it. I stay swamped burying bodies."

Willow laughed as she exited Noah Tannehill's house. Nothing like ghoulish humor to brighten a girl's day.

Leaning against the passenger-side door of Willow's SUV, Genevieve watched her grandchildren roll a ball of snow destined to become the torso of a snowman. "You'd think they'd get tired of snowmen, but they don't."

"A field of fresh, unspoiled snow is difficult to resist," her sister responded. Helen remained inside the vehicle, but had the back passenger window rolled down.

Genevieve frowned. "I wonder what's keeping Willow so long? At this rate, she'll have to reschedule her vendor appointments. It could prove to be a problem with only six weeks to the wedding."

"Maybe she's flirting with Noah Tannehill."

Genevieve whipped her head around and looked at Helen with interest. "Now, why would you say that?"

"He's gorgeous. I saw him in the post office around Thanksgiving. He's the kind of pretty that makes a room full of women burst out into excited giggles in his wake."

"Oh." Genevieve glanced toward the house. "Interesting. I do wish she'd show some interest in men again. But as far as I know, she hasn't dated since Andy died."

"Actually, she has been dating some."

The words struck Genevieve like a dart to the heart. On the one hand, she was thrilled to learn that Willow had taken that all-important step in moving forward with her life. And yet it hurt Genevieve that Willow would tell her aunt about it, not her mother. "I see."

"Stop it, Genevieve," her sister warned. She exited the SUV and stood beside Genevieve. Helen knew her better than anyone alive, so it was no surprise that she correctly surmised what Genevieve was thinking. Helen added, "There's no need to get pissy about this. Last summer, Willow talked about it with Brooke when we all met in Texas at your Fourth of July get-together at the family lake house. I just happened to overhear."

Genevieve's sidelong look was sharp enough to cut steel.

Helen continued. "Okay, it's possible I intentionally eavesdropped. The girls were downstairs in the playroom, and I'd come in to mix more Bloody Marys. When I heard Brooke mention the word *divorce*, my ears couldn't help but perk up."

"Mine would have, too," Genevieve conceded.

"Willow was reassuring her sister that life did go on after a relationship ended. Then she said she spoke from experience and that her heart had healed to the point where she'd wanted to date again. She signed up on a dating app."

Genevieve's mouth dropped open in shock. "Willow?"

Helen responded with a knowing nod. "Surprised me, too. She said she'd been on two first dates that didn't click. She had seen another man four times before deciding it wasn't right. Brooke had just asked her if she'd slept with any of them when Drew ran into the house yelling for his mom. It was right after that boat ride where Lucas played Dastardly Boat Driver."

Genevieve recalled the moment. Drew's laughter and excitement had attracted the attention of the entire gathering. He'd giggled his way through a description of his "wild and wooly best ever" tube ride. It made everybody smile.

"Anyway," Helen continued. "I cornered Willow afterward."

"I'm sure you did," Genevieve replied in a snippy tone. Helen wasn't one who let a chance to learn juicy details pass her by.

"Willow told me that she'd been dipping her toes back into those waters but intends to go slow. Very slow."

"And you didn't tell me about it?"

"She asked me not to."

Genevieve folded her arms, torn between hurt and curiosity. She pointed out, "You're telling me now."

"It was last summer," Helen said with a shrug. "I figure the statute of limitations has run out on my promise."

"Hmm."

Helen gave her sister a considering look. "Hmm, what? I know that tone."

"I don't know. Willow's dating again is just...curious."

"Because Andy was the great love of her life? You think she should take more time to mourn? You waited an age after David died to go out with a man, as I recall."

"No, that's not it at all. Everyone mourns differently, and Willow is the only person who can know when it's right for her to move on romantically. I just—" Genevieve shrugged. "I've spent more time with her in the past year than the previous five years put together. I'm picking up on something...I can't put my finger on exactly what it is...but I'm beginning to wonder if there's something she didn't tell us about her marriage. I wonder if they were having problems."

"Willow and Andy? Seriously? Why would you think that?"

"Just...I don't know. There hasn't been one thing in particular. Little comments she's made from time to time. They made my antennae go up."

"You haven't asked her about it?"

"With my history on the subject? Not hardly."

"Understandable," Helen observed with a nod.

Genevieve's and Willow's rocky relationship had begun when her eldest daughter first brought Andy Eldridge home to meet the family. At the time, Genevieve and Willow had been very close, and Genevieve had been looking forward to meeting the man who put such bright stars in Willow's eyes. But unfortunately, Genevieve hadn't liked Andy that day. Something about him had sent her Spidey senses fluttering. Something struck her as off. She'd mistrusted him and refused to give Willow her blessing.

Willow didn't take kindly to that. Genevieve's unfounded suspicions about Andy caused damage to her and Willow's relationship even to this day. They'd never gotten back to the closeness they'd shared before Andy came into their lives.

Not that Genevieve hadn't tried. Andy proved himself over time, and Genevieve apologized to both her daughter and her beau for withholding her blessing. And yet Willow never quite forgave her. Their closeness appeared to be a thing permanently in the past. By the time he'd popped the question, Genevieve had been more than ready to dive in and throw a spectacular wedding, which she'd done.

Willow's attitude had warmed during the wedding planning. The girl had a natural affinity for such a task, and they'd made a good team putting the event together, well, except toward the end when she went a little Bridezilla and didn't like anything her mother suggested. Nevertheless, Genevieve had begun to believe that their troubles were behind them.

Then, shortly after the honeymoon, Andy accepted a job offer and moved Genevieve's daughter to Tennessee.

Genevieve never felt like she had a place in Willow's new life. News that Drew was on his way a short time later both thrilled Genevieve and broke her heart. She'd always dreamed of being a local nana. Learning to be a long-distance grandmother required a change of attitude, but she'd quickly learned to treasure the experience.

Now, though, she lived fifteen minutes from her grands. It had taken disaster for her old dreams to come true. While she never would have wished widowhood on Willow—been there, done that, understood the heartache—she was thrilled to have her babies close. Mostly thrilled, anyway. She'd get this disruption to her new life figured out. "Well, her marriage to Andy isn't the issue here."

Helen drummed her fingers against the car door. "Maybe not, but this could be a piece to the puzzle that is Willow. We should feel out Andy's parents when they come up to help Willow with the kids before Jake's wedding."

"No, just let it lie, Helen. I'm happy Willow is dating again. More than anything, I want her to handle widowhood better than I."

"You did just fine. You raised four awesome children."

"I did that, and I'm very proud of them." Genevieve's lips lifted in a rueful smile as she added, "I wouldn't have said that this time last year. They weren't awesome children a year ago."

"True. The boys, especially, were stubborn mules. If their grandfather had known the damage he would do to your family by the manner in which he bequeathed his ranch to y'all, I wonder if he'd have done things differently."

"Maybe. It would have been nice to avoid World War Prentice. And yet it worked out in my favor because I moved to Lake in the Clouds, and I love it here."

"I'm glad. You're happy, and the Prentice family is better now."

"I think so. I hope so. The wounds my family suffered are real. They may be scabbed over, but they're not entirely healed. It takes time."

"You have time."

Genevieve thought about her birthday rushing toward her like an F5 tornado. "Time is our most valuable commodity, and we waste so much of it when we are young. I wish my children would recognize that and not repeat my mistakes."

"What sort of mistakes?"

A kaleidoscope of scenes from her past flashed through Genevieve's mind, and the sting of tears came with them. A dozen responses to her sister's question hung on her tongue. She voiced the one uppermost in her mind. "I don't want to be old with an empty life, Helen."

"Well, thank you very much," Helen said with a sniff.

"Oh, don't be that way. You know what I mean."

"I don't think I do."

"Well, we were talking about men and dating, for one thing. Not sisters. I have the best sister in the universe. She's *always* there for me. If I don't say often enough just how much I love her, how important she is to me, and how I'd be lost without her, then I am a wretched human being."

"You are a wretched human being."

Genevieve leaned over and rested her head on her sister's shoulder. "I love you, too."

They passed a few moments in silence and watched as Drew struggled to lift the second snowball and place it on top of the first, assisted by his four-year-old sister. Then Helen said, "This seems to be a good time for me to bring up something I've wanted to mention to you."

"That sounds a bit ominous."

"Not ominous. On topic, I think. But frank."

"When are you not frank, Helen?"

"So sue me," she said with a shrug. Then she drew a deep breath, met her sister's eyes, and exhaled in a rush. "You're doing it again."

Genevieve blinked. "Doing what again?"

"You're losing yourself in Prenticeworld."

Genevieve's defenses flared. "What do you mean?"

"Where the hell is Vivie? She's disappeared."

"Don't make fun of me," Genevieve snapped. "That nickname was just a phase." She'd tried calling herself Vivie when she'd first moved to Colorado, but it hadn't fit.

"Well, call yourself what you want, but *that* Genevieve was a lot of fun. That Genevieve was focused on reinvention and revitalization. That Genevieve went snowmobiling and danced across an Alpine meadow. This Genevieve..." Helen's voice trailed off.

"What?" Genevieve said testily.

Helen lifted her nose into the air. With lemon in her tone, she said, "Babysits."

Genevieve folded her arms. "I don't babysit. I have nana playdates with my grands. What's wrong with that? I've been waiting for eight years to be able to go and have special times with them."

"Nothing's wrong with it. I know how much you love Emma and Drew and enjoy spending time with them. But..."

"But what?"

"Do you know how often you've turned down an invitation from friends and family because you had to babysit? You skipped the bridge club's Telluride ski-and-spa trip."

"I took the children to see the Eternity Springs hot-air balloon festival that day."

"You totally blew off the Friends of the Museum winter gala."

"That wasn't because of the children. I didn't have a date."

"Half the people there didn't go with dates. You were too tired to go because you spent the day sledding with Drew and Emma."

Genevieve started tapping her toes. She felt like she was under attack. "Look, I've waited a long time to be an in-town grandmother. Playdates are important to me. Doing things with Emma and Drew when it's just the three of us has added a new and special dimension to our relationship."

"Fine. If that's what you want, great. I'm just pointing out that it's a change—a big change—from what you said you wanted when you moved here. You even missed a meeting with Gage Throckmorton and the architect about The Emily renovations. You claim the project is special in your heart, and here you go alienating Gage. So much for Vivie finding love again."

"I rescheduled! Gage wasn't upset. He understands grandchildren, and I am not setting my sights on him. And for the love of a good cabernet, would you stop using that name!"

"Okay, Nana."

She said it in such a snippy tone that Genevieve couldn't stop herself from firing back. "You're just jealous."

Helen folded her arms and arched a brow. "Oh? Of what?"

"I'm spending time with them instead of you."

Pursing her lips, Helen studied Genevieve with narrowed eyes. Then, after a moment, she nodded regally. "I concede the point. I had a year with the new Genevieve when I didn't have to compete with anyone for your time. I enjoyed that. I miss that. I miss you."

Genevieve sighed as the starch went out of her. Helen's complaint was valid. Genevieve had missed the sister time with Helen, too.

Helen continued, "However, this isn't only about

me. It's about you, too. This is a caution. I see you slipping back into your old ways, where you always put your children's needs, wishes, and desires before your own. You worried about backsliding last year when we arrived home from Europe and discovered that your children had descended upon Lake in the Clouds. Well, you handled your children just fine. It's your grandchildren who have you tumbling down the mountain. Those grandchildren turn you to mush, Genevieve. You don't want to be old and empty and alone? Then you need to find some balance."

Darned if those tears didn't flood her eyes again. Genevieve blinked them away. She kept her gaze focused on Emma and Drew as she asked, "I've hurt your feelings, haven't I, Helen? I'm sorry. That's the last thing I ever want to do. I meant what I said earlier. You truly are the world's greatest sister."

"Thank you. But look, you're not responsible for my feelings. You certainly don't owe me any particular percentage of your time. Maybe I get a little green-eyed and lonely when you choose the kiddos over me, but that's on me. Not you."

"I don't choose them over you, Helen."

"Okay, maybe that's not the best word choice. It's a weird sort of sibling rivalry that doesn't involve siblings and reflects poorly on me. However, remember what Mama always said to us. 'Begin as you mean to go on.' You need to set some nana boundaries, Genevieve. Right now, you host nana camp every single day."

"Playdates. We have playdates. And I want my nana playdates!"

"I'm not saying you shouldn't have them. I'm saying that time is precious, and you need to be in charge of yours.

What if Willow decides to make this move permanent?
Will daily playdates become permanent, too? Will you ever
be free to jet off on a last-minute trip with me again? This
brings us to Bora-Bora. You never gave me an answer."

Genevieve winced. "I want to go. You know I do.
But when we talked about a sisters' trip this winter, I
didn't know I'd be hosting a wedding in March."

"At the risk of pissing you off even more, I'm going
to point out that you aren't hosting the wedding. Jake
and Tess are doing it, and they've hired someone to
oversee planning and execution. Times have changed,
Genevieve. Children are marrying later in life and
paying for their weddings—as well they should. You're
an honored guest at this wedding, not the hostess."

"Okay, you're right about that, but Willow needs my
help with the children."

"So that's your answer about the trip. It's nana time,
not sister time."

"We could go later—"

"I'm leaving next Tuesday."

Genevieve drew in a quick breath. "You're going
without me? You're going alone?"

"Not alone. Linda Bartlet is going with me. You are
welcome to join us if you'd like."

Helen might as well have slapped Genevieve across
the face. She'd invited Linda Bartlet? "But it's supposed
to be a sisters' trip!"

"Well, that's how we originally planned it, yes."

"You couldn't wait for me to be able to go?"

"I could have. I chose not to wait. You're not the
only person growing older, Genevieve. The sands of my
hourglass are draining, too. If I don't go to Bora-Bora
now, I may never get another chance."

Genevieve closed her eyes. Helen was right. Their lives could change in an instant. Genevieve had learned that hard lesson early when her husband died from a heart attack at the ripe old age of thirty-nine. None of us were guaranteed another day, and advancing age made that all the more apparent.

If she didn't make that South Pacific trip now, she might never see that part of the world.

And yet she'd dreamed of nana playdates since Willow and Andy announced their engagement. She wanted to make memories with her grands while she had the chance, memories that would live on in the little ones' minds long after she was gone.

She wanted both. She wanted to be Supernana *and* the new Genevieve she'd been becoming over the past year. While the nickname Vivie didn't suit, the spark of newness and life it represented did. But it didn't end at Nana and Genevieve/Vivie, did it? She had the "mom" part of her to consider, too. Mom could also use some TLC.

Genevieve desperately hoped that Willow's presence in Lake in the Clouds would lead to a continued improvement in their mother/daughter relationship. She loved her daughter wholeheartedly and wished desperately to reclaim that closeness they once shared. Things were better than they'd been, but issues remained. For instance, Genevieve still wasn't sure what she'd done to drive the wedge deeper between them when Andy died. She'd like to know, but she guessed she didn't *need* to know. She simply wanted it fixed.

She couldn't fix it if she was in Bora-Bora.

"Oh, Helen. I'm so torn."

"I understand." Helen gave her shoulders a shrug.

"Honestly, I do. I'm trying to make the point that I don't care if you decide you want to babysit—excuse me, have a playdate—eight hours every day. Just make certain that Genevieve is doing what is right for her, rather than Mom and Nana doing what her family needs of her."

Her sister understood. Genevieve's eyes filled with tears. "You're the only person who sees all three of me."

Helen quipped, "The three faces of Genevieve. Ooh, someone should make a movie."

Recognizing the reference to a 1950s movie classic, *The Three Faces of Eve*, Genevieve gave her head a toss. "Now, there's a great idea, although the plot needs tweaking. Instead of strangling her daughter, the protagonist chokes her sister."

"Made you murderous, have I?"

"Yes. No. I don't know." Genevieve heaved a sigh. "I hear you, Helen, and I appreciate what you're trying to say, but I'm so mixed up right now. The ground is shifting beneath my feet. It's a question of roles and reinvention and balance. Who do I want to be now that I've finally grown up? I thought I had it figured out six months ago, but I think the only thing I've figured out is that I'm a snowflake."

Helen spurted a laugh. "You? A snowflake? In what universe?"

Her gaze on her grandchildren, Genevieve corrected. "Actually, I'm a clump of snowflakes. I'm a snowball."

"You'd better get back into the car, Frosty. You've been out in the cold too long, and your brain has frozen."

"Not frozen. Transformed. I've transformed. Spring

and summer and autumn are long gone. Now I'm winter. I'm thousands of individual snowflakes clinging together."

Her sister made an exaggerated roll of her eyes.

Warming to the imagery, Genevieve ignored her. "But here's the deal, Helen. My winter is in a constant state of change. When the sun comes out, I start to melt, which changes my shape. When another cold front rolls in, I refreeze. Then it snows, and I catch some more flakes. Right now, I'm a big fat snowball perched on an incline. I'm teetering, and I could start rolling any time. Straight downhill and headed for a tree trunk. No, wait. Make that a gravestone. I'm a snowball ready to roll into a grave marker."

Clapping her hands together, Genevieve added, "Splat."

"Okay, that's it. I'm honestly a bit concerned at this point. Hypothermia can do strange things to a person." Helen turned toward the children and called, "Emma? Drew? Y'all finish up your snowman. Everybody needs to get into the car to warm up. Your mom will join us soon."

More quietly, she murmured, "I hope. I will start honking the horn if Willow doesn't show up soon."

"I am a little chilled," Genevieve admitted. Chilled and confused, which was only natural, considering that her life-role desires were pulling her in different directions.

Helen grumbled. "Too bad we don't have a Saint Bernard with a cask of brandy in the backseat."

"I could use a drink. And someone warm to snuggle up against."

"Now, there's the most sensical thing you've said

in minutes, Genevieve!" Helen exclaimed. "Why don't you call Gage and invite him to dinner?"

"I'm not going to date Gage Throckmorton. It's only been a year and a half since he lost his wife. He's not ready for a new relationship."

"I don't know. Men tend to move faster than women following a loss."

"Well, romance is the last thing on my mind right now."

Helen shot her sister a meaningful look. "Maybe it shouldn't be."

"Drop it, Helen." Genevieve's gaze shifted toward Noah Tannehill's home. "I do wish Willow would hurry along, however. We are wasting time, and that is a crime." Genevieve looked at her sister and smiled. "Thank you." She hugged Helen hard and repeated, "Thank you so much."

"You're welcome." Then, following a moment's pause, she added, "Um, what for?"

"Because you're right. As usual."

"That's true, although exactly what am I right about in this case?"

"I need a plan, some organization. I need to guide the snowball downhill. I need to find a balance between Mom and Nana and Genevieve."

"Hear! Hear!"

"It will have to wait until after the wedding, though. As much as I'd love to go on the South Pacific trip, I just can't. When my kids need help—truly need it— I'm going to help. It's in my DNA. Willow needs help until after the wedding. I cannot switch granny gears until after the I dos are done."

"Granny gears? Genevieve, please, no! You can't stand the word *granny*."

"But I like the alliteration. So sue me."

"Do not ask me to use that word. I'll call you Vivie, but I'm not touching *granny*. After all, I'm six years older than you are."

Genevieve laughed as Emma came running toward them, her cheeks red with cold and her eyes shining. Drew followed on his sister's heels. Both children were dusted with snow. Genevieve's heart swelled with joy. She went down on one knee, heedless of the snow and the twinge of pain the movement caused her knees, and opened her arms.

Her grandchildren ran to her for a hug. Drew was safe and in her arms. Emma was safe, in her arms, and babbling about a lopsided snowman.

Willow approached from the direction of the house, a bemused expression on her face. And beside Genevieve, always beside her, Helen stood ready to help.

Genevieve met her daughter's and sister's gazes, thought about New Year's Eve, and said, "Muffle."

"Excuse me?" Willow asked as Helen snorted.

"My guiding word. I haven't been paying attention to it, but that will change."

Helen folded her arms and spoke in a false snippy tone. "You intend to muffle my advice?"

"Did I say that? I didn't say that."

Willow gestured toward her SUV. "Can you two continue this argument while I drive? I'm already late for my meeting with the caterer."

"Excellent idea." Helen turned and spoke to the children. "Drew, get into the car. Emma, come here, sweets. Let me buckle you in."

Genevieve climbed into the backseat and sat between her grandchildren. Once Helen settled into the front passenger seat, Genevieve leaned forward and placed her hand on her sister's shoulder. "I'm not muffling your advice, Helen. It's the noise. It's always about the noise. You know what noise does to snow, don't you?"

"Hon, I haven't a clue."

"Avalanche."

Willow glanced at her aunt as she started the car. "What is she talking about?"

"It's beyond me. Maybe we really should run by the ER. Perhaps she's had a TIA."

"No, I haven't had a stroke. I'm muffling. I'm searching for that balance you've convinced me I need in the quiet. I can't stop the melt, but I can control the roll."

Helen glanced at Willow. "Your mother is a snowball."

"That's silly, Nana," Emma declared.

"Sometimes a little silly is exactly what a nana needs." Genevieve sat back in her seat, determined to enjoy the drive. Enjoy the afternoon and evening and tomorrow and the day after that. She would enjoy her role as the mother of the groom six weeks from now.

She could do this. She *would* do this.

After all, age need not be necessarily measured as time already lived. In terms of the time Genevieve had yet to live, statistically speaking, she was still middle-aged. Sixty was the new forty, right?

Yeah, well, tell that to your knees.

Well, snowballs didn't have knees, did they? So she could—she would—enjoy this roll downhill.

Right toward the gravestone in the cemetery at the end of the road.

Splat.

Okay, this new attitude of hers needed some fine-tuning.

She turned her gaze toward the window and the snow-covered mountain meadow. Where did the time go? She'd been thirty-nine ten minutes ago, facing her fortieth. Now, sixty. That old saying about youth being wasted on the young...so much truth. And yet so silly to bemoan a birthday. Wasn't she still on this side of the grass? Wasn't she spending glorious time with her grandchildren, watching them grow and learn and thrive, despite losing their father so young?

Just like her children had lost their father. *Oh, David. I wish you could join us on playdates. I wish you could be here to watch Jake marry the woman of his dreams. I wish you'd been here to grow old with me. I'm so lonely.*

Tears welled in her eyes, and as she furiously blinked them away, Emma's small hand stole into hers. "It's okay, Nana. Don't cry. I'm here."

Out of the mouths of babes. "I know, sweetheart. I'm so glad. So very glad."

The rest she'd get figured out.

In time.

Chapter Five

NOAH HAD PUT THE task off for as long as possible, but his online order had been delayed. He was down to two cans of beans and half a loaf of bread. Even more serious, he was out of coffee. He had to go to the grocery store again.

After his last venture into town, he'd decided that the only thing worse than going to the post office in Lake in the Clouds was making a local grocery run.

A shopper had two stores from which to choose for groceries: a national chain store and a small mom-and-pop, been-there-forever type of place called simply the General Store. He preferred the anonymity of the chain store, but the mom-and-pop carried local and regional brands he'd come to love. So, for the Mocha Moose Morning Blend coffee beans and the Rocky Mountain Road ice cream made over in Eternity Springs, he'd brave nosy Nettie Parkin, who ran the register at the General Store.

The place closed at seven. Having learned by experience that Nettie was most inquisitive early in the day, he timed his arrival for six thirty. With his list in hand, he entered the store, grabbed a grocery cart, and headed for the produce. Potatoes. Onions. The tomatoes looked sorry, so he skipped those. He'd just tossed a handful of garlic bulbs into the cart when he heard an excited voice exclaim, "Mr. Tannehill! Hi, Mr. Tannehill! It's me. Drew. Remember me? I haven't seen you in so long!"

Noah looked up to see the boy, wearing sneakers, a coat, and Spider-Man pajamas, darting toward him.

"What are you buying, Mr. Tannehill? Is that garlic? My nana uses garlic when she makes lasagna. It's awesome. She made it for us this week, and she has this little plastic roller thingy that you put the garlic inside and roll it and the peel comes right off the garlic. It's way cool. Have you ever seen that? I think they should make one big enough for onions, but Nana says she's never seen one of those. Maybe I'll invent it when I grow up. What else are you buying? We're buying Froot Loops instead of eggs for breakfast. Can you believe that? I ask and ask and ask and Mom never lets me have them, but this time I wore her down 'cause she's so tired from getting ready for the wedding. Do you like Froot Loops?"

"Take a breath, kid." Noah frowned down at Drew. "I don't want you passing out and keeling over here in the bananas."

Drew giggled. "I'm just excited to see you. I talk a lot when I'm excited."

"I think you're excited all the time." Noah placed a bunch of bananas in his shopping cart. "So, your mom is getting married?"

"No. Not my mom. My uncle Jake. The wedding was gonna be in Texas but the building burned down so now they're getting married here and having the party at my nana's lodge. My mom is planning the party because it's her job and Uncle Jake and Aunt Tess—she'll be my aunt after the wedding—had to work. Want to come to the party? My mom told me I could invite a friend. It's in five days. Will you come?"

Noah was taken aback. "I'm not your friend."

"Oh." The boy's face fell. He shoved his hands into his coat pockets and scuffed the toe of his sneaker against the floor. "Okay."

Noah felt like a heel. He hadn't exactly been Mr. Cheerful for the past year, but he didn't go around kicking puppies or children. Instead, he immediately attempted to backtrack. "I mean, I'm sure your mother meant a friend your own age."

"I don't have any friends my age in Lake in the Clouds. Not yet. I'm trying to make friends but it's hard 'cause I'm homeschooled and Lake in the Clouds doesn't have a co-op or pods for kids like me. Mom is sad about that. Once Little League starts next month, it will be better, and I'll make lots of friends. Now all I have is my sister. She's only four. Her birthday is soon, though."

"Look, kid. I'll be your friend, but I don't need to go to any wedding reception."

Noah's words flipped Drew's switch, and he brightened. "Since we're friends, can I come over to your house and play? We can have playdates like I have with my nana. Will you let me help you make dollhouses? I really want to do that."

"Hold on. Hold on. Don't get ahead of yourself."

Noah wanted to abandon his grocery cart and head for the exit. "I don't think that's a good idea. Your mom wasn't very happy that you came over to my house the first time."

"She'll be happy when we 'splain it to her. You'll see. I'll go tell her now." He darted toward the back of the store and disappeared around an endcap holding a selection of nuts.

Noah gave a quick retreat serious consideration. He could grab the bare necessities and head for the register. Or he could continue shopping and hope that Mrs. Eldridge would get control of her kid.

Based on how she'd stormed his fortress, she undoubtedly would try to rein in Drew. She'd been the quintessential mama bear protecting her child—all the while worrying that she was overprotecting him. He'd liked that about her. Nevertheless, it wouldn't hurt anything for Noah to shift into speed-shopping mode.

He grabbed a couple stalks of broccoli, some carrots, and a bag of lettuce, then breezed by the bread and snagged a loaf. Now at the back of the store, he turned to roll past the meat cases, loading up on protein. He deliberately did not look down the aisles as he passed, doing his best to be a stealth shopper.

To no avail.

From behind him came Drew's voice. "Mr. Tannehill!"

Noah closed his eyes and sighed.

"Mr. Tannehill! You're still here. I'm so glad. I was worried when you weren't by the bananas."

A second little voice piped up. "Drew says you'll help us because you're his friend."

Noah glanced over his shoulder to see a little girl in

blond pigtails and pink pajamas staring up at him with big green eyes rounded with worry.

Oh hell. A little girl. I can't deal with little girls. They reminded him of Maddie.

"Our mom is crying in the grocery store," Drew said. "She only cries when she's in her room or the bathtub and she thinks we can't hear her, but she's crying right now in the yogurt department. Anyone can see her, and she'll hate that."

Noah abandoned his cart without thought and started toward the children. "What happened?"

"I don't know," Drew moaned.

The girl piped up. "I told Mama that Mimi wants us to bring creamer for Grampy's coffee. She looked at me, and then her eyes got wet, and she sat down on the floor and started crying."

Noah put the clues together. "Mimi and Grampy are your grandparents?"

Both children nodded. Drew said, "They came to visit us. They're going to Uncle Jake's wedding, but they came early to help Mom with us because she is so busy getting everything ready. They just got here today."

"Are they here in the store?" Noah asked, hoping help was at hand. The girl shook her head. Drew said, "No. They're staying in one of the cabins at Raindrop Lodge where we live, and they were tired from the trip so they are going to watch TV and go to bed early."

"Our mom put groceries in their cabin before they got here," the girl added. "But she forgot that Grampy likes coffee creamer. So I told her and it made her cry!"

Drew bit his lower lip. "I tried to ask Mom what was wrong, but she just held up her hand. That means to wait and give her a minute. But she's been sitting there for way more than a minute."

"And we're not supposed to sit on the floor in the grocery store," the girl said, wrinkling her nose. "It's gross."

Drew nodded. "If the mean lady at the front sees her, I'm afraid of what will happen."

Drew was talking about Nettie Parkin. Noah shared his concern. He headed for the dairy department, where, sure enough, he found Willow Eldridge sitting on the floor with her hands covering her face. Her shoulders shook. She was definitely crying.

"Um...ma'am? Willow?"

She ignored him. Noah didn't like the sensation of looming above her, so despite the pain the action caused him, he went down on one knee. He placed his hand on her shoulder. "Hey, now. What can I do to help?"

A good ten seconds passed before she finally responded. "Watch my kids so I can have a safe nervous breakdown."

"Can nervous breakdowns ever be safe?" Noah wondered aloud.

"I can't have a dangerous one because of my kids." Sighing heavily, she lifted her head and met his gaze.

It was a gut punch.

Noah hadn't seen such misery in a woman's eyes since Daniel's wife, Cheryl, visited Noah in the hospital.

He wanted to wipe the look from her face, which was shocking for Noah to realize.

He hadn't felt the urge to comfort a woman since Cheryl's visit, either.

He felt it now, and that scared him spitless. "I recommend an axe."

Willow gave him a blank look. "Pardon me?"

"Chopping firewood is a great way to release tension.

Of course, it's not exactly an after-dark activity." And of course, the moment the words were out of his mouth, his mind went there. *After-dark activity*. Tangled sheets and sweat-slicked skin. His body responded to the thought.

Now? His libido picks *now* to return? After a year's hiatus? While he's kneeling on the old tile floor of the General Store? Sheesh.

Noah immediately attempted to recover. "Of course, there's always bowling."

She sputtered a laugh and swiped the tears from her cheeks. "Bowling."

"Nothing like slinging a sixteen-pound bowling ball down the lane to work off steam. Although you should probably stick to twelve or thirteen pounds. The lanes in Lake in the Clouds are on the north end of town. On State Street. They're open until ten." Then, Noah did something he couldn't begin to explain. He added, "You want to go?"

What did I just say?

Willow's expression turned incredulous. "Bowling? Now?"

"I want to go bowling!" Drew exclaimed.

Just who is having the breakdown here?

"Are you better now, Mama?" Emma asked. "Did you get a boo-boo?"

Willow shifted her gaze away from Noah and toward her daughter. "I'm okay, honey. I'm sorry I worried you."

Okay, he needed to recover and fast. Noah attempted to rise and do it gracefully, but he had to grab hold of the dairy case and wrench himself up. Damned if Willow didn't pop up onto her feet and try to help him. *Great. Just great.*

A disembodied voice spoke over the General Store's intercom system. "Attention, shoppers. The store will be closing in ten minutes. Please make your way to the checkout counter now."

In the meantime, Drew was bouncing from one foot to another. "What about bowling? Are we going to go bowling with Mr. Tannehill? Please, Mom?"

Noah racked his brain for a way to ward off this nonsense in the wake of his runaway mouth. He couldn't spend the next hour or, God forbid, two hours around this family. In the company of a preschool-aged girl. His nightmares that night would have nightmares.

Luckily, Willow tossed him a lifeline. "No. We can't go bowling. You're in your pajamas."

Noah wasn't about to point out that there really wasn't much difference between a grocery store and a bowling alley where children's fashion was concerned. Not in Lake in the Clouds, anyway.

Unfortunately, Drew did it for him. "Why is it okay for us to wear pj's to the store but not the bowling alley?"

"Because I said so."

Noah exhaled a silent sigh of relief. She'd rolled out the definitive mom response. He was safe. Now he needed to scurry back to his cart, grab coffee, and head for the checkout. Nettie didn't abide stragglers at closing time.

"Nobody will care," Drew said. "I'm not ready to go home yet. Besides, it's too late to take Grampy's creamer to him. He'll be asleep. I think we should take it to him early in the morning and have breakfast with them. That's a good idea, don't you think, Mom?"

Emotion flickered through Willow's eyes, though

Noah couldn't put a name to the type of emotion it was. Pain? Anger? Despair? It was there and gone so fast he couldn't be sure. However, Noah's stomach sank when she pursed her lips, shifted her gaze between her children, then lifted it to meet his.

Willow's bright smile didn't reach her eyes as she said, "Actually, I do think that's a good idea, Drew. Thank you, Mr. Tannehill. We'd love to go bowling with you tonight."

Noah reached for a Hail Mary, an excuse to withdraw the invitation. He came up blank. Well, he could fall back on being the crusty curmudgeon of Lake in the Clouds. Throw out a "never mind" and turn and walk away.

His gaze settled on the boy who had gone from shuffling foot to foot to hopping up and down in joy.

Sure, and kick a few kittens on your way out. Maybe run over a puppy or two on the drive home.

He was stuck. He was going bowling.

Well, gutter ball.

Willow set the bag containing cereal and powdered creamer into her floorboard, then buckled Emma into her car seat with fingers that trembled. Was she really taking her children to a bowling alley at bedtime? With a virtual stranger? Had she lost her mind?

Yes, very probably.

After the little surprise her mother-in-law had sprung a short time ago, who could blame her?

It had followed a perfectly lovely "welcome to Lake in the Clouds" dinner Willow and her children had hosted for Andy's parents at the restaurant in the lodge. Then, while walking back to their cabins, Maggie had slipped her arm through Willow's and intentionally slowed her down while the children ran ahead with Tom. Then, with her sweetest of smiles and soft Southern voice, she'd said, "Willow, dear, I have some difficult news to share. There is no easy way to do this, so I'm just going to lay it all out."

Oh no! Willow braced herself to hear that one of them was ill.

Instead, Maggie lobbed a grenade. "It's regarding Jenna Randall."

Willow reeled backward in shock. Jenna Randall had been the Other Woman. Tom and Maggie knew? Andy told his parents about her? And they'd never let on to Willow that they knew?

More betrayal from Team Eldridge. Willow shuddered, suddenly wishing she'd brought more than a heavy sweater to keep her warm in the chilly nighttime mountain air. She was cold clear to the bone.

Willow had to clear her throat to ask, "You knew about Andy's affair?"

"We learned about it a few months after we lost him. Jenna reached out to us and told us the whole sad story. Tom and I were shocked and disappointed, Willow. We raised our son better than that. However, there was a child involved. Our grandson. We've been involved in AJ's life since he was born."

A son.

Willow had known that Jenna was expecting Andy's child. He'd told her himself when she confronted him after she'd spied him kissing a redhead at a company Christmas party. Coming on the heels of her own recent miscarriage, the news about his mistress's pregnancy had cut Willow to the core.

Andy had been contrite. He'd claimed to want to stay in the marriage, but Willow had known it was over. There was no getting past this depth of a betrayal. Nevertheless, for her children's sake, she'd taken a few days to think her decision through. She'd told him she was leaving him, and he'd gone out and killed himself by driving like a fool—and almost killed Drew in the process.

Another son. Drew and Emma had a brother. In a croaking voice, Willow asked, "His name is AJ?"

"Yes. Andrew John Randall. Named after his father, of course."

Of course. Never mind that Andy already sired one son named Andrew John. Willow was halfway surprised Jenna wasn't calling her son Drew also.

Willow had never wanted to know anything about Jenna Randall's baby. The woman had yet to give birth when Willow had directed her lawyer to settle a portion of Andy's life insurance money on the child after he was born. Then, she'd washed her hands of the entire situation. Or so she'd believed.

Sudden anger whipped through her. "Maggie, I understand why you have a tie to that boy, but it's different for me and my family. If you and Jenna Randall are looking to establish some sort of sibling relationship between my children and AJ, this is not the time. Maybe when my kids are older and—"

Maggie interrupted. "She's dead, Willow. Jenna Randall passed away suddenly a few weeks ago. Tom and I brought AJ to live with us."

Whoa. Willow stopped short. Her thoughts were

a whirlwind. *That poor little boy has lost both his parents.*

Maggie continued, "I've hired a nanny, and she's staying around the clock while we are here in Colorado. AJ is still adjusting to his new home and needs the stability of being in his own bed each night right now. Otherwise, we'd have brought him so you could meet him."

"Oh, no, Maggie." Willow held up her hand, palm out. "Hold on just one minute. I need to process all of this. I'm not sure that my kids—"

The older woman interrupted again to deliver the second part of her one-two punch. "Remember that colonial down the street from us that you admired so much over the years? Well, we found out that the owners were about to put it up for sale, so we snapped it up for you. Our gift to you and the children. It's time you brought them home to be raised as Eldridges, Willow, which is befitting of their heritage."

Willow gaped at her mother-in-law. "Maggie, you bought a house for us? In Texas? Without asking me?"

"You love that house," she defended. "We won't force it on you if you don't want it, but it wouldn't have lasted a day in this market. We had to jump or miss our chance."

A combination of anger and despair whipped through Willow. This was too much. Way too much, coming at her too fast. "I can't do this now, Maggie. I am up to my eyeballs in wedding prep, and I do not have the mental bandwidth to add anything else to the mix. This discussion will have to keep until after Jake and Tess's wedding."

"It can't wait. We must leave directly from your

mother's brunch on Sunday morning to catch our flight home. Our nanny has a commitment."

So. Do. I. Willow knew it would do no good to scream at her mother-in-law, no matter how badly she wanted to do so. "I'll think about it."

Willow knew she wouldn't move to a house down the street from the Eldridges and their newly expanded family, no matter how much she loved the home's floor plan, but she wasn't lying when she said she didn't have the mental capacity to think the whole thing through at the moment. Plus, she'd need to take her mother's wishes into consideration before she made any decision about where she, Drew, and Emma would make their permanent home. That meant she'd finally have to come clean with Mom. *Ugh.* "I'll call you next week, Maggie. That's the best I can do."

Andy's mother released an aggrieved sigh. "Well, I guess. All right."

"And please, Maggie. Please don't say anything about this to my mother while you're here. The thought of the children and me moving to Texas will cause a shi— It will upset her. This is a special week for my brother and his bride; it wouldn't be fair to them to disrupt that."

"Very well."

"I have your word?"

Maggie nodded. "Yes, Willow. I'm not unreasonable."

That claim ended the conversation, and Maggie and Willow caught up with Tom and the children at Cabin 11, where the Eldridges were staying during their week in Lake in the Clouds. After saying their good nights, Willow escorted the children on toward Cabin 17.

She'd overseen bath time in a daze, her emotions a stew of shock, devastation, and anger. Then, needing a distraction and food for breakfast, Willow gathered up her children and escaped to the General Store.

Now, she still wasn't ready to return to the ghosts of betrayals past that awaited her back at Raindrop Lodge. Neither did she want to think about houses and Texas. So what the heck? Forget about bedtime. *Let's go bowling!* With a sexy, secretive stranger who was not Santa Claus.

Noah Tannehill. He'd been nice to her tonight.

A truck in the next row flashed its lights at her. Noah. She gave him a little wave, climbed into her vehicle, and started the engine. When he'd told her to follow him, she hadn't argued. She'd been glad not to think about where she was going. She wanted to put her brain on cruise control.

She didn't want to think about Maggie Eldridge or houses in Texas or toddlers named AJ. Andrew John.

I should have hired a nanny for the kids this week myself.

When Maggie and Tom Eldridge offered to come for the wedding a few days early in order to help with the children, Willow was pleased to accept. It was crunch time for the event. She had her hands full, as did her own mother. Having babysitters available should have made everything about this week more manageable. Instead, she had a crisis on her hands.

If Maggie spills these beans to Mom? Willow shuddered at the thought.

Drew tossed her a lifeline by interrupting her musings as she turned left out of the General Store parking lot. "Have I ever been bowling before, Mom? I don't remember."

"No. This will be your first time."

"I can't wait!"

Emma followed up with her most oft-used phrase. "Me, too!"

A sense of disembodiment gripped Willow as she followed Noah's truck to State Street and turned right. She couldn't believe she was doing this. It was so out of character for her.

Or was it really?

She was basically running away from a problem. That was right in her wheelhouse, wasn't it? It's what she'd been doing since Andy died, something she'd come to Lake in the Clouds having vowed to change.

"Yeah, well, change shmange. I'm not ready yet," Willow muttered as she flipped on her signal and turned into the parking lot at Mountaineer Lanes.

Red, yellow, and white neon lights flashed, illuminating the angles and planes of Noah Tannehill's face after he parked his truck and began to approach her vehicle. It gave him a devilish look. Willow also noted his limp and recalled how he'd struggled to stand at the grocery store. How in the world could he bowl?

The rumble of balls, crash of pins, and whir of a ball return greeted the foursome as they walked into Mountaineer Lanes. Drew's eyes went round with wonder. Emma gasped with delight. Willow tried to recall the last time she'd gone bowling. Never with Andy. Too blue-collar of an activity for him. Maybe back in college on a girls' night? Nevertheless, it had been a long time ago. Willow recalled enjoying the activity tremendously, but she'd seriously hated wearing rental bowling shoes.

"I wonder if they'd let the kids bowl in socks?" she mused.

Noah tipped his ear toward her, but she could tell he hadn't heard her above the din. She pointed toward the children's feet and raised her voice. "Shoes."

"They can go in their socks. What size shall I get for you?"

"Could I wear my socks, too? I can't tell you how much I despise wearing rental—" Willow broke off abruptly as Emma took off running.

"Auntie!" The girl exclaimed.

Willow glanced over toward lane number six, where Aunt Helen was packing a bowling ball into a bag. Spying Emma, her expression brightened. She called, "Hello, babycakes! What are you doing here?"

From that moment on, events spiraled out of Willow's control. She introduced Noah to Aunt Helen, who had just returned from a trip to the South Pacific the previous day. "I'm shocked to see you here," Willow said to her aunt. "I would have thought jet lag would have you laid flat."

"It did all day yesterday and until about four o'clock this afternoon. I woke up wired, and it was my regular bowling night. I decided the exercise would do me good. We've just finished up. Come say hi to my friends. I've told them all about you, and they've been dying to meet you."

Helen introduced Willow, the children, and Noah to Stella James, a retired teacher; Andrea Holt, the secretary at First Baptist Church; and Kim Murphy, a vice president at a local bank. The church secretary said, "I hear you're doing a fabulous job with the wedding planning. The whole town is talking about it."

"It's been fun to work with new vendors. I think we'll have a spectacular day on Saturday if the weather forecast holds."

"I'm sure you will," the banker declared. "Allow me to mention that if you decide to set up shop in Lake in the Clouds, I hope you'll consider First Financial for your banking needs."

"Oh, hush, Kim," Stella chided. "We don't mix bowling and business, remember?"

The women turned their curious gazes on Noah. But before anyone could attempt a third degree, Drew's and Emma's excitement got the better of them, and they dominated the conversation, babbling on about bowling and bawling and wearing pajamas in public.

After responding with enthusiasm to the children, Aunt Helen gave Willow a considering look, then darted a quick gaze toward Noah. She declared, "Well, it appears that much has happened during my absence. I'll be anxious to hear all about it."

Willow warned her with a stare. "Not now, Aunt Helen."

"No, not now. You have a full plate, what with the wedding only a week away. You need to be sure and take care of yourself. You're already looking a bit pinched around the eyes."

"Gee, thanks," Willow drawled.

"I call 'em like I see 'em. Tell you what—why don't I take Emma and Drew off your hands for a bit? I'll share my bowling expertise with the children, and you and Noah take some time to yourselves in the tavern." She gave Noah a brilliant smile and added, "Have a beer on me. I run a tab."

Before Willow quite knew how it happened or managed to mount a protest, Helen had spirited the children away. Within minutes, Drew and Emma rolled balls in a lane with bumpers in the gutters. Willow sat across from

Noah in a booth inside the Let 'Em Fall Tavern, the bowling alley's bar-and-grill, where she could observe her children from her seat.

"What will you have to drink?" Noah asked her.

For a moment, Willow simply stared at him blankly.

"A beer? Wine? A bottle of bourbon?"

She gave a little laugh. "I'm sorry. I'm a little discombobulated. What just happened out there?"

"I think we ran into a force of nature."

"My aunt Helen. Yes, that's a good way to describe her. She and my mother are a lot alike, although I will say that Mom is more subtle in her efforts. I'm sorry if you felt forced into forgoing time on the bowling lane."

"Not hardly. I had no intention of bowling myself, anyway," Noah said.

"You didn't?"

"Not with this bum leg, no. So, a drink? I'm buying, though."

Willow grinned. "You don't allow strange women to buy you drinks?"

"Should I tell your aunt you referred to her as strange?"

"Whoa. You play dirty." Immediately, she wanted to bite her tongue. *Suggestive, there, Willow? You're out of practice talking with handsome men.*

"Darlin', if you only knew," he fired back automatically. His expression arrested as if he'd spoken as indiscreetly as she. After clearing his throat, he added, "So, um, what will you have?"

Okay, I'm going to pretend that never happened. "Beer, please. The Mountaineer lager."

"Excellent choice." He signaled the bartender and called, "Two of my usual, please, Jace."

"Your usual," Willow repeated. "So you're a regular at the bowling alley, but you don't bowl?"

"The microbrewer owns the bowling alley. I like the beer and prefer coming here over the brewery itself. People leave me alone."

"Oh." Then, letting curiosity get the better of her, she asked, "So, what happened to your leg?"

Noah frowned. "Kind of a personal question, isn't it?"

"You saw me crying into the yogurt," Willow said with a shrug. "That pretty much did away with my inhibitions."

Willow looked away from his keen-eyed stare and focused on her children. Emma's blond pigtails swayed as she rocked back and forth, watching her bowling ball roll slowly down the lane. Willow should get her phone out and take a picture or two of this first, but she had a personal rule about phones at the table.

She shifted her gaze back toward him, an apology on her tongue. He spoke before she could.

"I injured my leg in a fire," he said in a tone and manner that declared the topic closed. He followed immediately with, "So why the tears?"

Well, guess she'd asked for that, hadn't she? Willow was spared an immediate reply by the arrival of a server carrying two glasses of beer. After setting them on the table, he asked, "Anything to eat?"

"Not for me, thank you," Willow said with a smile. "We've already had dinner."

"Large pizza. The works," Noah said.

"You must be hungry." Willow hoped to distract him from the topic of her tears, so she plowed ahead with food talk. "Is the pizza here good? My mother orders from Pizza Planet, and it's pretty good. My kiddos will eat pizza every day if I let them."

"It's excellent here, believe it or not. Drew and Emma might want some as an after-dinner snack. Why were you crying, Willow?"

So much for distraction. Willow slid her thumb along the side of the glass, scooping up a bead of condensation as she sought an explanation that wouldn't bare her soul.

"Is something the matter with Drew?" Noah pressed.

"Drew?" Her head came up. "Why would you ask that?"

"When he asked me to come to your family wedding, he—"

"Whoa," Willow said, interrupting. "He what?"

"He invited me to Uncle Jake's wedding," he replied, the faintest gleam of a twinkle in his golden eyes. "Your brother?"

Willow nodded, sitting back hard against the padded seat of the booth as he continued. "He said you told him he could bring a friend. Apparently, he considers me his only friend in Lake in the Clouds."

That took Willow's breath away. Her heart twisted. "Oh, Drew. He breaks my heart. Truly he does. I've been trying to help him find other children his age to befriend, but it's been challenging. I should have signed him up for youth basketball, but the season had already started when we moved here, and I decided to wait for baseball. That starts next week." She brushed at a crumb on the table, summoned her nerve, and asked, "Did you accept his invitation?"

"What?" Noah's brows arched. "No, of course not. I'm a recluse, don't you know? I don't do weddings."

Willow didn't know whether to be relieved or insulted. "But you do bowling alleys?"

"A man needs his pizza. Nobody delivers all the way out to my place. You're attempting to deflect. Talk to me about your meltdown. That seemed to be more than wedding jitters."

She considered telling him it was none of his business, but that felt rude in light of the kindness he had shown her. She decided to share half the story. She told him about her in-laws' arrival and the news Maggie had relayed about buying her a house.

"That's some gift," he responded. "Comes with some strings, I'll bet."

"Strings. Yarn. Rope. Chain. Spools and spools and spools of it."

"You didn't tell her to keep her house?"

"No. She literally just sprung this on me. The situation is more complicated than just a house. I need time to think everything through and speak to her with kindness. I know her heart is in the right place. They are my children's grandparents, and they love Drew and Emma. I don't want to alienate them. I think it's important for children to have family in their lives."

Had she not been watching him, she'd have missed the grimace that flashed across his face. A story there. Was Noah Tannehill a divorced father, perhaps?

His voice was rough as he added, "I know it's tough to be a single parent."

"Enough about me and my problems. Do you have children, Noah?"

"No." He closed off then as sure as a submarine hatch. He picked up his beer, shifted in his seat, and watched the action on the bowling lanes. For reasons she couldn't pinpoint, Willow wanted to cry again.

They sat without speaking for a few minutes, and the

arrival of his pizza was a welcome distraction. "Try a piece," he suggested.

Willow didn't need a slice of pizza, but it did smell delicious, and eating would help get past this awkwardness, she hoped. "A little one, thanks."

"Think Drew, Emma, and your aunt are ready for a pizza break?" Noah asked.

Willow shook her head. "Aunt Helen doesn't eat pizza."

"She's a healthy eater?"

"Not necessarily." Willow smiled crookedly. "You should see her pack away chicken-fried steak. No, her anti-pizza stance is somehow tied with an argument, bet, or combination of the two she had with one of her husbands. She swore she wouldn't eat another piece of pizza the rest of her life, and as far as I know, she's held to it."

"Wow. That's some dedication."

"That's my auntie. As far as the kids go, I can tell they're having too much fun to want to stop."

They observed the children for the next few minutes while they ate. Both kids appeared fascinated by the ball return. She grew concerned when Drew kept sticking his head in front of the return to peer into the void in anticipation of the ball's arrival. "He's going to get his head thunked if he keeps that up," she fretted. "I've seen my aunt warn him twice."

"He'll learn."

"The hard way," she grumbled.

"Then he won't forget."

Willow sighed. "True. It's just difficult to watch and not jump in. But he needs to learn to listen, and better he gets hit by a bowling ball than a car."

Noah lifted his beer in a toast. "Famous words of mothers everywhere."

At that very moment, a ball popped out from the return on the lane where the children were bowling and conked Drew on the nose. Both Willow and Noah winced as they watched the boy let out a squeal and hold his nose. Then Willow very determinedly turned away from the window and focused solely on Noah. "You're right. The pizza is fabulous. I've wondered what to provide for the tear-down crew after the wedding. This will be perfect. Thank you for solving my problem."

"You're welcome. So, how is it that you're planning your brother's wedding instead of him and his bride?"

She shared the story of the New Year's Eve destruction of their wedding venue and Willow's reasons behind the move to Colorado. He asked her about her work as an event planner, and she told a couple of her more entertaining stories. She'd just launched into her favorite tale about a Nashville politician, a proposal, and a pickle factory when Drew and Emma rushed into the tavern, Aunt Helen on their heels.

"Mama. Mama. Mama." Drew's eyes glittered with excitement. "Guess what. Aunt Helen wants to have a sleepover at her house! Can we go, Mama? Please? Pretty please?"

Emma clapped her hands together. "I want to go, too, Mama. Say yes, please? Fast, because we have to be there for the cuckoo serenade, and then we'll go right to bed."

"Hold on. Hold on a minute."

Willow glanced at her watch. It was twenty minutes to nine, already an hour past their bedtime. School wasn't a problem because she'd worked ahead with

Drew in anticipation of the wedding week, but they'd never stayed over at Aunt Helen's before. She'd never invited them. "Auntie?"

Helen waved her hand dismissively. "It will be fun for us. Plus, it'll give you a chance to have a little"—her gaze darted briefly toward Noah—"alone time before the wedding crunch begins."

"But Maggie and Tom arrived today, and they're planning to spend tomorrow with Drew and Emma."

"Not a problem. I'm working a shift at the reception desk at the lodge tomorrow morning. I'll bring Drew and Emma home before eight. In fact, we'll stop at the bakery and bring breakfast for everyone. How about that? As I recall, the Eldridges aren't super-early birds."

Emma clasped her hands prayerfully and begged. "Please, Mama? Please? Auntie Helen has extra toothbrushes we can use."

"And we're already in our pj's," Drew pointed out.

"Hurry and decide, Mama. The serenade!"

Willow laughed. "Okay. Okay. Go. Go."

The children gave her quick good-night kisses. Helen held out her hand and wiggled her fingers. "Keys, please. I'll need to take your car because of the car seats."

Willow reached into her handbag, withdrew her keys, removed the cabin key from the ring, and handed the rest over. The kids rushed toward the door, anxious to get to Helen's before the top of the hour. "See you in the morning," Helen said, following the kids. "Noah, I understand we'll see you at the wedding on Saturday. Bye now."

The wedding. Oh jeez. Willow called after her aunt. "Wait, I need your keys."

"My car isn't here. I rode with Stella. You'll take her home, won't you, Noah?" Without waiting for a response, Helen turned and followed the children, giving them a royal wave on the way out.

Willow was horrified, embarrassed all the way to her toes. "I can't believe she just did that," Willow murmured. She started to slide out of the booth to stand up. "I need to catch them. I am not on your way home, and that's not—"

He reached out and took her arm, stopping her. "It's okay. I don't mind."

"But—"

"Seriously. Settle down. It's a nice night for a drive around the lake. So, what's the serenade?"

She closed her eyes and released a laugh with only the slightest hint of hysteria. "Cuckoo clocks. Aunt Helen has a wall of cuckoo clocks in her condo."

"A wall of them?"

"At my last count, an even dozen. She could have added more since my most recent visit."

"That's . . . interesting."

"Go ahead and say it. We all do. It's cuckoo. My aunt Helen is the most levelheaded, down-to-earth person otherwise, but when it comes to her clocks, she's a child."

"I think that's kind of cool. I'm not sure I'd want to try to sleep at her home, but hobbies are good."

"Like your dollhouses?"

He hesitated a long moment, then nodded. "Yeah."

She wanted to ask him more. After Drew visited Noah's home, her son talked nonstop about his experience. Willow had researched dollhouses as fire-instruction tools and incorporated the information into his lessons. Drew loved it. Willow was curious about Noah's background.

He'd said he'd injured his leg in a fire. And those scars on his hands looked like burns. Had he been a firefighter? Drew thought so, but Noah certainly wasn't talking. Not about dollhouses. Not about himself.

But at least he was talking about some things. And, apparently, taking her home.

Like, after a date.

Willow took an extra-large sip of her beer.

"You want another one?" Noah asked.

Willow saw that he still had two-thirds of his drink left. Embarrassment stained her cheeks and she smiled sheepishly. "No, thank you. I'm good. I should probably be heading home soon. I have a full day of wedding prep tomorrow." She grabbed a napkin and wiped crumbs off the table. Following a moment's silence, she added, "Noah, about the wedding..."

Noah raised his hand and gestured toward the bartender for the check. "Don't worry. I'm not going to go."

"Of course not." Willow winced the moment the words emerged from her mouth. "Wait—that sounds horribly rude, and that's not what I meant. Drew invited you, and if you'd like to attend, we'd love to have you. It's going to be a fun party. When I said 'of course not,' I meant why would you want to come? You don't know the bride and groom, and you barely know us. Although the food is going to be excellent. Maybe you'd like to come for the meal? That's as good a reason as any. In fact—"

"You're babbling, Willow," Noah said.

"I am. I'm sorry. I'm nervous."

"Why are you nervous?"

Because this feels a whole lot like a date, and the idea terrifies me.

Willow had tried getting back into the dating game after Andy died, but she'd quickly thrown in the towel. Dating had changed in the past decade, but not in a good way. She wasn't ready to go down that road again. She might never be prepared. She didn't trust her own judgment.

He has such gorgeous eyes.

Heaven help me. Willow gave a little laugh. "Why am I nervous? Oh, let me count the ways. I'm in charge of a party for two hundred people in a new venue with new vendors on Saturday. I said the food would be excellent, but honestly, I can't be positive. The caterer has never served this big of a crowd before. Plus, my son and daughter will be the ring bearer and flower girl, and I've misplaced the pillow and basket. What kind of a wedding planner am I if I can't keep up with my kids' stuff?"

The bartender brought the check. While looking at it, Noah asked, "Is that why you were crying into the cottage cheese?"

"It was yogurt!" Willow insisted. "Get your dairy straight. And stop responding to everything I say with a question."

"Do I do that?" He grinned when Willow balled up her napkin and threw it at him.

"You're deflecting. My brothers tried the same thing with me. You're the one who got me into this mess. You can at least make a little effort here. Tell me something about yourself, Mr. Mystery Man. I dare you."

Chapter Six

TELL HER ABOUT MYSELF? Noah had already told her more than he'd told anyone in months.

But what had he expected when he'd allowed her aunt to maneuver the two of them into the Let 'Em Fall Tavern for a beer? He'd known they wouldn't sit here in silence. Of course she'd ask questions. Get-to-know-you queries. The type of questions one often asked on a first date.

This wasn't a date.

But all of a sudden, it sure felt like a date.

Gee, thanks, Drew. The dratted little kid had invaded Noah's comfortable gloom and drawn him out into the light.

Well, he'd allowed it to happen, so now he needed to pay the price. He'd allow Willow to get to know him. Up to a point.

He took a fortifying sip of his lager, then said, "All

right. I grew up in Denver. I went to the University of Colorado on a football scholarship."

"You did? What position did you play?"

"I was a kicker. I had a good leg."

Noah frowned into his beer, wishing he hadn't mentioned the word *leg*. He'd already said all he intended to say about his injury. He braced for her to ask the natural follow-up question: *So why do you limp around?* Instead, she said, "My brother Jake—the groom—played quarterback for the Rice Owls. His senior year, they beat Texas, which is my alma mater. He still rubs it in every chance he gets. So, what was your biggest victory in college?"

Noah relaxed. This he could talk about without being defensive. In fact, this he could talk about and have some fun with. "I guess it would have to be my senior year. I kicked a field goal with three seconds left in the game to get the win and a trip to the Rose Bowl."

"You did?" Willow was obviously impressed. "Who did you beat?"

He finished his beer and rolled his tongue around his cheek before answering. "The Longhorns."

She literally gasped out loud. "You did not!"

For the first time in longer than he could remember, Noah laughed. "You're right. I kid, I kid. We were terrible."

Willow laughed right along with him. "*You* are terrible."

"But I was a good kicker. I actually got drafted by Buffalo."

"That's awesome. Did you play in the NFL?"

"A couple of years, yes. I was sidelined with an injury my third year, and after that, I was done with football. I had other things I wanted to do." And that, he decided, was enough talking about himself. He tossed a pair of twenties onto the table. "So, you ready to go?"

"Let me pay for—"

"No. My invitation, my check."

"Actually, Aunt Helen—"

Noah's tone held a note of exasperation as he said, "I've got it, Willow."

Wearing a little grin, she nodded gracefully and rose from her seat. Noah had a moment alone when she excused herself to use the restroom, and he took the time to question his sanity. What the hell was he doing?

This had definitely taken on the feeling of a date. Although it had been so long since he'd been out on a date he couldn't be sure he remembered right.

That aunt of hers couldn't have been more obvious with her ploy to shift this bowling distraction into the date zone. Willow had appeared just as appalled about the woman's shenanigans as he.

Well, just because the woman tried her maneuvering didn't mean that he and Willow had to cooperate. Even if Noah did want to date again—and he absolutely did not—no way could he date Willow Eldridge. She had a four-year-old daughter. Deal killer right there.

Damned if he wasn't feeling a bit of regret over that truth.

Tannehill, you are not yourself tonight.

Then, it was as if he heard the echo of Daniel's voice in his mind. *Yeah, you are. You're finally acting like yourself again. It's about damned time you shrugged off the sackcloth and ashes. They don't suit. You don't deserve them.*

"Well, hell," Noah muttered.

Then, for something to do while he waited for Willow, he carried the cash for the tab over to the bar. "Thanks, Jace. Great as always."

"Glad you enjoyed it. Say, who's the looker you're with tonight? I haven't seen her in here before."

"Her name is Willow. Willow Eldridge."

Jace snapped his fingers. "The event planner. I've heard of her. She's related to Helen McDaniel somehow, isn't she?"

"She's her niece."

"So, how did a loner like you hook up with her?"

"It's a pizza, not a hookup," Noah snapped back. "I never figured you for a gossip, Jace."

"I'm a bartender. Gossip is my wheelhouse."

"Well, don't gossip about Willow. She's a nice lady. Emphasis on *lady*."

Jace held up his hands in surrender. "My bad, bro."

Both men turned to look at Willow as she emerged from the ladies' room, putting a stop to the conversation. Noah noticed she'd tidied her hair, but she hadn't put on any lipstick or touched up the minimal amount of makeup she wore. He liked that about her.

"Are we ready?" she asked him.

"Yeah." Noah gave a nod to the bartender. "See you next time."

"Pizza was great," Willow added with a smile.

It seemed natural for Noah to place his hand on the small of her back as he opened the door for her and escorted her outside. They left the clack and clatter of the bowling alley behind and stepped into the quiet of the small town, settled down on a school night. A single streetlamp combined with the red, white, and yellow of the bowling alley's neon sign to illuminate the parking lot. A gentle breeze swept the pine scent of the forest down from the mountains.

He walked her to his truck and opened the door for her. She observed, "You're an old-fashioned guy, aren't you?"

"The way my parents raised me." Noah shut the door and walked to the driver's side of his truck. He climbed into the cab and started the engine.

His stereo came on automatically and played the throaty, smoky voice of Norah Jones. As Noah pulled out of the Mountaineer Lanes parking lot, he tried to recall the last time he'd been alone in a vehicle with a woman. Maybe in the ambulance after the accident? He remembered a female paramedic. But no, there'd been two paramedics working on him that day.

And it had been a totally different atmosphere. That had been chaos. The vibe now was, well, intimate. He noted that Willow was tapping her foot. *Don't be nervous, Goldilocks.* He was nervous enough for the both of them.

Which was stupid. Once upon a time he'd been a smooth operator. Once upon a time seemed like a lifetime ago. But he didn't need to be smooth tonight. This was a ride home. Not a date. He cleared his throat and reached for something—anything—to break the silence. "So, what are you serving for supper at this shindig?"

"Steak," she replied immediately, her tone holding a slight note of relief. "Rib eyes. There will be other choices for those guests who don't eat beef, but Jake and Tess are Texans." She then rattled off a menu that gave Noah a moment of regret for refusing the wedding invite.

When they exhausted the topic of the wedding, she appeared more relaxed. Noah was, too. They continued their drive in easy silence. So easy, in fact, that Noah did yet another crazy thing. He cracked open a window on his life.

"I am...I was...a firefighter."

She waited for him to elaborate. When he didn't, she said, "That was my guess. Are you on disability? Because of your leg?"

"I'm not disabled. The leg will heal with proper rehab, which I'm doing. Getting stronger by the day. I had another surgery in December. Hopefully, it'll be the last."

"Want to tell me what happened?"

"Nope. I don't talk about it."

"I figured that, too," Willow said. "I understand. Believe me, I understand."

Noah glanced at her. He could barely make out her features in the truck interior's ambient light, but he could see the wry twist of her lips in the shadows. He wanted to ask her what injury she didn't talk about, but he couldn't do it. Not when he wasn't prepared to share his own pain.

Frank Sinatra followed Norah Jones on his playlist, and the sound of "Summer Wind" filled the silence as he approached the entrance to the Raindrop Lodge property. There, he noted a line of three exiting cars waiting to turn onto the road. "Something going on at the lodge tonight?"

"Hmm?"

He slowed his truck and flicked his turn signal. "It's late for guest departures."

"Oh. Those aren't guests. We closed to guests this

morning. Those are probably members of the cleaning crew. My mother insisted that the lodge be deep cleaned top to bottom before wedding guests begin to arrive. That starts happening tomorrow."

"Hmm." Noah made the right turn into the property. "This is a busy road. That can be a treacherous intersection."

"Oh, we know. Aunt Helen has been trying to get a stop sign approved for months. You do not want to get her started talking about it. She'll go on quite the rant. I swear she will make a voodoo doll of the guy who issues permits and stick pins in him."

Noah laughed. Again.

Willow directed him through the resort property toward the cabin where she and her children were staying. Approaching it, Noah debated what his next move should be. Just pull up in front of the cabin and wait for her to get out of his truck? Should he walk her to her door? That would be weird, wouldn't it? Presumptuous. This wasn't a date.

You invited them out, bought beer and pizza. That's sort of a date.

What if she asked him to come inside for another beer or a nightcap? Should he accept? Her children weren't there.

What would it hurt? He liked Willow Eldridge. She was attractive. She was intelligent and intriguing. That day he met her she'd charged into his home protecting her cub like the biggest, baddest mama grizzly in the forest. Tonight in the grocery store, she'd been a wounded little fawn who made him want to kiss her hurts and make them better.

Slow down, Tannehill. That way there be dragons.

Besides, she'd recovered fast. The woman who'd shared a pizza with him had her mojo back. She'd been friendly and funny and kind.

Very appealing.

He wanted to walk her to the door and give her a good-night kiss. He'd like to cup her face in his palms and tilt her head up. He'd like to see the moonlight wink in her eyes before he slowly lowered his mouth to hers. He'd take his time about it, go slow and sweet. Taste her, explore a little. Hold her. Make it count.

It had been so long since he'd held a woman in his arms. She'd be warm, and he was so cold. He'd like to soak in her warmth.

Whoa. Just whoa. This intersection definitely needed a stop sign.

She was a mother with two kids, and he had no business thinking about kissing her. He'd just pull up and drop her off. He wouldn't walk her to her door. She wouldn't ask him in. If she did, he'd say no.

Wouldn't he?

"This is it," Willow told him as they arrived at what was literally the end of the road.

Noah pulled his truck into the cabin's semicircular front drive. He shifted into park and hesitated. Was he going to lift his hand to the ignition switch?

Just as he started to move, Willow spoke. "I was leaving my husband the day he died because I'd discovered he'd had an affair and that his lover was pregnant. Today my former mother-in-law shared the news that the child—a boy—is now an orphan because his mother recently passed. My in-laws have taken him in to raise. He'll be in their lives and, therefore, my children's lives. In my life."

Holy hell. What a kick in the balls. How did Noah respond to that revelation? He needed to say something, but all he could come up with was a low whistle followed by "Damn, Willow."

She wasn't done. "My mother-in-law wants us to move down the street and become one big, happy family. I love her, but that isn't happening. That's why I turned into a basket case in the dairy case. Thank you for being so kind tonight."

With that, Willow Eldridge unbuckled her seat belt, exited the truck, and all but ran to the cabin door.

"Okay, then," Noah said aloud. No wonder she'd been bawling in the grocery store. He would have skipped the dairy and gone straight to the beer-and-wine aisle.

He waited, ensuring she made it inside before shifting into gear and heading out. His mind was spinning. He'd known that something had hurt her, but having heard the details? Wow. Willow Eldridge might well be as battered up as he.

He was halfway back to the highway when his phone rang. Willow. "Thank you for tonight. You don't know how much I needed the rescue," she said when he answered.

"This wasn't a rescue," Noah said flatly, fiercely resisting that idea. He'd given her a helping hand— that was all.

"I guess you'd have an opinion on that as a firefighter."

"Former firefighter," he corrected.

"We'll have to agree to disagree on the rescue part. I hope you'll allow me to say thanks."

He hesitated, then said, "That's not necessary. You already thanked me."

"Words aren't enough. Let me do more."

His heart went *ka-thunk*.

"I'm talking a fabulous meal. An open bar. Company and conversation if you want it. Solitude if you'd prefer. Noah, please be my plus-one at my brother's wedding on Saturday?"

He drew in a deep breath. It'd be a mistake. He didn't want to socialize. He wasn't fit for it.

There was bound to be dancing. A dance with Willow? Holding her close. Sharing her heat. *Yeah, right. On your bum leg?* All he'd be able to manage was a sway.

However, they *were* serving rib eyes. He exhaled in a rush and asked, "What time shall I pick you up?"

"You look beautiful, Mom," Lucas Prentice said to Genevieve as he offered her his arm to escort her up the aisle of St. Vincent's Church.

"Thank you," Genevieve replied. "I must say, you look outstanding yourself all decked out in black tie."

Lucas fiddled with the bow tie at his neck. "I'm trying not to complain since I know this is what Tess wants. Jake would have been happy with us all wearing jeans and T-shirts."

"At least you're getting to wear your boots."

"True." Lucas leaned down and kissed his mother's cheek. "So, shall we do this, mother of the groom?"

"Absolutely."

Her second son escorted her up the aisle to Pachelbel's Canon. She sat in the front row next to her sister, who took hold of her hand and squeezed it. Helen had regaled her with tales of her travels over a long lunch earlier in the week, and Genevieve had suffered a severe case of FOMO about missing Tahiti and Bora-Bora. But Genevieve was a good sister. She'd listen to Helen's stories and hear how much fun she'd had. Without Genevieve.

At the altar, the men took their places. Lucas stood beside Jake. Gazing at her sons, Genevieve could feel her heart give a little hitch. She leaned toward Helen and spoke softly. "Isn't it wonderful to watch Lucas standing up as Jake's best man? A year ago, they weren't speaking and avoided each other like the plague. Today, their grandfather's estate issues are settled, and the boys are back to being brothers. I'd begun to lose hope the healing would ever happen."

"It's a happy day," Helen replied.

And it was. Brooke and then Willow marched down the aisle and took their places as attendants to the bride, followed by the flower girl and ring bearer, Emma and Drew. Genevieve got a little misty-eyed as she viewed her children and grandchildren standing at the altar. She couldn't help but be sad that David wasn't here to share this beautiful family event.

At the signal from the organist, Genevieve rose to her feet. Her heart filled with joy to see the love shining in Jake's eyes as he watched his bride walk down the aisle to join him.

The church was packed. Tess, who had no blood family, had family nonetheless. She'd been bubbling for days over how many of her friends had accepted their invitations. Genevieve couldn't understand why the young woman was so surprised. Everyone who knew Tess loved her.

Her heart full, Genevieve's gaze drifted away from

the happy couple and touched on Willow. Her daughter shone in her role as an event planner. Everybody around town was talking about it. Willow'd had everything organized and running smoothly as the guests began to arrive. With Maggie and Tom in town, Genevieve had even been relieved of babysitting duty. That had been both a joy and a regret.

She wouldn't have missed a minute of these past three months with her grands. And yet, what she would have given to go with Helen on her trip. How to fulfill these two parts of herself? *Three parts*, she amended as her gaze returned to the bride and groom. She focused on Jake's face. He looked so much like his father. So handsome. So full of life and love as he spoke his vows to the woman he loved. *David, you would be so proud.*

Now her teary eyes overflowed, and she reached for the handkerchief she had ready in the hidden pocket of her gown. *Dang it, my mascara will run. I'll be a raccoon in all the photographs.*

Then, like always, just when she needed it, Helen slipped her arm through Genevieve's and gave it a squeeze, offering silent comfort and support. Genevieve made it through the rest of the service with dry eyes, taking dozens of mental photographs.

"Wasn't it a beautiful ceremony?" she observed as she and Helen settled back into the car taking them to Raindrop Lodge for the reception.

"Just lovely," Helen agreed. "Tess and Jake make a gorgeous couple. I'll tell you who else makes a gorgeous couple—Willow and Noah Tannehill."

"He's a fine-looking man. I'll admit this date caught me by surprise. The first I heard about it was this morning when she told me she and the kids wouldn't be sharing this car with us out to the lodge. She was so busy I didn't have a chance to quiz her about it."

"Oh, I have the scoop on that."

"You do?" Genevieve whipped her head around to stare at her sister. A ribbon of hurt fluttered through her. *I've babysat Willow's children darn near daily for the past three months. Helen has been on the opposite side of the world for over a month, and she knows more about what's going on in Willow's life than I do?*

Genevieve had thought she and Willow had made significant progress over the past year. Guess she'd been wrong. "What do you know?"

Helen explained about running into Willow, Noah, and the children at the bowling alley. "Drew told me he'd invited Noah to the wedding, but he didn't think he'd come. I, of course, encouraged it. I like to think I may have helped a little bit in facilitating his presence here this evening."

"Hmm." Genevieve had heard about the sleepover at Auntie's house, of course. The children mentioned it at the rehearsal last night. They hadn't mentioned Noah Tannehill. Neither had Willow breathed a word about the man until she'd mentioned he'd be driving her to the reception.

"Willow and Brooke both look lovely in pastel green. Tess couldn't have chosen a more flattering color for her attendants. It was nice of her to include Jake's sisters in the wedding party, don't you think?"

"I do." *Tess is thrilled to have sisters. She told me so. She tells me things. Even living a thousand miles away in Austin.* "I'm thrilled to have Tess join our family. I love her."

"Me, too." Helen nodded. "It's nice that the Eldridges can join us, though it must be a difficult, bittersweet

moment for them. The last Prentice-family wedding
they attended was when Willow married Andy. I'm sure
they always miss him, but it must be worse at times
like these."

"Have you spoken to Maggie and Tom this week?"
Genevieve asked.

"No. Maggie stepped out of their cabin as I drove
by one day, but I was late to a meeting and didn't have
time to stop and talk to her. We exchanged waves."

"Hmm. That's about all I've managed, too. It's been
such a crazy-busy week, and I know Willow was grateful to have the extra help with the children because your
week was jam-packed, as well. I hope to get the chance
to visit with them tonight. They're still family, as far as
I'm concerned."

"Speaking of family, I don't want to be Debbie
Downer at a happy event, but you need to know this because she's working tonight. Our manager gave notice
this afternoon."

"Lana did? No! Why?"

"Her husband has been diagnosed with Alzheimer's.
She's going to devote all her time to his care."

"Oh no. I hate to hear that. I knew she was worried
about the possibility." Genevieve clicked her tongue. "I
saw him at the store earlier this week, and I could see
a significant decline from the last time we met. Alzheimer's is such a horrible disease."

"It is. And scary. It's one of those great 'what-if' dis-
eases. I swear, Genevieve. I'm praying for pneumonia.
Dr. Theimer always said pneumonia was God's gift to
old people. A heart attack wouldn't be bad, either, as
long as it was the widow-maker type. Do they call it a
widower-maker when a female has one?"

"I don't know. Can we change the subject, please? This wedding is a happy event."

"Fine." Helen paused a few beats, then added, "I worry about strokes, too."

"Helen!"

Her sister laughed and patted Genevieve's lap. "I'm done. I don't know about you, but I'm ready for the cocktail hour and the appetizers. That truffle mac and cheese is calling to me."

Traffic slowed down unexpectedly at that point. Genevieve noticed but didn't overthink the delay until their car came to a complete stop. Helen leaned forward and spoke to the hired driver. "What's up?"

"Don't know, ma'am. Traffic has come to a standstill."

Genevieve frowned. Willow was still back at the church, her presence required for after-ceremony photographs. Genevieve knew she had hired off-duty policemen to facilitate traffic at the entrance to the Raindrop resort. Maybe Willow should make a call.

She slipped her phone from her evening bag and dialed her daughter. The first call went to voice mail, so she tried again. This time, Willow picked up. "Mom?"

"Just thought you should know traffic is shut down on 16."

"You're kidding."

"Afraid not."

"Thanks for the heads-up, Mom. I'm on it."

Genevieve returned her phone to her bag and said to Helen, "Willow is checking. There's probably a herd of mountain goats in the road or maybe a fender bender ahead."

Helen scowled and shook her head. "I don't think so. I'll bet you dollars to donuts that something nefarious is happening here."

"Why do you say that?" Genevieve asked, gazing at her sister in surprise.

"Because..." Helen folded her arms and spoke with a huff. "We're having a big event at Raindrop. Our biggest ever. I'll bet my favorite fur coat that weasel Nelson Camarata is up to his nasty tricks."

"You don't own a fur coat."

"That's beside the point. Nelson Camarata is messing with Jake's wedding. You just wait and see."

"Why would the mayor do that?" Genevieve asked.

"Because he's a control freak." Helen tossed her head, sending her dangling earrings swaying. "From the day he was elected mayor of Lake in the Clouds, he declared himself the Grand Poobah of everything that happens in our town. He was already a member of the homeowners association board at Mountain Vista Retirement Community, and that's where he and I started butting heads."

"Oh dear." Genevieve winced. Her sister was not a fan of her HOA. That was one of the reasons Genevieve had decided to buy a house when she moved to Lake in the Clouds instead of joining her sister in the luxury retirement community.

"I swear, give that man one little smidgen of power, and he thinks he deserves all of it. He thinks he's the god of Lake in the Clouds, and he's not."

"No, that would be Gage," Genevieve dryly interjected.

She and Helen shared a smirk at that. Genevieve's claim wasn't far from the truth. Gage had a lot of power. The Triple T Ranch established by Gage's great-something grandfather had once owned almost all of the land upon which Lake in the Clouds had been built.

Each time they'd sold off a parcel, they'd maintained an interest in the property and attached strings, which effectively gave Gage a vote in how the land was used even now, more than a century later. In fact, Genevieve's first interaction with the man had been in a squabble over her and Helen's purchase of the Raindrop Lodge property. Luckily, they'd moved beyond adversaries and had become friends.

Helen snorted and continued her diatribe. "You are correct, Genevieve. Our mayor is actually Nepotism Nelson, and I called him out on it. His son is the chief of police. His daughter runs the water department. His nephew is head of Planning and Permitting, and he is the reason why we haven't gotten the stop sign we need at the lodge yet. Someone needs to do something."

Genevieve's phone rang. "It's Willow. I'll put it on speaker. Hello?"

"Mom, you won't believe what happened. I just talked to my hired cops. The police chief called for a license-and-registration check on all outbound vehicles on Highway 16 between five and seven p.m. tonight."

"Oh no. What can we do about it?"

Willow's disembodied voice rose from the phone. "I think it's time to pull out the big guns. Perhaps a call from Gage Throckmorton to the police chief will take care of it."

"Good idea. Gage and the Triple T Ranch probably have the stroke to get this done."

"I don't have Gage's phone number. Would you text it to me?"

"Sure. Unless you would rather I phone him about this?"

"I'll do it," Willow said. "This is my job."

"All right." Upon ending the call, Genevieve located Gage Throckmorton in her contacts list and forwarded the information to her daughter. Her sister observed, "You know, Noah wasn't the only fine-looking man in the church today. Gage wears a suit very well. When are you going to ask him out on a date?"

"Stop it, Helen. It's not that way with me and Gage."

"Yet," Helen said with a pointed look.

"Well, *yet* might never happen. I'm not sure I want it to happen. He's still mourning his wife and I've been single a very long time. I'm accustomed to and comfortable with being alone."

"Well, now, that's just a shame, Genevieve." Helen clicked her tongue and added, "Times are a-changing, though, aren't they?"

Genevieve was saved from making a response when her phone rang again. It was Willow.

"FYI, Mom," her daughter said. "I spoke to Gage. He's calling the mayor now to remind him of the water contract that's due for renegotiation and to tell him to call off his dogs on us. The contract is a big deal and important to the mayor. Gage says we'll be moving again in minutes."

"Excellent news," Genevieve said. "It's nice to be on the right side of a person with power."

Willow continued. "We're going to push the schedule for everything back twenty minutes. It shouldn't be a problem at all. I'll see you soon." Willow disconnected the call.

Helen folded her arms over her chest and fumed. "Nelson is such a weasel. He's done this to be pissy because he wasn't invited to the wedding."

"Why should he have been invited to the wedding?"

Genevieve shook her head in wonder. "That's ridiculous. He's never met Jake or Tess."

"I know," Helen agreed with a scowl.

Genevieve rolled down her window and stuck her head out to see how long the line of cars stretched. "It looks like we might be beginning to move."

Helen brightened. "That was fast. Love to see Nepo Nelson taken down a peg or two. The man is—"

"Enough of him, Helen," Genevieve interrupted. "We have a celebration to attend. Let's think happy thoughts."

"You're right. Happy thoughts. How about this? What a difference a year makes, right?" Helen took hold of her sister's hand and gave it a squeeze. "Why, this time last year, we were knee-deep in planning our renovation project at Raindrop. Now we're all spruced up and open for business and hosting our first wedding. You weren't talking to your children. They weren't talking to each other, and now we're all one big, happy family."

"Yes." And yet a ribbon of unease fluttered through her. *What a difference a year makes.* Something about that sentence didn't sit well with her at the moment. Was it because Helen knew about Willow's date to the wedding and Genevieve hadn't? Because the sight of that new pearl necklace Helen had bought on her trip had given rise to Genevieve's own green-eyed monster? Maybe because this wedding reception marked an ending for Genevieve as well as Tess and Jake's new beginning?

Helen was right. The Raindrop Lodge project was officially done. Zach Throckmorton's Independence Construction company had completed the last of the new cabins they'd planned for the resort earlier this month.

The decorating was completed the previous week, just in time for the wedding guests' arrival. The project that had brought Genevieve to Colorado was finished. Over. Kaput. The sands of its hourglass were empty.

Happy thoughts, mother of the groom. Happy thoughts. "I see champagne on ice. Why haven't we broken into it?"

"Because when I asked you if you wanted a glass as we left the church, you said no."

"And you listened to me?"

Genevieve reached for the bottle, but Helen slapped her hand. "It's too late now. We're turning into the entrance. We'll be at the lodge before you can wrestle the cork free. Knowing your luck, the wine will spray, and we'll both get wet. I don't know about you, but I don't want to look doused and soused in the wedding pictures. Wait two minutes and get a glass from a passing waiter."

Genevieve stuck out her tongue at Helen. She hated when her sister was right.

Helen sniffed. "I wouldn't want that nasty thing in my mouth, either."

The old saying from their childhood lifted Genevieve's spirits, and she laughed. "Oh, Helen. I'm so happy for Jake."

"I know. Me, too. So, who do you think is next in line? Lucas? Willow? Brooke?"

"Not Brooke. It's too soon after the divorce. And Lucas? Who knows what goes on in his mind? He's been running since the day he was born. I don't know if he'll ever settle down. And Willow?" Genevieve lifted her shoulders. "Sounds like you're in a better position to know what's going on in her mind than I am."

"Now, Genevieve," Helen chided.

"Don't 'now, Genevieve' me."

"You are in a strange mood, aren't you? Well, I guess it's your due. Your baby just got married. It's natural for your emotions to be jumbled up."

The car stopped in front of the lodge, and a waiting attendant opened the door. Genevieve looked up at the building and her pique melted away. Raindrop Lodge and its surrounding grounds looked lovely.

Festival lighting defined a party perimeter between the lodge and the lake. Round tables draped in the colors of the sunset surrounded a temporary dance floor. A string ensemble played softly in the background during this, the cocktail hour, and the dinner that would follow. Once dancing kicked off, a DJ would take over the music duties to boost the party atmosphere.

Genevieve got her glass of champagne and began to make the rounds greeting guests. The crowd skewed younger than at Willow's and Brooke's weddings, where the guest list had included more Prentice-family friends. Jake and Tess had invited a few Lake in the Clouds locals they'd gotten to know during their time here last spring, so Genevieve did know people. It was just a different wedding than previous family celebrations. She wasn't throwing this wedding. She wasn't the hostess. She was a guest. That's how it should be with the bride and groom in their thirties, right?

Right.

So why did it make Genevieve feel like an old cow put out to pasture?

She was just being emotional, like Helen said. She needed to get over herself and enjoy the evening. The wedding party arrived and was introduced to much fanfare. Jake gave a little speech thanking everyone for coming, then he and Tess enjoyed their first dance.

"They're a beautiful couple," came a familiar voice from behind her.

Genevieve smiled genuinely as she turned toward Gage Throckmorton, who stood beside his son Zach. "Hello, you two. Aren't they, though?"

Zach said, "Your whole family is looking mighty fine tonight."

"Why, thank you, Zach." Genevieve leaned over and gave his cheek a kiss. "By the way, you did a fabulous job with the dance floor. Jake and I took a practice spin on it last night. It's smooth as can be."

"I'm glad. I think a temporary dance floor is a wise investment for Raindrop. I'll bet y'all develop quite a destination-wedding business after this. I know the folks in town are hoping to see that happen."

Gage nodded his agreement. "They want Willow to stay around and manage that part of your enterprise. She's been a rock star throughout these arrangements."

"I heard that," Willow said as she and Helen came up beside them. "The last thing I feel like right now is a rock star. Gage, I've been looking for you to thank you. I'm afraid we'd all still be lined up on the highway if you hadn't been available to bail me out."

"No thanks necessary," Gage replied.

"Nelson Camarata and his nonsense needs to be stopped," Helen snapped. "He gets my goat. You should do something about him, Gage."

"Nah. I have my hands full with ranch business. Except for special circumstances like today, I let the town take care of itself." Gage winked at Genevieve's sister and added, "Why don't you take him on? You could do it. It would be fun to watch. Oh, and by the way, welcome home, traveler. How was your trip?"

With that, Helen was off and running. By now, Genevieve also could describe the over-the-water bungalow where her sister had stayed in Bora-Bora. She could converse about the dozens—maybe hundreds—of types of fish Helen had seen while snorkeling. Genevieve knew all about the kayak trip and the booze cruise and scented lotion at the Tahitian resort. So when Willow, God bless her, interrupted to suggest they take their seats for dinner, Genevieve spontaneously reached out and hugged her.

Willow laughed. "Hungry, Mom?"

"Just wanted to congratulate you on a job well done."

"Hold that thought until the end of the night. Knowing my luck, Mayor Camarata will decide to send the fire marshal out to check our sprinkler systems and shut down the kitchen during dinner service."

"Don't even go there." Genevieve slipped her arm around her daughter's waist and gave her a squeeze. "Now, I'm going to go have that steak I've been thinking about all week."

Dinner proved to be as fabulous as billed and the company as pleasant. Since Genevieve's children and grandchildren all participated in the wedding party, they were seated at the head table. At Genevieve's table for eight, Willow had placed a lovely mix of Texas friends and new friends from Colorado. And Helen, of course.

So, Genevieve got to hear all about the snorkel trip yet again.

When Helen finally quit holding court, Gage turned to Genevieve and asked, "So, is Willow remaining in Lake in the Clouds after this, or is she returning to... where was it? Kentucky?"

"Tennessee. Nashville." Genevieve took a sip of water. "I believe she plans to stay through the traditional end of the school year, even though she's homeschooling Drew—successfully, I'll add, which boggles my mind. What a lot of work that is! Anyway, what she has planned beyond Memorial Day, I'm not certain."

"Man, it would be tough on you for her to take those grands and go after you've had them around for six months, wouldn't it?"

"Definitely," Genevieve replied honestly.

"When Zach's brother got divorced and his ex took our little guy down to Durango, it liked to have killed me." Gage lifted his water glass and took a sip. "Now I build my calendar around my opportunities to visit with him. Luckily, I only have to drive a couple of hours to see him. I would hate to be an airplane ride away from my grandson."

Genevieve offered him a sympathetic smile. "It was awful, especially when the children were babies. They change so quickly."

Gage's gaze shifted toward Willow, who stood speaking to a server near the cake table. He said, "Well, maybe Willow will decide to stay in Lake in the Clouds and build a business as an event planner here. Hey, I have a great idea!" Gage lit up with a smile that was so filled with delight that Genevieve smiled back at him before he even shared his great idea. "Why don't we hire her to plan our grand-opening shebang for The Emily?"

"Oh." Genevieve's smile froze as the old Yogi Berra quote flittered through her mind. *It's déjà vu all over again.*

A little over a year ago, in what her family had come to call her great getaway, Genevieve had fled her life in Texas to make a new one in Colorado. She had thrown herself into the renovation of the Raindrop Lodge project—and then her son had shown up to "help."

Now, her partner in the only other truly interesting thing she had going in her life—the theater renovation—wanted to, in effect, turn that over to Genevieve's daughter. And she couldn't refuse without looking like a bad mother!

"That would be fabulous," she replied, keeping her smile on her face—barely—as her steak turned into an anvil in her stomach.

"Yeah, wouldn't it?"

He was so proud of himself. Genevieve was suddenly reminded of David. Men could be so clueless sometimes.

She was glad for the distraction of the speeches and the mother-son dance. After that, the party began in earnest.

The playlist was a nice mix of current tunes and classic, pop, country, and universal appeal. Gage asked her to dance to Frank Sinatra's "Summer Wind," and Genevieve allowed herself three minutes to do nothing more than enjoy the sensation of once again being in an attractive man's arms.

Her sister's words from earlier drifted through her mind. Did she want a "yet" with Gage Throckmorton? It was a lovely thought...but an intimidating one, too. It had been a long time for her.

The dance put Genevieve in a mellow mood. As Gage escorted her back to their table, her gaze sought out each of her children in the crowd. First, Jake and

Tess, because Tess was now one of hers. Next, Willow stood on the dance floor with Emma and Drew, the trio holding hands as they danced to the change-of-tempo "Shout." Genevieve spied Lucas holding court over a bevy of females near the bar. It took her a moment to locate Brooke, but she finally spotted her with friends from Texas at the photo booth.

Her chicks were all doing okay. They'd all abandoned the nest and, despite a damaged wing or two, were still flying.

And, hang it all, she was flying, too.

Gage excused himself after returning her to their table. No sooner had he departed than Helen all but shoved a fresh glass of champagne into Genevieve's hand. "Here—we're going to drink to my new project."

"Your new project?" Genevieve asked. "What new project?"

"I'm going to get us our stop sign."

"Good. How do you plan to do that?"

"Gage gave me the idea. He told me to take on Nelson, and that's exactly what I will do."

"Take on Nelson Camarata?"

"Yes. My next project. I'm going to run for mayor! The election is in August."

Genevieve gaped at her sister.

"I'm going to run on an anti-nepotism platform and promise that my first act as mayor will be to rid our city government of everyone with ties to the old goat."

"There won't be anyone left."

"Precisely." Helen clinked her flute with Genevieve's and beamed a high-wattage smile. "It's really too bad that tomorrow is Sunday. First thing Monday morning, I'm going to go to the courthouse and file my paperwork."

"That's wonderful, Helen."

Helen was going to run for mayor. Helen had a new project.

"You'll make a great mayor." Genevieve reached over and gave her sister a hug. Then, speaking into her ear because the music volume had increased with a new song, she added, "I'll be right back. Gonna run to the ladies'."

She rose and left before Helen could get a good look at her eyes. Instead of turning toward the lodge and the restrooms, she headed for the lake.

At that point, Genevieve did something not unheard of for a mother of the groom at a wedding. However, it usually happened earlier in the event and not with such sudden ferocity.

Genevieve Prentice burst into tears.

Chapter Seven

AS PATSY CLINE BELTED "Crazy" from the sound system, Noah decided the song couldn't be more appropriate. He was slow dancing beneath the stars with Willow Eldridge in his arms. Nothing had felt this good in a very long time. Never mind that his leg was killing him.

Willow was a dream. Tall and lithe, she flowed like water around the dance floor despite his less-than-graceful lead. She looked fabulous in a frothy green dress that made him think of mint ice cream. *She's a Dreamsicle.* Used to be an ice-cream bar by that name when he was a kid. *Wonder if they still make them?*

They didn't speak, but the silence was comfortable. Though they stood at the edge of a crowded dance floor, it somehow felt as if the two of them were alone.

Noah pulled her a little closer, wallowing in her warmth. He shut his eyes and turned his face into her hair. *Roses*, he thought. *She smells like roses.* He felt the stirrings of desire and hummed along with Patsy. *Crazy.*

He wanted to kiss her. He wanted to nuzzle her neck and nip her ear just below the diamond stud. He wanted to taste the champagne on her lips and know the heat of her breath. It would be so easy to go with this moment and do what felt so natural.

Noah lifted his head. His gaze met Willow's and—

Something tugged at his slacks. He ignored it. *Tug. Tug. Tug.*

Willow said, "Emma, what are you doing?"

The little girl stood staring up at him with her mother's eyes. "My turn, please."

Aw, hell. "Uh."

"I want to dance. You can lift me up. That's what Uncle Jake and Uncle Lucas do. You've danced with Mama long enough, Mr. Noah. It's my turn."

Willow looked at Noah, waiting for his response. What was he supposed to say? *I can't deal with little girls*? Yeah, right. Willow would think he was a perv or something. Why was Emma here yanking on his britches, anyway? Wasn't it past her bedtime?

"Emma," Willow scolded, though she didn't take her gaze off Noah. "You're being impolite."

On the defensive, he attempted to explain. To excuse. "I can't carry her. My leg..."

It worked—damn his weak-ass soul for the cowardly excuse. Willow's expression melted with sympathy. "Of course. Emma, leave Mr. Noah alone. Go ask Nana to dance with you. Or Aunt Helen."

"They're girls."

"So what? Girls can dance with girls."

"But I want a man."

Willow laughed, and Noah thought he heard her mutter, "Yes, well, don't we all?"

Noah suddenly needed to get away—from the little girl, the oh-so-appealing woman, and everyone. Being around all these people was making him a Patsy Cline poster child. Crazy crazy crazy. He had to escape. "Tell you what, Emma. Dancing with your mom is just about the best thing ever. I'll let you take my place."

Coward that he was, Noah let his hand slide away from Willow's waist. He placed her hand in her daughter's and beat a retreat.

Damn, he hated himself.

So what else was new?

He snagged a drink from a passing waiter's tray and headed off into the darkness away from the party, his thoughts as black as midnight. What the hell had he been thinking when he accepted Willow's invitation? He had no business trying to mix with normal people.

Oh, it had started out well enough. In the early part of the event, he basically had been a date in name only.

Since Willow and the children had been members of the bridal party, they'd been required to be at the church long before the guests arrived. Noah hadn't needed to pick anybody up. He had driven Willow and her kids from the church to the lodge, but nothing about that ride had been date-like, either. She'd spent almost the entire time on the phone with her assistant, a "day of" coordinator, for which she'd apologized profusely. "I don't know what I was thinking," she'd said when she'd hung up the phone. "I knew I'd be working for most of the wedding. I'm so sorry, Noah."

"Hey, no worries at all. I get a steak dinner out of it."

An excellent steak dinner, it had turned out. Even the

company during the meal had been tolerable since he'd been seated next to Drew and the boy rarely shut his mouth. Didn't matter if it was full of food, something his mother chastised him about each time she caught him at it.

After dinner, he'd felt obliged to ask Willow to dance. He'd been thinking about kissing her, and then the tug on his pants and a pretty little girl staring up at him with stars in her big green eyes—it had transported him back to another place, another time.

Daddy already danced with me. Your turn, Uncle Noah!

Noah took a swig of his drink, and the smooth, smoky bourbon slid down his throat like angel tears.

"You're a shit, Tannehill," he murmured. "She's just a little girl. Go back and ask the little girl to dance."

He turned around, gazed toward the dance floor, and two events captured his attention. First, Willow and Emma were indeed dancing. Well, a version of dancing. They were holding hands, hopping around, and giggling. Under other circumstances, he might have smiled at the sight. The second event was somewhat alarming.

Genevieve Prentice rose abruptly from her table and headed his way, her expression distressed. As she drew closer, he saw that she had tears spilling from her eyes and rolling down her cheeks. What in the world had happened?

No one else appeared to have noticed Genevieve's flight. Acting on instinct, Noah melted back into the shadows as she rushed by.

Genevieve disappeared into the darkness along the shoreline of Mirror Lake.

Well, hell. Noah stood frozen in indecision. He

needed to make amends to Willow's daughter for his yellow-bellied retreat back there, or it would plague him like a chigger bite for weeks. He glanced back toward Willow. She and Emma obviously weren't devastated by his action. But Genevieve. Something must be really wrong for Genevieve to dash off from her son's wedding reception.

Noah watched to see if she recovered and returned. While doing so, he remembered his own mother at Daniel's wedding. She hadn't wanted to miss a minute of it. A smile touched his lips at the memory. She'd whined about having to go to the bathroom because it took her too long to shimmy in and out of her spandex shapewear, or as she called it, her "suck-it-ins."

Noah waited for the length of one whole song and debated going to tell Willow what he'd seen. Knowing his luck, she'd hand the kid off to him, check on her mother, and then be gone for the rest of the night. Noah gave it another minute, then wandered in the direction that Genevieve had taken.

He saw her standing on one of the small fishing docks staring out at the water. He stopped, pursed his lips in thought for a moment, then made a quick detour before advancing to approach her. "Did the music get too loud for you, Genevieve?"

She jumped. "Oh, Noah. I didn't see you."

"I'm sorry if I startled you. I saw you standing alone out here, and I thought you might be getting away from the noise for a few minutes. Thought you might be thirsty." He handed her the fresh cocktail he'd snagged from the waiter. "My compliments to your bartenders. These are excellent."

"It's all Willow's doing. I had nothing to do with it."

Well, that was definitely a bitter note he heard in her voice. Moonlight reflected off her face and illuminated the tear streaks on her cheeks.

Okay, now what do I do?

Turning around and leaving would probably be the kindest thing. However, Noah kept thinking about his own mother and how in her last days, she relived the favorite memories of her life, including Daniel's wedding day. So he said, "I may be way off base here, and I'm probably out of line, but I know what it's like to want to hide and nurse your wounds. Sometimes it's easier to talk to strangers than friends. If you'd like to talk, I'm happy to listen. I give you my word it will all stay right here."

She appeared startled and a little embarrassed. "Oh, Noah. Thank you, but I'm fine. It's nothing. Just a little mother-of-the-groom moment."

"Okay."

"And I did need a break from the music."

"I understand. Me, too."

Genevieve sipped her drink. "I hope you're enjoying the evening."

"I am. That rib eye was the best I've had in ages." And he wasn't going to talk about himself or how he'd become Willow's plus-one. Or was he Drew's plus-one? He still wasn't exactly sure how that fell out.

"Good. My steak was excellent, too. Willow was a little worried about the catering, but they've done a fine job. Everything's been great. She's done an excellent job."

"That she has."

"Gage Throckmorton wants to ask her to plan the grand-opening event for The Emily. It's the old movie theater downtown that Gage and I have been working together to renovate. It's named for his late wife—he lost her to cancer not too long ago—and we're having a big gala when it opens."

"That's nice." Wasn't it? He thought he might have detected that bitter note again. Was she angry at Willow over something? All righty, then. He was gonna beat feet. He had zero interest in getting into the middle of family drama.

Now to ease his way out.

Then Genevieve sighed heavily. "Actually, Noah, I'm feeling a little put out about it, and that makes me feel like a queen B. Throw in the fact that my sister just announced that she's decided to run for mayor . . . well, I'll be honest. I'm jealous of them."

Yes. Well. Crap. Apparently, Genevieve was taking him up on his offer to listen. What the hell had he been thinking? "Um . . ."

He didn't know what to say, so he took a sip of his drink.

Genevieve didn't appear to mind, because now that she'd gotten started, she kept on going. "I'm right back where I started sixteen months ago. Sixteen months is a long time when your sands are free-falling, I'm telling you. I've wasted sixteen months, and I don't have sixteen months to waste!"

"I'm sorry. You've lost me, Genevieve."

"I have nothing to do! I decided to move to Colorado sixteen months ago, ready to make a fresh start and a new life and be someone who is more than Mom. Now Raindrop is finished, and The Emily might as well be, and all I am is my gravestone!"

"Okay, I was with you for a bit, but I'm gone again."

"She made a great meat loaf!"

Meat loaf! He really should go find Willow. No, maybe the groom or the other brother or both of them. Or maybe this called for the entire Prentice family. Well, everyone except that precious little girl who brought to mind another little angel. A little fatherless angel.

Stop it! The last thing they needed was for Noah to follow Genevieve down Maudlin Road.

"Oh, I'm sorry, Noah. I probably sound a little crazy, don't I?"

"Um...I don't think I'll answer that."

She chuffed a little laugh. "A lot crazy, then. I was trying to make a point to my children a while back, and I asked them what epitaph they believed was appropriate for my gravestone. Except for Lucas's meat loaf suggestion, everyone agreed on one word—*family*. Family has been the focus of my life."

"That's...nice?"

"It is. Yes, it is! Only, I grew too dependent on my family. My family was my life. But it smothered my children and me, so I did something about it. I started a new life."

"That's great." Wasn't it?

"So why am I back at the beginning? I love the time I spend with Emma and Drew, but dammit, I want Bora-Bora, too! Why does family have to be both a lodestone and a millstone? I no sooner find some balance in my life than my chickens come home to roost, and it's so hard to say no because they're cute and fluffy, and they grow up so fast."

Noah decided that keeping his mouth shut was the best thing to do under the circumstances, so he took another sip of his drink and listened.

"So I give up Bora-Bora, but I'll always have Bogart and Bacall, only, let's give that to planner chick, which truly is a smart idea, only, what am I going to do with my life because it's wrong to waste a minute of it because of sands, you know? I have a big birthday this year."

Drew obviously got his run-on sentences from his grandmother. Despite his best intentions, Noah couldn't help but ask, "Sands?"

"'Like sands through the hourglass, so are the days of our lives.' Daytime TV. A soap opera. My life is a soap opera. The most boring one ever!"

This was getting out of hand. "I can see that you have some issues to work through, Genevieve, but I worry that you will regret doing this tonight. What I hear is that you are passionate about your family. This is a family event, and I'm sure you've felt passionate about it. If I may, I'll share a piece of advice. My mom expressed regret until the day she died for the forty minutes of my brother's wedding reception that she missed because she got stuck in her shapewear."

"Oh no!" Genevieve said with true horror in her tone. "She didn't."

"She did. You need to go back to the party, Genevieve. Jake and Willow will notice you're gone, and they'll worry about you."

"You're right. I know. Noah, I apologize for dumping all of this on you. I don't know what came over me. You didn't deserve it."

"Don't worry about me. Actually, I was happy for the distraction. I've been battling a few ghosts of my own tonight."

"Oh." She blinked up at him. "Do you want to talk about them?"

"Nope. I think we both should get back to the party and the business of having fun. Come with me, Genevieve, and next time something slow comes on that doesn't require a lot of movement on my part, will you honor me with a dance?"

"Yes. I'd love to dance with you, Noah. Thank you."

It turned out that just as they reached the reception area, the Righteous Brothers' "Unchained Melody" began to play. Noah gave her a questioning look. "This one?"

"Perfect."

"Fair warning, with my bum leg, I sway more than move."

"Even more perfect." He set their empty glasses onto a bar tray, took her into his arms, and they began to dance. They didn't speak throughout the first verse, then Genevieve said, "I danced to this song with my husband at our wedding. David was a swayer, too. Not because he had a leg injury, but because he had two left feet."

Genevieve's wistful tone suggested that her meltdown might be over. Thank God.

Over Genevieve's shoulder, Noah caught sight of little Emma Eldridge. She was running around the tables chasing another little girl. Maybe after this, he would track her down and give the dance a go.

Then again, maybe not. Obviously, she hadn't been as traumatized by his refusal as had he. He probably should just let that idea go.

Genevieve lifted her face toward him and smiled. "I'm sorry I subjected you to my emotional tizzy, Noah."

"Don't worry about it. Today's an emotional day, and it sounds like you're at a turning point in your life. Sometimes you have to spit those words out before they can start making sense to you. I understand that."

"A turning point. Yes. I just need to find a new project."

Noah frowned, opened his mouth to speak, but then thought better of it. Not quickly enough, because eagle-eyed Genevieve spotted it. "What? You don't think I need a new project?"

"Not exactly. Look, it's not my—"

"Tell me."

He shrugged. "Okay. I think you need a new passion. I mean, your family is obviously your passion, which is all well and good, but it sounds to me like you need something else to care about that's more than a project."

"I'm not looking for romance."

"I didn't mean that kind of passion. Well, it could be that kind of passion, but I'm thinking more along the lines of an interest like travel or hiking or spelunking."

"Spelunking?" she said with a laugh. "I hardly think so."

"I'm talking about something that isn't finished when your activity connected to it is finished. You're passion-ate about your family. Is there something else that pops to mind? What about travel? You mentioned Bora-Bora earlier. Willow told me she knows you wanted to go with your sister to the South Pacific, but she thinks you didn't go because of her kids."

"She told you that? You know, Willow and I are over-due a heart-to-heart talk." Genevieve exhaled a sigh. "I do enjoy traveling with my sister, but I don't know that I'd label traveling a passion. It's a lot of work."

"Well, think about it. Don't look for a new project. Look for a new passion. That's my advice, and it's worth exactly what you paid for it." The song was drawing to an end—thank goodness. Noah figured he'd stepped outside his comfort zone plenty far enough already.

"I will think about it. Thank you, Noah. You've been so kind to a crazy old woman."

"Not crazy." *I claimed that song earlier tonight.* "And you are far from being old."

"I like you, Noah Tannehill."

"I like you, too, Genevieve Prentice. Thank you for the dance."

Noah escorted Willow's mother back toward her table, and then he truly did need to get off his feet. He headed back toward the lakeside bench that had been his original destination before Genevieve rushed past him. Happy to find it unoccupied, he sank into the seat with a little groan. *I've lost my ever-lovin' mind.*

He had maybe three minutes of peace. He wasn't even that surprised when Drew sat down next to him. "Hi, Mr. Tannehill. I hardly got to talk to you at all today."

"You talked to me plenty."

"Not about your dog. I heard you have a dog! I want to know more about him. Why didn't I meet him when I visited your house? I love dogs. I want a puppy so bad, but Mom won't let me have one until we're settled. I don't know when we're going to be settled. Are you having fun? Are people being nice to you? I hope so. I've told everyone you're my friend, but sometimes, that's when they act like bullies. It's 'cause they're jealous. How come you walked away into the dark? I wanted to go after you and make sure nobody was mean to you, but Mom said to leave you alone. Are you okay, Mr. Tannehill?"

Not to Noah's surprise but to his consternation, the

boy's little sister took a seat at Noah's other side. She spoke to her brother. "Don't be stupid, Drew. He's not okay. He has a bad boo-boo on his leg."

Then little Emma Eldridge leaned over and killed him. She kissed Noah's knee.

～✒️～

Willow worked into the wee hours of the morning following the wedding reception overseeing the cleanup. She would have liked to sleep in, but duty called early Sunday morning when she and the kiddos went to her mom's for the final event of the wedding weekend: a brunch Genevieve hosted for family and out-of-town guests. She had insisted that Willow be nothing more than a guest at the event, and Willow happily complied.

Maggie and Tom attempted to corner her and discuss their "gift," but Willow successfully avoided the conversation. Before they left to drive to Durango to catch their flight home, she promised Maggie a phone call on Wednesday. When their car pulled away from Genevieve's curb, Willow drank a celebratory glass of champagne and ignored her mother's curious look.

After the brunch, her family dispersed. Jake and Tess headed off to the Maldives on their honeymoon, Lucas traveled home to Texas, and Brooke resumed the extended tour of Europe she'd interrupted for her brother's nuptials. Before gathering up her children and carting them back to Raindrop Lodge, Willow summoned her courage and asked her mother to meet her for coffee on Monday morning.

After that, Willow decided to ignore the anxiety

Maggie Eldridge had introduced into her world during the past week and give herself a lazy Sunday afternoon.

It was heaven. The weather was fabulous, and the kids played outside most of the time. They were tired, too, so they didn't wander off for once. Willow sat in the sunshine, read a book, and tried not to think about tomorrow.

Confessions of secret keeping about her marital troubles and seeking advice for life-changing decisions could wait another day. If she spent a little of her downtime dreaming about Noah Tannehill, well, a little fantasy didn't hurt a girl, did it?

But like always, Monday morning did arrive. Willow had hired an off-duty employee of Raindrop Lodge to watch the children for a few hours. The talk she needed to have with her mother required privacy and zero interruptions—neither of which she'd get if her children were around.

Willow put hard rock on her stereo and thrummed her fingers nervously on the steering wheel as she approached her mother's home. She'd stopped at the bakery on her way for cinnamon rolls. If ever a conversation needed sugar courage, this was it.

She pulled into the drive, shifted into park, and shut off the engine. Where was she going to start?

Probably that god-awful Christmas party. Willow would sit down at her mother's kitchen table, open the bakery box, and spill the whole ugly story while eating some sugar with her crow.

Her mother had been right about Andy all along. She had been right, and Willow had been wrong. Not only wrong but spectacularly wrong. Colossally wrong.

Willow wondered if one of the reasons she'd found

it so hard to forgive her mother for not liking Andy at the start was because, deep down inside herself, Willow knew, or at least suspected, that her mother was right.

Genevieve Prentice had wicked-good instincts.

Willow moaned softly and scooped up the bakery box. She opened her car door and stepped out into the crisp mountain morning. Birdsong trilled in the air, and the springtime breeze was just right to hear the rush and bubble of the creek below. Her mother's traditional red geranium brightened the front porch.

Willow girded her proverbial loins and headed for the door. She rapped twice and tried the knob. Unlocked. Stepping inside, she called, "Mom?"

From upstairs came her mother's voice. "Willow, is that you?"

"Yes."

Following a moment's pause, Genevieve called, "I'll be down in a minute."

"Okay." Willow set the bakery box in the middle of the table and took two plates from the kitchen cabinet. She hesitated at the coffee bar. Should she make a pot or stick with the single serve? Willow could drink coffee all day long, but her mother usually cut it off after her two morning cups.

Deciding to start with a single cup, Willow began the prep. She'd just put two scoops of dark roast into the filtered basket when her mother breezed into the kitchen. She was dressed for going out in black denim jeans, a white shirt, and a black-and-white vertically striped sweater. She wore wooden earrings and a matching necklace she'd taken to fancying. Pretty dressed up for morning coffee in the kitchen, Willow thought.

"Sweetheart. I'm so sorry. Didn't you get my text?"

"You sent a text? When?"

"Last night."

Willow tugged her phone from her pocket and checked the screen. She hadn't received a text from her mother. "You didn't send me a text."

"I didn't?" Frowning, Genevieve pivoted and exited the kitchen. She returned a moment later with her phone in her hand. "I'm such a doofus. I accidentally scrolled one name too far and sent it to Winstead Dentistry. Oops." She crossed the room and gave Willow a hug. "I'm sorry you made the trip, honey, but I can't visit this morning. I'm on my way out of town. A car is coming for me in—" She glanced at the digital readout on the oven. "It'll be here any minute."

"Wait. You're going out of town? Today? Why? What happened? What's the emergency?" Thinking of her siblings, she added, "Did someone have trouble after leaving Lake in the Clouds?"

"No, no. Everyone is fine. As far as I know, anyway. I'm going away for ten days. Well, almost two weeks, counting travel time, because I'm going to mosey. If one actually moseys in a Maserati. I'll be back a week from Friday. I don't want to miss my hair appointment Saturday morning."

"A Maserati! Mom! What is going on?"

A wicked twinkle entered her mother's eyes. "Apparently, I caught Helen's travel bug while hearing her describe the fish in the South Pacific Ocean for the seven hundredth time Saturday night."

"You're not going to Bora-Bora!"

"Not in a Maserati, no. I'm driving to New Mexico. But first, I'm going to Aspen to pick up the car."

"You bought a sports car. Oh, Mom. You're doing it

again, aren't you? It's another getaway? Have you put this house up for sale?"

"Willow!" Genevieve exclaimed. "You're not listening and you're jumping to conclusions. I'm renting a Maserati from a luxury car service in Aspen and driving it to New Mexico."

Now? Just when Willow had finally stoked herself up to tell her mother the truth about the disaster of her life. "Why?"

"Driving a car like that through the mountains will be an adventure."

"Yes, I can see that it would be, but why are you going to New Mexico?"

"Immersive drawing classes." Genevieve's expression lit with delight. "It's something I've always wanted to try."

Since when? This was the first Willow had ever heard about it.

This must be another one of Aunt Helen's wild hairs. The two of them must have cooked this scheme up after having one too many glasses of champagne Saturday night.

Genevieve continued, "The class had a last-minute cancellation, so I snapped it up."

"Wait. Auntie isn't going with you?"

Her mother sounded almost gleeful as she said, "Nope. It's just me."

"I don't understand."

"Well, I don't have time to explain." Genevieve opened the drawer of her built-in desk and removed an envelope of cash, which she slipped into her purse. "Where is that extra phone charger of mine?"

She snapped her fingers and exited the kitchen.

Willow followed her mother into the great room, where she tugged a charger free from a wall plug. Willow's gaze locked on the wheeled suitcase and matching tote waiting beside the front door, and her world narrowed to the set of Louis Vuitton. *No! Mom, you can't leave. Not now. I have to decide what to do.* "But Mom. I *need* you!"

Genevieve turned around, the cord dangling from her hand, her eyes glittering with exasperation. "Willow, I'm sorry, but *I* need this trip. I love you and the children to the moon and back, but the world can't always revolve around your needs. Today, I'm making myself a priority. I need some balance in my life. I'm sure you can find another babysitter for the next two weeks."

This isn't about babysitting! "But Mom, wait a minute."

"I don't have a minute," Genevieve said, heading for the door as the bell chimed. "Here's my car."

Willow stood in speechless shock as her mother greeted an older man wearing a blue polo shirt and khaki slacks who stood on the front stoop. "Mrs. Prentice? I'm Mark with Allied Car Service."

"Wonderful to meet you, Mark. I'm ready to go."

He gestured toward her bags. "Is this it?"

"Yes."

The driver took the bags. Genevieve returned to the kitchen for her purse, then hurried past Willow, pausing only to brush a quick kiss on her cheek. "Bye, hon. Please lock up when you leave. You have a key."

The front door shut behind her with a firm thump.

Willow stood in her mother's living room, dazed and dismayed. The sound of a trunk slamming shook her from her stupor, and she rushed outside. Her mother was climbing into the back of a black sedan. "Mom? Mom. Mom! Listen, please!"

With one leg in the car, her mother halted and Willow hurried to say, "I didn't come for babysitting. I wanted to have a heart-to-heart talk with you. About Andy and everything. I want to try to clear the air."

For a long moment, Genevieve stood frozen in place. Then she lowered her sunglasses and peered over their top toward her daughter. "You have spectacular timing, Willow."

Willow gave her a troubled smile. "Apparently so."

"Oh, honey." Genevieve's fingers drummed against the car door for a good fifteen seconds before she lowered her leg to the ground and stepped away from the car. "I've wanted to have this talk with you for years. I can stay."

Okay, good. Willow expelled a sigh of relief, but then the expression on her mother's face gave her pause. The excitement had gone from Genevieve Prentice's countenance. A minute ago, she'd been happy and eager. Now, her mother looked disappointed and tense.

Willow's stomach dipped. This was wrong. She shouldn't expect her mother to drop everything just so that her grown daughter could cry on her shoulder about things that happened years ago. No one was bleeding. This wasn't a matter of life and death. *Grow up, Willow. Mom obviously has something going on. You need to stand on your own two feet here.* "Mom? This trip is important to you, isn't it?"

Genevieve gazed at Willow solemnly. "Yes, it is."

"Then you should go. This conversation has kept for a decade. There's no reason why it can't keep for another two weeks."

"Are you sure?"

Maggie Eldridge would push for an answer on Wednesday, yes, but Willow suddenly knew what she needed to do. She needed to be brave like her mother—for herself and for her children.

"I'm sure, Mom. You go ahead to New Mexico."

"We will have this talk when I get home?"

"We will."

Her mother's shoulders sagged with relief. "Great. I really need to attend this class. C'mere and give me a hug."

The moment of being wrapped in her mother's arms ended all too soon for Willow. However, the whirlwind of emotion churning through her had settled a bit with her mother's hug. She was able to think more clearly. As the driver went to shut the door, Willow took a big step forward and called, "Hold on a second. Mom, one thing. Why is a last-minute drawing class in New Mexico so important to you?"

"Ask Noah."

"Noah? Noah Tannehill?"

"Yes."

Now Willow *really* didn't understand. "What does he have to do with any of this?"

"He has everything to do with this. Ask him to explain about my passion. The tock is clicking. Let's go, Mark."

The driver shut the door. Her mother smiled and waved through the window as the sedan pulled away from the curb.

"Passion?" Willow watched the car depart, a sense of disbelief rolling through her. "What could Noah possibly know about my mother's passion?"

Chapter Eight

WHEN NOAH FELL INTO bed the night of Jake Prentice's wedding, he was done with people. He slept in on Sunday morning and did chores around the house that afternoon. Monday morning, he started a new project in his workshop. By the time the crunch of tires warned him of an approaching vehicle on Wednesday afternoon, he'd had his recluse hat firmly back on his head. He hadn't left his property once.

Whatever was coming up the lane wasn't big enough to be a delivery truck. Noah scowled down at the piece of balsa wood he'd painted a rich purple.

"Now what?"

At the sound of his voice, Marigold lifted her head from her bed in the corner. Her big brown eyes stared at him balefully. None of her six three-week-old actively nursing pups were distracted from the business at hand.

Noah debated his next move. He could rise from his

workbench seat and investigate the intruder. He could stay right where he was and wait to be found. Or he could escape out the back door and hide in the woods.

That last wouldn't work. Mari would shake off her pups and lead the interloper right to him. He might as well wait for the trespasser to track him down or leave. Besides, he had a niggling suspicion about who might be driving the car whose engine had just shut off in front of his house.

This time, it only took Goldilocks about four minutes to track him down in his workshop. Of course, the open door and music from his stereo provided some hard-to-miss clues. Noah wasn't surprised when Willow Eldridge walked into his workshop. She looked . . . well . . . how to describe her? Gorgeous went without saying. But she was a Viking queen, tall and regal, and judging by the heat flaming in her eyes, ready to go to war. Despite being somewhat forewarned, the first words out of her mouth flabbergasted him.

"Are we dealing with a Mrs. Robinson situation here?" Willow asked, her arms folded and her toe tapping.

Noah dragged his gaze away from the way her arms pillowed her breasts. "Excuse me?"

"*The Graduate.* The movie."

"Uh . . . Dustin Hoffman?" Noah sputtered a laugh. "From, like, the seventies?"

"Nineteen sixty-seven. I looked it up. My mother wasn't even in kindergarten yet at the time. As a modern woman, I should be able to say, *You go, girl*, but I'll be honest—I've never been a fan of the age-gap trope."

"Whoa. Whoa. Whoa. Whoa. Hold on just one minute. Are you seriously accusing me of sleeping with your mother?"

"Yes! No! I don't know," she said as she paced back and forth just inside the workshop doorway. Sunlight beaming through the opening caught a glimmer of fire in her hair that he hadn't noticed before. A little strawberry in that blond. How had he missed it? He'd always had a thing for strawberry blondes. "What the hell, Noah? You should have told me you were dating her."

"Dating her! Did she tell you that?"

"No, but—"

Exasperated, Noah interrupted. "Something put that idea into your head."

"Not something. Someone! Okay, maybe I don't really think y'all are role-playing classic movie characters, but something happened at the wedding."

Noah ran his hand down his face as he put some clues together. Talk about a minefield. He exhaled heavily. "Willow, don't get me wrong. Your mother is a lovely woman, and I don't know what anyone has tried to tell you about what they think they saw at the wedding, but—"

"Wait a minute. Something happened at the wedding? *What* happened?"

"Nothing happened. I had an innocent conversation with your mother beside the lake."

"Nothing? Well, I've been stewing on your 'nothing' since Monday."

"What happened Monday?"

"My mother left to go to Aspen to pick up a Maserati and drive to New Mexico, where she's taking ten days of drawing lessons. But before she left, she told me to ask you to explain about her passion."

"Ah." The proverbial light bulb went on.

"'Ah'? That's all you have to say? 'Ah'?"

"Pull up a chair, Willow. There's one at the desk over by the window. Watch out for the dog."

"Drew says that you have a dog. He's been pestering me ever— Oh! You have puppies!" Her mother's passion problem momentarily forgotten, Willow went down on her knees and began cooing and oohing. "He didn't say you have puppies."

"I didn't tell him. I was afraid he'd hike over the mountain at dawn."

"What kind are they? How old are they? How many boys? How many girls?"

"She's a stray who wandered up. I suspect someone dumped her when they realized she was pregnant. The pups—four girls, two boys—are three weeks old. Ready to find homes in another three." He paused and pinned her with a stare. "You in the market for a dog?"

"They're going to be big dogs, aren't they?"

"Marigold is mostly a golden retriever, I believe. Maybe full-blood. Father is unknown, but based on the size of those feet, yes, they'll be big. The vet told me to tell potential adopters to be prepared for seventy-five pounds for the males and sixty-five pounds for the females."

"Marigold?"

He shrugged. "She was a round puff of yellow when she waddled up here. Seemed to fit."

"She's beautiful. The puppies are too precious."

"I repeat. You in the market?"

Willow sighed. "Drew's been asking for a puppy for forever. I've put him off because our living situation was up in the air."

"Is it still up in the air?"

"Not as much as it was. This morning, I kicked the teeth out of the gift horse's mouth."

Noah didn't have to think too hard to make sense of that. "You told your kids' grandmother you didn't want her house."

"Yes. I'm not moving my family to Texas. But we're not returning to Nashville, either. I'm putting our house on the market. What happens next is still a work in progress. And that means I've got a lot of big decisions to make before I'm ready to let Drew have a dog. Now, you and these precious pups have attempted to distract me from my mission. Tell me what went on between you and my mother at my brother's wedding."

Since Willow appeared to be perfectly happy sitting on the workshop floor amid the puppies, he didn't mention the desk chair again. Instead, he returned his attention to his project. Picking up his paintbrush, he explained. "Genevieve had a bit of a meltdown at the wedding, and I witnessed it. We talked. She spilled her guts. I gave her a piece of advice. Apparently, she took it to heart. That's pretty much the story."

"That doesn't tell me anything. Why did she melt down? What advice did you give her? And what on earth does it have to do with *passion*?"

Noah covered another shingle the size of his fingernail in purple paint. He didn't need to be so meticulous, but over the past couple of days, he'd found that he enjoyed the detailed work. "I picked up some signals, but I'll be the first to say that I barely know your mother, so I could be totally wrong. Take everything I say with a grain of salt. Deal?"

"Deal."

"She came to Colorado in search of something. I don't think she's found it yet. She's jumped into projects. Projects are all well and good, but they have an ending. I told her she needed a passion. Something that doesn't have a completion date."

"Oh," Willow said, the light dawning. "Drawing lessons. She's looking for a hobby?"

"A passion. Something in addition to her family." While Willow considered what he'd shared, Noah carefully placed the painted shingle on the drying tray. A dozen more to go. He picked up another one and wetted his brush.

Meanwhile, Willow picked up and cuddled the pup who had finished his meal and become interested in the laces on Willow's sneakers.

"What else did she say to you?"

"I really don't want to get in the middle of family drama."

"I think it's too late for that, Noah. Mom sent me here." When he grimaced, she laughed. "Hey, anything is bound to be better than me thinking you're playing Benjamin Braddock to Mrs. Robinson. I had to watch the movie again last night after the kids went to bed, you know. I couldn't remember much about it other than the music."

"Great music." Noah carefully stroked color on the tiny shingle.

Willow gazed at him with interest. "You like Simon and Garfunkel?"

"I do."

"Me, too. Although they've been a source of trauma for me."

Noah finished painting the shingle and reached for another. "How so?"

"Oh, it was like fifteen or twenty years ago. My mother was in Las Vegas chaperoning one of my little sister's cheerleading group competitions, and Mom went to see Simon and Garfunkel in concert at the MGM Grand. It was their Old Friends reunion tour. She splurged on a ticket way up front. I've heard the story so many times I feel like I was there myself. Anyway, my aunt Helen was so jealous. I mean, *Wizard of Oz* Emerald City green. She's six years older than Mom, and she was growing up when they were popular. It still gets her goat when that concert gets mentioned." Willow paused, then added reflectively, "Maybe that's why my mind went to Mrs. Robinson so quickly."

Noah decided it was safe enough to tease. "Well, Genevieve is pretty hot."

"I know. She should have a man in her life!" Willow declared.

"Has there been anyone since your father?"

Willow lifted her shoulders. "No one serious. No one she brought to family events. Well, except for...hmm." Willow scooped up a second puppy and clucked and cooed over it.

Noah wasn't going to ask. He wasn't. "Hmm?"

"It's only a friendship thing, but she invited Gage and Zach Throckmorton to our family Fourth of July celebration in Texas last summer. Gage is a recent widower. He's not dating. But he and Mom have become friends."

"She's working with him on another project." Noah dipped his brush in paint. "She mentioned it during her, um, our conversation."

"Her meltdown." Willow set the puppies down and rose gracefully to her feet. She bent over, gave all the non-actively-nursing pups a belly rub, then wandered over to his desk and grabbed the chair he'd pointed out to her upon her arrival. Instead of turning it toward him and taking a seat as he'd expected, she tugged it over to his workbench and sat beside him. "Can I help?"

"Can I trust you with a paintbrush?"

She scowled at him. "Yes."

He handed her a clean brush, a stack of rectangular planks, and a drying tray. "These will be white."

"Cool."

He returned to his shingles. For a few minutes, they worked in companionable silence. Willow interrupted the quiet by asking, "What did my mom say about our own John Dutton?"

"John Dutton?"

"The television show *Yellowstone*? The rancher? Kevin Costner?"

"Ah. Yeah." Noah shrugged. "I don't watch much TV."

"Never mind that. What did my mother say about Gage Throckmorton? I think they would make a great couple. He danced with Mom at the wedding. Did you see that? I had hoped that he would ask her to dance. It was part of my evil plan when I made the seating chart. So, what about Mom and Gage?"

Once again, Noah found himself in a pickle. *Well, Genevieve, if you didn't want me spilling your secrets, you shouldn't have sent your daughter to me.* "The conversation wasn't so much about him as it was about you. I guess Gage suggested they hire you to plan the grand-opening party for their theater renovation. It took a little wind out of your mother's sails. She recognizes that you'll do a fantastic job, but she had some ownership over that project and..." Noah shrugged.

Willow winced. "Oh no. It's just like with Jake. He swooped in and hired Tess to do the interior design for the lodge. That was Mom's project, too."

Noah finished painting the final shingle and dropped the brush into a jar of water. He planned to tackle the fencing next, so he reached for a clean brush and the pot of pink paint.

Willow carefully painted what would be the planks for a wraparound porch. Her next comment proved her mind remained on her mother. "She said she needed balance. What is she trying to balance? She is passionate about her family. I think...oh. Oh, of course. The kids. Her grandchildren. I asked her to babysit too much, didn't I?"

Willow groaned and closed her eyes and dropped her head back. "Of course I did. She never once told me no. She wouldn't, would she? Not after all the times she bemoaned the fact she couldn't babysit for me because we lived in Tennessee while she was in Texas. I was so busy with the wedding, so fretful about Drew and happy to have help whom I knew I could trust that I never stopped to look at it from her point of view."

Willow set down her paintbrush and a completed plank and covered her face with her hands. "I don't know what's wrong with me. I screw up so much where my mother is concerned. Once upon a time, she and I..." Her voice trailed off. "I don't know why I'm telling you all this."

"Like mother, like daughter," he said, his tone dry.

Her mouth twisted in a wry smile. "I went over to her house to tell her the whole sad story about Andy and his girlfriend. She was on her way out of town. I'd worked myself up to finally spill all my secrets, and she gives me the brush-off."

"I'd like to point out that I am not and have never been trained to be a counselor. Or a priest. Confessions aren't my area of expertise."

"Good, because I didn't come here to confess anything. Even if my mother-in-law tried to make me feel like the biggest sinner on earth; I'm not so certain she's going to talk to me again anytime soon."

Noah shrugged. "Her loss."

"Relationships are complicated, aren't they?" Willow said with a sigh. "I have the best mother in the world. I honestly do. She and I were close until we weren't, which was my fault. Part of that, I think, was normal growing-up stuff. Mom and I needed to learn to relate as adults in addition to the mother-child relationship. But after Drew was born, and I realized my marriage wasn't all I'd hoped it would be, well, I closed off. I didn't want to disappoint her."

Noah had enough talk about family and relationships at the moment. Abruptly, he set down his paintbrush and the piece of fence railing. "Time for the puppies to go outside to play. Want to help?"

"Oh, I'd love that. I need something to get my mind off my problems. Guess I can use some balance myself. Just let me finish this plank first."

"So, are you going to take one of these puppies? Or—" Noah waggled his brows. "How about two of them? One for each kid."

"We can't get a puppy, much less two of them. I'm not sure where we'll be living in a couple of months. I have to get a job. I don't know if we'll stay in Lake in the Clouds, move back to Texas, or try somewhere totally new. I can't deal with puppies and two kiddos while trying to move."

"Where do you want to live?"

"I think . . . here." Her teeth tugged at her lower lip for a moment. "That's another thing I wanted to talk about with my mother. Based on the interest I've fielded in the wake of the wedding, I think I could establish a nice little event-planning business and work as much as I want. The kids are happy here. I thought Mom would be happy to have us here, but now I'm unsure. When she moved from Texas to Colorado, she basically ran away from home. So I have to ask myself..." Willow paused and shrugged. "Is it fair for home to follow her?"

Noah let out a low, near-silent whistle. "Well, I'm smarter than to jump into the middle of that one. You're on your own."

"Appreciate you."

Smirking, Noah walked over to the pen he'd fashioned to keep the puppies corralled but that still allowed Marigold the ability to come and go at will. The dog rose as Noah stepped into the enclosure. He gave the mama a good neck scratching, then observed, "You know, Willow, you pick out the puppies you want, and I'll keep them here until you're settled."

Willow snorted but didn't look up until she'd finished painting the plank and placed it on the drying rack. "You're just afraid you won't be able to find homes for all the puppies."

"No," he said, putting as much innocence into his voice as he could muster. "Look at them. Who will be able to resist them?"

She looked at the pups, and her expression turned to mush. "You fight dirty."

"I fight to win."

"Hmm."

He scooped up two pups and held them out toward Willow. She rolled her eyes, dropped her brush into the water jar, then rose and walked toward the puppy pen.

Noah handed the two pups to her, then gathered the other four into his arms. To Marigold, he said, "Take some quiet time if you want, Mama. We'll keep your babies safe."

As if she understood him, Marigold turned three times in a circle, then lay down and closed her eyes.

They carried the puppies outside. "Where shall we put them down?" Willow asked.

Noah led her around the far side of his workshop, where he'd used logs to outline a play area for the pups. He'd piped water from the outdoor spigot to a trough and had a basket of chew toys and balls for the little destroyers to demolish. "Why, look at this!" Willow exclaimed with delight. "It's better than a doggy daycare."

"It makes my life easier—that's all." Noah set his wiggling wags down inside the enclosure, then turned the spigot to add a little water to the trough.

For the next ten minutes or so, Noah and Willow played with the puppies, though in reality, he spent most of the time watching Willow. With every puppy tumble and tail wag, the tension within her eased. She was a ray of sunshine on the partly cloudy afternoon, her laughter lighthearted and joyous, her manner playful and carefree.

He'd thought of her often since the wedding. Thought about that almost kiss.

He had no business thinking about kissing her. Willow Eldridge and her curious little boy and her precious little girl were complications he didn't need.

She glanced at her watch. "I'd better be going. I need to pick up Drew and Emma from art lessons soon. Want help carrying these darlings back to their mama, or is it still playtime?"

"I should probably get back to my workbench."

Willow cooed and cuddled three of the pups, leaving the other three for him, and headed back toward his shop. As she passed the SANTA'S WORKSHOP sign that had lured Drew to trespass back in February, she jerked her head toward it. "Puppies and dollhouses. I'm not so certain that's not a legit sign."

Noah gave her a guarded glance.

"That is what you call those fire-demonstration things you build, right?" Willow asked.

"Yeah."

One of the puppies managed to wriggle its way onto her shoulder, and she laughed. "Hey, you. Get back here."

Noah plucked the puppy off her and carried the little boy by the scruff of his neck back to his mama. Soon, all six pups were nuzzling around Marigold for an after-playtime snack, and Noah was walking Willow to her car.

"I meant what I said about the puppies. Two of them. Or one. Bring the kids. Let them choose."

"Oh, Noah."

"It would make Drew and Emma so happy. You know it would."

She sighed. "All right. I'll think about it."

"Promise?"

She gave an exasperated roll of her eyes, but a grin flirted on her lips as she said, "Yes, I promise."

It was the grin that did it.

Willow was happiness, brightness, and warmth, and Noah's resistance melted away, ice sliding toward the sun. Lifting his hand, he tenderly cupped her cheek.

His voice was low and a little gruff as he suggested, "How about we seal it with a kiss?"

Her tongue slipped from her mouth and moistened her lips.

Noah lowered his head, and at the first touch of her soft, sweet lips, heat—blessed heat—blasted through him.

Balance, shmalance. Willow had stepped off a cliff and was in free fall. She hadn't been kissed like this in ages. Maybe ever. How his lips could be both soft and firm at the same time she didn't know, but she also didn't care. They drew her into this swirling, spinning, heady world of sensation. Of *need*.

He tasted sweet...sugary sweet...and she recalled the bowl of gumdrops she'd seen on the desk in his workshop. *Candyman.* When his tongue stroked her lips, slipped between them, and met hers, it sent the liquid heat of desire zinging through her veins. Her knees melted, and she sagged against him, knowing instinctively that Noah Tannehill would catch her.

They were a perfect fit, her curves slotted to his angles as if custom-made to go together. She breathed in his scent—woodsy, spicy, and just a little sweaty. And sexy. Noah was sexy. The heat from his body seared into her and stoked her own warmth. Her passion. *There's that word again.*

It had been so long. So long since a man's arms had held her. So long since she had felt anything near this level of desire. It was exhilarating. It was frightening.

She was falling faster and faster, and he held her closer, kissing her deeper. This was no simple good-bye kiss. It was tangled sheets and magic hands and shudders and moans. Willow was seconds away from hitting the ground and having her way with him.

Luckily, Noah had more sense than she because he lifted his head and took a backward step. Willow felt bereft as his arms slid away from her.

His voice raspy, Noah said, "Art."

Willow blinked. "Um, what?"

"Class. Um...art class. You, um, don't want to be late. The kids. Don't you have to pick up the kids?"

My kids! She'd forgotten all about Drew and Emma. The heat that bloomed in her cheeks had nothing to do with passion and everything to do with embarrassment. "Oh. Oh, yes. I'd better go."

Noah reached around her and opened the driver's side door. He stood there, grimacing, and rubbed the back of his neck. "Yeah...um. Willow...uh...I...um...that was...whoa."

"Yeah." She managed a shaky smile. "Me, too."

"I don't mean for you to get the wrong impression," he added with a note of warning.

"No. Me, either," she said quickly. "I'm not looking for any complications. Believe me."

"Neither am I. I just got...well...carried away. You pack a punch, Ms. Eldridge. I lost my head there for a minute."

"So do you, Mr. Tannehill. I think it's safe to say we both got carried away. So, I'll...um...be going." Her cheeks stinging with embarrassment, Willow slid behind the wheel.

Noah looked like he wanted to say more. "Willow?"

She looked up at him, waiting.

"I'm dragging around a lot more baggage than half a dozen puppies. I don't want there to be any misunderstandings. Don't look to me for anything beyond friendship. In all honesty, I'm not sure how good I can be at that."

He looked so troubled. Willow felt her embarrassment fade as her heart melted. "Hey, you've been an excellent friend to me, Noah. You don't owe me anything. No expectations here."

He nodded. "Okay, then. Well, I'm glad you came by."

"Me, too." Grinning, she reached for the door. "So good to have the Mrs. Robinson question cleared up."

His hand darted out and caught hold of the door, preventing it from closing. "Think about the puppies."

Willow groaned and rolled her eyes. Noah wore a satisfied grin as he shut her door. She started the engine, shifted into gear, and drove away from his home. As if she'd be able to think about anything other than that kiss for the next, oh, millennia.

Truth be told, she was feeling a little gobsmacked. Not by the kiss itself. That hadn't come as a complete surprise. If she were honest with herself, she might have come here today looking for it.

Because . . . he'd been about to kiss her on the dance floor.

She'd known her mother was no Mrs. Robinson. Had Genevieve been attempting to play matchmaker by sending her to Noah with her passion comment? Maybe. Willow had made herself fair game to this sort of stuff from her mother when she invited Noah to the wedding. Nor could Willow have explained that he was Drew's guest as much as hers. Her mother wouldn't have bought it.

She wasn't sure that she had bought it herself.

As she pulled onto the highway leading into town, her heart raced like a horse at Churchill Downs.

"Calm down," she lectured herself. He'd warned her off, hadn't he? He wanted to be friends. Just friends. Okay. Well, she'd meant what she'd said. She needed a friend a lot more than she needed, well, more. But my, oh, my. That kiss. Noah Tannehill's kiss.

So he had baggage. She had a baggage car. A baggage train. A baggage aircraft carrier.

Wonder what his baggage was all about? Maybe if they became better friends, she'd find out.

Wonder what he thought about friends with kiss benefits? Just kissing. Necking. Making out. Good grief. What was she, twelve?

More like sixteen and hormonal. Besides, judging by the rate at which the kiss had heated up, it would go way beyond kissing seriously fast.

She glanced at her reflection in the rearview mirror. She wasn't a teenager anymore. She was thirty-three and sex-starved.

Somebody ought to write a song about that. Maybe somebody already had. If not a song, there was undoubtedly a *Cosmo* article about it. Although, maybe *Cosmo* was for younger women. She didn't know. She hadn't looked at a women's magazine since Emma was born, and she'd had to deal with two kids while standing in the checkout line at the grocery store. Even before that, she'd gravitated toward *House Beautiful* instead of *Woman Beautiful*, which was probably why Andy ended up with "Bimbo Beautiful."

Do. Not. Go. There. She absolutely would not ruin this lovely moment with Noah by bringing that…that…baggage into it.

So, she turned on her music and picked a classic rock playlist as she completed the trip to pick up her children, enjoying the hum of life in her blood that lasted for the rest of the day.

On Thursday, Willow returned to their prewedding morning routine with schoolwork for Drew and activities for Emma. Her daughter was busy creating a forest full of pipe-cleaner animals while Drew and Willow tackled multiplication at the kitchen table. Then, the sound of tires crunching on gravel drifted through the open windows and announced a visitor's arrival.

"Someone's here!" Drew said, looking up with delight. He set down his pencil.

"Don't even think about it. Back to work, kiddo." Willow rose and walked toward the front room as a knock sounded on the door.

"It's me," called Aunt Helen.

"Come in."

The door swung open, and Helen blew inside. After greeting the children and getting hugs, she spoke to Willow. "I know it's a school day. I'm sorry to interrupt, but I only need a few minutes. I have a couple of things out in the golf cart I'd like to show you if you can steal a minute."

"Sure we can!" Drew piped up.

"You sit right back in your chair," Willow said to her son. She smiled at Helen. "Always good to see you, Auntie. Drew is working on his own right now, anyway. Emma, want to take a break and play outside for a few minutes?"

"Can I bring my animals?"

"You may. Put them in a grocery sack, and they'll be easier to carry."

"Okay," Emma replied.

Drew whined. "But Mom—"

Willow cut her son off with a *Don't start* look. Emma scrambled down from her chair, pulled a plastic sack from a cabinet, and loaded it up with pipe cleaners. Then Emma and Willow followed Aunt Helen outside.

One of Raindrop Lodge's electric utility vehicles sat in the circular drive at the front of the cabin. Willow saw that the vehicle's bed contained several signs as Emma dashed toward the woods opposite the house. She called, "I'm going to put my animals in the woods, Mama."

"Okay. Just don't go beyond the play area."

"I won't!"

As Emma scampered off, Aunt Helen turned to Willow and asked, "What in the world is your mother doing in New Mexico?"

"You don't know?"

"No. I haven't talked to her. I missed a call from her on Monday, but she left a voice mail saying she was going to New Mexico for ten days. She didn't say why, and she hasn't returned my calls or texts other than to text back saying she arrived safe and sound and would call when she came home."

"That's good to know. I've been a little worried about that."

"So what's the skinny?"

"She's taking a drawing class at an artists' colony. She wants to find her passion."

Aunt Helen's jaw dropped. A wounded look fluttered across her eyes. "Without me?"

Willow didn't know how to respond to that, so she tried changing the subject. "What do you want to show me?"

"I'm canvassing votes."

"Already? That was fast."

"For my logo. I had Sylvia Lawrence do a mock-up, and these are my choices. I like the graphics of all three, and I'll probably use them all, but I need to settle on a color palette. I can't make up my mind."

"Hmm." Willow picked up the top sign and studied it. The words MCDANIEL FOR MAYOR were fashioned in the four colors of the Colorado state flag—blue, red, white, and gold. A second version was done in American red, white, and blue. Willow eyed the third and asked, "I love the white and lavender, but do the colors represent something?"

"The state flower. The columbine."

"Oh yes. Well, it's probably my favorite, but I think the Colorado flag colors are a stronger message."

"Good point. Thank you, sweetheart. So, tell me more about your mom and this artists' colony."

Willow sighed, but recognizing the terrier aspect of her aunt's character, she knew she might as well spill all her beans. Well, some of her beans. She wasn't ready to talk about Noah with her aunt. She gave her a recap of what she knew, including the Maserati, which had Aunt Helen's eyes bugging wide. Willow said, "I think Mom needs a new interest, and she's thinking art might be it."

Aunt Helen had a hint of sulk in her voice when she said, "Good for her. I'm glad, except I don't know why she had to do that right now. I need her to be my campaign manager."

"Oh wow." The idea of it made Willow grin. "The Bennett girls are large and in charge, hmm? Lake in the Clouds will never be the same."

"That's the idea. Ol' Nelson should have told his

nephew to give me my stop sign the first time I asked, and we could have avoided all of this. Now I'm going to take his job, break up his little kingdom, and send all his little princes and princesses home. But I need help to do it." She paused and eyed Willow speculatively. "Wait a minute. What was I thinking? You're a professional planner. You can be my campaign manager! You're staying in Lake in the Clouds, aren't you? You're not moving back to Nashville?"

"Mo-om!" Drew shot from the cabin door like a bullet. "I finished my worksheet. We're done for the day, right?"

Saved by the hot rod, Willow thought. "Wrong. But you can have a five-minute recess."

"You're such a meanie," Aunt Helen said, her eyes twinkling.

"True. But we still have a geography lesson to do."

"Then I won't keep you. Just tell me you're not going to move back to Tennessee and break your mother's heart. You'll make a fabulous campaign manager."

"I love you, Auntie, but I can't be your campaign manager. My plate is full, and your instincts were right, to begin with. Mom is the right woman for that job. Now, I think you'd be smart to send her a text today asking her to take the position so that when she finally turns her phone on, she'll see it before she plans another self-discovery journey."

"Another one?" Helen's eyes went round and wide. "She's doing something else?"

"I honestly don't know."

Aunt Helen's expression grew troubled. "I thought the campaign would be something your mom and I could work on together. It seems like I've hardly seen her since we returned from our Germany trip in December. I miss her."

"Aw, Auntie." Willow reached over and gave her aunt a hug. "Tell her that. I know she missed you, too, while you were on your South Pacific trip. She had a serious case of FOMO."

"Hmm." Helen shrugged, not yet appeased.

Willow encouraged her with a smile. "Just when is this election?"

"The end of August. The twenty-sixth."

"Well, I'm not going to manage your campaign, but you can count on me to be a volunteer."

That obviously caught her aunt's interest. "So you *are* staying in Colorado?"

"I need to talk to Mom about it before I decide. I want to be certain that this would be right for Mom, too. After all, she moved to Colorado to start a new life." Willow's heart gave a little twist as she gave voice to the doubt that had been niggling at her mind. "I don't know if it's right for her old life to follow her."

Helen opened her mouth, then shut it. Then she opened it again and closed it again without saying a word. This was very unlike Aunt Helen.

Willow's stomach sank. "Okay, say it. What has Mom told you?"

Helen shook her head. "No. It's not that. Not her. Your mom hasn't said anything. It was me." She drew a deep breath, then exhaled loudly. "What can I say? I acted like a green-eyed teenager. I got jealous of all the time your mother was spending with Drew and Emma. She went all 'supernana' on me, and I felt left out."

"Oh, Auntie." Willow caught her breath at her own blindness. She'd never thought about the situation from

Helen's point of view. How many times had Willow's mother canceled on her sister to help care for her grand-children? "I'm so sorry."

Helen held up her hand, palm out. "No, I was wrong."

"You were right." And this was one more thing to add to the list of things to talk about with her mother. "That's why I'll wait and have a long, heart-to-heart talk with Mom before I decide where the kids and I will settle."

"She'll want you here."

"Yes, I think you're probably right. But it needs to be the right thing for all of us. I want us all to be comfort-able. I'll promise you this. If the kids and I end up here, there will be a lot more Genevieve time to balance out the nana time. I didn't see what was happening before. I do now."

"You're a good girl, Willow Eldridge. And please, believe me when I say I'm delighted you're going to stay in Lake in the Clouds."

"We're *probably* going to stay. We'll need to find a place to live, of course, and I need to do some-thing about daycare over the summer. I'm not going to homeschool next year. It's way too much work."

"Y'all can stay here in Cabin 17," Aunt Helen said quickly. "We're in no rush to list it for rental."

"That's bad business, Auntie."

"It is family. I know you'll want a place of your own eventually, but you take your time finding the right place. Find the best neighborhood for the children. Oh, Willow. This will make your mother so happy—if she ever tears herself away from naked men."

"Naked men?"

"You said it's a drawing class, didn't you? Surely

they'll be studying the human form. What sort of lame drawing class would it be otherwise?"

"Oh, Auntie."

Helen winked and called, "Drew? Emma? I'm leaving. Give me a hug and tell your mother to bring you to the lodge for lunch because it's pizza day."

"Pizza day!" Drew yelled.

"Pizza day!" his sister repeated. Both children darted from the forest and ran to give Auntie Helen her hug.

After the geography lesson and a science unit that involved a walk through the woods looking for beetles, Willow herded the children up to the lodge, where Helen convinced Willow—easily—to allow her to sub for Nana and take the kids into town to swim in her condo's indoor pool. She also handed Willow two cards. The first was for the real estate agent who'd helped Willow's mom buy her house. The second card advertised a business belonging to the daughter of Raindrop Lodge's accountant—Little Ducklings Daycare.

Willow went back home and called them both.

Chapter Nine

NOAH'S HEAD WAS STILL spinning from kissing Willow when Gage Throckmorton dropped by the Hideaway to discuss replacing the fence that separated their properties. Noah jumped at the chance for some physical labor and declared himself ready to work the following morning.

Gage was skeptical. He intended to have a couple of his ranch hands do the job. But Noah's leg was back to 80 or maybe even 85 percent, and he thought that fence building would be as good physical therapy as what his PT guy had him doing. He insisted that he do half the labor and pay half the expenses.

He was shocked as hell when the boss man himself showed up Friday morning with a UTV loaded with supplies.

The first day he and Gage worked together, they hadn't done much talking beyond what was necessary for the job. By the end of the second day, Noah called the man friend.

Gage somehow got Noah to open up. In the beginning, their conversation revolved around typical stuff—sports, favorite brews and whiskeys, and barbecue methods. Then almost without Noah's notice, the sly older man began slipping in questions. Before he realized it, Noah had revealed how he'd injured his leg.

"A firefighter, huh?" Gage had said. "I have a lot of respect for you guys. Takes big balls to go into a burning building."

"Former firefighter," Noah shot back. "I'm not going back."

"Physical disability?"

Noah wouldn't lie about that. Nor was he inclined to offer an explanation. He said simply, "I'm ready for a change."

Gage let a long moment pass before he shrugged and changed the subject to barbed wire.

Noah was happy to discuss fencing. He didn't owe the rancher any details about his injury or the events surrounding it. Yet he chewed on the exchange for the rest of the afternoon, and when he finally swallowed it, it sat in his stomach like sour milk. So when they finished working for the night and Gage dropped him off at home, Noah found himself spewing his guts. "I'm dealing with some PTSD. Had a fire get tricky on us. Lost some folks."

"Damn. That's rough." Gage clapped him on the shoulder. "Like I said before, I have nothing but respect for firefighters. So, you up for another day mending a fence?"

"I reckon so."

"Tomorrow is Sunday. The only work I want to do is haul supplies. Bring your fishing gear. We'll be near my favorite fishing spot on the Triple T. Since we're not drawing wages for our work, I figure we've earned a day on the creek, don't you?"

"I won't argue against it." Noah grabbed his work bag from the back of the UTV, then posed the same question he'd asked of Gage at the end of the past two days. "Hey, Throckmorton. Don't you need a puppy?"

"No, Tannehill. I damned sure don't."

As was his habit, Noah headed first to his workshop to tend to Marigold and the pups. After that task, he went inside, showered, and threw together something for dinner. He was hungry. This physical work had given him a better appetite than he'd had in months.

He decided to drag out the Crock-Pot and make something more substantial for his evening meals from here on out.

Sunday morning, Gage gave Noah the option to ride along with a ranch hand on the UTV loaded with fencing supplies or use one of the Triple T's horses and accompany Gage on horseback. Noah liked to ride, and he judged his leg was ready to handle it, so he accompanied the rancher. They spent two hours positioning supplies along the fence line, then headed for Gage's fishing spot.

In a state filled with breathtaking vistas, this one had to rank among the top ten. A rainbow of spring wildflowers carpeted a meadow ringed by towering, snowcapped mountains. A frothy, bubbling creek wound its way through the center of the field. It was hands down one of the most beautiful spots Noah had ever seen.

"What a hidden gem," he said.

"Isn't it? Our family is blessed. Now, let's get to work and catch us some lunch, shall we?"

The trout all but jumped onto Noah's flies, and he caught his limit within the first hour: three brown trout and a rainbow. Gage struck out but didn't seem to care, especially once Noah offered to share his catch for their lunch.

"Honestly, I like the casting as much as the catching," Gage told him when he sat around the fire Noah had built. "There's something so relaxing about getting a line wet, don't you think?"

"I totally agree." Noah handed over two of the trout he'd cooked in the foil pouches with seasonings Gage had brought along.

"Thanks. Doesn't seem right that I let you catch, clean, and cook, and now I'm gonna eat half of what there is."

"Hey, it's your creek. Your slice of heaven. I'm thrilled you've shared it with me. This has to be one of the prettiest spots in the state."

"It was my late wife's favorite spot on the ranch. Emily and I talked about building a getaway up here. Came close to doing it a time or two, but when it came right down to it, we liked it unspoiled. Decided this little campsite would do us."

They ate their fish in silence but for a couple of smacks and hums of pleasure. Seasoned simply with butter, onion, salt, and pepper and baked in foil pouches over the fire, the fish was five-star cuisine.

"Delicious," Noah said, licking his fingers when he'd polished off the last bite.

"Very good. Excellent job, Chef Noah." Gage balled up his foil, wiped his hands with a paper towel, then deposited his trash in a bag. He stretched out his legs and leaned back on his elbows. "I could almost take a nap."

"Go for it. We're not on a clock."

"Yeah, but my bones are too old to get comfortable on this hard ground without an air mattress under me, at least. Last time Emily and I tent camped up here, we needed to airlift in all the gear we needed for the night." He sighed and smiled bittersweetly. "This is the first time I've come here since she died."

"I'd heard through the grapevine that you lost her to cancer." Noah flicked his gaze toward the older man, uncertain what Gage needed from him now. "You doing okay?"

"Yes. Yes, I am. I'll admit I had a few moments while in the water. Maybe that's why I proved to be such a lousy angler today."

"As good an excuse as any, I'd say."

"I had a good marriage," Gage observed, his gaze on the bubbling mountain stream. "Emily wouldn't have liked that I've avoided this place. She wouldn't approve of quite a bit of what's gone down since her death. I had a falling out with my kids. Still paying the price for that with my daughter. Had a falling out with God. I was one unhappy SOB, I'll tell you."

Noah scooped a handful of pebbles off the ground and began tossing them toward the water. "Losing someone you love is damned hard."

"Losing anyone is damned hard. It didn't matter how much money I had or how much stroke my family has in the area. Hell, in the entire state. Didn't matter how many prayers I said or what sorts of bargains I tried to make with the Almighty. I couldn't save my Emily. I was powerless. Made me so damned angry. Made me mean. What good does any of it do if you can't save the one person who means the most?"

Gage muttered a curse and rolled to a sitting position. "I'm sorry. I don't know what got into me to give me diarrhea of the mouth. That's just wrong after a most delicious meal. Guess being up here is getting to me after all."

"Shoot. Forget about it. I get it, Gage. I absolutely get it. Why do you think I'm hiding out at my grandfather's cabin in Lake in the Clouds?"

"Hell, I knew there must be a reason I liked you so much. You ready to talk about that?"

Noah considered it. "No."

Gage nodded. Both men rose and spent a few minutes tending to the campsite and packed up their horses. They made the ride back to Noah's place in companionable silence. As Noah unloaded his gear from the packhorse, Gage said, "I hope you're ready to get back to work in the morning. I'd like to get this project finished by the end of the week."

"Shouldn't be a problem."

They discussed a few logistics for the coming days, and as Gage prepared to depart, he met Noah's gaze and said, "Anytime you feel the need to talk, Tannehill, I'm your man."

"I appreciate it."

Noah wasn't ready to talk today, but maybe soon. He had the feeling that sunshine and puppies and physical work might be pulling him out of the black hole where he'd existed for the past year.

Kissing a beautiful woman hadn't hurt anything, either.

On Friday afternoon, almost two weeks after Jake and Tess's wedding, Genevieve sat in the back of a luxury sedan and sipped from a bottle of sparkling water while a driver ferried her home from Aspen to Lake in the Clouds. Driving the Maserati through the mountains had been a kick but had totally worn her out. In hindsight, she should have arranged to drive the sports car one way instead of round trip. Next time she did something like this, she'd know better.

Not that there necessarily would be a next time. She had enjoyed the experience, but she couldn't say she was passionate about it. Same with the drawing classes. Oh, she'd loved the setting—a large estate outside of Santa Fe with private bungalows. The food was fabulous, and the company interesting and eclectic.

She'd have enjoyed it more if Helen had been with her.

Won't my sister love to hear that?

Based on the tone of some of the texts from Helen that she'd found on her phone when she'd turned it on this morning, Genevieve had some explaining to do. Oh, she'd known to expect that. One of the selling points of the workshop was that the time was "unplugged." Guests were asked to send the estate's emergency phone number to loved ones upon arrival, then turn off their phones and not turn them on again until departure.

Genevieve loved that part of the event. The time away from a screen of any kind had been restorative. In addition to the time spent with her sketchbook, it allowed her to think and to dream and to plan. She now had a nice long list of potential passions to explore.

Of course, her phone had blown up this morning, but she'd expected that, too.

She'd read through the messages, answered all that needed a response, and promised to call everyone by the end of the day tomorrow. Now she was ready to be home. She thought she'd probably call Helen and Willow once she arrived and had some privacy. Her driver was nice and friendly, but no way could she tell her sister about the male model they'd sketched while the driver could overhear.

Finally, he made the turn onto her street. Genevieve was surprised to see Willow's car parked out front. Immediately, worry assailed her. Had something happened? No one had called her this afternoon. Making sure, she checked her phone for missed calls. Nothing.

Oh no. Is something wrong with Helen?

No. This was probably about the air clearing Willow wanted to do, but still.

Reaching into her purse for her keys, Genevieve spoke to the driver. "Paul, that's my daughter's car parked in front of my house. She's not supposed to be there, and I'm a little worried that something is wrong. I'm going to dash on inside as soon as you stop."

"Sure thing, Ms. Prentice." He goosed the gas pedal, and the car accelerated, pulling into her driveway a few seconds faster, something Genevieve appreciated. She opened the door the moment it was safe. The driver called, "Good luck."

She darted toward the front door, the quickest way into the house. Her heart pounded. Her mouth was dry as sand. Even as she attempted to fit her key into the lock with shaking fingers, she tried the knob. It turned. She rushed inside. "Willow?"

Three things hit her at once. Lights blazed in the kitchen. Andrea Bocelli played on the sound system. The aroma of garlic and olive oil drifted in the air.

Genevieve relaxed just a little bit. "Willow!"

"Hey, Mom!" Her daughter emerged from the kitchen, a smile on her face and a tea towel slung over her shoulder. "You're home!"

"Is something wrong? What's wrong?"

"Nothing's wrong. I decided to have a welcome-home celebration for you. I knew you'd be hungry from traveling, so I made Tuscan chicken. It's almost ready."

Something is wrong. "The kids are okay? Helen? Your sibs?"

"Yes, Mom. Everyone is fine."

Well, something wasn't fine. Genevieve knew her daughter. This was about more than a decade-overdue talk. "Okay, then. I'd better see to my driver."

Fifteen minutes later, Genevieve's bags had been deposited in her room. She'd changed her clothes, washed her face, and done some deep breathing to bring down her pulse rate. With a glass of wine in her hand, she sat at the kitchen bar and waited for her daughter to tell her what the heck was going on.

"You made an early dinner for us."

"I did."

"So, where are the children?"

"At home with a babysitter."

"A babysitter?" Genevieve drew back in surprise. "Who?"

"Her name is Olivia Brinkley. I found her through a friend of Auntie's. She's sixteen, and this is the second time I've used her. The kids love her."

"That's good." Genevieve sipped her wine.

Willow set a plate of charcuterie on the bar in front of Genevieve. "So, tell me about the art class. Did you enjoy it?"

"I did. But I'd rather you tell me why you're here, Willow." Genevieve chose a piece of cheese. "I know you wanted to talk, but this is a lot of effort. It feels bigger."

Her daughter grimaced, then topped off her own glass of wine. "I had hoped to ease into this conversation with some small talk, but you always did say it's best to pull the bandage off fast. That said, I'd rather start with the easiest and work my way up. Okay?"

Genevieve made a sweeping gesture. "This is your show."

"All right. Well, then. Here goes. Remember how I talked about guiding words on New Year's Eve? How I told you that mine for the year is *listen*? Well, I listened to you. I went and talked to Noah like you suggested." Then, because she couldn't help herself, she added, "I asked him if you two had a Mrs. Robinson thing going on."

Genevieve choked on her cheese. She took a sip of wine to wash it down before saying, "You did not!"

Willow offered her mother a napkin. "I did. You threw me a loop with the whole passion thing."

"Willow Anne," Genevieve scolded.

"Don't fret. I never really thought that, and Noah set me straight. I need you to know that I heard you, Mom. I did some hard thinking. I've made some decisions, but I want to run them by you before they're set in stone. You have veto power. No hard feelings if you choose to exercise it." Willow met her mother's gaze and stressed, "I totally mean that. Okay?"

Warily, Genevieve said, "Okay."

"All right. First, I'd like to make our stay in Lake in the Clouds permanent, but I intend to be mindful of your need—of all of our needs—for balance. To that end, after-school and summertime childcare will be handled by Little Ducklings Daycare while I try to get an event-planning business off the ground. Emma starts kindergarten in August, and I don't intend to home-school either her or Drew for the fall semester. In the meantime, you're welcome to take them out of daycare for nana playdates whenever your heart desires."

Genevieve folded her hands prayerfully in front of her face. "Oh, honey."

Willow rushed on, anxious to get everything on the table before her mother offered a comment. "Auntie said we could continue to stay at the cabin at Raindrop, but I'm going to start looking for a house. Actually, I have started, but nothing appropriate is on the market right now. I wouldn't have made an offer before having this conversation, but I wanted—"

"Oh, honey!" Genevieve repeated, rising from the bar stool and rushing toward her daughter. She threw her arms around Willow and hugged her hard. "I'm thrilled. Truly, I couldn't be happier. This is the most wonderful news."

"I'm glad you think so. We need you, Mom."

Genevieve's heart caught. Tears stung her eyes. "Oh, honey. You don't know how badly I've missed being needed by you."

"Well, if that's the case, some of the other stuff I have to share will knock your socks off."

"That sounds ominous."

Willow gave Genevieve a crooked smile, then reached for her own wine. "It's nothing that won't keep until after dinner. Please, let's lighten the mood so that we don't spoil the chicken?" When Genevieve nodded her agreement, Willow continued. "I hope you're ready to jump right into campaign mode. Auntie has a meeting scheduled for ten o'clock tomorrow morning."

"So I understand. I had about one thousand and one e-mails waiting for me when I turned on my phone this morning."

"How did you like being unplugged for so long?"

"I'll be honest. I loved it." Genevieve glanced ruefully toward her phone as she added, "It made me feel young again."

"Oh, Mom. You are so not old. Tell me, how much fun was it to drive a Maserati?"

They talked about the car and the classes while Willow finished preparing their meal. Over dinner, the conversation turned to the events in Lake in the Clouds. Genevieve asked a few leading questions about Noah Tannehill. Still, Willow apparently hadn't seen him, but for that one visit Genevieve had sent her on. Dang it. They talked about Helen's campaign, Emma's new shoes, and Drew's latest scrape. Genevieve frowned and thought back over the past weeks. "Why, is that his first set of stitches since Christmas?"

"It is," Willow confirmed.

"Wow. I hadn't realized that."

"Even more, this one was totally not his fault. Emma tried changing him into a frog with her fairy wand, and he accidentally backed over a log and clipped his arm on a rock."

Genevieve clapped her hands and grinned. "Well, there you go. Smart boy to back away from a girl with a fairy wand. This chicken is fabulous as always, Willow. It's truly one of my favorite meals ever."

Willow accepted the compliment with a nod, then added, "Save room for dessert."

Genevieve's eyes gleamed. "We have dessert?"

"From Cloud Puffs," Willow said, naming the local bakery. "Death by Chocolate."

"Well." Genevieve set down her fork and sat back in her chair. For Willow to bring out the chocolate—serious chocolate at that—whatever news she had to share wasn't good. "Okay. I'm not waiting any longer. Tell me what's happened to upgrade this conversation from overdue to a calorie bombing? What do I need to know about Andy?"

Tears filled her daughter's big blue eyes and overflowed to spill silently down her cheeks.

Genevieve grabbed a tissue from the box at the end of the bar and handed it to Willow, who said, "Mom, it's bigger than just Andy. I hardly know where to start. "

❧

Gage and Noah set the final fence post at three o'clock on Friday afternoon. By five, as the Triple T Ranch work utility vehicle Gage drove approached Noah's place, the older man observed, "I'm so hungry that my belt buckle is rubbing against my backbone."

"I offered you half of one of my sandwiches at lunch," Noah replied.

"If you didn't need two, you wouldn't have brought two. I needed you to work harder than I needed to fill my old man's belly. I wanted to finish up today. That said, I wouldn't object if you could find an apple for me in your house when we get there. Or maybe a hunk of bread. A side of beef."

Noah grinned. "How about beef stew and biscuits? I put it all in the Crock-Pot this morning before you picked me up."

"Son, you are a king among men."

Noah grinned, something he'd been doing a lot this past week. Working alongside Gage and talking about everything and nothing to pass the time had been a catharsis neither man had expected, but it was clear both were better for it.

Now that they were back at his place, and since Gage had expressed his hunger so eloquently, Noah saw to getting food served right away.

"You're a good cook," Gage observed. "This is mighty fine beef stew."

"Learning to cook is part of the job when you're working in a firehouse. Firefighters like tasty, simple food and lots of it. Beef stew was always a basic."

"Well, me and my belly thank you." Gage patted his stomach with both hands. "I was getting...What's that term the kids use when being hungry makes them cranky?"

"Hangry. *Hungry* and *angry* combined."

"That's it. Hangry no more," the older man declared with satisfaction. "Right now, I'm happy as a dog with two tails. Work's done. Belly's full."

Noah grinned. "Can I get you anything else?"

"Actually, you can. Got any whiskey around here, Tannehill?"

"I keep bourbon." Noah gestured toward a cabinet.

Gage nodded with satisfaction. "Pour me a glass, and then go show me these puppies you keep trying to push off on me."

"I can do that."

Noah poured two glasses and led the rancher out to the workshop.

"I've enjoyed working with you, Noah," Gage said

as they stepped inside and Noah flipped on the lights. "I'll admit it. I hate to see this time end. We will have to...whoa..." He gazed around the workshop. "You do some serious work here. This is a well-equipped shop."

"It's good for my mental health to get out and work with my hands. This workshop saved me. It's only been lately that my leg has healed to the point to allow me to work like I have with you the past week."

Gage nodded toward the shelving along one wall. "These are the fire-training dollhouses you told me about?"

"Yes," Noah confirmed.

"Interesting." He flicked a slide open and shut. "I'd like to see a demonstration sometime."

"I can arrange that."

Gage tested another couple of slides, then wandered over to the workbench where Noah's latest project was coming along slowly. Very slowly. His day work stringing barbed wire had cut his woodworking time down to one or two hours in the evenings, tops.

"Well, look at this." Gage leaned over and studied the Victorian dollhouse. Admiration filled his tone. "That is excellent detail work, Noah."

"I believe if you're going to do something, you might as well do it right. It's the way my parents raised us."

Gage gave him a sharp look, and Noah inwardly cursed. He'd just dropped a great big clue with the *us* there, hadn't he? He waited for Gage to follow up with the logical question, but perhaps the mulish set of Noah's jaw warned him off. Gage simply shrugged and said, "Some little lady is gonna be a lucky one. Does she know what she's getting?"

"No. It's a surprise." Noah didn't want to say anything more. He strode to stand beside the puppy pen. "I thought you wanted to look at the pups?"

"I'm getting to it." Gage opened then shut one of the miniature window shutters. "You on a deadline to finish this dollhouse, like for a birthday or something?"

"No."

"Good. For a minute there, I was afraid all that fishing I made you do might have delayed you and disappointed some little darling."

Noah heard a slight change in his friend's tone. A tightening. Not understanding it, he watched Gage closely as he responded. "You didn't make me do any fishing, old man. Get that out of your head. You didn't make me do anything except get off my ass, and that was good for me."

"Well, I'm glad."

Noah noted that Gage had begun massaging his hands. That wasn't an ordinary habit of his friend's. A touch of arthritis? Maybe some tendonitis? He'd worked hard with his hands the past week.

While Noah considered this, Gage abruptly straightened from his study of the dollhouse and crossed the workshop to stand beside Noah. He asked, "So, is Marigold a good mother?"

"She's been very attentive. But she's been spending more time away from the pups as she begins to wean them."

"That's nature's way."

Was the rancher looking pale? Hard to tell in this light. Noah turned toward the doorway leading to the building's apartment. "I'm going to get some water. You want some, Gage?"

"I still have my whiskey."

Noah decided to make him drink a bottle of water. It was easy to get dehydrated at this altitude. Alcohol only made that worse. With long, quick strides, he hurried through the shop into the apartment, where he grabbed two bottles of water and, just for safety's sake, stuck a packet of aspirin in his pocket before returning to Gage.

The man had picked up a puppy while Noah had been in the apartment and was scratching him behind the ear. "You feeling okay, Gage?" he asked.

"Yeah. I'm fine." He accepted the water Noah offered and drained half of it in one sip. "I probably didn't drink enough water today. I know better." He returned the puppy to the pen and changed the subject. "So, there's something I've been wanting to ask you. What would you think about being introduced to my niece? She's a nice woman. College educated, just moved back home after living in Florida for a few years. Pretty, too. Unfortunately, she's not had a lot of luck in the romance department."

That managed to distract Noah from his concern. "Thanks, but I'm not in the market."

"That's what I figured. I saw the way you looked at Willow Eldridge at the wedding. And by the looks of things, those kids of hers have you wrapped around their little fingers, too."

"Hold on there." Noah held up his hand, palm out. "That was just a favor for a friend."

"Uh-huh." Gage gave him a knowing grin, looking more like himself.

Noah relaxed. "No, seriously."

Gage gave a disbelieving snort, then bent to pluck a

ball from the toy basket Noah kept nearby. He threw it into the middle of the cavorting dogs.

The two men watched as a black-snouted male battled a solid gold female for a red rubber sphere. Noah felt compelled to open up a bit. "Look, my life is too big of a mess to involve other people in it."

Gage gave him a sidelong look. "Is it really? Looks to me like you have a nice thing going here. A little lonely, perhaps."

"I have some investments, but I don't have a job. I live here cheaply alone, but I can't hole up here indefinitely. At some point, I'll have to do something to make a living."

"Not a lot of profit in dollhouses?"

"Not hardly," Noah scoffed. "Especially when you don't charge for them."

"Yeah, it's hard to make any money when you give stuff away. How long has it been since your injury?"

Noah didn't like talking about the events of that god-awful day, but after working with Gage on the fencing, he respected the man too much to be rude to him. "A little over a year now."

"How many surgeries did you have on your leg?"

Noah sighed. "Three major. Six total."

"So all that physical trauma plus the mental fallout..." He shrugged. "Seems to me you haven't needed to expend much thought figuring it out until now. I wouldn't sweat it too much if I were you. If you want to see the woman, see the woman. Willow's a good one."

Considering that he'd been hiding from her ever since that kiss, Noah didn't think that was a likely outcome. It was time to change the subject, so he rolled out his usual question. "You're going to take one of these pups, aren't you?"

"Actually, I am."

Whoa. He hadn't expected that. "You are?"

"Yeah. We always had Labs at the Triple T. Great bird dogs. Lost our last one not long before we found out that Emily was sick, and neither of us wanted a new dog at that point. I haven't given it any thought until you started hounding me about it the last few days."

"You don't want to go back to Labs? You can't count on these dogs growing up to be hunters."

"No, I like the idea of a mutt. So, are you going to let me have the pick of the litter?"

That question stopped Noah. "Actually, can I get back to you on that? I sort of promised first pick to...someone else...but I'm not sure if they're still interested."

"'Someone else.' Let me guess. Willow Eldridge?"

"Her kids."

"Is the—" Gage broke off abruptly as a strange look came across his face. He reached into his pocket and pulled out his blue bandanna. "You must have put a lot of pepper in that stew of yours. I'm sweating like a big dog."

It had been a long time, but Noah instinctively switched to professional mode. "C'mere." He took Gage's arm and led him back to the bench. "You having chest pain?"

"No. Not really." After Noah's challenging look, he added, "Maybe a little discomfort."

"How long has it been hurting?"

"Look, Tannehill, there's no need—"

"Answer the questions, or I'm calling 911 right now."

Gage huffed a sigh. "It started while we were working today."

"It's getting worse?"

"A little, yeah." His voice was tight.

"Do you have any history of heart problems?"

Gage shook his head. "No."

Noah snapped out the rest of his questions at a rapid pace. "High blood pressure? High cholesterol?"

"No."

"What meds do you take?"

"I don't take any meds. I don't trust doctors."

"Why am I not surprised?" Noah muttered. "So, tell me about your pain. What does it feel like?"

"Just some pressure on my chest."

"Do you feel it anywhere else?"

"Maybe...kinda...here." He lifted his hand and rubbed his jaw.

Noah reached for his phone. "One last question. Scale of one to ten. How bad is the pain?" He was already punching in 911 when Gage responded.

"Ah, hell. I don't know. Maybe a seven?"

Waiting for the operator to answer, Noah handed over the aspirin. "Take these now."

In quick, succinct language, Noah requested an ambulance be sent to his address for a suspected cardiac event. Assured that help was on the way, he turned all his attention to his friend.

"I'm having a heart attack, aren't I?" Gage asked, his tone grim.

"Maybe. Can't know for sure without an EKG."

"Unless I keel over dead. Then it'd be a pretty good guess."

"Personally, I'd rather wait for the EKG." Understanding that what Gage needed now was distraction, Noah asked, "So, which of the pups strikes your fancy?"

Gage scowled at him. "You trying to distract me from the fact I'm at death's door?"

"Yes," Noah replied matter-of-factly. "This doesn't have to be a heart attack, Gage. It could be angina. It could be something else. Maybe it is just too much pepper in the stew."

"Damned good stew, though," Gage said, attempting a smile.

Noah kept it light. "Glad you think so."

"Hope it doesn't kill me," Gage quipped.

Noah chided him with a look, then tried to change the subject back to the dogs. He didn't want Gage focused on death. "So, what about the puppy? You looking for a boy dog or a girl?"

Gage wasn't buying the distraction. "What's with the hard sell on the mutts when I'm sitting here with an elephant on my chest?"

"I'm attempting to help you remain calm. It's in the handbook." Noah made a show of pursing his lips in thought, then added, "I think. It's been a while since I checked."

Gage snorted. "Just my luck to get a firefighter instead of a doctor."

"I thought you didn't trust doctors."

One corner of Gage's mouth lifted in a half smile, acknowledging the hit. "What the hell is calming about puppies? They're the biggest bundle of nerves in the world."

"True, but look at them. They're cute bundles of nerves. It makes me happy to watch them play. The thing is, they can't be left to puppy-on all the time at this point. It's time to start training them. Gotta get those good habits going before the bad ones set in. I know you know that. I've seen you with horses. I'll bet your dogs were always well trained."

Sitting hunched over with his hands on his knees, Gage stared toward the pups but gazed into the past. "They were. Emily wouldn't have it otherwise. Dogs were a helluva lot easier to train than our kids. That's for damned sure." Gage paused a moment. Shut his eyes. "My kids. I think Zach's the only one in town this week. Will you call him for me?"

"I will. Want me to call him now?"

Gage used his bandanna to wipe his brow again. "No. Wait. Maybe I should. If I croak..."

"I think you should be thinking positive about now, Gage. I'm not a doctor, but I will tell you that the fatal heart attacks I responded to went like..." Noah snapped his fingers.

Gage nodded solemnly. "Widow-makers."

Noah was relieved to hear the wail of an approaching siren. "Slang term and only anecdotal evidence, but I'm not too worried that I'll have to find a spot for one of these pups that isn't the Triple T Ranch."

Gage gave him a weak smile, then reached into his pocket and handed over his phone. "Maybe call him once I'm in the meat wagon?"

"Will do. They won't allow me to ride with you, but I'll follow along behind, so I'm there to bust heads if I think they're taking too long."

"Appreciate ya."

Noah gave his shoulder a squeeze. "I'm going to wave the driver down so he'll know where to come. Keep an eye on those pups for me, would you?"

"I'll do that. And Tannehill? If Willow's kids don't want the girl dog with the white fiddle on her face, she's the one I'll take. She's a feisty little thing."

"Noted. I'll check with Willow and keep you posted."

The EMTs didn't take long to get Gage loaded into the ambulance and headed to the hospital. Noah scrolled through the contacts list on Gage's phone, looking for Zach's number. When the call went to voice mail, he hesitated.

Noah knew that the Throckmorton father and son had a rocky roller coaster of a relationship. Gage had spoken about it more than once while they'd worked on the fence. Apparently, Zach and his dad had all but come to blows this past weekend over a misunderstanding about something to do with a bid Zach's construction company had made for a local project in which Gage had an interest. It stood to reason that Zach might not want to talk to his dad today, but leaving a "there's been a medical emergency" voice mail wasn't cool.

Noah disconnected the call and dialed the number from his own phone. Zach answered on the second ring. "Independence Construction. Zach Throckmorton speaking."

"Zach, this is Noah Tannehill. I'm calling about your dad." By the time he finished his conversation with Zach, he had his workshop locked, and his keys in his hand.

He arrived at the hospital no more than ten minutes behind the ambulance that had brought Gage in and sat down to wait.

Chapter Ten

WILLOW HAD PROMISED HERSELF she wouldn't cry. She'd done all right in that regard during her mother's time in New Mexico, but now that the moment of truth was here, she could no longer hold back the tears. She was a wreck.

Which was why she had to come clean with her mother tonight. About Andy. About everything. Because she needed her mother like she'd never needed her before. *Heaven help me.*

Since Andy was at the center of everything, Willow had brought a trifle for dessert. It was a subtle bit of personal symbolism. He was a trifle, a trivial thing at this point. He was of no consequence.

Yeah, right. Willow swiped at the tears rolling down her cheeks. Dead and buried and still throwing hand grenades into her life.

"Honey, talk to me." Genevieve grabbed another tissue and handed it to Willow.

"I'm trying. It's hard." Willow needed to ease into this tale, so she removed the dessert from her mother's refrigerator and set the trifle in the center of the table. As she spooned crisis-worthy-sized portions onto dessert plates for her mother and herself, she tried to explain. "I need to say this first, or it will get lost, and it's too important to get lost. I need to start with an apology, Mom. I'm sorry I got into such a snit over your initial dislike of Andy and then used it as a wedge to come between us. I hope you'll forgive me."

Genevieve shut her eyes for a moment, and when she opened them again, they glowed with approval, gratitude, and happiness. *I should have said this years ago.* Willow handed a dessert plate to her mother.

"Oh, honey. I made my share of mistakes, too. Of course I forgive you, and I hope you forgive me, too. Honestly, I think we went through some normal family growing pains. It's especially challenging when the first child in a family gets married, because you've never done it before. It's hard not to make mistakes the first time around. I wish I'd done many things differently when you and Andy got together."

Willow took a fortifying bite of chocolate. If not for the AJ part of this, she could have stopped right here. Her mother always had been one to accept an honest apology and generously extend her forgiving heart. But Willow's guiding word this year was *listen*, and she was listening to her own heart tonight.

She couldn't skip straight to the *Mom, I need you* stuff. Her mother deserved to hear the words.

Besides, Willow hadn't had enough chocolate to say the most brutal stuff yet. "The apology is only part of it, Mom. Before you left on your New Mexico trip, I told you that I wanted to clear the air, so I need to tell you everything."

"Okay." Genevieve nodded encouragingly.

"It's a bit of a list," Willow warned.

Genevieve gestured toward their dessert plates. "Which is why you brought Death by Chocolate. I understand. Get on with it, child."

"Yep. Okay, here goes. Number one on the hit parade—I was divorcing Andy. The day he died, I told him I wanted him to leave."

Her mother dropped her dessert spoon. "You what?"

"I told Andy I wanted a divorce."

"Oh, Willow." Genevieve covered her mouth with her hands. "Why?"

"Where do I start? Remember that Leonardo Di-Caprio movie where he plays a con man who forges checks and pretends to be a pilot?"

"I do. He was so handsome in a pilot's uniform."

"Well, Andy Eldridge could have been a script consultant."

Genevieve looked bewildered. "Andy. Your Andy?"

"He was a terrible husband, Mom."

"What happened? What did he do?" Then Genevieve's eyes flashed with sudden, fierce anger. "Did he hurt you? The kids?"

Willow should have realized her mother's thoughts would go to abuse first. Last May, the family discovered that her sister, Brooke, had been in a physically abusive marriage. "He never hit me. Never hit the kids. No, Andy took his meanness in an entirely different direction."

"*Mean*," Genevieve murmured. "That's the last word I would have used to describe Andy Eldridge."

"If I start at the beginning, this might make better sense, though I'm not exactly sure where the beginning was. Maybe by our third date. That's when I decided that Andy was the perfect guy for me."

"I remember."

Willow shrugged. "He was charming and handsome and funny and smart. He always knew exactly what to say to make me feel special. I fell head over heels in love with him."

Genevieve closed her eyes, wincing as if pained. She cleared her throat. "That was such a hard time for us. I didn't handle it well at all. You fell for him so fast and so hard. It scared me. You threw away your dreams and found new ones so fast."

"I know. You were right to be scared." Willow sighed heavily and admitted, "Your instincts were right all along, Mom."

"Explain."

Willow stabbed at her dessert with her spoon. "Oh, in the beginning, everything was perfect. He was perfect because perfect was all that he let me see. In hindsight, he was working on me even back then. Changing me. And yes, changing my dreams. He was subtle about it, planting little thoughts and ideas that acted like little wedges between me and you and me and my siblings. I didn't see, did you?"

"You and I created our own great big wedge, Willow," Genevieve pointed out. "I told you I didn't like Andy."

"Yes, but that was right at the beginning and then you changed your mind and tried to make things better. The thing is, Mom, he never said anything bad about you."

Genevieve lifted her gaze from her dessert to meet Willow's. Willow saw that her words had shocked her mother. "Seriously?" Genevieve asked.

Willow nodded. "He never said anything, but he had this way of asking questions that slithered around in my mind, creating doubt. For example, he'd say, 'Is it healthy for you to be so close to your mother?' When I look back on our wedding, oh, Mom, I feel so terrible. So ashamed."

Now a wary note entered her mother's eyes. "Why?"

"I cut you out. Here you were, gifting Andy and me with the wedding of my dreams, and there toward the end, I turned into Bridezilla. I'm so sorry. I was selfish. Unfortunately, I was listening to Andy, who was whispering in my ear, 'It's your special day. You are the only one who matters.'"

Genevieve stood and began picking up the dishes, not meeting Willow's eyes. Her voice was a little tight as she asked, "What about the mother-daughter spa weekend?"

"Mom, I'll deal with the dishes." Willow frowned. "What mother-daughter spa weekend?"

Her mother wrinkled her nose and carried the dishes to the sink. "No, I need something to do with my hands. Andy told me he was treating us to a mother-daughter spa getaway at the Four Seasons. But he called and canceled at the last minute because you were so angry at me over the brand of vodka I ordered for the signature cocktails."

Willow's voice went deadly quiet. "That sonofabitch. Mom, I didn't care about the vodka. He cared about the vodka. And there was never any mother-daughter spa day scheduled that I know about."

"I see." Her mother began loading the dishwasher, her motions getting a little jerkier, the actions a little louder with every dish she placed. Willow had loaded the dishwasher as she cooked, so her mother didn't have much cleanup to do.

"Okay then," Willow continued. "Moving on. Andy took the job in Nashville without discussing it with me first."

Standing at the sink, her hands sunk in soapy water, Genevieve muttered, "This just gets better and better."

Willow stared down at her chocolate-filled spoon, and her stomach took a sick little roll. She set down the utensil, rose, and carried her dessert plate to her mother. "I know. Looking back on it, I can't believe I went along. He convinced me I was wrong for not being thrilled about this big opportunity he had been offered. I convinced myself that I wanted to live in Nashville, that moving away from our extended families would make us stronger as a couple."

"Why?"

"He said we needed to cut the apron strings, to depend on each other instead of our families."

Genevieve put the last plate into the dishwasher and slammed the door.

"You're thinking awfully loud, Mom," Willow observed, her tone wry. "*Seriously, Willow, you fell for that?* and *I thought you were smarter than that.*"

An inadvertent smile flashed across her mother's face. "You can hear that, hmm?"

"Loud and clear. I can't argue with it. What I came to understand is that what Andy wanted was to cut me from my herd."

Genevieve muttered a curse, reached out, and flipped

on the garbage disposal. As the grinding noise filled the kitchen, Willow picked up the leftover trifle from the table, covered it with plastic wrap, and returned it to the refrigerator, all the while trying to collect her thoughts. She needed to keep to her script and say what she needed to say, make the points she wanted to make while she had her mother's attention.

Because she never, ever wanted to revisit this subject again.

Then, of course, she still had to drop the AJ bomb. And share the new bit of bad news she'd received from Maggie this morning about Tom.

The garbage disposal went silent. Willow said, "It wasn't all bad, Mom. Honestly, I was happy in Nashville for a long time. And you know Drew and Emma mean the world to me. Andy was an excellent con man, Mom. He had me totally fooled. I did love him for a long time. I was enthralled. Maybe I turned a blind eye to a thing or two, but what wife doesn't? I needed him to be as perfect as he appeared to be. I think—and please don't take this the wrong way—but I think that not having a father during my teenage years had a bigger effect on me than I ever realized."

Tears flooded her mother's eyes, and Willow wanted to call back the words. Except, they were the truth.

Genevieve wiped her hands on a dish towel and said, "Chocolate's not enough. I need booze."

She marched from the kitchen and headed for her great room bar, Willow assumed as she followed behind. Sure enough, her mother removed a crystal highball glass from the cabinet. "Want one?"

"I'm good, thanks."

Genevieve poured a generous shot of bourbon, tossed

it back, then poured another. *Oh, Mom. Better pace yourself. I'm just getting started.*

Genevieve's voice sounded weary as she said, "I recognized the void being without a dad left in your sister's world, even before the trouble last year, but I thought you were okay." She swirled the whiskey in her glass. "I thought you were happy with Andy."

"I was. Honestly, Mom. For the most part, I was. It wasn't until Drew was born that I began to see what he was doing."

Willow wrapped her arms around herself and paced her mother's great room. "At first, I couldn't put my finger on what was wrong, and even when I did, I thought I must be mistaken. But deep down, I think he was jealous of Drew."

"Oh." Genevieve's brow creased as she considered the idea. "That's not unheard of in some marriages. It's crummy. I never saw any sign of it. He always seemed like a very loving dad. I thought he was an adrenaline junkie and should have curtailed some of his hobbies once the children came along, but you didn't seem to mind."

"I did. I just couldn't say it. Andy would blow. He was Andy Eldridge, a loving husband, son, and father to the outside world. I'm not sure anyone else saw how controlling, critical, and demanding he was. At home, it was his way or the highway."

"That bastard," Genevieve muttered. Her mouth set into a grim line, she carried her drink into the media room, where she had hung pictures of her family on one wall. Willow followed and studied her mother studying the photograph of Andy taken during a climbing expedition in Ecuador. "That sorry SOB."

Willow drew in a deep breath. Here was her moment of truth. *But heaven help me, this is so danged hard.* "There's more, Mom. I found out he had a lover."

She turned away from the photographs and met Willow's gaze, a combination of sympathy and fury gleaming in her eyes. "Oh, Willow."

"Yeah." Willow took comfort from her mom's reaction, and as a result, she opened up a little more than she had intended. "I was clueless. He promised he'd always remain faithful to me and our marriage, and I believed him because he was so devasted by the affair Tom had when Andy was a teenager."

"Oh." Genevieve slowly nodded. "I'd forgotten about that."

"Andy so often railed on about the damage it did to their family that I never worried about it. Even during those last months when I had nagging little suspicions, I dismissed them. Despite our problems, I never dreamed he'd cheat on me."

"Well, I don't see you ever putting up with that."

"No. But Mom, that's not the worst of it."

Warily, her mother said, "Okay?"

"The worst of it is . . ." Willow's voice trailed off. She didn't want to do this. She knew her mom. Genevieve Prentice would blow a gasket.

"Honey, just tell me," Genevieve said, exasperation in her tone. "It can't be *that* bad."

Oh yes, it can. "Brace yourself, Mom. Andy got his girlfriend pregnant. When the Eldridges came here for Jake's wedding, they told me the woman had a son. She named him Andrew John. They call him AJ."

"Oh my God!"

"It gets even better." Pressure built in Willow's chest,

and for a moment, she thought the tears would erupt again. Instead, the anxiety turned to ice. She was ice. She had to be frozen to get through this.

"AJ's mother has died, leaving him orphaned. Maggie and Tom are raising him."

Genevieve's mouth gaped. "Why, they're older than I am. How can they possibly keep up with a toddler? They have to have help."

"Yes. They have a nanny."

"Still, that can't be easy."

"No, it can't. I imagine that's partly why Maggie asked me to move to Texas with the kids. To incentivize the process, they bought us a house."

"They what?" Genevieve shouted.

Willow relayed the details of the proposition Maggie had presented. Her mother's back got stiffer with every sentence, her eyes angrier. Willow tried to put some calm into her voice as she finished. "Don't worry, Mom. I told her no. Like I said earlier. We want to stay here in Lake in the Clouds. Maggie didn't like it. She argued that Drew and Emma need to know their brother."

Genevieve gasped audibly. "Their brother. Oh my God. I hadn't made that connection. What happened to the mother?"

"She had an aneurysm. She was driving. It happened very fast."

"Oh my God." Genevieve lifted her hand to her mouth. "Was the boy with her? Was it just like with Andy? That poor child!"

"No. She'd dropped her son off at daycare before it happened."

"Thank God." Genevieve took a long sip of her drink. "I cannot believe Maggie. She bought you a house?

Why, the nerve of her. The next time I talk to her, I'll give her a piece of my mind."

Now for the fun part. Willow found she could use a little of her mother's liquid courage. "Mind if I have a glass of your bourbon, Mom?"

Genevieve waved her to go ahead. In the time it took Willow to fix her drink, her mother didn't appear to have moved so much as an eyelash. Take that back. Half of her drink was gone. She said, "Willow, why do I feel you still have a big old heavy shoe to drop?"

Willow swirled her bourbon. "You always did have excellent instincts."

"Let's hear it."

Willow took a long sip of her drink. It was good whiskey, but Willow wasn't accustomed to drinking liquor straight. It burned her throat. "Maggie called me this morning. Tom had a stroke."

"Oh no. How bad is it?"

"It's bad."

"Oh, that's terrible. Poor Tom. I'll have to—" She broke off abruptly and shot Willow a look sharp enough to cut glass. "Oh, no. Oh, no no no no no. Willow, tell me she did not ask you to take care of that child."

Willow answered by taking another sip of her drink. Another long sip. She thought she could probably get used to it.

"Willow!"

The tears were threatening again. "What was I supposed to say, Mom? Maggie has a crisis on her hands. Her husband may well die. She needs help so she turned to family."

"That's a tenuous family connection at best. What about the mother's family? Surely she had someone."

"Maggie said there is no one. She's in a bind, Mom. She has no one else to turn to for help."

"So, call Child Protective Services," Genevieve fired back. "That's their job."

"C'mon, Mom. You've heard Tess's stories about her time in the foster care system."

"Oh, all right. Not CPS. But surely there's someone—"

"This little boy is Drew and Emma's brother."

Genevieve sighed heavily. "Don't you think your plate is full enough already, Willow? You're a single mother with two children. You're homeschooling your son. You're living at a tourist lodge. Not ten minutes ago, you told me you wanted to try to get a new business off the ground. How are you supposed to do that with a toddler in tow?"

These were all arguments Willow had made with herself. She didn't like arguing against all the points she herself recognized as valid. She was in between a rock and a hard place here.

"I'm not taking him to raise. I'm taking him in only until Maggie can work something else out."

"Fine." Genevieve threw out her hands, causing the liquid to slosh out of the glass. "You'll keep him for a little while, and in the meantime, your children will bond with this boy. So they'll suffer another loss when you send him back to Maggie. What will that do to them?"

"Dammit, Mom! What am I supposed to say? You are exactly right. I don't want to bring my dead husband's love child into my home! I don't want to look at AJ and be reminded of all the times my husband lied to me because he wasn't working late like he said he was. I don't want to feel like pond scum because I can't see an innocent child but instead see the sins of his parents. All of that is true. But he's an orphan. He *is* innocent. He *is* Drew and Emma's brother. I need to be able to look them in the eyes when they grow up."

"I understand all of that. I do. I'm saying there has to be a different solution, something that's good for AJ and you and your family. Because I know you, Willow. I know you better than anyone else on this earth. Involving yourself with this little boy will break your heart. You told me earlier in this conversation that I had good instincts. You said *listen* is your guiding word for the year. Well, listen to me, daughter, because my instincts tell me that taking this child into your heart and home will explode in your face. I won't let you do this. I'll...I'll...oh hell."

Genevieve drew a deep breath, then exhaled in a rush. "I'll go to Texas and take care of the child until Maggie can make permanent arrangements."

A lump the size of a golf ball formed in Willow's throat. Her heart melted. "Oh, Mom. You have the most generous heart of anyone, anywhere. You are always, always, always trying to fix things for your children. Thank you for the thought, but you can't fix this. This isn't your problem. You have your passion to seek out and your balance to achieve. AJ is my problem, not yours."

"Well, I suppose that's true," Genevieve said, her tone and her body language grim. "It would be some serious backsliding on my part, wouldn't it?"

Then Willow's mother did something entirely out of character. She uttered a primal scream and threw her glass at Andy's picture, knocking it off the wall. Both the frame and the crystal crashed on the tile floor and shattered.

"Whoa, Mom. That was your Baccarat."

Eyes flashing, Genevieve looked at Willow and declared, "I am so sorry that Andy Eldridge is already dead, so I can't murder him myself."

"I know, Mom," Willow said in a soothing tone.

"I'm so beyond furious with him!"

"I know, Mom," she repeated. "Believe me, I did my share of throwing things."

"How will you manage? A toddler, Willow? And two more? You'll be run ragged."

A little bubble of hysteria rose within Willow. "I haven't told you about the puppy."

"Puppy! Oh, Willow. You have to be kidding me."

"I don't think I am." She told her mother about Noah Tannehill's puppies, finishing that part of her tale by saying, "It's your fault. You threw me under the puppy bus by sending me over there. You and your passion."

"I didn't know about the puppies. I was hoping the topic might lead to a more interesting discussion between you and Noah."

It had, but Willow saw no benefit to going into that particular subject with her mother right at the moment. "Think about it, Mom. As terrible as this sounds, if Drew and Emma get a little brother and a new puppy simultaneously, what will they like best?"

Genevieve shook her head and clicked her tongue. "Oh, that is terrible."

"I called Drew's counselor this afternoon and explained the situation. She advised me on how to explain AJ to my kids, and she agreed that a puppy was a great idea. Actually, she thought two puppies might be the ticket."

Genevieve covered her mouth with her hand, but Willow heard the little horrified snort of laughter. "Oh, heavens. Willow. Two puppies and a toddler? None of them potty-trained, I imagine. Just how old is this child?"

"Not quite two."

Genevieve shook her head as she stared at the mess of broken glass lying on the floor. "And when is all of this happening?"

"His nanny is bringing him tomorrow." Sighing, Willow added, "I have to talk to Noah about the puppies."

"Lovely." Genevieve glanced up and met Willow's gaze. "Emotional issues aside, it will be pure hell for you."

"All I can do is take it one day at a time. Look, let's not forget that AJ is Maggie's grandchild, and Maggie wants him. She's not going to leave him in Colorado indefinitely, and I'm not moving back to Texas. I've made that decision, and you gave it your official seal of approval."

"Yes, I did, didn't I? Thank God for that piece of timing. You know I'm sincere."

"Yes, Mom. I'm certain you want us in Colorado. I'm also certain that I don't want Emma to be forced to make excuses for me in thirty years if AJ grows up to be a great person like Tess, and he asks his half sister why I dumped him into the system when his grandfather had a stroke."

"Y'all could blame it on me," Genevieve said with a shrug. "I'll be dead in thirty years."

"No, you won't, Mom. You'll only be ninety. By then, ninety will be the new seventy."

"Heaven help me. Heaven help you and your siblings."

Genevieve's stare returned once again to the broken glass and damaged frame on the floor, and the amusement faded from her expression. "Oh, Willow. This isn't fair. This so isn't fair to you. Where are my scissors? It's not enough to knock that asshole's picture off the wall. I want to cut it into tiny little pieces."

"Mom. Please. I can't deal with it when you use the a-word. And remember what you always taught us. Fair is what happens in October in Dallas. Does Colorado have a state fair? Where and when? I'll need to learn that if I'm going to raise my children here so I can adapt your wisdom."

"I honestly don't know." Her mother sighed heavily. Looking as if she'd aged ten years in the past ten minutes, she ambled toward the wall and the broken glass on the floor. As she bent to pick up the mess, Willow said, "Wait, Mom. Let me get a broom."

"I have a pair of scissors in the junk drawer in the kitchen. Bring those, too, please."

Willow couldn't believe she was smiling as she left the media room. She hurried to the laundry room, where she retrieved a broom and dustpan. Then, spying three pairs of scissors in her mother's neatly organized junk drawer, she grabbed two of them.

Returning to the media room, Willow stopped short. "Oh my God, Mom!"

Genevieve Prentice held her hands clasped against her breast. Her white cotton blouse was stained red with blood. She offered Willow a shaky smile and said, "Well, this day keeps getting better. Honey, will you drive me to the hospital, please? I'm going to need stitches."

Chapter Eleven

THE EMERGENCY ROOM DOORS swished open, and Zach Throckmorton strode inside, worry creasing his brow. Noah set down his coffee and rose from his seat, walking forward and greeting Gage's son with a smile. "It's not a heart attack."

"Thank God." Gage's son's shoulders sagged with relief. "So, what's wrong with him?"

"Angina. The doctor will explain everything. They know you were on your way. Press that buzzer"—Noah gestured toward a button mounted beside the door that led back to the exam rooms—"and tell them who you are. He's in room five."

"Great. Thanks, man. For everything. If you hadn't been there..."

"No problem. I'm glad I was around."

"At least he listens to you. More than he does to me or my brother or my sister."

As Zach disappeared from the waiting room, Noah

returned the January edition of *Car and Driver* magazine to the rack. He tossed his Styrofoam coffee cup
and candy bar wrapper into a trash can and glanced at
his watch. Twenty minutes had passed since he'd seen
Willow accompany her mother into the ER. Knowing
hospitals, she might be another hour. Or twelve.

He might as well go. He could call Willow tomorrow
and ask her why Genevieve's hand had been wrapped
in a bloody bandage.

He *would* call her tomorrow.

No more running and hiding like a kissing coward.

He took two steps toward the door when it whooshed
open again, and Helen McDaniel walked in. She went
directly to the attendant at the intake desk. "I'm here
for Genevieve Prentice. Her daughter is with her now,
but she and I are switching places."

After being directed to room number two, Helen was
buzzed back. She never saw Noah.

He wandered over to the watercooler, filled a paper
cone, and sipped from it. Slowly. He'd emptied it and
was debating a refill or tossing it into the trash when
the ER room door opened, and Willow walked out. He
crumpled the cone, threw it away, and followed her
outside. "Willow!"

She stopped and turned around. "Oh. Hi, Noah."

"I saw you come in. How's your mom?"

"She's okay. She cut her hand. Needed stitches.
What are you doing here?"

He gave her a brief synopsis of what had happened with
Gage, and she replied, "Oh no. I hope he'll be okay."

"Me, too. So far, so good."

Willow closed her eyes and sighed heavily. "This has
been a day for bad medical news."

Alarmed, Noah asked, "Oh yeah? More than your mother? Not one of your kids, I hope?"

"Kids are fine." Willow's brief smile thanked him for his concern about her children. "They're home with a babysitter. It's their grandfather. He had a stroke, and he's not doing well at all."

"I'm sorry to hear that," he said.

"It's been quite the day. I told my mother about my husband and his baby mama. She didn't take it well, which is why she ended up in the ER."

"Sounds like quite a story for quite a day. Want to go somewhere to tell me about it? I've wanted to talk to you. I owe you an apology for—"

"Noah, is that you?" a male voice said, interrupting.

Noah went stiff and still.

A second person said, "Hey, Noah Tannehill! It *is* you. Guys, look who's here. I told everyone your family's place was somewhere in this neck of the woods. Daniel brought me fishing around here one time."

Noah closed his eyes at the sound of the two very familiar voices and wished himself a million miles away.

"I'll be damned. What are the chances?" a third voice asked. "Noah. You're looking good, man. How's the leg?"

Like his brother always used to say, wish in one hand and crap in the other and see which fills up faster. Noah opened his eyes and tried to smile as he turned and faced a trio of men with whom he used to work. "Guys. Where's Sanderson?" Noah asked, referring to the fourth member of their crew. "If you three are here, he can't be far away."

"He's why we're here. Dumbass broke his arm.

He's in the ER getting it set. Should be about done, we hope."

Noah knew these men. Adrenaline junkies all. "Climbing accident? Flip a vehicle while off-roading? Bad hang-gliding landing?"

"No. We've come here to fish. Arrived last night. Staying out at a nice lodge on Mirror Lake. Raindrop Lodge. You know it? Anyway, Sanderson was putting gas in the car and tried to step over the hose and tripped."

"Clumsy bastard."

"He's lucky he only broke his arm."

"Enough about us." The unmarried man in the group turned a flirtatious smile on Willow. "Who is this lovely lady?"

Noah reacted instinctively and placed a hand at the small of her back. "Willow, let me introduce you to Mark Stevens, Jason Brock, and Lyle Keene. I used to work with them. Guys, this is my friend Willow Eldridge. Her mother and aunt own the lodge where you're staying."

"Oh yeah?" Jason said. "Great place. We're in the lodge rooms. They're clean and comfortable and the food is great."

Lyle nodded. "Next time we come, we'll plan ahead and book early enough to score a couple of the cabins. Those look sweet."

"They are sweet," Willow said with a smile. "My children and I have been living in a cabin at Raindrop since we moved to Lake in the Clouds after Christmas. We're getting our own place soon, but I know my kids will be sad to leave."

Noah figured that was enough small talk, and he'd

opened his mouth to say their good-byes when Mark plunged a knife into Noah's heart by asking, "How are Daniel's wife and daughter doing? I haven't seen them since February when Cheryl asked me to fill in for Daniel at Maddie's school's daddy-daughter Valentine's dance. I keep meaning to go by and visit, but you know how it gets. It's a crazy time of year with Little League."

Willow turned a curious look Noah's way. He didn't want to talk about Daniel or Cheryl or especially Maddie to her or anyone. He attempted to fade the question by focusing on sports. "I know you're busy with baseball, Mark. How is your older boy's arm coming along? Has he made his mind up about staying behind the plate, or is he thinking about giving pitching a try after all?"

"He's happy being a catcher."

Jason observed, "I don't see a cane, Noah. Does that mean you're ready to come back to work?"

"Hot damn," Lyle said, delight in his voice. "I didn't even notice. Look at you. You look great."

"You are coming back to work, aren't you?" Mark asked. "We sure miss you."

Noah suddenly had a boulder in his throat. If only they'd left the hospital five minutes earlier, this whole tableau could have been avoided. An awkward silence stretched until Willow's hand slipped around his arm in silent support. Noah was able to say, "I, uh, haven't been cleared yet."

All three men's gazes shifted to Noah's leg. They didn't know that the main problem remained inside his head. Mark cleared his throat, then said, "The station isn't the same without you around."

"He's right," Lyle agreed. "Nobody plays bad eighties

music when I'm trying to sleep anymore. That was your specialty."

"You coming back for the Memorial Day ceremony this year, Noah? It's the station's twenty-fifth anniversary. The chief is putting together a really nice remembrance presentation for our fallen. Of course, I'm sure you know about it already, with Daniel being your brother and all."

Noah couldn't have responded to that question had his life depended on it.

Willow, God bless her, stepped up and saved him. "I'm sorry to interrupt, but I need to check on my children. They're home with a babysitter, and we didn't expect a trip to the ER with my mother."

Noah's former coworkers took the hint and said their good-byes. Noah's instinct was to flee to his truck and burn rubber back home. Except he was having trouble making his feet move.

"C'mon, Noah. Let's get out of here before we see someone else we know. Where are you parked?" When he motioned toward his pickup, which was three spaces over from where they stood, Willow nodded. "Let's go in your truck. You're closer."

"Okay." Because Noah knew that he was going to have to tell her about Daniel, and he was steamed about it because he wasn't ready, his voice had a bite to it when he asked, "Where are we going?"

"Well..." Willow offered him a crooked grin. "The first official meeting of the Lake in the Clouds Emotional Wrecks Club can't happen at my house. My kids are there. We could go up to the lodge, but we risk running into your buddies again. How about the Mountaineer Lanes? I've been scheduling some campaign events for my aunt, and I happen to know that there's no league bowling tonight."

Noah closed his eyes and rubbed the back of his neck. "Sure. That'll be fine."

Tejano music drifted from the open window of a car driving by as Noah hit a button on his key fob. Lights flashed and the door locks thunked their release. Once inside the truck, Noah started the engine, but rather than place his car into gear and exit his parking spot, he sat with the engine idling. Eventually, Willow asked, "Noah?"

"Turns out I'm not feeling the bowling alley for this. Mind if, instead, we head back to my place? I think I'd be more comfortable limiting attendance at this self-help meeting. Also, I have emotional-support puppies."

She laughed softly. "Actually, I think that's a good idea. First, let me call home. I need to make sure all is well there and that the kids and the sitter are cool with her putting Emma and Drew to bed."

With that task completed and her maternal concerns addressed, they headed out of town. Willow suggested that she bring her own car so that he wouldn't need to take her back for it, but he preferred the return drive to riding alone for twenty minutes right now. Neither one of them spoke during the trip. Willow sat with her head tilted back against the headrest, her eyes closed.

Acting instinctively, he reached over and took her hand in his. She glanced at him and smiled, then closed her eyes once again.

Noah's thoughts returned to the scene in front of the hospital. What craptastic timing. And yet having Willow beside him when it happened...maybe it was meant to be.

Arriving home, he debated skipping the workshop and heading straight for the comfort of his great room, but Noah was a man of his word, and he'd promised puppies. Besides, the apartment might not be as comfortable as the house, but it came a close second. The outdoor lighting tied to motion detectors switched on, illuminating the workshop's surroundings as he parked by the side entrance and switched off the engine. "We're here."

Willow opened her eyes and sat up. "Another five minutes and you might have heard me snoring. I'm exhausted. "

"I'm right there with you. It's been quite the day. Why don't we go inside and veg a bit before we kick off our...what did you call this?"

"Emotional Wrecks Club."

"Right." He snorted a laugh. "How about we delay the opening gavel and veg a little first? Talk about nothing more serious than puppies."

Willow smiled and opened the passenger-side door. "Well, puppies can be serious." As she got out and walked around the front of his truck, she passed the SANTA'S WORKSHOP sign and added, "So can Santa Claus. With talk about the Easter Bunny abounding all around, Drew is beginning to put two and two together. He made a couple of discerning observations, and earlier this week, I was afraid he was about to pop the dreaded *Is Santa real?* question. We both avoided it. Honestly, I think he suspects but doesn't want to know the truth."

"Nothing wrong with that. A smart kid will milk an extra Christmas or two of Santa gifts out of it." Noah opened the door and escorted her inside the building.

"Okay, I'm confused." Willow gazed around the space. "This is really nice, but I thought this was your workshop. Have you remodeled since I was here?"

A pair of bar stools sat at the bar that separated the galley kitchen from the living space, where a couple of floor-to-ceiling bookcases flanked a stone fireplace. Furnishings were basic and chosen for comfort rather than style—an upholstered chair and ottoman with a good reading lamp to the side of the fireplace, a sofa long enough for Noah to nap on, end tables to put drinks, and a rug here and there added to help protect the wood floor once Marigold wandered into his world.

A circular staircase led to the loft bedroom and a bathroom upstairs. A barn door made from wood that matched the flooring led to his workshop and the downstairs powder room.

"No. We came in the side door. The apartment has always been here. The workshop is through there." He gestured toward the barn door. "Puppies are this way."

Noah slid the door open, and the yips and yaps of puppies filled the air.

"Aww..." Willow said in that melting voice that females tended to use around pups. It made Noah smile.

"Are any of them spoken for?" Willow asked.

"Gage wants the girl with the white fiddle face. She's over in the corner. See?"

"She's cute."

"If you want her, she's yours. I warned him that you'd have the pick of the litter if you decided you wanted one before they were weaned."

"They're all cute. I'm happy to choose a different puppy."

When she started to step over the fence, he cautioned, "Wait—I haven't cleaned the pen all day. Take them out one or two at a time to play."

"You sure? You're not afraid of them making a mess?"

"Floors clean. What would you like to drink?"

"Whatever you're having. In a plastic or paper cup, if you have one. No sense risking a repeat of today's rush to the ER."

Noah returned to the workshop a few moments later carrying brandy snifters filched from the picnic supplies. Recalling that she'd favored the old-fashioned served at her brother's wedding, he made two of those. He discovered Willow cuddling a sleeping pup and sitting not on the floor but at his workbench. Delight lit her expression. "Noah, this is fabulous. It's what you worked on last time I was here, isn't it? What we painted?"

"Yeah." He set her drink on the workbench beside her.

"This isn't one of the dollhouses you set on fire."

"No." With a mixture of pride and dismay, he watched her study the dollhouse. He probably wouldn't get out of the upcoming conversation without telling her why he'd built the toy—one more thing he wasn't ready to talk about.

"I love all the detail. Have you made this furniture, too?"

"Some of it. I made the beds, tables, and chairs. The really small stuff or intricate pieces like that"—he gestured toward a miniature china cabinet—"I ordered."

"It's just fabulous." Willow gazed up at him in speculation. "I'm pretty sure you told me the day we met that you didn't make dollhouses for children."

"This is my first one. I'm just fooling around with it," Noah responded. Then, anxious to change the subject, he gestured toward the puppy she held. "Is that the one?"

"The one?"

"You're adopting a puppy, right? I've been calling him Paint because of that inch of white on the tip of his tail."

"That begging note in your voice makes you sound like a puppy," she teased. "Actually, I did tell my mother today that we were taking one of your pups. I told her we might take two."

"Seriously?"

She shrugged, and in an instant, misery clouded over the light in her eyes. She rose and walked back to the puppy pen. "This one in my arms is a boy. If I wanted to take a girl puppy, too, which one would you recommend?"

"The one with the socks way in the back. Here, let me get her." Noah stepped into the pen and scooped up the puppy, pausing to give Marigold a good scratch behind her ears when she lifted her head and gave her tail a couple of thumps in greeting. "She's a sweetheart."

Willow accepted Socks and handed Paint back to Noah, who snuggled the sleeping pup close to his litter-mates. "She's so cute. They're all so cute. I don't know how I can choose."

"Bring the kids over. Let them choose. One for Emma. One for Drew."

That's when the misery cloud began to leak and rained down her cheek. "I absolutely am not taking three puppies."

"Ah." Noah was able to put the clues together pretty quickly. "Their grandfather's stroke. You're taking in the baby?"

"He's a toddler now. What else can I do?" She gave him a rundown of the arguments she'd made to her mother and her mother's responses in return. "I understand where she's coming from. I do. If I were in her shoes, I'd have thrown the glass, too."

The pup in Willow's arms stirred and opened her eyes. Willow smiled down at her and cooed and scratched her ears. Noah sort of wished he were a puppy. "When is all this happening?"

"Tomorrow. The nanny is bringing him tomorrow. I'm not prepared. I have nothing a toddler needs or requires. I think I can borrow a crib from the lodge for a night or two, but I'll be scrambling for supplies. Until I see what sort of sleeper AJ is, it'll probably work better for Drew and Emma to share a room. They won't like that. I'll need to look at the current real estate market with a new eye."

An idea fluttered through Noah's mind, and his gaze slid over to the dollhouse sitting on his workbench. "Willow, I have a crib you can use."

"You do? One you made?" At Noah's nod, Willow tilted her head and studied him. Then, softly, she asked, "For whom did you make the crib, Noah?"

Well, hell. "Guess I'm gonna have to do this. Let's go sit in the other room where it's comfortable."

Willow moved to return Socks to the pen, but Noah stopped her. He picked up their drinks and headed for the apartment. "Bring the dog. Emotional-support puppy, remember?"

There, he set the drinks on the coffee table and flipped the switch to ignite the gas logs in the fireplace. He needed some sort of background music. Did he have any dirges on his playlist?

No, but he did have some old-time country western. Hank Williams could come pretty close. Recalling the dance with Willow at her brother's wedding, he went for Patsy Cline turned down low.

Willow sat on the sofa in front of where he'd placed her drink. Noah knelt beside the fireplace and flipped open the woodbox where he'd stored a selection of dog toys. As he dug through the box, he began. "I owe you an apology."

Surprise filled her voice. "For what?"

He pulled a toy made of braided yarn from the box, then sat on the floor and looked up at Willow, holding her gaze. "I want to apologize for ghosting you. After we sealed the deal."

After they'd kissed.

"Oh. Well. Yes, I did wonder if I misread things." Willow set down the puppy, who scampered over toward Noah.

"No. Not at all. You knocked my socks off." He offered the toy to the puppy, and they began the tug-of-war. Willow sipped her drink and waited. He quirked a smile. "Not going to make this any easier on me, are you?"

"Not my job to make things easy."

Noah nodded. "It scared me. When I'm scared, I run away. It's what I do. What I've been doing since I watched my brother die."

"Oh, Noah. I take it back. Can I make it easier? Don't feel like you have to tell me anything. Seriously, we're good."

He grinned at her, reached into the toy box, grabbed a ball, and tossed it to her. Willow was quick, and she caught it. "You're offering to be my emotional-support person?"

"I guess I am."

Noah scooped up the puppy as he rose, walked to the sofa, and dropped beside her. He set the puppy on his lap, but an intelligent girl, she crawled halfway into Willow's. Noah draped his right arm around Willow's shoulders and stroked the puppy's back with his left. He drew a deep breath and began. "Firefighting is in my blood. Truly was the family business. I'd always known that when I stopped playing football, I'd head for the fire academy, and that's what I did. My grandfather, two uncles, and my dad were all Denver firefighters. Daniel—my brother—and I worked out of the same station where our dad had been chief."

"Was Daniel older than you or younger?"

"Older. Daniel was our lieutenant." Noah paused and reached for his drink. A little fortifying inner fire to get through this. "He wasn't on shift that night. He wasn't supposed to be at the station. The call came in from an old warehouse on the edge of downtown. Four-alarm fire. Our truck was first on the scene. We were a crew of three. Me, John Wilson, and our driver, Mack Kulpa. John and I were clearing the building—had some homeless folk tucked away in nooks and crannies. It was going up fast, but we were getting the job done."

He shut his eyes and was catapulted back into the nightmare.

The heat. The smoke. *Cra-a-a-ck!*

Whoosh. Noah had lunged away, but a mountain slammed into him. *I'm down. Pinned down.* Agony. Radiating. Radiating. Radiating. *Can't move. Can't move. Can't move.*

Coppery-tasting fear washed through him. *Where's Wilson?* He had been right beside Noah. "Wilson, report!" Nothing. "John!"

Think. Think! He keyed the radio. "Firefighters down. Firefighters trapped. Second division. Charlie side."

The radio crackled. Kulpa, the driver, replied. "Cavalry is coming, Noah. Half a dozen more trucks are on-site, and crews are on the way up. The loo just arrived."

Daniel?

Yeah, of course his brother would show up.

"Wilson?" Noah tried again. "Talk to me, bud—" He broke off when a cough racked his body.

By the time he caught his breath again, he spied figures coming up the stairs. Two men crossed the smoke-filled room to him. Familiar faces. Harrison and Kemp. "Wilson?"

"We've got eyes on him, Noah. We're gonna get him out. First, though, let's get you loose."

A heavy wooden beam had pinned his left leg. At this point, the agony subsided because Noah didn't feel anything. He couldn't feel anything! More men arrived, and they went to work lifting and levering the weight off his leg.

"How's Wilson?" he asked.

The hum of conversation taking place around him briefly paused, and Kemp repeated, "We've got eyes on him."

Noah pushed himself up on his elbows, anxious about his crew buddy. That's when he saw his brother framed in the doorway at the opposite end of the warehouse.

Some part of Noah relaxed at that moment. Here was the big brother who checked the closet and beneath the bed for monsters, the hero who took back Noah's stolen lunch money and gave the third-grade bully a black eye for his trouble. Here was the person who always, always had Noah's back.

Their gazes met and held. Daniel nodded. *It's gonna be okay now. Big bro is here. Superman is here to save the day.*

Daniel headed across the room. That familiar no-nonsense stride.

And then, without warning, the floor fell, and Daniel Tannehill disappeared.

Noah was brought back to the present when he felt the brush of a tissue across his cheeks. Embarrassment washed through him as he opened his eyes. How long he had sat there without speaking, he couldn't say. "Oh hell. Was I crying?"

"No," Willow said, tucking the tissue into her pocket. "Just a little allergy. Pet dander, you know."

Crap. "Pet dander," Noah repeated with a snort. He shifted the puppy's position, more for something to do than because it needed doing. "That's embarrassing."

"Don't be embarrassed. Tears are sometimes a tribute."

If that was the case, Noah probably had enough tribute locked inside him to build a monument to compete with Mount Rushmore. He reached for his drink and slammed it back, then decided to be done with this. "Fire had weakened the floor's structural integrity, and it gave out beneath my brother's weight. He fell into the fire in the room below. They, uh, couldn't get to him in time. Wilson didn't make it out, either."

Willow set her hand atop his as compassion filled her eyes. "I'm so sorry, Noah. That's a tragic loss."

He nodded, unable to say more due to the lump of emotion that had formed in his throat.

After a moment of silence, Willow asked, "You've mentioned you've lost your parents, but do you have any other siblings? Any other family?"

He cleared his throat. "No siblings. It was just me and Daniel."

"So you two were close?" He nodded, and she suggested, "Tell me about him."

Noah opened his mouth to speak, then hesitated. "I don't know what to say."

"You're such a guy," Willow complained. Noah could tell she was trying to lighten the mood. "Did Daniel look like you? Was he into sports? What were his favorite movies? Tell me something the two of you did as kids that got you into trouble."

Her prompts proved to be just what he needed. Noah answered her basic questions, but it was the tale of childhood shenanigans that loosened both his tongue and the vise around his heart. For the first time since Daniel's death, Noah was able to remember his brother with a laugh, rather than tears.

When he finished the story about sneezing powder and a fan in freshman algebra class, he fell silent, his thoughts reflective. It had felt good to talk about his brother. Surprisingly good.

Then Willow asked a question guaranteed to spoil his mellowing mood.

"Did Daniel have someone special in his life?"

"Two someones," Noah replied. "Daniel was married. He had a daughter. Madeline. Maddie. She's a little older than Emma."

"Oh," Willow breathed. "Oh, I see." She brightened with a smile. "You made the dollhouse for Maddie."

"No!" Noah quickly responded. "I didn't. I made it for..." He shook his head and said, "Look, my brother's wife and I aren't in touch. I haven't seen her since before the accident."

"You didn't go to your brother's funeral?" Then, before he could respond, she answered the question herself. "Your leg. You were in the hospital, I imagine."

He nodded. "For two months. It was a tib-fib fracture. Six surgeries. Another month in a rehab hospital. Discharged home but still tethered to daily outpatient rehab appointments for another three months. As soon as I was sprung, I headed here. I've been here ever since."

"So, why don't you see your sister-in-law?"

He shrugged. "Our last visit wasn't...pleasant. She came to see me in the hospital. She wanted to know what had happened inside the building, so I told her. I told her the ugly truth and then sent her away. Told her to stay away. She's stayed away. I'm sure she blames me. I sure as hell blame myself. He wouldn't have been there if not for me."

"Are you certain of that?" Willow's expression had turned doubtful. "From what you've said about Daniel, he sounds like the kind of guy who would have gone in whether he was on call or not. So would you. That's who you are. It's hardwired into you."

Noah suddenly needed to move. He rose from the sofa and walked over to the toy box, where he tossed the tug rope into its depths. Then he glared at the gas logs, wishing it were a wood fire so he could pick up a fireplace poker and stir the logs. He needed to do something physical.

He settled for giving the toy box a good, solid kick and dumped it over. Thinking this must be a new game, the puppy leaped down from Willow's lap and made a beeline for the toys. Noah linked his fingers behind his head with his elbows extended wide. He stared blindly at a rawhide bone that had spilled from the box. "I can't face his wife and daughter, okay? I can't. I just can't. I'm a coward."

The springs in his sofa squeaked when she rose and approached him. Noah tensed. Her touch was as gentle as a feather when she slipped her arms around his waist and rested her cheek against his back.

He closed his eyes against the pressure building behind them. His chest was tight from churning emotion—regret and grief and guilt. So much guilt. As fresh today as the day of Daniel's funeral. *"Time heals all wounds" is a damned lie.*

A shudder swept over him. Noah knew he was about to seriously lose it, so he pulled away from Willow and turned to flee.

She stopped him. She stepped in front of him and stopped him with a hand against his chest. Sincerity gleamed in her gaze and echoed in her voice as she stated, "You're not a coward, Noah. You're just not ready yet."

Then she went up onto her tiptoes and kissed him tenderly.

That one small expression of faith in him was all it took.

Noah broke. He kissed her back. He wrapped his arms around her and pulled her hard against him. Moving his lips over hers, he plunged his tongue into her mouth and poured out his anguish and his pain. Seeking comfort. Seeking oblivion. Seeking that warmth that was Willow.

What he found was heat. Willow kissed him back. She molded herself against him and circled his neck with her arms. Her fingers sank into his hair. She tasted like honey and heaven, and when she moaned against his mouth, his blood ran hot and burned away the memories that plagued him. The nip of her teeth against his lower lip banished all awareness beyond the woman in his arms.

He backed her against the wall, the pressure of her body pressed against him, both pleasure and pain. Her hands moved urgently across his back, and her nails scratched his neck. Noah shuddered. Willow groaned. He lifted her off the floor, and she wrapped her legs around him and sighed with pleasure.

He wanted. Oh, how he wanted. He buried his face against her neck and made her shudder when he found a sensitive spot below her ear. He rocked against her in that age-old rhythm that had him clenching his teeth and caused sweat to bead on his brow.

He could carry her upstairs to his bed and deal with this. She wouldn't protest. By all indications, she'd be an enthusiastic participant. And yet their timing was off.

"Wait." Noah tore his mouth away from her. He was tempted back by the sweet skin of her neck to press a string of kisses from her ear to her collarbone. She tasted so good. Smelled so delicious. He badly wanted to silence this kernel of conscience that was telling him to stop, except he couldn't.

"Wait," he repeated, stepping away from her but keeping his hands firmly around her waist. He was unable to make himself stop touching her. "This is bad timing, Willow."

"Why?" she asked, her voice thready.

"I'm a mess right now. Don't get me wrong. I'm very attracted to you. Have been since the moment we met. I would love nothing more than to take you upstairs to the bed in my loft this moment. But I have no business starting a relationship with any woman, much less a woman with children. I have nothing to give you. Maybe someday—"

"Hush, Noah." Willow put her finger over his lips. "No harm, no foul. I'm very attracted to you, too. Obviously. But the last thing I need in my life right now is a romantic relationship. That said, I like you, Noah. I could use a friend. Tonight. I would love to be your friend tonight."

Noah stilled. He did not want to make a mistake here, but he wasn't certain what the mistake would be. He needed a friend, too. Absolutely. But could she be looking for more? Could he? Was there any possibility that this could be more than a one-night, soft place to fall for one another? He wanted her. Oh yeah, he wanted her. But he wanted it to be right. "Okay, I may be reading this all wrong. I'm seriously out of practice here. Is this sort of like that support-person thing? Support-person sex?"

She laughed softly. "Maybe so. I don't know, Noah. I know that I'm feeling selfish right now. My life is a mess, and I can't see beyond tomorrow, but I want tonight for me. I haven't been with a man since my husband. If you want me, then I'll choose you. Just for tonight. Will you take me upstairs, Noah?"

"You're sure?"

"You think I'd make a little speech like that if I wasn't sure?"

He studied her, read the promise and the certainty in the steadiness of her eyes. A feeling began to uncurl inside him, and it took him a moment to identify it. Happiness. *I'll be damned.* "First one, hmm?"

"Yes."

His lips twisted ruefully. "Bit of pressure, there."

"Not really," she assured him, a gleam of amusement entering her eyes. "Not a hard act to follow, so to speak."

Noah's mouth lifted in a crooked grin. "What I should do is sweep you up into my arms like a romance novel hero and kiss you passionately as I carry you up the spiral staircase and then lay you across my bed."

He leaned forward and nipped her chin. Willow pouted. "That's not what you're going to do?"

"With this leg? That'd be pressing our luck. I'm afraid we'd both end up crumpled at the bottom of the stairs."

"Valid point."

"Besides, I need to make a run up to the house for necessary supplies. If I'm the first guy since numbnuts, I doubt you carry condoms in your handbag."

"True." Willow smiled brilliantly at him.

"I'll be quick as a minute. Well, getting to the house and back. Not once I'm in bed with you. There, I'll take my time. I promise. Although, fair warning, the first time might be quicker than we'd like because it has been a long time, but I'll make it up to you the second—"

"Go, Tannehill." Laughing, Willow pushed him toward the door. "Hurry."

"Don't change your mind while I'm gone!"

"I won't."

"Better put the puppy in her pen."

"I will."

Noah exited the apartment and hurried toward the house. Halfway there, Noah began to run.

Chapter Twelve

GENEVIEVE TAPPED HER FOOT on the wheel-chair's footrest while waiting for Helen to pull her car into the hospital's circular drive. She wanted to stand up. She wanted to pace and rant and rage. Instead, she had to sit quietly and exchange small talk with the poor orderly tasked with seeing her safely into her ride away from the hospital.

Finally, Helen pulled up in her Range Rover. Genevieve lurched from the wheelchair over the orderly's cautions. She climbed into her sister's vehicle, tossing the young man a smile over her shoulder. "Thank you so much, Steve. Have a nice evening, now. Good luck on that English exam."

She slammed the passenger door shut. "Get me out of here."

"Oh, Genevieve. Cool your jets. You've been here, what—four hours? Five?"

"I got four stitches in my hand. One per hour. I had time enough to have a colonoscopy or something else fun while I was there."

"Want me to turn around?"

Genevieve ignored the question. Her hand throbbed. Her heart ached. Hadn't Willow gone through enough already?

"Did you know about this, Helen?"

Warily, Helen asked, "Know about what?"

Genevieve's tone was flat and grim as she said, "Andy's baby mama."

Her sister gasped and whipped her head around to pin Genevieve with a look. "His what?"

"Baby mama. When Andy died, he left behind a pregnant girlfriend."

"He did not!" Helen scoffed.

"Yes, he did."

Helen's eyes flashed with fury, and she turned a corner a shade too fast. "Why, that asshole!"

Genevieve studied her sister closely. "You really didn't know?"

"No!" Helen exclaimed. "I'm totally out of the loop on this. Spill the tea, sister."

Genevieve did just that, hitting the highlights—or lowlights, as it were—about everything she'd learned from Willow today. When she was done, Helen let out a long, low whistle and a string of unflattering curses directed toward the late Andy Eldridge.

"I am so angry at that S.O.B.," Helen said when she wound down. "Surprised, too. I knew that their marriage had some rocky spots, but what marriage hasn't? Had no clue that he'd cheated on her. I certainly didn't know about any baby. I'd have told you that."

Genevieve believed her. "Willow never mentioned divorce to you?"

"Nope. Never hinted at it."

"Oh. I wish she'd talked to you." Genevieve realized that was true, too. "I wish she had talked to somebody. I'm certain her sister didn't know. Brooke wouldn't have been able to keep that kind of secret, either. We could have helped Willow through this."

"Are you sure?" Helen gave her a sidelong glance.

"Yes. I'm her mother. I know what it's like to be widowed."

"But you don't know what it's like to be the widow of an asshole, and besides, that made you Mommy Always Right."

Genevieve's feathers ruffled. "Excuse me?"

"Well, look at it from Willow's point of view. Because you were right all along, she had some crow to eat about Andy."

"I didn't want her to eat crow," Genevieve insisted. "I wanted her to have a happy marriage."

"I'll give you that." Helen slowed the car as the traffic signal they approached turned yellow, then red. Once the car had stopped, she looked at Genevieve and said, "But be honest. Deep down inside yourself, where Evil Genevieve lives, you preened a bit and did the *I was right* dance when she fessed up."

"Well, maybe. But I didn't let her see it."

"No, but she knows. She knows you."

"Okay, that makes me feel bad. I don't want her to hurt. Willow has enough hurt in her life, which is why Maggie Eldridge had no business dumping her problems on my daughter. Unfortunately, I can't even be angry at Maggie right now because of poor Tom. I know Maggie is going through hell. I understand her wanting to keep that cheating asshat's love child. AJ is her grandson. But the boy isn't Willow's responsibility."

"You are right about that, Genevieve," Helen agreed as the light changed, and they resumed their drive.

"I'm thankful Willow nixed moving to Texas, but I cannot believe she said yes to bringing him here to Lake in the Clouds, into her home. Why, that child is the—" Genevieve bit off the sentence.

"The what?"

"Never mind. It's too mean. I won't say it."

Interest in her gaze, Helen prodded. "Won't say what?"

Her lips pursed, Genevieve didn't respond, so Helen, being Helen, started guessing. "The bastard's bastard? The spawn of Satan?"

"The incarnation of betrayal."

"Ouch. How very Catholic of you. C'mon, Genevieve, he's just a child."

"Oh, I know. That's why I didn't say it. Look, I'm not blaming the baby. Truly, I'm not." Genevieve brought her hands to her head and massaged her temples with her fingertips. "It's a bad situation all around. So, I want to do what I can to change bad to good. But Willow is *my* child. I'm going to protect *my* child first. Every time she looks at that little boy, it will be an arrow through her heart. I don't want her to suffer that way."

"She's an adult, Genevieve. She gets to decide what works for her."

"I know. I recognize that. I acknowledge that."

Genevieve turned a fierce look her sister's way as she continued, "But that doesn't mean that Willow won't be my baby until the day I die. If she's tied to the railroad tracks and I see a train of pain bearing down upon her, I'll do everything possible to get to her with a pair of scissors in time."

"I know, honey," Helen said in a placating tone.

"The rest of the world can protect Andy Eldridge's love child, but I'm going to watch out for Willow!" Genevieve declared. Then with a sly self-satisfied smile, she added, "That's where you come in."

"Me?" Helen reflexively tapped the brake. "You've lost me."

"Careful!" Genevieve checked the side mirror to see if they were in danger of being rear-ended. Luckily, the road behind them was clear. She returned to her point. "Look, what do we really know about this little boy? Just what Maggie told Willow. Maggie's interests and ours are not aligned. And who's to say that the child's best interests align with Maggie's? AJ needs someone looking out for his best interests. Under ordinary circumstances, I'd volunteer, but in this case, I'm one hundred percent Team Willow. So that leaves you."

"Me! Why me?"

"Because if you agree to become AJ's advocate, you will put his needs first. With your legal background, you know what questions to ask, or you know the people who know what questions to ask. And you'll make sure all the legal i's are dotted and t's crossed in any agreements that are reached."

"I hate to admit this, but you're ahead of me, Genevieve. What questions are you talking about? What agreements?"

"For one thing, we need a DNA test. We need to confirm that this child is Drew and Emma's half brother. We need to know more about the mother than the fact that she's dead. Is Maggie being honest about her not having any other family? If so, we need to investigate what other options might be available. I'm thinking that a private adoption might be the perfect answer for AJ. He's not even two years old. Childless couples across America are desperate to have a little one to love. I feel certain there's an exceptional family out there who would welcome him into their family and love him unconditionally. I don't doubt that we could find parents for him who would be willing to allow Maggie to be a part of his life. Maybe Emma and Drew, too, if that's what Willow wants."

"Why, Genevieve Prentice. When did you think of all of this?"

"Those four stitches took a long time."

"I was with you most of that time. We were passion planning."

"I think we need a new name. That sounds nasty."

"Hey, it's your idea."

"Not exactly, but that's another story, and I don't want to get distracted. Will you do it, Helen?"

"Be AJ's family advocate? Do you know what you're asking, Genevieve? If I agree to do this..."

"You will do it to the best of your ability. Yes, I know. You were an excellent attorney before you retired. You are outstanding when you go legal-beagle investigator mode."

"I'll be Team AJ all the way," Helen warned.

"I'm counting on it. It means that tomorrow when I meet that little boy, I won't need to feel guilty about being Team Willow. I can put my child's needs first because my sister is on the job. She has my back. Like always."

Helen nodded and slowed the car as they approached an intersection. "Not to change the subject, but here's another missing stop sign."

"Oh my stars." Disgust laced Genevieve's voice as she dug into her handbag for her phone. "I don't know if I can take photos with one hand."

"Here, I'll pull over to the curb."

"I'm afraid your campaign manager is getting off to a slow start," Genevieve said as she nudged the button to roll down her window.

"Yes, that is apparent." Helen pulled to the side of the road, then reached across the console with her foot on the brake to help Genevieve take the photograph. "At least the streetlight is working. Although, does it look like it's flickering to you, Gen? I need to make a note of that."

Helen was putting together a traffic-safety presentation to make to the city council next week. Because she considered their reception of her suggestions for necessary improvements to be a foregone conclusion, she expected to use the information in her campaign.

"No, the light is steady. Ouch," Genevieve grumbled as she accidentally bumped her hand. "This hurts."

"I can't believe you managed to cut yourself. You're not usually a klutz."

"I'm not usually DEFCON ten angry." She rolled up her window.

"Is DEFCON ten a thing?"

"I don't know, Helen. That picture was blurry. You need to hold it steady if—"

Clink. Clink. Clink. Genevieve and Helen were startled at the rap on the driver's side window. Genevieve leaned forward and spied the end of a metal flashlight and a uniformed figure standing outside the car. Helen muttered a curse. She pushed the button, and the window slid down. "Hello, Ralph."

"License and insurance, please."

Helen rolled her eyes at her sister as she reached for her purse. "Aren't you going to ask us if we're having any trouble, Officer? We are two little old ladies parked by the side of the road, fumbling with our phones."

"Speak for yourself," Genevieve muttered.

Helen handed over the requested documents. "They haven't changed since you stopped me last week, Ralph. May I inquire as to the reason why we're being stopped?"

"You were already stopped."

"He has a point, Helen." Genevieve offered the policeman her friendliest smile.

"You are stopped, and you don't have your flashers on. That's a moving violation, so I must write you a ticket. I'll be right back."

Helen opened her mouth to protest, and Genevieve elbowed her in the side to shut her up. "My hand, Helen," she whined. Loudly. "I must get home. As soon as possible." Sotto voce, she added, "Please let's not make a trip to the ER and the jail on the same day."

Helen punched the button to roll up the window against the night air and snapped, "A moving violation when we're stopped? Isn't it nice to know that Lake in the Clouds has our own Barney Fife?"

"This is why you keep me in your life. Hardly anyone else is old enough to know what the heck you're talking about."

"That's not true. Your kids watched *Mayberry* reruns on TV while growing up."

"They did not." Genevieve waited a beat and added, "It was called *The Andy Griffith Show*."

Helen wrinkled her nose toward her sister. "Well, everyone in my building knows who Barney Fife is."

"You live at a retirement center."

"A senior condominium community," Helen corrected. "And Ralph is an idiot."

"I won't argue that. Get the ticket dismissed tomorrow. Take me home. I'm not kidding about my hand throbbing."

Helen huffed. "The things I do for you."

"I know. Love you, sister."

"Love you, too. Hand me your phone, and I'll retake that fuzzy picture."

Clink. Clink. Clink. Helen rolled down the window and held out her palm to accept the ticket. "Oh, thank you, Ralph. You are such a—"

"Don't say it," Genevieve murmured. "Don't say it."

"Public servant. Good night." She rolled the window up, flipped on her signal, and pulled out onto the street. "So, when is AJ due to arrive?"

"Sometime tomorrow afternoon. I told Willow I'd pick up the kids right after lunch and babysit until she was ready for them to meet."

"Oh, Genevieve. Of course you did. Mom to the rescue."

"That's what I do, Helen. That's what I do."

⤙⤚

Willow lifted her face to the hot water pelting her from the showerhead and smiled. The shower was invigorating. She felt rejuvenated and tingled from head to toe.

When she realized she was singing, embarrassment washed through her.

The shower door opened, and Noah started to step inside, a gleam in his eyes and unmistakable proof of his intentions leading the way. Willow held up her hand, palm out. "Down, boy. There's no more time for that."

"But—"

"I told my babysitter I'd be home by eleven."

"I can be quick," he begged, wagging his brows.

"Snooze, you lose, handsome." Grinning, she swatted him on his most fine ass and scooted past him out of the shower, grabbing a fluffy blue towel from the floating shelf to dry off.

By the time Noah showered, Willow had dressed and gone downstairs. She decided she wanted one more look at the puppies before she left, but as she walked toward the pen, she got distracted by the Victorian dollhouse. A faint smile hovered on her lips. The man certainly paid attention to detail.

She'd bet he'd made this for his niece, whether he'd admit to it or not. A pink-and-purple color scheme had preschool girl written all over it. Willow knew this for a fact. Weren't pink and purple Emma's favorite colors?

When Noah joined her, she was hunkered down before the puppy pen, scratching Marigold behind the ears. "Still trying to make a choice?"

"Actually, if it's all right with you, I'd like to bring the children out and let them pick. Drew will choose right away. Emma will hem and haw, but my instincts are telling me that in light of AJ's arrival, it will be a good thing."

"Of course you can bring the children out. In fact,

that's a nice segue into something else I want to talk to you about."

"Oh? What's that?"

He clasped her hand in his and tugged her toward the door. "Since you need to be home by eleven, let's talk about it on the way."

Willow was curious, but she felt too mellow to be too curious. She didn't really want to think much at all. Tomorrow was going to be a seriously tough day, and she would need to do plenty of thinking then. For now, she just wanted to settle back into his leather seats and veg.

So she wasn't thrilled when, after pulling out onto the highway and heading back into town, Noah said, "About that crib."

Don't look a gift horse in the mouth, Willow. "Oh yes. That's really nice of you to offer, Noah."

"Well, the thing is, I have more than a crib. This was a family retreat, and we always had a nursery. When my niece came along, we updated everything. I have the whole shebang—changing table, a high chair, toys, a bathtub. Pretty sure there are some diapers, too. Willow, my house has five bedrooms and four baths, plus the workshop apartment. I think you and the kids should move in here."

She sat up straight. "What?"

"I want to reassure you that as much as I enjoyed tonight—which I did. Very much. More than any night in years. Decades, even. Maybe ever. But back to the point, as much as I enjoyed tonight, I'm not trying to set up a repeat. Not that I wouldn't love a repeat, but that's not what we agreed to, and I had this idea before I ever dreamed that we'd end up in my loft. I have all this space, Willow, and I'm not using it. Move into my house. I'll move into the apartment. I spend all of my time in the workshop anyway. You can take your time finding the right place for you and the kids. Pay rent if that will make you feel better."

"Noah. I don't know what to say. That's ... incredibly generous. Probably a little crazy, too. I'll have three children, Noah."

"They'll be in daycare this summer, right?"

"Yes. I'm lucky that Little Ducklings had room for AJ. I called them as soon as I got off the phone with his grandmother. But ... " Oh, it would solve so many problems.

And, perhaps, create entirely new ones.

Was it a good idea for her to be around Noah daily? She feared she could totally fall for this man.

"Just think about it, Willow," he said, taking hold of her hand. "It's an option for you. No pressure from me one way or the other."

"I will." And she did. They remained silent for the rest of the ride back to the hospital to get her car, their fingers linked, the mood between them comfortable.

"Thank you," Willow said as he pulled into the hospital parking lot. "Seriously, Noah. Thank you. For everything. Tonight was ... "

"Spectacular. Magnificent. Mind-blowing. The best I've ever had. For me, anyway."

Willow smiled. "For me, too."

The parking places around her car were taken, so he found a spot a few rows over and parked. As he reached for his door handle, she said, "You don't need to walk me to my car."

He gave her a chastising look, then exited his truck. As they walked toward her car, she fumbled in her purse for the keys and finally found the fob. The headlamps flashed as she unlocked the door.

Though crowded with cars parked near the emergency room, the hospital lot was relatively empty of people. Noah reached around Willow and opened the driver's side door for her. She smiled up at him. "Good night, Noah."

"Good night, Willow."

She went up on her tiptoes and kissed him, lingering long enough to make it sweet but not long enough to turn it to steam. When they parted, she slid into her seat and started the engine. She went to shut the door, but he held it open. "There's something else I want to say. I'm not sure why except it's almost like I have this ghost kicking my ass telling me to say it. To thank you. Tonight was something else for me, Willow. Something more. You helped repair something inside of me."

"You did that for me, too, Noah. Thank you."

"So, we make good medicine together?"

"We do."

"Why do I suddenly feel like a snake oil salesman?"

"Better than a televangelist with a wife, three mistresses, and an offshore bank account."

"I don't have good enough hair to be a televangelist with a wife and three mistresses and an offshore bank account."

"Hmm. You may be right." Willow clicked her tongue. "It's that cowlick that makes you always look just a little bit mussed that scores you down from Mr. Perfect Hair. Bye, Noah."

"Bye, beautiful." He shut the door and moved to the front of the car while she backed out of the parking spot. She gave a wave, tapped her horn, and drove away smiling.

Forty minutes later, she crawled into bed, still smiling.

Chapter Thirteen

NOAH WOKE UP EARLY and made a game plan for the day. The first order of business would be to give the whole house a good cleaning.

Noah seldom utilized the rooms upstairs. While the space wasn't dirty, it needed sprucing up—a good dusting, cobweb patrol, a once-over in the bathrooms just to freshen things. He would run the vacuum and put fresh sheets on all the beds. Even if Willow decided not to take him up on his offer, what would it hurt to wash the sheets?

Absolutely nothing. Back in the day, Noah's mother always made sure to launder all the linens in the cabin at least twice a year. Daniel's wife, Cheryl, continued the practice after Mom died. Noah was the one who'd fallen down on the job. "Par for the course."

He tackled old ghosts right along with the chores, and by the time he had the downstairs ready for guests, he'd done more thinking about his brother than he'd done in many a month. The exercise proved to be cathartic. As he threw the last load of sheets into the dryer, he was feeling surprisingly upbeat. When Willow called, he answered the phone with a smile on his face. "Good morning."

"Good morning."

"Did you rest easy last night?"

"I slept like a babe, believe it or not."

"Nothing like vigorous exercise to aid healthy sleep."

"Yes, well, it proved to be a miraculous medicine. But on to the reason for my call. I wonder if you regained your senses overnight."

"Well, I did dream about you, so..."

She laughed. "Enough flirtation, Noah. I'm calling about your offer of a roof for our heads. No harm, no foul if you've second-guessed the idea."

"No second-guessing here. I actually spent some time this morning dusting." And sweeping and mopping and sanitizing.

"Oh no. Don't do that. We will be responsible for cleaning."

Noah's lips lifted in a smile. "So, you're moving in?"

"I'm serious about giving you a chance to change your mind."

"Not gonna happen. I'm happy to have you. Honestly."

"And you're truly okay with moving into the loft? I feel terrible about kicking you out of your bed."

"One of my beds. And actually, I now have a special fondness for the loft bed, and I may have started sleeping there anyway, no matter what was going on in the big house."

"Well, in that case, as long as our visitors arrive

as planned, I guess you can count on us staying there tonight."

"Great."

"You and I will need to sit down and establish some guidelines, and yes, I will insist on paying rent. I suspect my mother is going to hover around us today. She'll probably have dinner with us. Would you like to join us, too? It won't be anything fancy. Maybe takeout. Maybe pizza. It'll likely be an early meal, too. I'm guessing between five and six. Travel is hard on little ones. I'll bet AJ and his nanny will go to bed early."

"I'd love to have dinner with you."

"Great. I'll touch base with you when we're headed your way."

"Perfect."

"Noah?"

"Yeah?"

"I don't know how to thank you."

"You just did, Willow. Good luck this afternoon."

After the phone call, Noah kicked it into high gear. He moved his clothes and toiletries into the loft apartment and went to work upstairs. He soon had the nursery set up and bedrooms ready for Emma and Drew.

Ready, but too generic. Glancing around the room that would be Drew's, he thought, *Too sterile. Too impersonal.* It needed some stuff. A little paint wouldn't hurt, either.

Frowning, he took a mental inventory of the attic. When Mom and Dad sold his childhood home and shipped all the Christmas decorations here to their mountain getaway, hadn't they included a box of his and Daniel's things? He thought he remembered seeing them in the attic.

By noon, he'd done a lot, but he still had a few final touches he wished to make in Emma's room. They required a bit of work in the shop. So Noah placed the starship *Enterprise* made from a LEGO set on the shelf he'd hung on a wall in Drew's room, then headed downstairs and out to his workshop.

~✦~

As Willow grilled cheese sandwiches and heated tomato soup for lunch, she debated how to explain the sudden appearance of AJ Randall in their lives. She didn't lie to Drew and Emma. However, she also didn't think she needed to get into nitty-gritty details about their father's misdeeds.

News like this traveled through the Prentices like a stomach bug during a family road trip. So far this morning, she'd fielded phone calls from her mother, her aunt, her sister-in-law, and her brother Jake. They'd offered advice, counseling, support, and management oversight in turn. Her brother Lucas's call had been two full minutes of cussing out the memory of her husband without pausing to take a breath. Her sister, currently in France, had sent a sympathetic e-mail and promised a phone call once their time zones allowed for better communication.

Checking the bread, she judged the sandwiches ready and murmured, "Okay, game on." Then, in a louder voice, she called, "Drew, is the table set?"

"Yes, Mom."

Emma called, "I put the napkins on."

"Thank you, baby. Drew, come get the sandwiches, please." She carried the saucepan to the table and filled the bowls with tomato soup. A favorite of her children, that much was true, but comfort food for herself, too.

She waited until both children had polished off half their sandwich before saying, "So, kiddos, I have some good news and some bad news. The bad news is that Grampy is sick, and it's pretty serious. He's had something called a stroke."

"Is he gonna die?" Drew asked.

"Mimi says the doctors tell her they don't think he will die from this stroke, but he's going to be sick for a while and will need lots of care and help to get back to feeling like his old self."

Drew took a bite of his sandwich, his brow furrowed in a scowl. "Oh no. It's another bad thing, Mom. That's two."

"What?" What was he talking about?

Before Willow could figure it out or question him, Emma tugged on Willow's sleeve and asked, "What's the good thing, Mama?"

"The good thing is that Mimi and Grampy have been taking care of a little boy, and now he's going to come to stay with us until Grampy gets better. He's almost two years old, so Emma, you'll get to be a big sister. Drew, you're such a great big brother already."

"I've always wanted to be a big sister," Emma said, her eyes brightening with happiness.

Drew shrugged. "He's not even two? That's just a baby."

Obviously, her son wasn't interested in a baby brother. Good. Willow continued. "The even better good thing is that our friend Mr. Tannehill has offered to let us stay in his big house until we can find our perfect forever home in Lake in the Clouds. That means that both of you and the little boy—his name is AJ—can have your own rooms."

Now Drew's eyes went as round as his Harry Potter costume glasses. "Mr. Tannehill? We're going to live at the Hideaway?"

"For a little while."

"With Mr. Tannehill?"

"Well, not with Mr. Tannehill. His workshop has an apartment, and he'll live there. You are not to pester him all the time, Drew. He and I will speak tonight and establish ground rules about what you're allowed to do and not do when you're there."

"Probably like not touching his tools in his workshop."

"I expect that will be one of them. Also, not going into his workshop at all without permission," Willow emphasized. She held her breath, waiting for questions about AJ. If they got too uncomfortable, she had the nuclear distraction bomb to drop—puppies.

"Will we still go to Ducklings school if we have a new brother and new house?" Emma asked.

"Yes, honey."

"Okay, then. I like being a Duckling. Miss Caitlin is the nicest teacher ever. Can I have more soup, please?"

With that, the dreaded conversation appeared to be done with only minor drama and zero trauma. If only the rest of the day could progress that easily.

Genevieve arrived shortly after they finished lunch and took the news about their pending change of address with aplomb. "That is interesting. So, does this change our plans? Do you still want me to babysit this afternoon? How can I be of the most help to you?"

"I think the children will be fine meeting AJ when he arrives. If you want to stay and help keep them entertained, I'll continue packing. I did a bit already this morning. Being vagabonds, we don't have much, thank goodness."

Almost all of the kitchen supplies, the bedding, and the furnishings belonged to Raindrop Lodge. Their personal items amounted to their clothing, toiletries, toys, books, a few electronics, and the contents of their pantry and refrigerator. Considering that they'd lived in this cabin since January, Willow wasn't sure whether she should feel good or ashamed about being so foot-loose at this point in their lives.

"We probably have time to take one load over to Noah's before your guest is due to arrive," Genevieve pointed out.

"I don't think that's necessary. If you wouldn't mind taking a few boxes in your car, I think we can get everything in one load, Mom."

"I'm happy to load up my car. I'm sure Helen will have room in hers, too, if there's anything you and I can't fit."

"Auntie?"

"You didn't think she'd miss this event, did you?"

"Now that you mention it, no."

At a quarter to two, the nanny sent Willow a text saying they were about an hour away. With the packing completed, Genevieve took the children to the lake to fish while Willow retrieved the housekeeping cart from the storage building and tackled the cleaning of Cabin 17. The physical work helped settle her nerves, and she'd just finished the task and was tugging off a pair of yellow rubber gloves when a knock sounded on the door. Willow glanced up to see Noah standing on the threshold and offered him a genuine smile. "And what brings you here?"

"I thought you might need help moving boxes."

"Thank you, but we're already loaded up. We didn't have all that much to move."

"In that case." He tugged a flask from his pocket and held it up. "Need a little liquid courage?"

"I don't," she said with a laugh, "but you might ask my mother. She's strung pretty tight today. She and the kids went over to the lake to fish."

"Getting a line wet is a good way to relax. It wouldn't surprise me if all that fishing Gage did last week didn't help save his life."

"How is he doing? Have you heard anything?"

"I have. He called me this morning. Zach came by to talk." Noah gave his head a little bewildered shake as he added, "Gage offered me a job."

"Oh? Doing what?"

"Things Zach should be doing, if you ask me. They want me to step in and take some of the workload off of Gage's shoulders."

"I thought the foreman had taken over all the day-to-day work of the Triple T Ranch. That's what Mom told me Gage told her, anyway."

"I think that's right. But in addition to the Triple T Ranch, Gage also owns other real estate in the area and pieces of local businesses. That's all held under the umbrella of an entity called Throckmorton Enterprises. Plus, he has the charitable foundation."

Willow nodded. "Mom's partnership with Gage in The Emily is organized under the Throckmorton Foundation."

"He wants to stay involved with the charity, but he wants me to do his work for the Enterprises organization."

Willow could tell from his tone that he had reservations. "You're not interested in the job?"

"I told Gage no, which was why Zach came to talk to me." Noah gestured toward the housekeeping cart and asked, "Are you done with this? Want me to take it back where it belongs?"

"Sure. I'll show you where it goes. I'm done here. The cabin will only need linens and a fresh dusting to spruce it up when the lodge gets a rental. So, back to this job. Why does it sound like your no didn't mean no?"

"Because Gage wouldn't accept it," Noah replied, exasperation in his tone. "I told him I'm not qualified for that sort of job, but he says he can teach me everything I need to know. Then he sent Zach to tag team me and play on my sympathies." The cart's wheels rattled on the stone path as Noah pushed the housekeeping cart back toward the storage shed. "I guess it worked. I told him I'd help out temporarily. Just until they can make permanent arrangements."

"Hmm," Willow said.

They walked a little bit without speaking. Then Noah asked, "What do you mean 'hmm'?"

"You and me and our temporary arrangements—I wonder which of us will have the longest 'temporary.'"

"Probably better that we don't think about it," he said, his tone rueful.

"Yes. Probably." At the storage shed, she showed him where to store the cart, then they walked toward the lake to join her mother and children. Genevieve happily turned over the children and the fishing poles to Noah while giving Willow a questioning look that managed to convey about twenty-seven questions.

Willow was willing to answer maybe twelve of them, tops.

And she'd have to answer them another time because just then, Aunt Helen arrived at Raindrop Lodge in a car plastered with campaign signs. Genevieve snickered and said, "Told you she'd show up."

Aunt Helen parked in her usual spot close to the lodge's side nearest the business office, climbed out of her car, and waved them to join her. Genevieve suggested, "Why don't you stay here with the children? Let me see what she wants."

"Okay."

As her mother walked off, Willow knelt beside Emma to help her tie her shoe and looked up at her son. "Drew. Stop. Take a breath. Give Mr. Tannehill a chance to answer your first question before you ask a second one. Better yet. Stop asking questions. He's liable to change his mind."

"No! You won't, will you?" Drew turned a pleading gaze upon Noah.

"Don't worry. And I don't mind—"

Aunt Helen called, "Willow! Willow? Please join us for a minute. I have a campaign question."

Willow snorted. To Noah, she said, "That's a lie. She's going to quiz me about you."

He chuckled. "I knew what I was getting into when I invited you to stay at the Hideaway. Go talk to your mother and your aunt, Willow. I've got the kids."

"You sure?

"I'm sure. We're good."

Willow gave Drew and Emma her best mom look

and told them to behave, then walked to join her mother and aunt, who swept her into a hug. "Honey. Noah Tannehill? Color me impressed. I need all the deets."

"There are no deets," Willow lied. "He has a big house and a separate apartment."

Genevieve and Helen shared a skeptical look, then her mom asked, "And he's come over here now because...?"

"He's a friend, and he's offering me support. Just like the two of you are doing."

"But we're family," Aunt Helen pointed out.

"Friends and family. Like the saying goes, it takes a village." Her phone pinged, and she read the text. The nanny. Willow's stomach made a slow roll. She felt nervous. She felt a little nauseous. She was overwhelmed. "They're here."

Genevieve suggested, "Why don't you ask her to meet on the lodge's front porch? That way you'll have a moment to collect yourself after seeing the boy."

"Good idea." Willow texted the instructions, then glanced up from her phone and over her shoulder to find Noah watching her. Had he sensed her turmoil? Both children had abandoned their fishing poles. Drew babbled on about something while throwing rocks into the lake. Emma clasped Noah's hand and swung it back and forth, back and forth. He held Willow's gaze, nodded, and winked. *You've got this.*

She heard the words as clearly as if he'd spoken them aloud.

A car approached the Raindrop Lodge parking lot and pulled into an empty spot. The driver's-side door opened, and a dark-haired woman who appeared to be in her late twenties climbed out from behind the wheel.

She walked around the back of the car and opened the back passenger-side door, where inside, Willow could see the figure of a child strapped into a car seat.

The dark-haired woman took less than a minute to release the child from the car seat. It felt like an hour.

They couldn't see anything once the woman set the child on his feet. The car door slammed shut with a *thunk*. The front passenger door opened, and the woman removed something from the seat. *Thunk. Beep. Beep.* The door closed and locked.

With a rolling suitcase and diaper bag in one hand and the child in the other, the woman walked toward the front steps of Raindrop Lodge.

Willow got her first good look at the little boy, and her heart stood still. Standing beside her, Genevieve said, "Oh my."

Aunt Helen blew out a soft whistle. "He's Emma without the pigtails."

Willow swallowed hard. "And Emma looks just like her father."

A storm of emotion swept over Willow at that point. *Mom is right. Every time I look at AJ, I'll be reminded that Andy cheated on me.*

It would be so hard to ever love this poor little boy.

Shame washed through Willow. That was so wrong. She was a better person than that. Sins of the father should not be visited upon the child. She didn't accept the idea of generational sin. Not in her head at least.

Apparently, her heart had some work to do.

I'm human, far from perfect. I'll try, but...

Who knows? Maybe the fact that he looked like Emma would make AJ easier to love. Stranger things had happened.

Her mother took hold of Willow's hand and gave it a comforting squeeze. "We've got this."

Together, they walked forward to meet Andy's youngest. Willow wished she had that flask Noah had brought, after all, because her mouth was dry as sand. Her mother called, "Hello! Welcome to Raindrop Lodge."

The woman turned toward them with a smile tinged with relief. "Thank you. I'm Monica Brandt. This is AJ."

Willow opened her mouth, but she couldn't get any words past the sudden lump forming in her throat.

Genevieve continued. "I'm Genevieve Prentice. My sister, Helen, and I—" She made a half turn and gestured toward Aunt Helen. "We own Raindrop Lodge. And this—"

"I'm Willow," she said, finally finding her voice and a smile. "Welcome."

"I'm so glad to finally meet you," Monica said brightly. "Maggie has spoken about you a lot."

"I imagine she has," Willow replied, her tone rueful.

Her mother and Aunt Helen continued to stare at the toddler. Monica smiled uneasily. Eventually, Aunt Helen said, "We're being rude. Excuse us, Monica. It's just that genetics are fascinating."

"Oh." Understanding dawned in the nanny's expression. "Maggie has shown me photographs. AJ looks a lot like his sister."

"Exactly like her," Genevieve said. "I've always thought Emma had her mother's nose, but now..."

Willow stiffened. "She does have my nose."

"Hmm."

Helen stepped forward and said, "Why don't we sit on the back verandah at the lakeside corner? We'll be able to keep an eye on Drew and Emma from there. I'll order drinks and snacks for us. Milk and cookies for the child?"

Monica Brandt said, "I'm sure he'd love that. First, though, where might I find a restroom? I'm about to burst. And AJ could use a diaper change."

Yes, the fumes wafting from Andy's son were unmistakable. Genevieve and Helen looked at Willow, who sighed. "I'll show you."

Could there be a more appropriate beginning?

In the ladies' room, while the nanny disappeared into a stall, Willow lowered the fold-away changing platform from the wall, then squatted down in front of AJ. "My name is Willow. I need to change your diaper."

"I poop."

"Yes, I can tell."

The diaper bag was well organized, and Willow efficiently managed the smelly job. However, she couldn't help but compare her diaper-change wiggle worms to this little guy, who lay mostly still and quiet while Willow worked.

The commode flushed, and the nanny emerged from the stall and walked to one of the sinks. Her gaze met Willow's in the mirror. "Thank you."

"No problem. Happy to help." *With this, anyway.* With the diaper change completed, Willow set the boy on his feet, disposed of the diaper, and washed up.

"Miss Mon, want wub," AJ said, tugging on the nanny's shirt.

Monica gestured to the bag on the counter beside Willow. "He wants his pacifier. It's in the diaper bag."

Willow remembered seeing it. She unzipped the bag and withdrew a pacifier with a stuffed animal attached—

a giraffe. "Emma had one of these," she observed as she handed it to the child.

"They're magic," Monica said as AJ popped the pacifier into his mouth. She took hold of the toddler's suitcase, leaving Willow to take the child's hand. Outside the restroom, Willow turned toward the hallway leading to where they'd meet her mother and aunt.

To her surprise, the nanny didn't follow. Instead, she planted her feet and began speaking in a rush. "AJ is an easygoing kid for the most part, but he's accustomed to a schedule. This last week has been rough on him, with everything that's gone on. I wrote everything down in a journal—his likes and dislikes. I wanted to make this as easy for you as possible."

Warily, Willow said, "Fabulous. Thank you so much."

"I'm leaving now."

Alarm wafted through Willow. "I thought you planned to stay overnight."

"It's been a long trip. Frankly, I've gone above and beyond. He's a sweet boy, but...I didn't sign up for this. He's not my kid. There's an empty seat on the evening flight if I can get back in time. I won't say g-o, because sometimes that makes him cry. Better I just slip away. Good luck."

Before Willow quite knew what had happened, Monica Brandt had disappeared out the front door of Raindrop Lodge.

"Not your kid?" Willow muttered. "You didn't sign up for it?" She glanced away from the doorway to the toddler, who looked so much like her daughter that it left her dazed and confused.

"You're Willow," Andrew John Randall declared.

"Yes, I'm Willow. And you are AJ. C'mon, AJ. Let's

go find..." *Okay, maybe just this once because of the nose crack.* "Nana."

Rather than drag the child's things all around the lodge, she left them at the registration desk. Then, with practiced ease, she lifted AJ, propped him on her hip, and went in search of her mother and aunt.

Chapter Fourteen

GENEVIEVE LICKED A DELICIOUS morsel of chocolate chip cookie from her finger and glanced toward the door. No sign of Willow or the nanny and the toddler returning from the restroom as of yet. "Okay. You ready?"

Helen saluted with her pen. "Ready."

"The jezebel's name was Jenna Elizabeth Randall. She wasn't a native of Nashville. Maggie thinks she was from South Carolina, but it could have been North Carolina."

"Jezebel." Helen snorted. "Did you get any numbers? Driver's license? Social?"

Genevieve scoffed. "No. Maggie doesn't remember numbers any better than I, and she's distracted because of Tom. I'm lucky to have gotten what I did out of her."

"All right. What else do you have?"

"Jenna met Andy at the country club where he golfed. She worked in the pro shop."

"I'll just bet she did," Helen agreed. "You confirmed she died of an aneurysm?"

"That's what Maggie said. She was listed as the emergency number for Jenna's work and daycare. The only number."

"So, she *could* have family somewhere!" Helen declared.

"Maggie says she doesn't."

Helen wagged her finger at her sister. "Well, it's in Maggie's best interests to believe that, isn't it, if she wants to keep little Andy Junior?"

"So, where do we start?" Genevieve tapped her index finger against her lip and thought a moment. "Do we hire a private investigator in Tennessee?"

"I actually have a friend who might be able to help us."

"I thought you might," Genevieve said.

"I gave him a call this morning."

"I thought you might," Genevieve repeated, a grin fluttering on her lips.

"He said to phone ASAP with any further info we could glean."

"Phone him right now. It takes a few minutes to change a dirty diaper."

Helen nodded in agreement and dialed the number. She connected with a man Genevieve surmised was an attorney with whom her sister had previously worked. Helen relayed the little information they knew about AJ Randall and his mother in a short conversation that ended just as Willow arrived with the toddler on her hip. Genevieve wondered aloud. "Where's the nanny?"

"Willow doesn't look happy."

"You think the nanny ditched us already?"

Willow walked up and put the baby in the high chair. "Pour me a double, please."

Helen filled a glass with milk from the pitcher and handed it to Willow. "The nanny scarpered?"

"She's outta here." Willow handed the boy a cookie. He shoved it into his mouth. "He's not her kid. She's done her duty."

All three women stared at AJ. Willow sipped her milk. "Well," Genevieve said. "What now?"

"Chocolate. Chocolate. And more chocolate. For me, anyway. Probably need to watch the kids' sugar intake, or I'll be paying for it later."

"They can have a couple cookies apiece, can't they?" Genevieve, in her guise of Nana, asked.

"Of course. Noah will polish off what's left. He has a sweet tooth."

"Oh?" Helen said. "And you know this how?"

A hint of color stained Willow's cheeks.

Well, isn't that interesting?

"We're friends."

"How friendly of friends?" Helen asked, wagging her eyebrows. "How's his leg injury doing? I haven't noticed him limping of late. Healing coming along? Doesn't interfere with, um, *activities*, I hope?"

"Auntie! I am not discussing my sex life with you and my mother."

"Spoilsport," Helen observed. She winked at Genevieve.

Willow rolled her eyes, and then in a defensive move worthy of a Sunday afternoon on the gridiron, she waved and called, "Drew! Emma! Noah! Come get cookies! They're warm from the oven!"

"Good play, Willow," Helen said. "Good play."

"More, peas. More, peas," AJ said.

"He wants peas?" Helen asked.

"He's saying *please*," Willow clarified as her children came running up the hill, followed by Noah.

Genevieve held her breath as Willow introduced Drew and Emma to AJ. It turned out that the children were more interested in the cookies than in their younger half brother. She was a little shocked when Willow referred to the boy as their "brother," and Emma and Drew didn't bat an eyelash. Noah glanced from AJ to Emma, then back to the little boy again, and said, "Hi, AJ. I'm Noah. Can I have a bite of your cookie?"

"Mine!" the toddler said, turning away and protecting his prize.

"Okay. Okay. I'll get three of my own." He did precisely that.

Willow explained to Noah that the nanny had unexpectedly returned to the airport. Drew shared news about fish, beetles, and ladybugs, while Emma attempted to interrupt with essential facts about butterflies and her suspicion that AJ had a stinky diaper.

"Already?" Willow groaned. She met her mother's gaze and said, "I am so not ready for this."

"I'm ready," Drew piped up. "Can we go see our new house now, Mama? I want to see my new room. Mr. Tannehill says he might have found something in his attic that I can play with."

"He did, did he?" Willow met Noah's gaze, and they shared a smile.

Genevieve met Helen's gaze, and they shared an entire conversation.

Ten minutes later, the group was on their way to Noah's Hideaway, Genevieve and Helen having offered to help with the move-in because they were curious more than because they were needed.

Genevieve rode with Helen on the drive out, and the sisters fleshed out their plans for their upcoming trip, which they'd dubbed the Fangirl Follies. So far, they'd gotten tickets to see Rod Stewart in Vegas, Jason Isbell in Nashville, and Jackson McBride playing a special benefit at his dance hall in Texas. "We're limited by the election timeline," Helen admitted with a sigh. "I'm bummed we won't be able to kick off our trip or close it with a Kenny Chesney concert. But you know, if I were to lose the election, we'd have a lot more latitude."

"You are not going to lose the election. Not with me as your campaign manager."

"Well, I haven't exactly seen you working your fingers to the bone."

Genevieve held up her hand. "I have stitches!"

"Well, it wasn't campaigning for me that caused that. It was your temper."

"You're right. I'm going to dive in tomorrow. You know, I thought about it during my walk this morning. Perhaps I'll discover that campaigning is a passion of mine."

"Uh-huh."

"It could happen. You've actually already given me another idea to try."

"Oh yeah?" Helen glanced away from the road long enough to give her a wide-eyed look. "Spill the beans."

"Not beans. Fish. Do you remember Jack Harrington? He was the banker I went out with a few times about five years or so after David died."

"I do remember Jack. He drove that classic Firebird, didn't he? The yellow one?"

"He did. But he also kept fish. Tropical fish. It was really quite fascinating. He did a lot of research into the kind of fish to group together in his aquariums. Plus, they're fascinating to watch. Mesmerizing."

"Yes, they are. If you're snorkeling in the South Pacific."

"Maybe I want to bring the South Pacific to my living room in December."

Helen shook her head. "I don't see it, but it's your passion. Speaking of passion, did you see the same sparks flying that I did between Willow and Noah?"

"I did."

"Very interesting that she's moving in with him."

Genevieve pursed her lips. "Well, not in the traditional sense of the term."

"We'll see." Helen drummed her fingers on the steering wheel and let a full minute pass before she spoke again. "I saw Zach Throckmorton in the coffee shop today. He said his dad is ornery as ever after his medical scare."

"That's a fair assessment. I went up to the Triple T this morning and fixed breakfast for him. He was in full grumble."

"Well now." Helen shot her sister an appraising look. "Wasn't that neighborly of you? And you with stitches in your hand, too."

"I'm accustomed to playing injured, and yes, I was being neighborly. Gage is my friend. I was worried about him. When we spoke on the phone last night, he spent half the conversation complaining about the changes his doctor wants him to make in his diet. I thought I'd show him that a heart-healthy meal can be delicious."

"It's difficult to make major lifestyle changes after decades of being set in your ways," Helen observed. "Which brings me back to this search of yours. Maybe you should make taking care of Gage Throckmorton your next passion."

"Maybe you should pay attention to your driving, Helen. You just missed the turn." Genevieve allowed the barest hint of a smile to settle on her lips as she added, "I think I'll see how it goes with the tropical fish first."

*

"I'm intrigued," said Noah, eyeing with interest the grocery sack Willow set upon the kitchen counter. "My mother was a wonderful person, but the only kind of mac and cheese she ever made came out of a box. With orange powder."

"Well, I warned you not to expect anything fancy, but homemade mac and cheese is Drew's and Emma's favorite celebration food."

"I don't care about food," Drew declared. "I want to see my room! Can we go see my room, please?"

Willow reached over and clapped one hand across her son's mouth and pointed toward the living room with the other. "Lower your voice, Drew. Remember, Nana is rocking AJ to sleep."

"He's getting close," Helen said, glancing away from her perusal of the bookshelves that lined one wall of the great room and toward the rocking chair where Genevieve tended the toddler.

Noah winked at Drew. "I'll show them their rooms if that's okay with you, Willow."

"Sure. Thanks, Noah." Emma and Drew began rushing toward the staircase. Willow added a warning note to her voice as she called after them. "Quiet feet! Let Mr. Noah go first."

He'd suggested the change to his name to make it easier for the kids, and the Eldridges had enthusiastically agreed. As he led the children up the stairs, Noah was surprisingly nervous, which was stupid. What did it matter if the kids liked the things he'd put out for them? Drew had his own things. Hell, Noah's stuff was old. Nothing used a computer chip to run. And Emma, well, she was female. What made him ever think he knew what a female might want?

"Wow!" Drew stepped into a room that still smelled like paint. "Oh, wow. A telescope. There's a telescope in the window."

"Don't touch the walls," Noah warned. "Paint is still wet."

He'd painted a fantasy galaxy on one wall—stars, planets, and a nebula. He'd gotten a bit carried away, but circles were quick and easy to paint. Once he'd remembered the telescope and all the books about space, well, he figured Drew was just about the right age.

Emma walked up to Noah and pulled on his pants leg. "Do I have a telescope, Mr. Noah?"

"No, sunshine. I have something else for you." Noah's nerves ratcheted up another notch as he led the little girl—Drew wasn't budging from his space—to the room next door.

Already decorated in pink-and-white ruffles and butterflies for Daniel's Maddie, the room now also included a child-sized table and two chairs he'd brought down from the attic. Atop the table sat drawing paper, coloring books, markers, and a brand-new sixty-four-count box of crayons.

This room had a bay window with a built-in window seat, making it the bedroom's centerpiece. He watched Emma's face as she saw what he'd placed there. "It's a house. The most beautiful thing I've ever seen!"

"Let me show you how it works." He crossed the room and after a moment's hesitation, went down on his knees. *Only a twinge of pain. Making progress.* Pleased, he focused his attention on wide-eyed Emma and smiled as he flipped up the latches that allowed the roof and walls to open, revealing the rooms inside. "It's a dollhouse. See? Here's all the furniture. You can move it around any way you like. Here are some dolls. You can make them be Emmas or Drews or mommies."

"Or daddies?"

Noah cleared his throat. "Daddies, too. Here are some clothes in this wardrobe. I made a couple of dogs, too. See?"

"Puppies! Oh, Mr. Noah! You made this dollhouse? All by yourself?"

"I did."

"Do you play with dolls?"

"No." Noah chuckled. "But I heard you do. So I made it for you."

Her eyes went round as the Earth on Drew's bedroom wall. "What? For me? For keeps?"

"For keeps."

"Oh, Mr. Noah, thank you! But why did you do this for me? It's not my birthday, and it's not Christmas, either."

"Well, when you asked me to dance at your uncle Jake's wedding, I was grumpy, and I wasn't very nice to you. I felt bad about that. I wanted to apologize, so I made you a dollhouse."

"That's okay, Mr. Noah." Emma threw her arms around him and hugged him hard. "We all get grumpy sometimes. Mama says I'm her little ray of sunshine. Maybe I'm just your little ray of sunshine, too."

"I guess you are."

"If that's not the sweetest thing I've seen in a month of Sundays," came Helen's voice from behind them.

Noah glanced over his shoulder. All three women were standing in the hallway watching the little tableau in Emma's room. Genevieve must have found the nursery because her arms were empty, her hands clasped over her heart.

Willow looked at him all sort of mushy. "This was for Emma all along?"

Noah shrugged and climbed to his feet. "I guess you found AJ's nursery, Genevieve?"

"I did. Everything is so nice, Noah. This is so generous of you to do."

"Drew can't wait for the sun to go down," Helen added. "You might not get him down for supper, Willow."

"Speaking of supper..." Genevieve linked her arm with her sister's. "Helen and I are going to skip out on that tonight if you don't mind, Willow."

"We are?" Helen looked at her sister in surprise.

"We have some campaign planning to do."

"Oh. Yes. That's right. We do."

"Emma, come give Nana a kiss good-bye," Genevieve said.

The little girl scampered to do so, and in another ten minutes, all the good-byes had been said, and

Willow's mother and aunt departed. "They didn't really want supper," Willow explained as she waved them off. "They just wanted to see your house."

"No problem. So, will you spring the four-legged surprise on them tonight?"

"You know, I think I'll save that for tomorrow. We've had plenty of excitement today already."

After dinner, Noah said his good nights and retreated to his workshop. He played with Marigold and the puppies, grateful that Drew's window faced opposite his puppy play yard. He went to bed that night and went to sleep more at peace with himself than he'd been since his brother died.

He didn't see the Eldridges the following morning, as they went their separate ways early. He spent the better part of the day with Gage fishing his favorite stretches of water on the Triple T. Late that afternoon, he sat at his workbench building a couple of dollhouses for a fire station in western Wyoming when he heard Willow's car drive up.

The knock on his door came less than five minutes later.

"Mr. Noah. Mr. Noah. Are you home? I love my new bedroom. I looked at the moon through the telescope, and it was huge. Mama says you have a surprise for Emma and me. Something we are really going to love! Mr. Noah!"

As expected, the puppies were a hit, although AJ was a bit timid around them. The debate over what to name the dogs dragged on for the better part of a week. Drew finally decided on Thor while Emma went with Anna from *The Avengers* and *Frozen*, respectively.

By the end of April, Noah thought he might need to rename his cabin from the Hideaway to the Come-on-

Inn. It seemed as if people were coming and going all the time. Willow's sister visited for a few nights as she returned from a European trip and prepared to leave again to visit Peru. Willow's newlywed brother and his wife visited, and then the single brother did, too. Noah didn't know whether they'd come to give him the evil eye or check up on Willow now that she had AJ around or, more likely, both, but it kept things lively. Genevieve stopped by frequently as the opening of The Emily theater approached. Helen dropped by almost as often for a campaign coffee klatch.

And they always brought their new pups to visit. Drew had somehow managed to talk his grandmother and great-aunt into each adopting a puppy. Upon learning that Noah was down to one, Gage had decided his Sadie needed a companion, so he took the remaining pup to the Triple T Ranch.

Most evenings, Willow joined Noah for a nightcap on the porch swing, and they shared the events of their days. They hadn't slept together since that first night. Still, the twenty minutes or so of porch time together each evening was almost as intimate. Some days Willow's attitude remained positive. Others, acting as a single mother of three wore her down.

AJ had been with the Eldridges just shy of six weeks the night Willow joined him on the porch carrying not her usual glass of wine but a pitcher of martinis. "That bad?" Noah asked.

"Tom had another stroke. They don't think he's going to make it."

"Well, crap." The kids' grandfather had been doing better. The grandmother had been making noise about bringing AJ back to Texas. "I'm sorry, honey."

"I don't know what I'm going to do, Noah. It's hard taking care of three children all by myself. Yes, I have Little Ducklings, and Mom helps despite her big talk about not babysitting, but it's still all on me. Plus, the kids will bond with him if he stays here much longer. Drew already thinks that sharing a name gives them a special link."

"And you? Have you fallen for him?"

She sighed and sipped her drink. "That's the million-dollar question, isn't it? He's a sweet little guy. He truly is. It's not his fault that his daddy was a jerk. Like the saying goes, it's complicated."

He put his arm around her shoulders, pulled her close, and pressed a kiss against her hair. "Anything I can do to help?"

"You're doing it. You've done so much for us, Noah. Every day. I wish there was something we could do to help you in return."

"You have. You do. You brought sunshine back into my life."

She took hold of his hand and squeezed it. "That's Emma. She's Suzy Sunshine."

It's all of you.

"Which reminds me. Have you started that dollhouse for your niece yet?"

"Willow..." She'd been pressing him about this for a couple of weeks now. Willow thought he needed to pay a visit to Daniel's family. Noah stepped away from her and gave her a gentle, playful swat on the rear. "Don't push."

"Not pushing. Just asking." She returned his swat while giving a cheeky grin.

"I haven't really had time. Gage has me working as

if I have a real job, and your aunt talked me up to the volunteer fire department chief here. They asked me to do a fire flow demonstration this weekend."

"You spend your time on the porch swing with me."

"Not complaining about it," he declared. "At all."

"Speaking of Aunt Helen, has she pestered you yet to sign up for a Christmas-in-July vendor booth?"

"No. Why would I need a vendor booth at the Lake in the Clouds Christmas market?"

"To take orders for your Victorian dollhouses."

"What?"

"Beware. Since Auntie is the chairwoman of this year's event, she wants it to be the best ever. She's looking at it as a campaign event."

Noah laughed. "She's relentless, isn't she?"

Willow shrugged. "You could make a house for your niece and use it as a sample at the market to take orders. It might be a nice little business for you. You could sell them on eBay, too."

Helen isn't the only relentless woman in that family, Noah thought. "Just what I need—another job. It's not enough that I'm whatever I am for Throckmorton Enterprises. Now I'll be an eBay entrepreneur and a fire—" He broke off abruptly.

"And a firefighter. Are you going back to work, Noah?" Then, after a pause, she added, "Back to Denver?"

"I can't fight a fire," he stated flatly.

"You wouldn't pass the physical?"

Mentally, he wasn't fit. He could no sooner go into a burning building than he could fly. He polished off his whiskey, then held his empty glass out to her. "Are you going to share those martinis or what?"

Willow arched a brow in surprise. She knew from past conversations that he ordinarily didn't drink gin. "Of course."

Determined to keep the conversation pointed in a new direction, he asked, "So, are you all ready for the theater-opening gala?"

"I think so. Mom is so excited. Nervous but excited." Concern dimmed her glow a bit as she asked, "How about Gage? Is he feeling all right? Is he going to be okay to come to the party?"

"Yes. He's doing fine. This was a wake-up call for him. He may gripe and grouch, but he's taking his doctor's orders seriously. He's working to unload stress from his life. Apparently, that's been a real issue with him—he's still running all the family businesses himself."

"Yes. Zach told me that's the main reason why he wanted to start his own business. He wanted to make his own decisions. His father wouldn't turn loose of anything."

"Well, he's turning loose now. Though I don't know why he's doing so with me. I'm not family, but he's asking me to help him make decisions that will affect his family. It's damned hard. I'm not a lawyer."

"But you're honest, and he trusts you. He has lawyers on retainer who can do the legal work. Let me share a little insight there. As someone who watched a family business tear a family apart, I think Gage is being pretty smart. If my grandfather had turned over management of his business concerns to his heirs instead of trying to control them from the grave, my family would have avoided a lot of grief."

"I hope you're right."

They sat without speaking for a few minutes, and Noah thought Willow might have relaxed a bit. Her next words proved him wrong. "I have something I need to talk to you about. I've been putting it off."

"That doesn't sound good."

"It's not bad. At least, I hope it's not bad. It's about the house."

"Oh, Willow. Don't worry. Whatever the kids broke can be fixed."

"No. No. It's not that. Well, it's sort of that. Drew did make a hole in the drywall in his room, but it was a small baseball-shaped hole, and I patched it. It's about our finding a permanent place to live."

Noah's stomach sank. "Oh."

"The last thing I want to do is abuse your hospitality and stay too long. The problem I'm having is that nothing suitable has come onto the market. My real estate agent tells me I'm looking for a unicorn."

Good.

"However, she got a call today about a piece of land. It's actually a pretty wonderful piece of land. Not far from here. We could build a house that suits us, but that takes time. Probably more time than you figured when you offered us your house."

"Now, Willow."

"Wait. I don't want you to say anything tonight, okay? I want you to take some time and think this over. Please. It's imperative to me that you are comfortable with this situation. We could always move somewhere else until our house is ready. But it's not simply the construction time. If you'd feel crowded... if it would be weird... I won't do it."

Weird? "What am I missing here?"

"It's that twenty acres of land across the highway. We wouldn't share a fence or a road like you do with the Triple T, but it's still close. Since you and I are...um...um..." She made a circular motion with her hand and sipped her martini.

"Since we're um, um," he repeated with a grin. "You want to define that for me, Ms. Eldridge?"

"Well, that's part of the problem. I'm not exactly sure what we are. We're friends, but are we more than friends?"

"I think so. Don't you?"

"I do, but the label is fuzzy. I know the l-word isn't appropriate."

"I don't know about that," he ventured. "I am your landlord."

She slapped his arm. "Ha ha."

"Do we need a label?"

"I think we need something, Noah. Especially if you're thinking about going back to Denver. It's a little like the situation with AJ. Those three children and I will become a family if we act like one for too long. If you and I sit on the swing and act like lovers each night...um..."

"I think technically we're already lovers."

"But we're not in love. I think I could fall for you, Noah. I could fall hard, and if a serious relationship is off the table for you, I think I would want to know that. Not tonight, but probably sometime soon. By the end of the summer, maybe. Unless you already know it's off the table tonight, and if so, go ahead and tell me. It won't kill me, but I would like your input before I make a decision on the property."

"Fair enough. I'll think about the land, and nothing is off the table tonight. Okay?"

"Okay." She smiled at him. "Good. I'm glad." She drew a deep breath, then exhaled with a sigh. "In that case, I have one more question."

Noah couldn't help but groan. Willow laughed. "No, you'll like this one. At least I hope you'll like this one. One of the moms I've gotten to know at daycare has invited Drew and Emma to spend the night with her kids the night of The Emily gala. Since my kids will be at the Wheeler's house, would you like to come back to my place for an after-party?"

The "hell yes" on his tongue froze. "What about AJ?"

"He's an excellent sleeper. Noise doesn't bother him. He rarely wakes in the middle of the night, and if he does, he's in a very sturdy crib. He can't climb out."

Noah held up his glass in a toast. "Here's to excellent carpenters."

Willow clinked his glass with hers. "Here's to a man of many skills. I can't wait to see what surprise you have for me next."

"I'm a man full of plans, Goldilocks. A man full of plans."

Chapter Fifteen

THE EMILY THEATER OPENED with a film noir gala that kicked off with a showing of *The Maltese Falcon*. Guests wore evening attire, a relatively rare event in Lake in the Clouds, with most women choosing styles that fit the theme. "Face it," Genevieve observed as she, Helen, and Willow watched the arriving guests from the third-floor office. "Nineteen forties fashion was simply the best. Classic and flattering."

"Well, ladies." Helen made a game show hostess sweeping gesture. "All I know is that we look gorgeous."

Genevieve and Helen both wore long gowns, Genevieve in gold and Helen in red. Willow had settled on a cocktail dress in basic black with a fitted bodice and pencil skirt that hit just below her knee. She wore her hair up and a vintage pearl choker.

"Well, you and I aren't too bad for a pair of old broads," Genevieve said to her sister. "On the other hand, Willow could be a star of one of the movies we're showing tonight."

"Because I look dead?" Willow asked.

"You know that's not what I meant. Glamorous. Lana Turner glamorous. Noah is going to swallow his tongue when he gets a look at you."

"Might be lots of tongue swallowing going on tonight," Helen commented. "Once Gage gets a look at you, Vivie."

"Stop that!"

Helen laughed, then continued. "Our favorite grumpy firefighter just arrived. He's wearing a suit. You know, it occurs to me that the next time we need to get involved in a fundraiser, we could do one of those calendars with sexy men. Think of our pool. Noah. Zach. Even Gage. No reason not to represent the sexy seniors. Or how about one of those bachelor auctions. Why—"

"Auntie!" Willow interrupted, laughing. "Stop. Just stop. I'm going downstairs now to meet my date." She picked up her evening bag from the desk, then stopped in front of her mother. "Mom, congratulations. You've done a fabulous job. I'm so proud of and happy for you."

"Thank you, honey. And thank you for all the work you did for tonight. I'm so glad that Gage suggested we use you as our event planner. You're really good at this sort of thing, you know."

"I know." Smiling happily, Willow gave Genevieve a hug, then exited the office.

Genevieve started to say something to her sister, but Helen held up her hand, motioning her to stay quiet. She walked to the door and cracked it just enough to ensure they weren't about to be disturbed. Then she turned the lock and said, "The e-mail arrived just as I left home."

"The DNA test came back?"

"Yes. Just as we expected ever since we saw how closely AJ resembles Emma, the test proves that he is Drew and Emma's half sibling."

Genevieve exhaled a long breath. "Okay, then. Well, we had to do that. So, on to step two?"

"Yes, step two. I'll call the brother in the morning."

"I don't know, Helen. I'm having second thoughts. Maybe we should tell Willow."

"Yes, in step three. We don't know anything certain yet. We have suspicions. We could be wrong. Just like with DNA, let's verify. Then in step three, we bring in Willow with facts and actionable information."

"Okay. You're right. We keep to the plan."

"And in the meantime, let's go downstairs and enjoy the party. It's your night, Genevieve. The theater is beautiful. You and Gage have done a fabulous job. So go downstairs and accept the adulation you so richly deserve. Maybe flirt a little with that handsome rancher."

"Oh, Helen."

"Oh, Helen, what? You're not dead yet, Gen. Of course, the man just had a heart attack. Maybe you should hold off on that for a while and let him recover. Until your birthday, at least."

"Don't mention the b-word," Genevieve said and led the way downstairs. "And Gage didn't have a heart attack. It was angina."

Her eyes twinkling, Helen gave a shrug. "So you have no excuse. Go flirt."

Genevieve gave her sister a look that equated to

flipping the bird without having to use the vulgar gesture. Helen laughed, slipped her arm through Genevieve's, and the Bennett sisters descended the stairs.

The theater restoration had turned out even better than Genevieve had hoped when she and Gage began the project. While the bones of the old theater had stood firm, time had taken its toll on the interior. Gage had worked with his construction specialist son on the structural renovations. Genevieve had been starting basically from scratch on the interior. She'd spent hours upon hours researching theaters built during the same period as the one in Lake in the Clouds. With a vision in mind, she'd worked with her own professional—Jake's new wife, Tess—to develop a design she loved.

It turned out splendidly. The murals painted in the theater were re-creations of historic travel postcards advertising some of Colorado's natural wonders—the Royal Gorge, Pikes Peak, and Garden of the Gods. She'd used forest green velvet for the curtains and the upholstery on the seats, and lots of gold braid and tassels.

The one place the color scheme differed was the founder's box, which sported a portrait of the theater's namesake and was done in the late Emily Throckmorton's favorite color of rose accented with gold.

Tonight, all three of Gage's children were attending the gala. Gage's recent health scare had been a wake-up call, not just for him but for his children, too. Life was short. It was a crime to waste a day of it.

Blast it, Helen. You had to bring my birthday up tonight of all nights, didn't you?

"Genevieve!" called a guest who greeted her as she began to mingle. "The Emily is fabulous. Congratulations."

"Thank you."

"I can't believe what you've done here," said another guest. "This was such a great idea. I've always loved this old building, but I never would have thought to try to save it."

Genevieve was talking to one of Lake in the Cloud's librarians when she felt a touch on her elbow. She glanced up to see Gage. He remained by her side and they worked the room as partners. It was lovely. People said such nice things; the praise was constant and genuine. Genevieve basked in the glow of it and in the approval she saw in Gage's eyes. All too soon, it was time for the first movie to start. She joined Gage on the stage at his request because he wanted to say a few words.

"You look lovely tonight, Genevieve," the rancher said to her as they waited for their guests to take their seats and the room to quiet down.

"Thank you. You're looking fine yourself. How are you feeling?"

"Good. Good. Getting tired of answering that question, though."

"Any time an ambulance has been involved, and you live in a small town, I imagine you can expect it."

"I know. I know."

At that point, Willow walked onto the stage carrying a wireless microphone. "I suggest you start talking, Gage. In my experience, that's the only thing that will shut them up."

Willow flipped the switch on and handed the microphone to him. He tapped it twice, then said, "Good evening, everyone. I want to thank you all for coming. I'd like to take just a couple minutes here before the movie starts to mention two incredible women."

First, he made a brief but heartfelt and beautiful tribute to his late wife that brought tears to Genevieve's eyes. Emily and Gage Throckmorton had shared a deep and abiding love, the kind of love she liked to think she and David would have enjoyed had he not been prematurely taken from her.

Gage finished by saying, "I can't begin to explain how much it means to me to be able to honor the memory of my movie-buff wife by dedicating The Emily to her here with you all tonight. Which brings me to the second incredible woman I need to mention. My family and I owe this joyous moment tonight to Genevieve Prentice." He looked at Genevieve and gave her an affectionate wink.

Genevieve's heart gave a little flutter. Working with him on this project had been a pleasure. He was a good man. Not an easy man, but one who was true to his word. She respected him and admired him. And, if she was being honest, she was attracted to him, too.

But that was not for tonight. Tonight was about Emily Throckmorton and The Emily.

Gage continued. "Genevieve had the vision to suggest this project as a way to honor my late wife, and the drive and fortitude to make it happen. While officially, Genevieve and I were partners in the project, the truth is that she was the boss, and I did what she told me to do. Those who know me know that's not how I ordinarily do business."

"No kidding," called his son Zach.

"Quiet in the peanut gallery," Gage fired back with a grin. "Genevieve put an enormous amount of time, effort, and thought into this restoration, and it shows, don't you agree?"

Pleasure at the praise washed through Genevieve as the crowd clapped enthusiastically.

Gage raised his voice to be heard over the noise. "So my hat's off, my glass is lifted, and I offer my most sincere thanks to my theater partner and friend, Genevieve Prentice. She is a special woman."

And Gage Throckmorton is a special man, Genevieve thought as she gazed up at his ruggedly handsome face.

"Now, for all our guests here tonight, welcome to The Emily. Make yourselves comfortable and enjoy the movies."

Gage escorted Genevieve off the stage to applause. She said, "Gage, I don't know what to say. Thank you so much. That was so sweet."

"I meant every word I said. You gave your all for this project, and it couldn't have turned out better. You're a treasure, Genevieve. It was a lucky day for Lake in the Clouds when you decided to make our little town your home."

Genevieve took her seat to watch the movie. *The Maltese Falcon* was one of her favorites, and she'd never seen it on a big screen before. She expected to be swept up in the story by Humphrey Bogart playing Sam Spade, private investigator. Instead, her mind wandered. Her mood plunged.

It was done. This project was over. What was she going to do now? What did she have that mattered?

The fish? Oh, she'd enjoyed the research. She'd decided to start small. After spending a lot of time investigating equipment, she'd purchased a small "practice" tank and the required accessories. Then, she'd bought her first two fish to see how long she could keep them alive.

So far, the fish experiment was going swimmingly. She found watching the tank relaxing, and when the children visited, they loved it. Genevieve was just about ready to dive into deeper water, so to speak.

And yet, as much as she enjoyed the activity, she wasn't passionate about it. She'd been passionate about restoring The Emily, but that job was finished. Maybe she could find another building to restore, but that idea didn't excite her, either. Been there, done that. What next?

This find-her-passion thing wasn't working out quite the way she had hoped.

At intermission, Genevieve made the rounds, thanking the guests for coming and receiving their adulations. It should have all been wonderful, but every "way to go" and "great job" scraped like sharpened fingernails against her heart. Needing a few moments of escape, she stepped outside into the cool springtime night air.

A half dozen groups of people congregated under the lights of the theater marquee. Genevieve heard the chimes inside the theater signal the end of intermission, and people began to return inside.

Genevieve remained where she was, standing just beyond the reach of the lights in the shadows. She wrapped her arms around herself and shivered, wishing she had brought her jacket. Despite having lived in the Colorado Rockies for a year and a half, Genevieve had yet to shake all of her Texan ways. Dressing for cool nights didn't come second nature to her yet.

"Here," came a familiar deep voice. Noah slipped his suit coat around Genevieve's shoulders, and warmth chased away the chill. "You and your daughter are just alike. Willow forgets her jacket more often than not."

"Thank you. I should probably refuse it, but I won't. I'm an old lady, and my skin is thin."

"Oh, don't give me that 'old' business. I know you recently signed up for a rock-climbing class at Lake in the Clouds Outdoors. That's not the action of an old woman."

"It is if she's crazy, too. I don't know what got into me, thinking that rock-climbing might become a passion of mine. Just thinking about doing it scares me, never mind actually tackling the activity. I let the guys at the outfitters shop talk me into it. They don't understand that I'm a chicken."

"Balderdash."

Genevieve jerked a glance up at him in surprise. "You sound like my sister."

"Where do you think I got the word? I love using it. It's much more satisfying to say than *bullshit*, which is the appropriate but impolite response to your statement. Willow has talked to me about her family. You have more courage than most people I know, Genevieve."

Danged if her throat didn't close and her eyes filled with tears at that. What was wrong with her tonight? Ten years ago, she could call herself hormonal. Well, that ship had sailed, hadn't it? At least she was in the shadows, so Noah wasn't witnessing her inexplicable meltdown. Again. All she needed was for him to tell Willow that her mother was crying on the street corner, and her daughter would launch into mothering mode.

She went on the offensive, hoping to deflect. "That's sweet of you to say. So tell me, why is it that I discover you lolling about in the shadows at every party I throw? You're missing the movie. Intermission is over."

"I know. I'm heading back inside. I just needed to

stretch this leg of mine for a bit. It's better if I don't sit for too long."

"Oh, of course. You've made such huge strides in your recovery I forget you were injured. My bad."

"Not at all. That's the way I want it. Besides, it allowed me to play the gentleman and loan you my jacket. Are you ready to go in?"

"No, not yet." Genevieve started to shrug out of his jacket, but he stopped her. "Keep it."

A figure moved out from the deeper shadows. Gage Throckmorton said, "Give Noah back his jacket, Genevieve. I'll give you mine."

"How long have you been standing there?" Genevieve asked as she handed Noah his coat. "Why aren't you inside watching the movie?"

Gage didn't immediately respond but waited as Noah gave a little salute before disappearing into The Emily. Gage slipped his jacket around Genevieve's shoulders. It smelled of the woodsy aftershave he wore, and she couldn't stop herself from inhaling a deep breath.

"My kids got to talking about their mother at intermission, and I got a little emotional. Needed a few minutes to myself. So I sneaked out the back door and walked up on you and Noah chatting. Didn't mean to eavesdrop, but I couldn't exactly help it. So, what's this passion talk all about?"

Genevieve didn't want to talk about it. She was feeling emotional herself. So she couldn't understand why she opened her mouth and spilled her guts to Gage. She explained about her conversation with Noah the night of Jake's wedding and her hunt for something—a grand passion—to give the winter of her life meaning.

"Winter of your life? Hell, Genevieve. You must

have been going to church over at First Community and listening to Reverend Mays's sermons. He's the most depressing minister I've ever known."

"I'm not explaining it properly. Gage, I'm lost. Not all that long ago, I made huge changes in my life. I re-invented myself. I breathed new life into my life. But here it is less than two years later, and I'm...well...back in the same old rut. I need something to live for. I need a reason to keep getting out of bed every morning. For the majority of my lifetime, that reason has been my children. That life is over. It's dead. I had the funeral for it."

"Most spectacularly, I'm told." Gage referred to the family dinner to which Genevieve had summoned her children for an old-fashioned tongue-lashing.

Genevieve continued. "I recognized that my old life was gone, and I attempted to move forward, to build something new here in Lake in the Clouds. I've tried to create a life with value and purpose, a life I'm passionate about. I've continued the charitable work I did in Texas, and that's good, but it's not filling the hole. I have my sister, thank God, but she has her own life and probably a new job soon because I cannot imagine she won't win this election. All I have are colorful fish and naked-man drawings and impending lessons on how to climb up the side of a mountain when there's a perfectly good road leading to the top. Why can't I find something to do with my life that I'm as passionate about? Something that fulfills me the way raising my family did?"

"Hell, Genevieve, I understand the struggle. Truly, I do, especially with my recent history. But, I have to ask, why now? Why are you looking for the meaning of life tonight of all nights? Why aren't you inside enjoying the fruits of your labors?"

Defensive, she fired back. "Why aren't you?"

"I'm mourning my wife."

"I'm mourning my life."

"Why?"

"Because it has no purpose. My life's work is completed, but I'm still looking for something to feel passionate about. That sounds whiny, I know, and I hate myself for it. I tell myself that Grandma Moses didn't start painting in earnest until she was seventy-seven, so I still have some time. Nevertheless, I think my chances of discovering some new interest just waiting to bloom into passion this late in life are slim to none. I blew up my old life, thinking that would solve everything. It did for a while because I had much to do to settle in. Now, I can find activities. I can find projects. But what do they matter? What does it all mean? Shouldn't my life *mean* something? Shouldn't I have a purposeful life? Shouldn't it be important? Raising my children was important. What does a person do when her life's work has ended, but she's still on this side of the grass?"

"You stay busy, that's what," Gage said. "Listen, I like Noah. He's a good guy, sharp as a tack, and quick to do the right thing. I get the point he was trying to make, but I think that makes a mountain out of a molehill. You don't need a grand passion that will consume you for the rest of your years to make your life rewarding, Genevieve. What you need is to fill your life with people you love, like, or admire. And have something to keep yourself busy for the next three to six months. After that, see where life takes you. Maybe it's fish. Maybe it is mountain climbing. Maybe it's throwing pots."

"Pottery? I hadn't thought of pottery."

"Well, put it on your list. Look, I understand your

fear. I feel it, too. You're right that life should be more than just waiting to die. I'll tell you this. Whoever coined the term *golden years* and made us think our retirement years were supposed to be easy sold us a bill of goods. Getting old isn't for sissies. It's an aching back and painful knees and sagging skin and bumps where bumps aren't supposed to be. It is loss. People you love pass on, and life gets smaller. You don't have the means or the energy to try to grow it again because, like you said, what's the point?"

"Are you trying to cheer me up, Gage?" she asked, her tone droll. "If so, you're doing a poor job."

"Give me a minute to make my point. I'm an old man. Takes me longer than it used to, but I can still get the job done. You are on the right path, Genevieve. You are actively growing your life."

He took her hands in his and gave them a squeeze. "It's not the things you do in life that make life rewarding; it's the people you do life with that make it your...oh hell. What is that term the young ones use?"

"Best life," Genevieve said. "Oh, I like that bit of philosophy, Gage."

"Well, good. Remember it. So, are you ready to go back inside? See what Sam Spade is up to at the moment?"

"I am."

⚓

The sound of a child's cries pulled Willow from the oblivion of sleep. AJ. She groaned into her pillow. She didn't want to open her eyes, much less pull herself from bed and take care of the toddler. She was exhausted, the good kind of exhausted from a night of being thoroughly loved, but nevertheless, bone-deep tired.

"Mama. Mama. Mama."

I am not your mama.

Immediately, guilt washed through her. AJ was just a little boy. An innocent little boy who missed his mama. He must be so confused.

"Mama. Mama. Mama. Mama."

Willow opened her eyes. The sun was barely up. Groaning, she started to rise, but a large, warm hand settled on her naked hip and stilled her. Noah's deep, masculine voice rumbled, "No. You sleep. I've got him."

Memories of the night skittered through her, and she couldn't help but smile. No wonder she was so tired. Nevertheless, AJ wasn't Noah's responsibility. This was her job. "I can't let you—"

"I have this. Go back to sleep, beautiful." He kissed her hair, released her, and rolled from the bed.

Willow vaguely heard the bang of his belt buckle against the wood floor and the rustle of denim as he pulled on his jeans. She should have argued with him. She would have done so, except exhaustion won out, and she drifted back to sleep.

When she awoke again, the bedroom was awash in sunlight. Willow sat up, stretched, inhaled a deep breath, and froze. "Bacon."

It was a shock to her system.

"He babysits and cooks breakfast?" she murmured aloud as she climbed from the bed. To say nothing about the great sex.

She really should find a way to keep him.

Following a quick shower and feeling like a new

woman, Willow searched for Noah. The house was empty, but she found a note on the kitchen counter. "Breakfast is in the warming oven. AJ and I have taken the dogs for a walk."

Noah, three dogs, and a toddler? Just where did he keep his Superman cape?

A few minutes later, with a mug of freshly brewed coffee in one hand and a breakfast burrito in the other, she went outside in search of Noah. She saw him walking across the wildflower-carpeted meadow leading down toward the spring. He pulled AJ in the red collapsible wagon used to haul things around his place. Marigold, Thor, and Anna scampered ahead of him, behind him, and ahead of him again.

As she watched them, Willow's breathing grew shallow. Andy's son and Noah. There, right there, was her past and, if not her future, certainly the possibility of one.

Suddenly, she was so afraid. She hadn't lied to Noah when she told him she had a wall around her heart. What was she doing hanging out with Superman? He leaps tall buildings in a single bound. If he wanted her heart, her little old wall wouldn't stop him.

Then what? Was she ready to finally move on from Andy's death? Was she brave enough to give her heart again? To Noah. And, maybe, to AJ.

She needed an answer. Soon. She'd thought she would have a couple of months to find her courage, but now that seemed like a stretch. Were the decisions being made for her? Were they out of her control? Had she already torn down the walls and left her heart unprotected?

All Noah needed to do was take it. It was right there

waiting for him if he wanted it. If he wanted it—there was the rub. Just because he babysat, cooked breakfast, and made sweet love to her didn't mean that the heart exchange was a two-way street. Just because she might be ready to plant permanent roots in his kitchen and his bedroom didn't mean he wasn't ready with a hoe to weed her out.

Oh, she was afraid. What should she do about her feelings for Noah? And what in the world was she going to do about AJ?

Hurrying back inside, she located her phone and called her mother.

Genevieve didn't answer. She'd had a late night with The Emily gala. Though ordinarily an early riser, she might still be asleep. Or out on her walk. Who knows—maybe she had scheduled a mountaintop sunrise yoga class, and now she was well into her day? She could be on her way for a day of shopping in Eternity Springs.

So, Willow sent a text: MOM, I NEED YOU.

Genevieve Prentice had changed over the past year and a half. She didn't automatically drop everything and rush to her children's aid like in days past. But Willow had used all caps.

Her mother would call.

Chapter Sixteen

AS NOAH WATCHED AJ'S new game of picking wildflowers and tossing them into the wagon, a sense of certainty washed through him. If he wasn't extra careful here, he would make a huge mistake. He never should have invited Willow and her crew into his Hideaway.

He scooped up a handful of stones and threw them down toward the creek, one by one. AJ wasn't even her kid, and he'd stolen a little piece of Noah's heart. Drew had owned a chunk of it since February. And Emma? All it took was one soulful gaze from those big green eyes of hers, and Noah had been a goner. He hadn't realized it, of course, because said heart had been encased in ice at the time.

The ice was a necessity in the aftermath of the fire that had crushed him. Crushed his leg, his heart, his soul. But then, he'd met the Eldridges, and they'd cracked the ice.

It would be so incredibly easy to surrender to his

need to love Willow and make a family with her and her children. He could stay here in Lake in the Clouds, work for Gage in the morning, and come home to Willow in the afternoon.

He could tell her he was all in.

But that would be a lie. He'd never fixed what was broken inside him, and until he did that there was no all in. Not for Willow, and not for himself.

He couldn't ignore the truth any longer—he'd been living only half a life. And Willow and her children deserved a whole life.

Hell, he deserved it, too.

Noah needed to climb back on the damned horse. Physically, his body was ready. Mentally? The time had come to face his demons and conquer them.

He needed to go back on the job. He needed to *do* the job. He needed to face his fears and fight a fire. If he didn't do this, he'd always doubt himself. If Noah didn't defeat his demons, he'd never be able to promise those precious children with confidence and authority that he could—he *would*—protect them.

He had to leave Willow to be worthy of Willow. Wasn't that a kick in the junk?

If—and it was a big if—Willow was even willing to go along with the plan. She may want nothing to do with a man who fought fires for a living. He couldn't blame her. After all, her precious children had already lost one father. Why risk putting them through that tragedy a second time? Sure, life wasn't guaranteed. A man could get run over by a car or an aggressive elk in his own mountain meadow, but firefighting was inherently a risky occupation.

When he told Willow he intended to return to Denver

and his job until he felt whole again, she might tell him to take a permanent hike. Who knows how long the process might take? And it sure as hell wouldn't be fair to ask her to pick up and move her family to Denver after she'd put so much effort into making a life for herself and her children here.

But if she was willing to wait for him, maybe someday he could return to Lake in the Clouds, marry Willow, and be a father to her children. Maybe have another kid or two. They could start a new life together. Maybe change the name of the cabin from the Hideaway to something forward-looking. Something bold and bright and full of life.

"Getting ahead of yourself, Tannehill," he muttered. Way the hell ahead.

First, he needed to talk to her. She'd said she was a big believer in communication. She wanted him to be truthful about his thoughts. He needed to tell her exactly what was in his heart.

He should begin with those three particular words. *I love you.*

It was a risk. Willow could hand his heart right back to him. But hell, if he was ready to face a wall of flames, shouldn't he be prepared for this?

Noah sighed and scooped up one of the puppies who'd come within reach. Thor. Cute little guy. He'd miss Thor and Anna when he left, but at least he'd have Marigold. The apartment he'd never gotten around to moving out of in Denver allowed one dog per renter.

So, was he doing this? Was he going to leave his sanctuary? His hideaway? Was he ready? Which was riskier to his psyche—staying here or going home?

Was Denver still home?

He heard the sound of a car engine and turned in surprise. "Genevieve?" he murmured. Why would she be dropping by this early on a Saturday morning? Especially since she'd had a late night herself.

"Oh hell." This couldn't be good news. Not Drew or Emma. *Please, God*, he prayed. He scooped AJ up into his arms and began to run. He arrived at the house after the SUV stopped in his circular drive but before Genevieve and her sister emerged from the vehicle.

Willow stood on his front porch, holding a cup of coffee and smiling at him.

Smiling. Not an emergency. Noah relaxed.

"Thanks for breakfast," Willow said. "Thanks times ten for the extra sleep."

She held out her arms for AJ, and Noah handed the toddler over, saying, "You're welcome. Is everything okay? The kids are okay?"

"Yes. I called the Wheelers first thing. The boys are still asleep, and the girls are playing dress-up. They're all going to story time at the library at two, and I'm picking them up at three."

"Okay." Noah and Willow both called hellos to their visitors. Noah studied Willow's mother and aunt as they climbed the front steps. Genevieve looked stressed when she returned the greeting, he realized. Carrying a tote bag, Helen appeared defiant. *That's interesting.*

They all went inside, the dogs darting in first, headed for the mudroom and their food and water bowls. Willow set AJ down, and the toddler headed for the toy box in the corner of the great room. He struggled to pull a bucket of giant building blocks from the box. Willow helped him, then once he was occupied, Genevieve asked her daughter to come sit down next to her.

"I know you wanted to talk to me, honey, but I beg your patience. I need to share some news and, frankly, I have a feeling that whatever you wanted to speak to me about is liable to be impacted by this."

"Okay," Willow began and if Noah wasn't mistaken, her cheeks began to flush. "That sounds ominous."

"Don't be concerned," Helen said. "Just lead me to the bar. I brought necessary supplies."

Noah stood beside the front door, uncertain whether he should stay or make himself scarce. "Can I help you with anything, Helen? If not, I'll head out to the workshop to give you folks some privacy."

"No. Please stay. We could use some ice and glasses. A shot glass if you have one. I'm making Bloody Marys."

Noah darted a glance toward Willow and saw that her wary gaze shifted between her mother and aunt. Okay, then. He sauntered to the wet bar at the far end of the great room, where he removed three tall glasses from a cabinet and filled them with ice from the ice maker. Next, he set out a shot glass, a cocktail shaker, and a spoon. Then, he sat on the floor beside AJ and began building the boy a tower with the blocks.

"Don't you want a drink, Noah?" Helen called.

"No thanks. I'm good."

Genevieve met her daughter's gaze and began. "I have some information you need to know. About AJ."

"Oh, Mom," Willow said with a groan. "What did you do?"

"Well, as you recall, when you first told me about AJ and Maggie's request, I wasn't thrilled."

"How does one forget that little trip to the ER?" Willow replied dryly.

"You know better than anyone how strong maternal instincts are. How we are moved toward protectiveness."

Helen said, "Oh, Genevieve, don't drag this out. Cut to the chase, why don't you?"

"Oh, all right. Maggie lost her son. She has a vested interest in keeping her grandson in her life. But we only had her word that AJ's mother had no other family, so we thought it imperative to establish that as truth. So, we investigated AJ's mother."

Having made drinks for the three women, Helen plopped a celery stick into each glass. "We did a DNA test, too. That's why this has taken so long."

Some of the color drained from Willow's face. She slumped down onto one of the bar stools. "Why? He looks just like Emma. He's Andy's."

"Yes." Helen placed a drink in front of Willow. "He and your children are half siblings."

Willow stared at her aunt for a long moment. "Wait a minute. You sampled my children's DNA without my permission?"

"It's a cheek swab. The test was done anonymously, so there's no record."

Genevieve said, "We needed to be sure before we took the next step."

"What next step?" Willow asked.

Genevieve and Helen met each other's gazes. Genevieve said, "Helen's research uncovered that Jenna Randall had an older brother. Damon Randall is in the service, stationed overseas at Ramstein Air Base in Germany. He and Jenna have been out of touch for some time."

"*Semi-estranged* is the term his wife used," Helen

said. "I called and spoke to her last night after the party. I was going to call this morning, but with the time difference..." She shrugged. "I didn't see the sense in waiting. We had a lovely call, considering the news I shared."

"You told her about AJ?"

"Let me finish, Willow," Helen said. "Damon's wife's name is Lisa, and she and Damon have been married for six years. They're due to rotate home to Edwards Air Force Base in California in August. They don't have any children, and I sensed that was a disappointment. Anyway, Damon had not been notified of his sister's death."

"Oh." Willow covered her mouth with her hand and grimaced at the thought. "So, you told her?"

"I did."

"Oh, Auntie. That's a horrible thing to have to do."

Ice clinked in Genevieve's drink as she gave the celery stick a twirl. She met Willow's gaze and said, "Auntie did not inform Lisa Randall that Jenna had a child."

"I wanted to," Helen said, "but your mother insisted that the decision is up to you."

"Oh wow. Wow."

Helen carried her drink around the bar and stood behind her sister. Willow couldn't see it from where she sat, but Noah had the angle. He watched Helen give Genevieve's arm a squeeze of encouragement before she turned a smile on him. "Would you be a dear, Noah, and join me outside? I'd like you to check my tire pressure. I swear my left rear tire feels to be running a little low on air."

"Sure, Helen." He fitted a blue block on top of a yellow, then handed the stack to AJ. "Why don't you build a house for Emma now, hot rod? She'll be home soon."

"Emmie!"

Noah rose and followed Helen outside. As always, the dogs came with him, and as he shut the door behind them, he said, "Am I correct that your tire doesn't need tending?"

"Smart man. Yes, my tires are fine. Those two need a little privacy."

"Should I grab the kid and bring him and the dogs outside?"

"No, let him stay. He's part of this, isn't he? Part of it, but not all of it. Why don't you show me this workshop of yours? Drew talks about it all the time. He tells me he's helping you build dollhouses to burn."

"We're building. We're not going to do the burning part. He's having trouble getting that part of it through his head."

Noah led Willow's aunt into his workshop, and he switched on the lights. Immediately, Helen's gaze went to the yellow-and-white dollhouse on his workbench. "It's like Emma's."

"I've made a few changes in the design, but yes, it'll be a lot like Emma's."

Helen studied the dollhouse before turning an admiring look his way. "And what lucky little girl will receive this when it's finished?"

Noah hesitated. "I may use it as a sample. Willow is encouraging me to take orders for them at the Christmas-in-July festival."

"That's a fabulous idea!"

"I'm not so sure."

"Why not?"

He picked up a paintbrush and tapped it against the table. "I'm healthy enough to return to work. I'm a fire-fighter, Helen. I think it's time I go home to Denver."

She remained silent for a long moment before saying, "I see. Well, I know that will disappoint many people around here, but you have to do what you think best. Have you told Willow you're leaving yet?"

"No. I'm still not sure of my schedule. I have a long way to go before I'm sturdy enough on my feet to be confident to carry anyone else along with me. I need to try to do this, Helen. Nothing says I'll be successful."

She snorted. "You'll do just fine. That said, if you will allow this old woman to give you a piece of advice? Whatever you do, communicate and be honest with Willow. She needs that. She deserves that."

"Yes, ma'am. I hear you. You have my word."

"Do you hate me?" Genevieve asked.

"I don't hate you," Willow responded. "I wish you'd said something to me before doing the DNA test, but I can understand why you did it the way you did."

"Will you tell him?"

"That's an easy one. I will, and I'll do it without hesitation or a smidgen of guilt. It won't be due to any ill will I may harbor toward AJ. It will be because two years ago, my brothers were estranged. If not for you and me and Brooke and Auntie, Lucas and Jake wouldn't have known a thing about the circumstances of the other's life."

Genevieve grimaced. "I have PTSD remembering that."

"I know, Mom. I also know without a doubt that in similar circumstances, both Jake and Lucas would each want to know that he was an uncle."

"Oh, Willow." Genevieve sat back in her chair. "You are so right. I never even considered that point. I can't believe I didn't think of it."

"It's the PTSD," Willow said, waving her point away. "How did Auntie leave it? Are the Randalls expecting another call from her?"

"Yes. Helen told Lisa Randall that after she verified the information she was given, someone would contact her with more information about Jenna Randall's estate. We figured if you didn't want to say anything about AJ, we'd send a generic box of something."

"You two are sneaky."

"You know your aunt."

"Oh, you hold your own with her, Mama."

"Thank you, dear. So, we're good? You're okay with my buttinskiness?"

"I want honesty. Truth. Zero secrets. I'm done with secrets, Mom. I know I've been the villain in this regard, so I have no room to complain. As far as I'm concerned, we're good."

"Excellent. So, since that's out of the way, why did you send up the bat signal this morning?"

"Stop it. That was the mama bear signal." Willow gave her mother a quick summary of the thought process that had led to her cry for help. "I don't know how this news about AJ changes anything. I don't know what to do."

"I think you know. I think you're ready. The fact that you sent up the bat signal for me tells me you are."

"What if I scare him off?"

"Then he's not the man I think he is. Better to know that now than before you invest any more of your heart."

"Mama! Mama! Look!" AJ held up a tower of blocks.

Out of the blue, tears stung Willow's eyes. "That's good, AJ."

Seeing Willow's reaction, Genevieve reached over and wrapped her daughter in a hug. "It's okay, honey."

"No, it's not. I'm not AJ's mama."

"I know, baby."

"He's a sweet little boy, but half of the time when he calls me Mama, the image of that woman in bed with my husband flashes through my mind. I think of how Andy lied to me, cheated on me, and betrayed Drew and Emma. How he betrayed our family. I cringe to say this, but I resent AJ, Mom. He's just a little boy, and I resent him. It makes me feel like pond scum."

Genevieve chastised her with a look. "Let's see. Pond scum who has taken that little boy into her home and cared for him and shown him affection."

"But—"

"No *but*s. I've seen you, Willow. Maybe it hasn't always been easy, but you've been sweet with that boy. I've admired you for it. You are not pond scum. You're human."

"But—"

"No *but*s! Tell me there are not moments you don't resent Drew and Emma."

"What? I never!"

"Oh, Willow." Genevieve's expression turned scornful. "Be honest. You're a single mom. Minor feelings of resentment are a normal emotion of parenting. They happen to everyone."

They do? Willow took a sip of her Bloody Mary.

"I certainly had my share. Still do. Why do you think I sold my house and gave away my dishes and ran away to Colorado?"

Willow giggled a little. Genevieve grinned. "Honey, remember what I always told you and your siblings growing up? Life is hard..."

They spoke simultaneously. "Wear a helmet."

Genevieve continued. "When you're single parenting, the hard part is amplified. One parent is hard, two is harder, and three—no matter who donated the DNA—is...well...I won't use *hardest*, because what do I use for number four? But you get my drift. When you have those minor feelings of resentment, don't ignore them or they might grow into major ones. That's when you can develop a legitimate problem. Instead, recognize that it's time for a little self-care. It's time to get a baby-sitter or take a bubble bath or sit down and read a good book. A novel. Something just for fun, not because you need to learn something."

Willow set down her drink and, impulsively, gave her mother a hug. "I love you, Mom. Thank you. You don't know how badly I needed to hear this."

"It'll be okay if his uncle wants to take him," Genevieve said.

"I'll be relieved. Does that make me a horrible person? Maggie will be devastated."

"Willow Anne! For once and for all, you are not responsible for Maggie Eldridge's feelings! Maybe if she hadn't been so selfish, she'd have raised a son who wasn't a cheating asshole."

"Asshole!" AJ repeated, having wandered unnoticed over to Willow's side sometime in the past few moments.

Genevieve clapped her hands over her mouth and said, "Oops. Sorry."

"Watch it, Mom." Willow gave her mother a mock scowl as she lifted AJ into her lap. "You don't want me to have to wash your mouth out with soap. Drew will tell you that is not a pleasant experience."

"Yes, he will, won't he? Speaking of Drew, why don't you let me pick him and Emma up at the library? I'll take AJ home with me now, too. It'll give you and Noah a little more private time since Helen and I interrupted your morning. Time for a little more"—she waggled her brows—"self-care."

Willow clapped her hand against her chest. "Whoa. Did you just offer to babysit AJ? Did the poles just reverse? Did the sun rise in the west and set in the east?"

"I did. You see, I've recently been reminded of a great big fat life truth. Living a purposeful life isn't just about finding balance or being passionate. The things you do in life don't make life rewarding; it's the people you do life with that make it your best life. I need to do life with AJ, who is Drew and Emma's little brother. Face it—I am a world champion nana. So why in the world wouldn't I spread that love around?"

"Why in the world?" Willow repeated. This time, the tears that spilled from her eyes were happy ones.

Chapter Seventeen

AFTER A SHORT DEBATE over car seat logistics, Willow handed her mother her keys and loaded AJ and the diaper bag into the backseat. She waved off her visitors, then turned to Noah. "It's a little after seven in Germany. I'd like to get this phone call off my plate before I do anything else. Would you mind holding my hand?"

"I'll be happy to. You want to sit on the swing?"

"I would love that."

The call proved infinitely easier than Willow anticipated. Between Aunt Helen's call and hers, Damon Randall had done some investigating of his own. He had discovered that his sister had a child when she died. He had already hired a private investigator in Tennessee to track the baby's whereabouts.

He and his wife very much wanted custody of AJ.

Willow explained about Maggie and her own connection to AJ's father. Damon Randall was quiet for a moment, then said, "I think my sister's son is a lucky boy to have you in his life."

Their hands clasped, Noah lifted her hand to his and kissed it.

After discussing various possibilities, Willow and Damon Randall settled on a plan whereby he and his wife would visit Lake in the Clouds at their first opportunity, which would be ten days from now. Emma's birthday, Willow noted. They would spend some time with AJ and formulate a plan for moving forward once the Randalls returned to the States permanently in August, including how to break the news to Maggie.

Damon was prepared to fight for custody if necessary. Willow had every hope that it could be avoided. He promised that he'd make sure that AJ remained close to Maggie and to his half siblings, too, if that's what Willow wanted. He sounded sincere, and she hoped that she could believe him. From what her aunt Helen had discovered about Damon Randall, Willow thought that she could.

When the call ended, Willow exhaled deeply, and the weight of Granite Mountain lifted from her shoulders. "Well, this has been quite the morning."

"No lie, that."

"You know what I'd like to do?"

He brushed a curl off her shoulder. "Tell me."

"It's a lovely day. I haven't been up to Inspiration Point since last summer. I'd like to go up there and hike to the waterfall. And you've never taken me for a ride on that motorcycle you have in the garage."

"Well, Willow Eldridge. I didn't know you're a biker chick."

"Stick around, Noah Tannehill," she teased. "You might be surprised by what you learn." Had she not happened to be watching him closely, she would have missed the shadow that flashed across his eyes.

She started to call him on it then and there, but like she'd said, it had been quite a day. She wanted the motorcycle ride and the hike. She wanted to exercise and commune with nature and forget about her worries and concerns. She needed to do some self-care that her mother had advised her about earlier. Whatever Noah had on his mind could keep.

His bike was a Honda cruiser. It had been his primary mode of transportation in Denver until he'd seen one too many accidents as a first responder. At that point, he'd brought it to the cabin. He gave her a thorough safety lecture and carefully fitted her with an extra helmet he had in his garage before they headed out.

The drive up to Inspiration Point was one switch-back after another, filled with magnificent views. While the helmet prevented her from experiencing the wind in her hair, she counted the opportunity to snuggle close against the driver's back as a fair trade-off. Shortly before they were to reach the official entrance to In-spiration Point, he veered off of the road and entered a gate marked with the Triple T Ranch logo. This was a route Willow had never traveled.

They rode on a dirt-packed trail for another five minutes before he parked at the edge of an aspen grove. He grabbed a pack from the bike's storage compartment saying, "Gage showed me this route to the falls. It's an easy hike and the views are spectacular."

Noah wasn't kidding. By the time they settled down for their picnic lunch near where the waterfall roared and sunlight painted rainbows in the mist, she was relaxed and filled with peace.

However, Noah looked like he was sitting on an ant-hill. Willow thought she might have figured out why.

Might as well get this over with, too. Can't deal with a problem until you know what you're facing.

Waiting until he'd finished his sandwich, she asked, "So, when are you going back to work?"

Noah coughed and choked. He grabbed his water bottle and took a long sip. "Okay. Wow. Well, I only decided that this morning."

Her stomach sank. But at least now she knew for sure.

"I don't want you to think I've been keeping it from you. Hasn't been much of an opportunity to discuss it. I wanted to explain, especially after last night. Last night meant something to me."

"It meant something to me, too, Noah." And she wouldn't cry because he was leaving. She simply would not cry.

Noah continued. "I don't want you to think I'm a love-'em-and-leave-'em type of guy, because that's the last thing I want to do. I don't want to leave you."

Her eyes widened in a combination of surprise and uncertainty. *What does he mean by that?*

He held up his hand. "No, I'm not asking you to move with me. That wouldn't be fair to you or the kids." His mouth twisted ruefully, and he added, "Or your mom."

"She would kill us both."

"No. Your aunt would get me first." He rose to his feet and held his hand out to her. "Walk with me?"

Willow let him pull her up. As they walked hand in hand, he guided her to a spot away from the waterfall where the sound rushed rather than roared. He lifted her onto a boulder, so they were at eye level. She could smell the fragrance of spruce trees in the air.

Noah stared solemnly into her eyes. "Willow, here's the deal. I'm in this. I have serious feelings for you. I have never been in love before, and we haven't known each other for that long, so I hesitate to leap out and throw down a declaration of love. I've never said those words to a woman."

Her heart had warmed and begun to pound. He looked so serious, so sincere, almost scared. *That's okay. Let this scare him. He should be afraid. Love is too important to treat lightly.*

So, she clarified. "Not even to your high school girlfriends?"

"Nope. Look, I know for a fact that I've never felt anything like this for another woman. I know I would love for you and Drew and Emma to be my family. But I can't ask that of you. Not now. Not yet. Because I have this other thing I need to deal with before I can commit myself to you. I have to know who I am before I can offer myself."

"Okay."

"I have to go back to work." He shoved his fingers through his hair. "I have to face the fire first."

"You have to face your demons."

"You understand," he said, relief in his tone.

"Probably not, because I'm not a firefighter. I'll listen if you want to tell me."

He spoke for twenty minutes, almost without a break. He told her why he made the decision that he'd made and why he wouldn't ask anything of her. A few times during the telling, Willow teared up. Could this day get any more emotional?

Yet she understood his reasoning. She supported his rationale. More than anything, she appreciated his honesty.

When he finally ran out of words, she leaned over and kissed him. "Thank you for telling me."

"You're cool with it?"

"Honestly, I don't know how I feel. Like I said earlier, it's been quite a day. So back to my original question. When do you plan to leave?"

"I don't know. I could go tomorrow, or I could wait a month. I could stay the summer. I could leave now and return for the Christmas-in-July event and the election-night party in August. I'm definitely going to be here for your mother's birthday. That's a party I don't want to miss. But I'll be honest—I worry that if I stay much longer, I'll never leave. In the long run, that wouldn't be good."

"Stay for Emma's birthday and then go," she suggested. "It's ten days from now. You'd be here to meet Damon Randall that way, and I would appreciate that. Plus, Emma would be sad if you missed her big day."

"Yeah." He filled his lungs with air, then blew out a heavy breath. "You ready to hike back to the bike?"

"Almost. There's something I want to say first. Noah, I have been in love before. I do know what love is. You go to Denver, and you face your demons, and then you come back to me and mine. I love you. We love you. When you are ready, you come back to the Hideaway, and we will welcome you home. We will be your home."

⊱⊰

The morning of Emma's birthday dawned bright with a cloudless blue sky, although afternoon thunderstorms were forecasted. Rain wouldn't spoil the fun, because

Willow had booked a party room at Cloudy Day Fun Time, the indoor amusement park in downtown Lake in the Clouds.

A former variety store on the town square, Cloudy Day was birthday-party central for the twelve-and-under crowd in Lake in the Clouds. It had bounce houses, indoor zip lines, and ball pits for the little ones. If kids didn't wear themselves out during the two-hour playtime before moving to the party room for the cake and presents, they weren't trying.

Noah thought it was a good choice. The distraction was necessary for the Eldridge kids. They'd taken the news that AJ would be leaving at the end of the summer with his uncle Damon, whom they'd met over Zoom, relatively well. But they weren't at all happy to learn that Noah planned to leave Lake in the Clouds tomorrow. He was scheduled to return to work the following Monday at his old station in Denver.

He couldn't say he was any happier than Drew and Emma.

He honestly didn't know if he could do the job.

His situation wasn't unique. Protocols existed for easing firefighters back into the usual rotation on a timeline they could successfully manage. It may take him a week. It may take him a year. Maybe he'd never have the strength to curb his monsters.

No way to know until he tried.

Wanting to spend some quality time with Willow's children before he left town, Noah had invited the birthday girl and Drew to a breakfast picnic, after which they'd go fishing at their favorite spot beside the creek. He'd consulted with Willow and chose Froot Loops for the menu.

He tried not to be too disappointed that Emma seemed more excited about the breakfast cereal than the new furniture he'd made for her dollhouse. However, when he brought out the barn he'd made to expand her dollhouse footprint along with the horses he'd carved, everything changed.

"I love them! Thank you, Mr. Noah!" She threw her arms around Noah's neck and hugged him hard. "I'm gonna miss you so much. I don't want you to move back to Denver."

"Me, either," said Drew with a mouth full of cereal. He swallowed, wiped his mouth with the collar of his T-shirt, and added, "I know you need to be a hero, but why can't you be a hero here in Lake in the Clouds? You're already a hero here."

"He's right." Emma gazed up at Noah and declared, "You're *my* hero."

Drew's eyes flashed with stubbornness. "No, he's mine! He saved me the day I got lost in the woods, and I thought I found Santa's workshop."

"Well, he saved me that time I heard a monster in my closet," Emma fired back, folding her arms. "He searched everything and chased it away so that I could go to sleep! So he's my hero, too!"

"Okay, but what about the time..."

While Drew and Emma squabbled, Noah played with Marigold and the puppies who had crashed the party. He could have told the kids to stop their bickering, but frankly, he liked hearing about his superhero status.

Eventually though, Drew made Emma cry, so Noah sent the boy back to the house for a ten-minute party time-out. Then he distracted Emma from her tears by offering to play horses with her.

The boy was back out exactly ten minutes later with a peace offering for his sister—a plan to build a corral fence for her horses using Popsicle sticks and glue. Emma was delighted by the idea. The three of them then discussed other items they could add to her growing dollhouse estate while they, along with the dogs, hiked through the forest to the fishing spot on the creek. Noah had stashed their fishing supplies there first thing this morning.

Unfortunately, the fish weren't cooperating, and soon the children abandoned their poles to hunt for rocks the appropriate size and shape for skipping. Noah sat with his back against a tree, watching them play, idly scratching Thor behind the ears while Marigold and Anna dozed at his feet. Noah's mood was bittersweet. He'd enjoyed this morning. He was going to miss Drew and Emma badly.

Wonder if he could talk Willow into bringing them to Denver for a visit? It'd be fun to show them around the firehouse. He'd run the idea by her before he left.

Noah gave Drew permission to wade into a shallow section of the creek to fetch a perfect skipping stone that he'd spied. The boy sat and removed his shoes, while Emma abandoned rock hunting in favor of picking up pine cones. Just as Drew prepared to step into the water, Noah noticed Marigold's head come up and her ears go forward. She'd alerted on something.

Immediately, so did Noah.

Something was wrong. Noah didn't know what. He didn't know how he knew it. He simply knew that he knew it. He rolled to his feet. "C'mon, kids. We need to go back to the house."

"Why?" Drew asked, a whine in his voice.

Emma's bottom lip trembled. "Is my party over already?"

"We can come back. I just want to check on your mom."

At that, the children shared a worried look. Drew reached for a shoe, and Marigold whined and took off. Noah muttered a curse beneath his breath. He scooped Emma into his arms and began to run, calling over his shoulder, "Drew. With me. Now!"

"Okay. Okay. Okay."

They had picnicked a good hundred yards away from the house. Noah had been a kicker rather than a wide receiver, so sprinting for the goal wasn't his forte—especially not on a leg held together with pins and rods. Nevertheless, he ran as if the hounds of hell were chasing him. Or, more accurately, redemption's gates stood ahead of him, drifting shut.

Standing at her kitchen counter, Willow poured a second cup of coffee and thought of her day ahead: introduce AJ to his aunt and uncle at ten, Emma's party at noon, sign the contract for the land across the street at four, then one last family dinner for Noah before he headed to Denver. Good lord. She was exhausted just thinking about it. Exhausted and, if she were being honest, a little sad.

They were all feeling a little melancholy about his departure, and she was glad her children got to spend this last special morning with Noah. They loved him. And, she knew, he loved them too. Just like she knew Noah had to go to Denver. He'd go, and he'd fight his fires. He'd do what he needed to, and then he'd return to her. She believed that. She had to believe that.

She moved into the living room and took out a wooden puzzle to occupy AJ while she turned her attention to assembling party bags. Willow enjoyed this particular activity. She and Emma had spent some good mother-daughter time choosing the trinkets and games to put inside the bags. Then they'd spent more time decorating the bags. Emma felt a little bad about not being here to make the final preparations, but Willow had assured her that the time spent with Noah was important, too.

With the favor bags ready to go, Willow had placed them in a plastic tote containing other party supplies and was mentally reviewing her schedule when AJ asked, "Mama. Play with me?"

She'd given up on any attempt to correct him about calling her Mama. Glancing at her watch, she decided she had twenty minutes to spare. "What do you want to play?"

"Cars."

"Sure. I'll play cars with you." They had a simple Hot Wheels track and about a dozen cars that had provided many hours of fun for both of her children. She sat down on the floor in the great room and helped him set up the racetrack. Soon, die-cast cars began to fly.

She and AJ had been playing for about ten minutes when Willow heard an ungodly crash outside. *What the heck?* She made her way to the living room window, expecting to see a tree fallen in the yard. She hoped it hadn't caused any damage. That was the last thing Noah needed to worry about before he left.

A glance outside didn't reveal anything amiss, when

she heard another sound—this time more like a crackling pop—and she couldn't begin to guess what it could be. A lightning strike? But the sky was cloudless and brilliantly blue as far as the eye could see. Yet something made the hair on the back of her neck prickle. She moved away from the window and picked up AJ, saying, "Let's go check on your brother and sister."

Closer to the front door than the back, she opened it. *Was that smoke? Oh God. That's smoke. Where's it coming from?*

Even as she asked the question, she knew. The workshop.

Still carrying AJ, she dashed around the side of the house.

Her first sight of the workshop stopped her cold. The building was totally engulfed. Walls. Roof. *Oh God. What do I do?* Even as she tried to form a plan, a boom sounded. A window exploded outward.

"What do I do?" She tried to think. Fire flow. What had Noah taught them about fire flow? He'd taught Drew! Drew would know. Thank heavens Drew was with Noah. Surely he'd still be with Noah. Drew had a tendency to go off on his own, but he'd stick by Noah's side. Wouldn't he? The boy was obsessed with Noah's workshop, but he wouldn't have sneaked in there today. Not today.

"Drew!" Willow called as she rounded the corner of the workshop, her prayerful gaze searching the window and the space beneath it. Nothing. Even as terror gripped her, she suddenly knew she was no longer alone. She turned around. Noah. Noah, with Emma in his arms and Marigold at his feet, running hard.

Drew wasn't with them.

Willow's heart dropped and despair rose within her. She extended her arm toward the burning building and cried, "Where's Drew? Why isn't he with you? Where is my baby?"

And suddenly, Noah was there by her side, wrapping his arms around her. "He's okay, love. He's with me. He's right behind me. He's okay."

Afraid she hadn't heard him right, she repeated, "He's okay? He's not hurt? He's not burned?"

Noah shook his head. "He'll be right here. He took his shoes off to go wading, so he had to put them back on. I didn't wait for him, but I heard him following us."

"Oh. Oh, thank God. Thank God." Just then, she heard her son's little voice calling from the forest, "Mama! Mama! Mama!"

Her knees went weak, and she started to sink to the ground. Noah caught her. "C'mon, love. We need to scoot back a bit."

Noah moved the group to a spot he considered safe and summoned Lake in the Cloud's volunteer fire department with a 911 call. He was still on the phone when Drew skidded to a stop next to Willow, his eyes round with worry. "Oh, this is horrible. Nobody was inside, were they? Nobody was hurt or killed?"

"No, thank God," Willow assured him.

Drew clapped both hands on top of his head. "It's still a terrible thing, though, right?"

Willow heard a note in his voice that put her on alert. This was the boy who survived the auto accident that killed his father. This was the boy who flipped out when he believed he'd watched a campmate drown last summer. Her son was fragile. He loved that workshop. Santa's workshop. She needed to be careful with him.

He'd come so far. She didn't want to trip him back into a cycle of broken bones and stitches.

"Yes, honey, it is a terrible thing, but it's a blessing because no one was hurt."

Having finished his call, Noah said, "That's right, buddy. Nothing is lost that can't be replaced. That's a good thing."

"But it's still a bad thing. A terrible thing. Right? Your apartment burned up! Your tools burned up! All our dollhouses are toast! That's awful!" He all but screamed the final word. "*Right?*"

"It's awful, yes, but—"

"Thank goodness!" Drew exclaimed. "I've been waiting and waiting and waiting."

"For a fire?" Noah asked, his confusion evident.

"For a bad thing. I've been so scared. Bad things always come in threes. Daddy died and Grampy is really sick and this is a terrible thing, so it's number three. But nobody got killed or hurt! And you can build a new workshop that's even better because you're a great builder, Mr. Noah. So this is the best bad thing that could happen. Everything is good now. Right? I can quit worrying!"

"You've been worrying," Willow repeated softly.

"Yes! But also, I was anxious for the good things. Because after you're finished with the bad things that come in threes, you have good things that come in threes. Now we'll have three good things. Right, Noah?"

"Sounds good to me." Noah met Willow's gaze, and he gave her a look she couldn't quite read.

The fire trucks and ambulance arrived at that point, followed quickly by Helen and then her mother. Gage showed up not long after Willow's family. Noah

explained to all that, based on the evidence he could
see, he believed the source of the fire was electrical in
nature. "I think the investigators will find the fire sim-
mered in the north wall for a while and traveled through
the wall before breaking through to the attic. It could
have been a short. It could have been a faulty outlet. I
had the electrician out two weeks ago to replace some
old wiring. Could have been he got some bad parts."

Ten o'clock rolled around while things were still
in chaos. Willow liked Damon and Lisa Randall right
from the first. Luckily, AJ did, too, and he was happy to
go off with them to the public park with plans to meet
at Cloudy Day Fun Time at noon for Emma's party.

Helen, God bless her, put herself in charge of the
dogs, loading them all up and taking them over to
Raindrop Lodge for the day. Drew was fascinated by
all the activities of the firefighters. Speaking to Noah,
Gage said, "I know that you could give him more
professional answers to his questions, but it appears
his mother needs your attention more than Drew. Why
don't you let me watch him watch the firefighters? You
see to your lady."

"Excellent idea," Genevieve agreed. "Why don't I
oversee Emma's bath and help her get ready for the
party?"

Willow wasn't prepared to argue with any of them.
Her mother and daughter disappeared upstairs, leaving Willow and Noah alone. "How about some swing
time?" he asked, taking her hand. He led her around to
the front of the house, facing away from the remnants
of his workshop.

They no sooner settled on the porch than the rain
arrived earlier than forecast. "There's a blessing," Noah

said. He draped his arm around her shoulder and pulled her tight against him.

"If only it had come two hours earlier."

He shook his head. "I wouldn't change a thing, Willow."

She drew back and questioned his sanity with a look. He grinned boyishly, and his eyes began to dance. "What?" she asked. "Are you going to score some insurance bonanza from a total loss of your barndo?"

"I'm hoping...planning...to score something a lot more valuable. Three good things. Emma." He leaned in and gave Willow a quick kiss. "Drew." Another quick kiss. "And you."

This kiss wasn't quick at all.

When he finally pulled away, Willow's head was spinning, and her heart was thudding so hard she feared it might explode from her chest like the window had from the fire.

Fire.

"What about Denver?"

"I'm not going."

"Because the workshop burned?"

"Yes."

"I don't understand. You didn't fight that fire. You didn't go into the burning building."

"You're right. I didn't. But I could have. I saw the structure on fire before I saw you. Before I saw AJ. I knew that I could go in. That's all I needed. I know that if I need to, I can. Drew was right. This fire was the best bad thing that ever happened. I love you, Willow Eldridge. I love your children. Will you marry me and let me stay home?"

Tears welled in her eyes and spilled down her cheeks.

"We'll have to change the name of the place. The Tannehill family won't be hiding away from anything or anyone."

"Good point. How do you feel about the Love Shack?" At her response, he added, "Do you want your eyes to get stuck in the back of your head, Willow? I would have thought your mother would have warned you about that."

Then, he kissed her so completely that Willow forgot what else she intended to say.

Except for yes.

Epilogue

GENEVIEVE PRENTICE THOUGHT IT hilariously appropriate that she turned sixty the day after Thanksgiving.

She'd planned her party with meticulous care. She'd invited her children months in advance and gave them special dispensation to miss a family Christmas if they'd all gather for Thanksgiving in Colorado and stay for a little birthday event on Friday. Yesterday had been nice, with dinner hosted by Willow and Noah.

Noah's brother's wife and niece had come from Denver for the day, which had been lovely. Little Maddie had gone wild over Emma's dollhouse, and Genevieve doubted Noah would be able to hold out until Christmas to give Maddie the one he'd made for her. They'd even had a video call with Maggie, AJ, and the Randalls from their home in California. Genevieve had been so pleased to see that Damon was a man of his word and kept Maggie involved in her grandson's life, especially since she mourned the loss of Tom, who'd passed away in September.

But Thanksgiving was over, and today was Genevieve's birthday. She had a surprise party to throw.

She couldn't wait.

At precisely 10 a.m., she dialed her sister's number. They had plans to go to Eternity Springs for lunch and an afternoon of shopping before returning for Genevieve's "little party" that evening. "Are you ready? I'm leaving my house now."

"Are you sure you don't want me to drive? It is your birthday, after all."

"Oh, I'm sure."

"All right. I'll just need you to make one little stop on the way if you don't mind."

Ah-ha! I knew it. "Oh? Where do you need to stop?"

"At Raindrop. I left my purse in the office there yesterday."

Sure you did. "Of course. No problem. No problem at all."

Genevieve had figured out pretty quickly that her family wasn't leaving her "little birthday event" plans alone. They were surprising her. The way she saw it, she was free to surprise them in turn. *Turnabout is fair play, kiddos.*

Wasn't it too much fun to see it playing out just like she had expected?

Her sister was all smiles when she climbed into Genevieve's car in front of Mountain Vista Retirement Community. "Happy birthday, little sister."

"Thank you, Madam Mayor."

"Has a nice ring, doesn't it?" Helen said, preening as she buckled her seat belt.

"It surely does. You're doing a great job, Helen. Only three months in and look at what you've accomplished." Genevieve checked her rearview mirror before pulling into traffic. "Rumor has it there's been a flurry of resignations at city hall."

"Yes. All relatives of the former mayor."

"Excellent news. I've also noticed some new stop signs around town."

"Six new ones installed within the Lake in the Clouds city limits this month." Helen waved at a neighbor out walking her dog, then took a moment to study her sister. "You look lovely today, Genevieve. I must admit I expected you to be down in the dumps because you've been dreading this birthday so much. But you're positively glowing."

"It's my new face cream. I have a sample in my purse. Remind me to give it to you."

Helen searched around the seat between her and Genevieve. "I'll get it now before we forget."

"You can't. Can you believe this? I forgot my purse, too! I left it at Willow's yesterday. We'll have to drop by and pick it up now on our way out of town."

"Oh. Well, maybe we should go to Raindrop first."

"No, we shouldn't. That would be completely out of our way."

Helen frowned. "But what if Willow isn't home? I'm sure I heard her say they were getting up early and going somewhere today."

Genevieve waved away the protest. "I have a key. Besides, I'm pretty sure I left it on the porch."

"Oh. Well, okay. That's all right, I guess."

"Yes, it is." Genevieve bit the inside of her mouth to keep her grin from spreading too wide.

They hashed over Thanksgiving dinner during the drive, with the consensus being that Noah made a nice, flaky piecrust and Willow had their mother's bread dressing down to a T. Next, talk turned to Christmas shopping status and Helen confessed to a first. "I only have two gifts left to buy."

"What? Today is Black Friday and you're almost done? Who are you and what have you done with my sister?"

Helen grinned. "It's all my new city manager's fault. We made a bet to see who could finish first."

"Nicole Vandersall is amazing," Genevieve observed. "She's a good hire."

"I know. Lake in the Clouds is in good hands with her. My own workload is a fraction of what it was when she came on board six weeks ago. I'm well on my way to being a figurehead mayor."

Genevieve frowned. "Does that bother you?"

Helen shook her head. "No, not at all. I ran for mayor because I wanted to fix things, not because I wanted a job."

"That sounds about right," Genevieve replied, unable to keep the smile off her lips as she turned onto the road that led to Willow's home—once one passed the Triple T Ranch property. Not that they would pass the Triple T Ranch property today. This was their destination.

Helen's eyes widened as she spied the hot-air balloon tethered to the ground in the middle of Gage Throckmorton's pasture. "Look at that, Genevieve. Isn't that part of Gage's ranch? What's he doing with a balloon on his property today?"

"Why, I do believe it *is* part of Gage's ranch." Genevieve slowed as she approached the open gate and turned into the pasture. "Let's see, why don't we?"

"Oh, Genevieve. We don't have time."

"Sure we do. The sands of my hourglass are just dribbling."

Helen sighed. "Have you been watching soap operas again?"

Genevieve drove her vehicle up close to the balloon, the envelope a swirl in a palette of blue, purple, teal, peach, and pink. "Isn't it pretty?"

"Your favorite colors."

"I know." Genevieve parked and shut off the engine. She got out of the SUV, removed a tote from her back-seat, and handed it to Helen as she exited the vehicle. "These are your boots. And a warmer jacket. You'll want to slip them on."

"What? What! What is this, Genevieve?"

"It's my birthday. So we're going up, up, and away."

"No, we're not! You said you'd never go up in a hot-air 'death trap.' You're afraid!"

"A little, yes. But I've spent thirty years listening to you tell me how wonderful it is, and I'm ready to try it."

"But...but...but."

"I trust you, and I trust our pilot. Helen, let me introduce you to Mark. I met him when I was in New Mexico. He works with the Albuquerque festival every year."

Helen gave a little laugh. "I can't believe this. You're right. I've been trying to talk you into doing this with me forever." A cloud crossed her face and she asked, "How long will this ride last?"

She's worried we'll be late to the surprise party. It took great effort for Genevieve not to giggle with glee. "Not that long. We're just going around the mountain.

Or, over it. I'm not sure which is the correct term. I know we need to get to Raindrop to, um, pick up your purse."

Helen shot her a sharp look. "You know."

"I've been around the block, Helen. Sixty times."

"Who let the cat out of the bag?"

Genevieve waved the question off. "Change your shoes, sister, and let's get this party started."

She was a little nervous, but when she'd decided to make an entrance—in a manner of speaking—she knew she needed to listen to her guiding word for the year and muffle her fears. The experience turned out to be as glorious as her sister had promised. It took Genevieve about five minutes to relax, and after that, she allowed the giddiness she was feeling to catch hold.

When they rose above the mountain and rounded a curve, and Raindrop Lodge, snuggled up against Mirror Lake, came into view below, Genevieve knew that the time had come to spring the birthday surprise upon her sister.

"So, Helen, I need your assistance. Call one of my kids and tell them the surprise party has moved outdoors. I want them and everyone you invited to the party to congregate in front of the lodge."

"You're ruining the surprise, Genevieve," Helen warned.

"Well, about that. Here's the deal. I appreciate the effort you and my children put into this party. I will point out that I specifically told you all I didn't want a big party, and I told you exactly what I did want."

"Yes, but you had to know we'd want to do more."

"I did. And I love you for it. Now, call one of my kids."

Jake answered on the second ring. Helen relayed the

instructions and disconnected the call as he began to ask questions. She said to Genevieve, "You can answer to them."

"Or not." Genevieve smiled at Mark, the pilot, and said, "We're ready when you are, Mark."

He saluted her and said, "Yes, ma'am."

They descended as they approached Raindrop. Genevieve could see a crowd begin to congregate outside. It was now or never. "So, Helen. A wise man told me recently that it's not the things you do in life that make it rewarding, but the people you do life with that make it your best life. I figure if you can do rewarding things with the people that count the most, it's a win all around. That's why Wednesday night, when the kids all came to my place for pizza, was so special. It's why yesterday meant so much. It's why today, on this birthday of all birthdays, I want to spend it with you."

"Aw, honey. That's sweet."

"Actually, not so sweet."

"Aw, honey, now I'm worried."

"It's my birthday, and I'm kidnapping you."

"I know. You took me on a hot-air balloon ride when I was supposed to be taking you to your surprise party."

"See, about that. It's *my* surprise party." She beamed a grin at her sister. "I'm taking you to Iceland."

"What?" Helen screeched like a barn owl.

"We've always wanted to see the aurora borealis. Nothing is guaranteed, of course. But Iceland is our best shot."

"The northern lights? Excuse me? I did not have booze in my coffee this morning. You have lost your effing mind. This sounds like something *I* would do!"

"I know. Isn't it great? See that helicopter over there? It's Gage's. It's going to fly us to the airport."

"The hell it is!"

Genevieve bent and picked up a large red duffel bag waiting in the basket. She handed it to Helen, then picked up the green duffel. "Would you help with this? When Mark gives the word, we're dropping them. Each package has a little parachute. It should open on its own. Right, Mark?"

"Yes, ma'am."

"Wait a minute. Wait just one minute. What is this?"

"Birthday presents. Everybody gets a present. My kids each get special ones. They're labeled."

"Who do you think you are? Oprah?"

Genevieve laughed. "Actually, that's almost true." She fished her phone from her pocket and navigated to the photos. She handed her phone to her sister, saying, "Everybody gets a car!"

Gaping, Helen looked from her sister to the phone. Seeing the first photo, she gasped. "Oh, honey." She scrolled to the second photo and then to the third. "Who did these? Did you do these?"

"I did. They're a birthday love letter to my family." Genevieve's voice rang with pride. "Those drawing classes were worth the money."

"David and his classic Mustang. You captured him perfectly. And his car! The kids will be over the moon." She looked up in horror. "You're throwing these out of a balloon?"

"They're packaged for it." She paused a moment, then asked, "You will go to Iceland with me, won't you?"

"Oh, Genevieve. I want to go, but how can I? Last year, I'd have gone in a heartbeat. But now I'm the mayor! I can't just up and take a vacation out of the blue. I made a commitment. What will people say?"

"They'll say that you've done more in three months than that last bozo did in three years. They'll say that your city manager has Lake in the Clouds running smoothly. They'll say that your sister anticipated your objections and dealt with them so that you could leave town with a clear conscience."

Helen narrowed her eyes. "What did you do?"

Genevieve offered her sister a self-satisfied smile. "In addition to filling Nicole Vandersall in on the plan and enlisting her help to free up your calendar, I arranged for a celebrity mayor pro tempore to cover for you until we return."

"A celebrity mayor! Who...?"

"Celeste Blessing from Eternity Springs."

"Oh," Helen said reverently. Everyone in Colorado knew Celeste Blessing from Eternity Springs. Nobody could do the job better. "But I don't have my passport. I'd need to pack a bag."

Genevieve proudly lifted her chin. "I have that covered. Remember yesterday when I ran to the store for more butter?"

"I do. It took you forever."

"Well, I didn't go to the store. I went to your place, used my key, and packed everything you'll need."

A note of admiration in her tone, Helen said, "Sneaky."

Genevieve recognized her due with a nod, then grasped her sister's hand and gave it a squeeze. "Come with me, Helen. Let's go find the northern lights. Let's live this life hard."

The balloon drifted lower. Gathered in front of

Raindrop Lodge, Genevieve's children began to laugh and wave upon identifying the occupants of the hot-air balloon's basket. Helen snorted a laugh. "You're really going to ditch your own sixtieth birthday party?"

"Surprise!" Genevieve replied. "I'm getting away. That's what I do."

Helen's gaze was warm as she met her sister's and said, "In that case, I guess I'll have to tag along."

"Excellent. I knew I could count on you."

Helen smirked as her gaze drifted over the friends and family gathered below. "You know, Genevieve, after all of this, I can't wait to see what you do for your seventieth."

"I understand it's the new fifty. Is it time to toss our gifts now, Mark?"

"Give it about ten more seconds."

They counted down like schoolgirls, and then the packages began to rain. Below, her family's reactions included surprise, delight, and joy, which shifted to confusion as the balloon started to rise.

Jake, her eldest, called, "Mom? Where are you going?"

"Iceland!"

Simultaneously, her four children shouted, "Iceland!"

Lucas added, "You can't go to Iceland!"

"Sure I can," Genevieve called back. "It's my birthday, and I'll fly if I want to."

Helen shook her head. "You're so lame, sister."

But as they approached their landing zone and spied Gage Throckmorton casually leaning against his helicopter with his arms crossed, waiting for Genevieve, Helen said, "Never mind. I take it back."

Acknowledgments

Every time I finish a book, I marvel at how lucky I am to make a living telling stories. It's the best job in the world, and I am so grateful to the team of people who make it possible.

First, my thanks to my family. My husband is my rock. He's supported me in this endeavor for more years than I care to count. He is and always has been my hero. To my children, their spouses, and my grandchildren, I love you all. Thank you for your love, your support, the happy pill photos you send when work keeps me home instead of out on Play Days, and learning to roll with my deadline craziness. I know it's not easy. Bless you all!

I must also thank my sister. She is truly the Best Sister in the World. She holds my hand, helps me plot, always answers my calls, and never fails to provide a room at the inn when I'm in need. And she gave me a wonderful niece who is all-in on Lake in the Clouds and my source for all things firefighting. Thank you, sweets! You were such a help to me with this book!

I also need to thank my dearest friend, Mary Dickerson. From those early days a million years ago at NRH Library till now, you have always been there to help whenever I need it. I truly could not write my books without you.

I also want to thank my publishing team. To my agents, Christina Hogrebe and Meg Ruley with Jane Rotrosen Agency, thank you for your help with everything Emily March. To Amy Pierpont, editor-in-chief of Forever/Forever Yours, Grand Central Publishing, thanks for your fabulous editorial insight and for your support of all things Lake in the Clouds. Thank you once again to Junessa Viloria for helping make my work the best it can be. Also, a huge thanks for the hard work and effort from everyone at Grand Central, including assistant editor Sam Brody, publicity and marketing director Estelle Hallick, publicist Allie Rosenthal, production editor Luria Rittenberg, and copyeditor Kristin Nappier. It's a pleasure to work with you all.

Finally, a great big shout-out to my readers. I am so very blessed to have you in my corner. Thank you for taking this journey with me. What a ride it continues to be. Here's to keeping our balance!

Reading Group Guide

QUESTIONS FOR DISCUSSION

1. In *Balancing Act*, Genevieve struggles with the fact that her sixtieth birthday was coming up. Have you ever experienced a milestone that intimidated you? What was it?

2. Noah and Willow both carry wounds from losses in their pasts. What do their experiences have in common?

3. Which character did you relate to most strongly? Why?

4. When Noah's workshop caught fire, he realized that he could overcome his fears and decided not to return to his firefighting job in Denver. If he had returned to Denver, do you think his relationship with Willow would have had the same outcome? How do you think their relationship would be different?

5. After the fire, Drew is happy because he believes bad things come in threes, and the fire would be the last event in a series of three bad circumstances. Do you believe that good and bad things come in threes? Why or why not?

6. Helen and Genevieve had a trip to the South Pacific planned before Tess and Jake's wedding. Genevieve decided to skip the trip to help her kids but is jealous when Helen returns with fabulous

stories from her trip. Do you think that Genevieve should have stuck to their original plan or do you think she made the right choice to stay home?

7. Willow is faced with a difficult situation when Andy's parents are no longer able to take care of Andy's son AJ. What are your thoughts on Willow being asked to take in and care for the child that her husband fathered with another woman?

8. Part of Genevieve's journey in *Balancing Act* includes finding a new passion. Have you ever made a big change in your life or discovered a new talent or passion?

9. Throughout *Balancing Act*, Noah is healing from emotional injuries as well as the injury to his leg. How do you think grief can change a person and how they handle situations?

10. As a firefighter by trade, Noah educates Drew on fire safety in his home. Do you have a fire safety plan and know two ways out of the rooms in your home?

VISIT **GCPClubCar.com** to sign up for the **GCP Club Car** newsletter, featuring exclusive promotions, info on other **Club Car** titles, and more.

@grandcentralpub   @grandcentralpub   @grandcentralpub

About the Author

Emily March is the *New York Times*, *Publishers Weekly*, and *USA Today* bestselling author of over forty novels, including the critically acclaimed Eternity Springs series. *Publishers Weekly* calls March a "master of delightful banter," and her heartwarming, emotionally charged stories have been named to Best of the Year lists by *Publishers Weekly* and *Library Journal*.

A graduate of Texas A&M University, Emily is an avid fan of Aggie sports, and her recipe for jalapeño relish has made her a tailgating legend.

You can learn more at:
EmilyMarch.com
Twitter EmilyMarchBooks
Facebook.com/EmilyMarchBooks
Instagram @EmilyMarchBooks
Pinterest.com/EmilyMarch

Book your next trip to a charming small town— and fall in love—with one of these swoony Forever contemporary romances!!

THIRD TIME'S THE CHARM
by Annie Sereno

College professor Athena Murphy needs to make a big move to keep her job. Her plan: unveil the identity of an anonymous author living in her hometown. And while everyone at the local café is eager to help, no one has an answer. Including the owner, her exasperating ex-boyfriend whom she'd rather not see ever again. After all, they ended their relationship not just once but twice. There's no denying they still have chemistry. So it's going to be a long, hot summer…unless the third time really is the charm.

SEA GLASS SUMMER
by Miranda Liasson

After Kit Blakemore's husband died, she was in a haze of grief. Now she wants to live again and give their son the kind of unforgettable seaside summer she'd had growing up. When her husband's best friend returns to town, she doesn't expect her numb heart to begin thawing. Kit swore she wouldn't leave herself open to the pain of loss again. But if she's going to teach her son to be brave and move forward, Kit must first face her own fears.

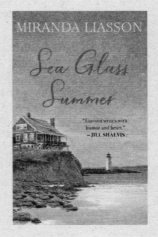

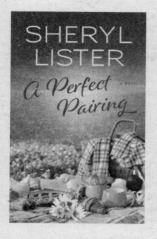
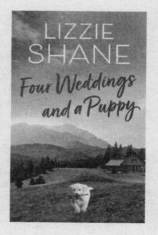

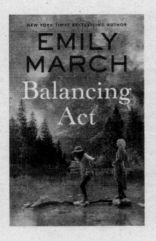

BALANCING ACT
by Emily March

After settling into life in Lake in the Clouds, Colorado, Genevieve Prentice is finally finding her balance. But her newfound steadiness is threatened when her daughter unexpectedly arrives with a mountain of emotional baggage. Willow Eldridge needs a fresh start, but that can't happen until she stops putting off the heart-to-heart with her mom. Yet when Willow grows close to her kind but standoffish neighbor keeping secrets of his own, she realizes there's no moving forward without facing the past...Can they all confront their fears to create the future they deserve?

FALLING FOR ALASKA
by Belle Calhoune

True Everett knows better than to let a handsome man distract her, especially when it's the same guy who stands between her and owning the tavern she manages in picturesque Moose Falls, Alaska. She didn't pour her soul into the restaurant just for former pro-football player Xavier Stone to swoop in and snatch away her dreams. But amid all the barbs—and sparks—flying, True glimpses the man beneath the swagger. That version of Xavier, the real one, might just steal True's heart.

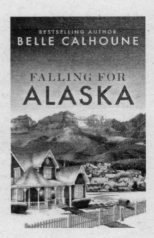

CHANGE OF PLANS
by Dylan Newton

When chef Bryce Weatherford is given guardianship of her three young nieces, she knows she won't have time for a life outside of managing her family and her new job. It's been years since Ryker Matthews had his below-the-knee amputation, and he's lucky to be alive—but "lucky" feels more like "cursed" to his lonely heart. When Ryker literally sweeps Bryce off her feet in the grocery store, they both feel sparks. But is falling in love one more curveball...or exactly the change of plans they need?

FAKE IT TILL YOU MAKE IT
by Siera London

When Amarie Walker leaves her life behind, she lands in a small town with no plan and no money. An opening at the animal clinic is the only gig for miles, but the vet is a certified grump. At least his adorable dog appreciates her! When Eli Calvary took over the failing practice, he'd decided there was no time for social niceties. But when Eli needs help, it's Amarie's name that comes to his lips. Now Eli and Amarie need to hustle to save the clinic.